Footsteps echoed on the marble floors outside the ballroom. Not rushing in panic to help, but advancing at a steady, inexorable pace.

Someone was coming to check for survivors.

I couldn't see the ballroom doors from where I knelt—there was a table in the way—but I heard them fly open. That end of the ballroom seemed to grow dimmer, as if a thin black smoke blew across the threshold.

"Look at this mess."

The voice was rich and soft, dropping into the awful silence like a knife sinking into flesh. It resonated in a way that set my teeth on edge—not because it was discordant, but because I could feel it in my whole body.

"What were they thinking? There's almost no one left to kill."

The hollow percussion of his boots cut across a quiet broken only by the soft, desperate moans and choking gasps of the dying. The pace was too slow and confident, a casual stroll through a garden of death.

He had to come from an Echo. A deep one, most likely. Pearson's last words whispered a chill into my blood: *It's them.*

I should have taken that mission.

Praise for Melissa Caruso

Praise for Rooks and Ruin

"A classic, breathtaking adventure brimful of dangerous magic and clever politics. This is a book that will thrill and delight any fantasy fan."
—Tasha Suri, author of *The Jasmine Throne*, on *The Obsidian Tower*

"*The Obsidian Tower* deftly balances two of my favorite things: razor-sharp politics and characters investigating weird, dark magic. A must-read for all fantasy fans."
—Emily A. Duncan, *New York Times* bestselling author of *Wicked Saints*

"Block out time to binge this can't-stop story filled with danger and unexpected disaster. From the fresh take on time-honored tropes to a crunchy, intrigue-filled story, *The Obsidian Tower* is a must-read."
—C. L. Polk, author of *The Midnight Bargain*

"Full of tension and immediately engaging.... Caruso builds a vivid universe... filling the pages with personality and depth."
—*BookPage* (starred review) on *The Obsidian Tower*

"With *The Obsidian Tower* [Melissa Caruso has] hit another level in terms of prose and tension. This is a truly excellent fantasy, and an epic beginning for a new trilogy."
—*Locus*

"Full of magical and political intrigue, Caruso's latest novel will surprise and delight fans and new readers alike. With rich worldbuilding, nuanced characters, and ratcheting tension, *The Obsidian Tower* is a fulfilling read from start to finish."
—Tara Sim, author of *The City of Dusk*

By Melissa Caruso

THE ECHO ARCHIVES

The Last Hour Between Worlds

ROOKS AND RUIN

The Obsidian Tower

The Quicksilver Court

The Ivory Tomb

SWORDS AND FIRE

The Tethered Mage

The Defiant Heir

The Unbound Empire

THE

LAST HOUR BETWEEN WORLDS

THE ECHO ARCHIVES: BOOK ONE

MELISSA CARUSO

orbitbooks.net

Copyright © 2024 by Melissa Caruso
Excerpt from *Notorious Sorcerer* copyright © 2022 by Davinia Evans
Excerpt from *The Hexologists* copyright © 2023 by Josiah Bancroft

Cover design by Lisa Marie Pompilio
Cover illustrations by Shutterstock
Cover copyright © 2024 by Hachette Book Group, Inc.
Maps by Tim Paul
Author photograph by Erin Re Anderson

Orbit
Hachette Book Group
1290 Avenue of the Americas
New York, NY 10104
orbitbooks.net

First Edition: November 2024
Simultaneously published in Great Britain by Orbit

Orbit is an imprint of Hachette Book Group.
The Orbit name and logo are registered trademarks of Little, Brown Book Group Limited.

The publisher is not responsible for websites (or their content) that are not owned by the publisher.

The Hachette Speakers Bureau provides a wide range of authors for speaking events. To find out more, go to hachettespeakersbureau.com or email HachetteSpeakers@hbgusa.com.

Orbit books may be purchased in bulk for business, educational, or promotional use. For information, please contact your local bookseller or the Hachette Book Group Special Markets Department at special.markets@hbgusa.com.

Library of Congress Cataloging-in-Publication Data
Names: Caruso, Melissa, author.
Title: The last hour between worlds / Melissa Caruso.
Description: First Edition. | New York : Orbit, 2024. | Series: The echo archives; book 1
Identifiers: LCCN 2023050698 | ISBN 9780316303477 (trade paperback) |
    ISBN 9780316303644 (ebook)
Subjects: LCGFT: Fantasy fiction. | Science fiction. | Novels.
Classification: LCC PS3603.A7927 L37 2024 | DDC 813/.6—dc23
LC record available at https://lccn.loc.gov/2023050698

ISBNs: 9780316303477 (trade paperback), 9780316303644 (ebook)

Printed in the United States of America

LSC-C

Printing 2, 2024

To Maya

Watching you grow from small, potato-shaped human
to best brainstorming buddy
has been one of the greatest joys of my life.

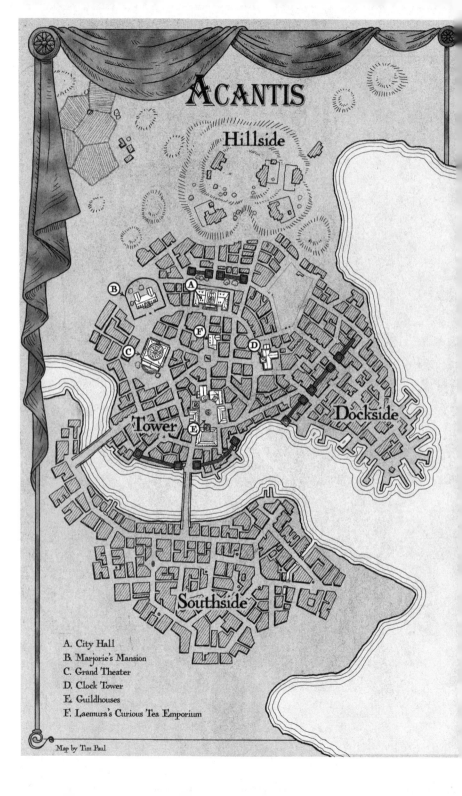

ACANTIS

Hillside

Dockside

Tower

Southside

A. City Hall
B. Marjorie's Mansion
C. Grand Theater
D. Clock Tower
E. Guildhouses
F. Laemura's Curious Tea Emporium

Map by Tim Paul

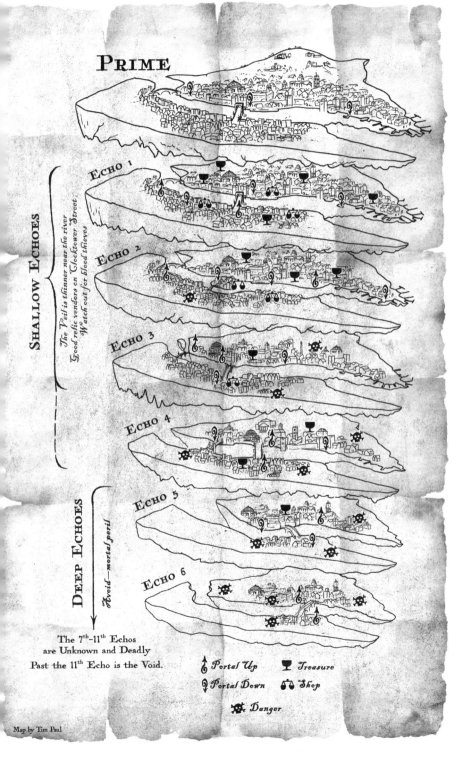

PRIME

ECHO 1

ECHO 2

ECHO 3

ECHO 4

ECHO 5

ECHO 6

SHALLOW ECHOES

DEEP ECHOES

The Veil is thinner near the river
Good relic vendors on Glocktower Street
Watch out for blood thieves

Avoid—mortal peril

The 7th–11th Echos
are Unknown and Deadly

Past the 11th Echo is the Void.

Portal Up   Treasure

Portal Down   Shop

Danger

Map by Tim Paul

REST WHEN YOU CAN

It's easy to fall into the wrong world.

It happens most often to children. Their grip on reality is loose to begin with, and when their imaginations wander, sometimes body and soul will follow. I've seen it happen. One minute the kid is there, playing in the dirt and whispering to themselves, and the next they've slipped down into an Echo. You have a tiny window, maybe five seconds, where they go a little transparent around the edges; if you spot it in time and you're fast, you can catch them. Otherwise someone like me has to go in after them, and that's dangerous work.

Adults can fall between worlds, too, though it's rarer. If you stumble into a spot where the Veil is frayed or torn, you may suddenly find that all the familiar things around you have gone strange and wonderful. Since Echoes are confusing, you might not be sure when it happened or how to get back.

Echo retrievals were always my favorite part of the job. In my years as a Hound, I'd rescued dozens of lost kids and a good handful of adults. I was the only active guild member with a perfect success record. When I brought them back home through the Veil between worlds, they all got this same dazed look at first—as if wandering through bizarre reflections of reality had changed them, and it seemed impossible that the world they'd left behind was still the same.

I felt a bit like that now. Two months at home with a newborn wasn't *quite* like falling into another world, but I'd had almost as little contact with my old life. Being out in public at a party surrounded by people felt strange as a half-remembered dream.

I haunted the buffet like a ghost of myself, stuffing candy-sweet grapes into my mouth more out of nervous reflex than hunger. I only had a few hours of freedom, so I had to make them count—but blood on the Moon, I'd forgotten how to talk to people.

It would be easier if Marjorie's year-turning party wasn't so... stuffy. Dona Marjorie Swift was on the Council of Elders, and her social peers packed the ballroom: the solid, serious merchants and bankers of the class that ruled the great city-state of Acantis, dressed in elegant tailed jackets or pale puffy gowns, all of them striving to impress. One of their pocket handkerchiefs probably cost more than my entire outfit, even counting my Damn Good Boots (a precious find, knee high in soft leather, practical *and* stylish). This was the first time I'd been able to squeeze back into them after my feet had swelled up so much while I was pregnant.

I searched the room for familiar faces, but it was hard to pick them out from the sea of muted colors. You'd think everyone would dress more festively to greet the New Year, but it was still the Sickle Moon for a few more hours, and that meant sober restraint was fashionable— so, drab colors and under-seasoned food. Not that I could complain; I'd been eating odd scavenged scraps since the baby came, with no time to cook or go to the market. I could hope Marjorie would break out more interesting fare after midnight. Some of the more fashion- able partygoers would have brought a sparkling white Snow Moon gown to slip into when the year turned, or a jacket that reversed to flash silver and crystal in the lamplight. I might get about one hour of a livelier party before I had to go home.

Still. It was a party, and I was here. Without the baby. Which felt more than a little like magic.

I'd hoped to see some of my friends from the Hounds, but the one Hound I glimpsed was Pearson, who only talked to me when he had a mission to assign. There were a few members of other guilds around; they might be my best bet. The guilds didn't care how much money you had or what quarter of the city you hailed from, only what you could do. I spotted a couple of Butterflies—a well-known actor in a silky cape talking to a friend who defied stodgy Sickle Moon fashion with his vivid iridescent eye makeup—and a vaguely familiar shaggy-haired youth with some kind of guild tattoo on their hand, maybe a Raven.

And . . . shit. There was Rika.

She'd cut her black hair along her jawline, but I'd recognize her anywhere. I'd seen that wiry back disappearing through windows or over walls too often. Been too late to stop those slender fingers from plucking some priceless object from its protections one time too many. Her gown was all smoke and silver, draping around her like she'd only just formed in this layer of reality from one of the Deep Echoes.

Rika was no Hound, sworn to guard and protect and seek and find. She was a Cat, light and nimble, velvet and hidden steel, and she was trouble.

She'd been chatting with an older woman in a violet gown, but she broke off, rubbed her arms, and glanced around as if she felt someone watching. Before I could look away, her grey eyes caught mine across half the ballroom.

Once she might have slipped me a wink or a wicked smile—but it was the first time we'd seen each other since the Echo Key affair. The usually mischievous bow of her lips flattened, and she turned back to her conversation.

The slice of cheese I'd just grabbed crumbled in my fingers. I wasn't ready for this. Not now, when I was a sleepless mess of under-baked feelings. There was too much I'd been trying not to think about before I went on leave to take care of Emmi, and Rika was at the thick of it.

Why was she here? Rika would never come to a party this rarefied for fun. She must be on business. And that meant she was here to spy, or to steal something, or maybe even to kill someone, though I'd never heard of her doing blood work. I had to tell Pearson. I had to figure out what she was up to. I had to—

No. I was on leave.

I'll take Emmi, my sister had said. *Go to the party. You need to get out of the house. But I'd better not hear about you doing a lick of work, or I swear to the Moon I'll put hot pepper powder in all your tea.*

I was here to have fun. To talk to people. Right.

It would be nice if I had any idea how to do that anymore. Socializing was a mysterious activity that Past Kem had done, irrelevant to Present Kem, who primarily existed to make milk and desperate soothing noises. Sure, a few of my friends from the Hounds had come by in the first week or two to meet the baby, some of them bringing gifts of varying appropriateness (my old mentor, Almarah, had been excessively pleased to give Emmi her first dagger, never mind that it'd be years before she could use it), but after that...well, it had been pretty lonely.

Apparently my sister had been right when she said I needed to get out of the house. It was unfair; no one that bossy should be right so much of the time.

I nibbled my cheese and wished I could drink. But my sister said the wine would get into my milk and be bad for Emmi, so that was out. I'd have to remember how to make words *and* say them to people all on my own.

"Kem. Hey, Kem. Didn't expect to see you here."

It was Pearson. He had a rumpled, worried look, all stubble and shadows. There was only one thing that ever meant.

"I'm not working." I gave it a bit of emphasis in case he'd forgotten. "I'm allowed to go to parties."

"Right, right." He laughed, as if I'd made a joke, and took a sip from his wineglass. "Listen, do you want a drink? Can I get you something?"

"Can't," I said shortly. "Nursing."

He blinked at me like some sad owl, and I relented a bit. "How are the Hounds doing?"

Pearson leaped on the opening. "It's not the same without you. We've got lots of good people, everyone's great, but nobody like you."

I grunted. "No one who can blink step, you mean."

"Well, yes, but also not much experience on hand at the moment. A lot of our best are on assignment outside the city." He licked his lips. "So, you know, I was wondering—"

"Did you see me on the active roster, Pearson? No. Because I have a baby, remember? Small, potato-shaped human."

"Right, of course, of course." He said it in the vague way you might acknowledge the existence of hippogriffs, or some other animal found in distant lands you'd only seen in woodcuts. "Motherhood. Splendid. Only we've run into something that looks like it might be big—just hints, but maybe some kind of power game stirring in the Deep Echoes—and we've got no one available with much Echo experience, so of course I thought of you." He flashed a tentative smile.

I gave him a flat stare. "It can't be urgent, or you wouldn't be at a party."

"Probably not, no," he agreed quickly. "So you could look into it in your spare time."

"My spare time." I rubbed my forehead. "You're not a father, are you."

"No, no." He seemed alarmed at the thought. "A bit damp, babies. And loud, I'm told. Not really my area of expertise."

"All right then, let me explain to you in four small words." I raised four fingers and then folded them down, one after another. "I. Am. On. *Leave.*"

He sighed, and his shoulders drooped. "Can't blame me for trying."

"I suppose not." I lowered my voice. "Did you know that Rika Nonesuch is here?"

"Really?" He was good enough not to peer around openly, but his eyes darted about the room. "She's bound to be up to no good."

I shouldn't ask. It was too much like work. But I couldn't help myself. "Any idea what she might be after?"

Pearson scratched his chin thoughtfully. "Could be looking to rob Dona Swift. Or to spy on the other City Elders—I think there are three of them here. Or she could be after the clock."

"Clock?"

He tipped his head toward the far end of the ballroom. "This supposed antique grandfather clock Dona Swift bought off a sketchy dealer. You only have to look at it to know it's not from *this* layer of reality. Could be a good fake, but I'd bet cold money it's from an Echo."

"That's just what we need." I shook my head. "Well, good luck. I'm not going to go finding things out on purpose, because I'm not working, but if I hear anything useful, I'll let you know."

Pearson nodded. "Thanks. Can't wait to have you back, Kem."

I grunted noncommittally as he moved off. There was no sense letting him know how comments like that currently plunged me into a whole inner crisis. Of course I wanted to go back to work; I missed the Hounds, missed seeing my friends, missed the excitement of a challenging mission and the satisfaction of a job done well. Stars, I missed just getting to walk around the city without a fussy baby strapped to me. But I also couldn't imagine leaving Emmi. I hadn't been away from her for an hour and it already felt *weird* to have my arms empty, as if part of my body were missing. I missed her funny little face, her wide wondering eyes, her tiny grasping fingers.

At the same time, damn. *Damn.* I could do what I wanted, and nobody was depending on me for every single little thing. I was just myself again, existing only for myself, for these few hours at least. I felt light and giddy, as if someone had untied heavy weights from my arms and legs.

Now, if only I knew what to *do* with all this freedom.

Dona Marjorie swept toward me with the inevitable momentum and grace of a galleon in full sail. Acres of suitably subdued forest-green skirts puffed around her, sleeves and bodice trimmed with modest ivory lace; emeralds winked with a splash of cheeky color in the tower of elaborately coiled and woven braids of her iron-grey hair. Her round brown cheeks beamed, dark eyes sparkling. She always seemed so genuinely happy to see me, and I never could tell for sure if that was because I'd saved her son's life or because she was just an absolutely delightful sugar puff who loved everyone. Probably both.

"Signa Kembral!" She threw her arms wide; I accepted her hug, a little embarrassed, as her voluminous skirts enfolded me. "I'm so glad you came. How's little Emmelaine? Is she sleeping?"

"No," I said, letting two months of despair come through a bit. "Not so you'd notice."

Marjorie shook her head. "Oh dear. Do you want me to send someone over to take her for a while so you can rest?"

"She screams like she's on fire every time I leave the room, and I doubt I could sleep through that, but thanks for the offer."

"Well, you just relax and enjoy the party, then." She patted my arm, then dropped her voice nearly to a whisper. "I'm glad you're here tonight. Just in case."

"What does *that* mean?"

Marjorie laughed, lifting her painted nails to her lips as if I'd made a slightly off-color joke. "Oh, you know, politics always get a little intense at the year-turning, that's all. Everyone's all fired up to charge out the gate with new legislation and new alliances as soon as it turns from a Sickle Moon to a Snow Moon, and the knives are out. It's good to have level heads like yours around. Don't you worry about it—focus on having a lovely night!"

My smile slipped from my face as she moved on to greet her next guest, her voice rising in welcome. *Great.* My first time in public in two months, and I'd picked a night when Dona Marjorie expected "politics" to get so wild my skills might be needed—and I doubted it was because she wanted a third at tiles. Maybe I should have worn my swords.

Suddenly a low, harsh, brassy music jarred the ballroom. It shook deep into my bones, reverberating in my teeth, seeming to come from the air itself. Just a handful of notes, each a deep *bong* like a punch to the stomach—and then silence.

A hush fell over the gathering, the kind that comes when a large number of people all hold their breath at once.

The clock. That had been the simple melody the city bells played before tolling the hour; it must be the grandfather clock Pearson had mentioned. He wasn't kidding about it being from an Echo, with a chime like that.

The whole party waited, but no hour rang. The room's other and more mundane clock, a marble antique on the mantel, still showed about ten minutes shy of nine o'clock in the evening.

A smattering of nervous laughter rose up, like a handful of pigeons taking flight to the ballroom's high ceiling. The murmur of conversation swelled back into its usual busy clamor, everyone no doubt telling one another *Oh, it's just the clock.*

I resisted the urge to go look at it. That would be too much like work. If it were dangerous, I'd feel obliged to do something about it; if it presented a puzzle, I couldn't resist trying to solve it. No, I absolutely should not cross the ballroom, weaving between partygoers with one muttered *Excuse me* after another, waving away a servant offering a tray of drinks, nudging an errant chair aside with a swish of my peacock-tail scarlet coat. The last thing I wanted to do was lurk around waiting for the crowd drawn by its disconcerting chime to dissipate, giving me a clear view of it at last. And under no circumstances should I approach it so close that my breath misted on its glass face, staring at it in fascination.

Fine. *Fine.*

I could see what Pearson had meant. The basic shape of it was dignified enough, a grandfather clock with a cabinet of shining dark wood, its round face gleaming. But the carvings surrounding the face were twisted and phantasmagorical, with staring eyes and strange creatures climbing and writhing up into a spiked crown. Each number was in a different style and size, some of them crazily elaborate or tilted off-kilter. The three hands formed wickedly sharp spears of shining steel that patrolled the numbers menacingly, threatening them with impalement.

A single fine crack marred the face, running from top to bottom, starting at the number twelve and snaking down like a bolt of lightning. Iridescent colors showed in the silvery ribbon of broken edge embedded in the glass. I reached out, curious, and ran a finger down its length to see if I could feel it.

The glass felt slick and unbroken. But I pulled away a bloody finger.

I cursed and sucked it. *That was stupid, Kem.* What did I think would happen, petting broken glass?

"Well, well. If it isn't Kembral Thorne, in the flesh."

That was the last voice I wanted to hear right now. She'd come up behind me without making a sound, and it was too late to escape.

I forced myself to turn slowly, as if I wasn't surprised, to face my nemesis, Rika Nonesuch.

STAY ALERT FOR DANGER

My traitor pulse flared up, but I squelched the old anticipation before it could flare to life. We were not going to have some duel of wits and spend all evening trading flirty quips as we attempted to outmaneuver each other. That was over.

"Rika." Her bare name was the closest I could come to a cordial greeting, after what she'd done to me.

"Here I thought you'd retired from polite society." Her grey eyes traveled up and down the length of me, as if to assess my current condition, or perhaps my fashion sense.

I was already feeling a bit defensive about both. I'd done my share of recovery over the years—knife wounds, the deeper scars of Echo magic, you name it—but having your abdominal muscles stretched out and your innards squashed for months on end left its own kind of marks, never mind childbirth itself. And I'd discovered to my chagrin when I tried to get dressed for the party that nothing quite fit the same way now that Emmi had deconstructed and rearranged my whole body. I knew damned well I should be in somber Sickle Moon colors like everyone else, but my scarlet Blood Moon overdress had fit best—more of a coat, really, with split peacock-tail skirts going to just below the knee in front and trailing nearly to my ankles in back—so that was what I was wearing. The neckline was, ah, *different* with my milk come in, however, and suddenly I was very conscious of it.

"Not retired," I said curtly. "You're not so lucky."

"That's right. You'll never retire. You're probably back on the job already. Up to anything dangerous tonight?"

Her tone was too bright, its false surface ease covering an intensity beneath. A faint flush touched her cheeks, as if from drink or dancing, and one tendril of dark hair hung artfully awry—but I hadn't seen her dancing, and there was no drink in her hand. What was she up to?

None of my damned business, that's what. Rika Nonesuch was not my problem tonight.

"No. I'm on leave."

"Your idea of a good time on a day off is to investigate some creepy Echo relic?" She shook her head. "You really know how to relax."

It was too like what she'd said right before the star diamond incident. *You need to learn how to relax. How to stop being a Hound for half an hour.* I'd trusted her, like an utter fool. Heat flushed up my neck.

"The last time you told me that, I woke up under a pile of garbage in a tenement cellar."

"Truth comes in a variety of astonishing guises."

I had no patience for her games tonight. "Why are you here, Rika?"

She executed a delicate shrug that set complex shadows to playing across her collarbones. "Do you always know why you do things?"

"Yes."

"Of course you do." She laughed, and there was an odd, bitter edge to it. "I don't know what fever came over me, thinking I should come talk to you, but it's past now. I suppose I should see a physicker if symptoms recur."

I'd been avoiding her gaze, but at that note of hurt I couldn't help a quick glance to see whether it was real.

Our eyes locked together with an almost audible *click*. Tension bracketed hers, grey irises shining with some silent electric message.

If I let myself fall into them, I could read it—the same way we'd once had a whole unspoken conversation across a room in little twists of expression at a boring political event we were both working.

It was so close. Whatever we'd once had, whatever heady combination of rivalry and teasing chemistry and *connection*, it was right there, prickly and alive and waiting just below the brittle surface of hostility, like water rushing beneath a skin of clear ice. I could pretend nothing had happened and slip into our old patterns; I could say something wry and warm and give her a little half-suppressed smile and hope things would somehow snap back to what they once were.

But I was flustered and grouchy and tired, and not ready to forgive her, and feelings were delicate things I no longer understood how to mend.

I covered the tightness in my throat with a scowl. "Fine. Don't tell me. But whatever job brings you here tonight, you'd better not do anything against Dona Marjorie."

"You always assume the worst of me, don't you." Her lips moved, but it wasn't really a smile.

"Hounds always prepare for the worst." I should have stopped there, but my anger at everything she'd thrown away between us surged up and spilled bitterly out of my mouth. "You should know that, after the Echo Key affair."

Rika's face went flat as a slammed door. *Whoops.* That might have crossed a line.

Cats weren't supposed to be caught. That was, in fact, the entire point of the Cats. Sometimes they helped the downtrodden secure justice they couldn't find within the law; mostly the city's elite hired them for steep fees to sabotage, steal from, or spy on one another—all the sort of tasks they didn't want sticking to their reputations, like mud on a fine silk cravat.

This meant Hounds and Cats had more of a direct rivalry than any of the other guilds. It was often a Hound's job to stop a Cat from fulfilling her mission, but as a professional courtesy it was pretty common to do so without actually *catching* her. Especially if they had a long history of doing each other small, thoughtful favors when they weren't striving to thwart each other—like returning a glove the Cat had dropped fleeing a burglary scene, or picking a lock so that a tired Hound on duty could get out of the rain. Or leaving each other little teasing notes if they were working the same building, or rescuing each other from annoying people at parties. In short, if they were friends.

Which, after the star diamond incident, we most certainly were not. So there was no reason I should feel a sudden rush of guilt, no matter *how* her face looked.

"I see." Rika's voice went sharp, losing all its usual silky richness. "That's how you're going to play this? Fine. I won't coddle you anymore."

She turned on her heel and stalked off.

I'd never once felt *coddled* in the presence of Rika Nonesuch. Either I'd scored enough points in our new enmity that she was taking the gloves off, or I'd been an asshole for no good reason and should go back home, curl up in a ball, and give up on talking to people ever again. By the sinking feeling in my stomach, I had an awful suspicion as to which it was.

A great shattering crash splintered my thoughts to pieces.

I jumped and reached for my knife. But it was just a drunken guest who'd staggered into one of Dona Marjorie's staff, knocking over a whole tray of glasses. I let out a relieved breath as the inebriated tailcoat apologized with slurred speech, trying to help the poor man— Carter, his name was; I recognized his curling mustache—while he waved the young guest off with far more patience and grace than I could have managed.

My nerves still jangled. Between this and my reaction to an innocent clock chime, I might be a little on edge tonight.

Time to prove that I *did* know how to relax, damn it. I scanned the room in desperation, looking for a friendly face.

A sea of conversation lapped at my ears, nearly all of it in the drawling, refined cadence of old money Hillside or the clipped precision of new money Tower district, which only made me feel more out of place. Laughter rose up above the crowd with the loose, uncontrolled ring of inebriation—everyone sure was drinking like it was a Wine Moon tonight. There had to be *someone* else in that crowd who I knew and liked. Someone uncomplicated and easy to talk to, who wouldn't leave me feeling like a mess of wet knots.

My eyes snagged on Dona Harking, talking to Marjorie over by the wine table. Ugh. He was the opposite of uncomplicated, all venomous elegance and a sparkling veneer of charm. Given what I knew about him—and the worse things I suspected—the only way I ever wanted to talk to the bastard was if it would get me the evidence I needed to land him in prison.

Pearson had made me back off from Harking. *You got the kids back, Kem,* he'd sad. *You did what your client hired you to do; you're not a city investigator. The job is done. Let it go.*

I was no good at letting things go.

Harking's gaze wandered and caught mine across the ballroom. He flashed me his classic wry smile and lifted his glass; I forced a small return nod. It was never a bad idea to maintain a certain level of politeness with City Elders, no matter what you thought of them.

The nod must have encouraged him, because now he was heading in my direction. It was far too late to act like I hadn't noticed and drift away. Every muscle in my abdomen tightened. *Here we go.*

"Signa Thorne," Harking greeted me. "I must say, I'm surprised to see you here."

"That's me," I said through a false smile. "Full of surprises."

He did me the courtesy of a chuckle. "Is this your plan for retirement, then? Attending parties with the city's elite?"

"I'm a bit young to retire." I couldn't keep an edge out of my voice. Leave it to Harking to discover something that annoyed me even more than Pearson assuming I'd come right back to work: assuming I was done with work now that I was a parent.

"So you're staying in the business, then?" His dark eyes glittered, assessing. "Teaching, perhaps? I'm sure there are many who would line up at the chance to learn to blink step."

It wasn't an unreasonable question. A lot of Hounds switched to teaching when they had kids, and to be honest I was considering it. But Harking's tone of breezy assumption made my jaw tighten.

"No, I'm going to keep working in the field." I threw it back at him with far more confidence than I possessed, out of sheer spite.

His lids dropped until his eyes were gleaming slits. "A pity."

"Oh? Because I'll uncover all your sketchy secrets?"

"Not at all." His tone was lazy, unconcerned. "Because a field Hound's work is dangerous, and it'd be such a shame if something happened to you, with your daughter so young."

The bastard was threatening me. He must know or guess how close I'd come to uncovering his crimes, and here he was, standing bold as daylight in Marjorie's ballroom and threatening me, because he was a City Elder and could get away with it. And he *dared* bring in Emmi.

I showed him my teeth. "I'm not worried, Dona Harking. I'm exceptionally hard to kill."

"So I've heard." He swirled the wine in his glass. "Nonetheless, Signa Thorne, a dog with pups ought to be careful where she sticks her nose."

"And a City Elder ought to know better than to try to intimidate a Hound. The guilds protect their own."

"My dear Signa Thorne, whyever would you think I was trying to intimidate you?" There was nothing innocent in the cynical grooves of his face. "It was merely an observation. I'm sure you'd never *dream* of overstepping your guild charter and meddling in city politics, so it's hardly relevant to your situation. Is it?"

And that was the crux of the thing. I couldn't go after him without a client; the balance of power between the guilds and the League Cities was too delicate, governed very precisely by intricate charters. You didn't mess with that. And the city would never investigate him so long as he remained rich and powerful enough to prevent it from doing so.

"Of course not," I ground out. "How nice of you to spontaneously express concern for my hypothetical welfare."

"Good, good. I'm so glad you're sensible enough to know your limits." Harking lifted his glass half an inch in a perfunctory salute. "If you'll excuse me, Signa Thorne, I should give my regards to my fellow Elders."

I glared holes into his back. Oh, I was *not* up to dealing with Acantis politics tonight. I itched to pick up my cold leads from the Redgrave Academy job and follow them right to the heart of all his nasty secrets, but even if I *had* a client, it'd be a while yet before I could go back to work. If I could bring myself to leave Emmi in someone else's care and go back at all.

I was thinking about work again. I rubbed my forehead. *Fun, Kembral. You're here to have fun.* There had to be *one* enjoyable conversation somewhere at this party.

And there she was, water in the social desert: Jaycel Morningray. Poet, duelist, socialite, occasional public nuisance, and an old friend from Southside. She was holding forth to a rapt audience as usual, wineglass in hand, with a loose confidence suggesting that said glass was neither her first nor her last of the evening. I started in her direction; Jaycel was an endless fountain of gossip and witty commentary, and she knew me well enough to understand when I wasn't in the mood to talk. I could let the wonderful sound of adult human words wash over me without any pressure to make them myself.

As I navigated the crowded ballroom toward her, a skittering motion caught my eye.

Something small ran under a table—a mouse? No, it had seemed... *shiny.* I paused, my brow bunching into furrows. Surely I'd imagined that sparkling iridescence, a trick of my tired eyes.

Unease prickled the back of my neck. I reached for the white damask tablecloth.

"Kembral darling!"

Jaycel had spotted me and was sauntering toward me. I straightened with a grin.

She was in fine form, flaunting an intricately embroidered dueling cape that hung dramatically from one shoulder, a gorgeous swept-hilt rapier riding at a cocky angle on her hip. Her short dark curls tumbled around her face in a careless way that seemed to come naturally to Jaycel but that many in the Acantis social circuit spent hours of artifice trying to emulate. There was nothing false in her broad smile at the sight of me, and gratitude surged in my heart at the welcoming sparkle in her eyes.

We'd grown up together in Southside, two kids running around the neighborhood. Mostly she got us into trouble, and I got us out of it, though occasionally we swapped.

"Jaycel. Stars, it's good to see you."

"Look at you!" She clasped both my shoulders, theatrical as always, gazing at me as if I were some precious family heirloom returned at last after being lost for three decades at sea. "You look good. Tired, but good."

"I am *so tired*," I admitted, with probably too much passion.

"Bah! We won't let it slow you down. I'm making it my *mission* tonight to find someone scrumptious to dance with you."

Wait, no. "What?"

She threw an arm around my shoulder, gesturing expansively with her wineglass. "It's a challenge! I know you're choosy, and the pickings tonight are slim, my friend." She shook her head. "But we can do this. *Together.*"

"Are you teasing me? I honestly can't tell."

"No, no, I'm deadly serious, darling. Now, let's see—you're a waxing Cloud Moon, right? A seeker of truth! Too bad Dona Swift has almost thirty years on you; she's a half Compass Moon, the journey and the homecoming both, which would be a perfect match. Ooh, if you're looking to make a salacious mistake—"

"When have I ever done anything salacious in my *life*?"

"—there's Dona Harking." Jaycel bit her lip. "I am deeply bothered by how relentlessly attractive he is."

"*Harking?*" That sent my eyebrows crawling up my forehead. "The man is morally bankrupt."

"Of course he is. That's half the draw." She shook her head. "Oh, I can't explain it to you. It's just—those piercing eyes. That sardonic smile. That *ass*." Her fingers flexed. "Plus, he's great in bed."

"*What?!*"

"Oh, relax. It's not like I married him. Sometimes it's not about personality. Well, for the rest of us, anyway—I suppose it always is for you." She let out an aggravated sigh. "I still can't believe you wound up with *Beryl Cascarion*, of all people, who is a walking set of abdominal muscles with a bit of scruff. You *say* you're not attracted to people that way—"

"I'm not."

"But the man has *no virtues whatsoever* aside from being easy on the eyes. Please don't tell me you fell in love with his mind."

She was drunk, I reminded myself. She was drunk, and not trying to be cruel. "Look, he can be really charming. He made me laugh, he made me feel like I was important to him, he made a fuss over me. It felt nice. I was a fool, all right?"

Jaycel clapped my shoulder. "You're not the first person to make a fool of yourself over Beryl Cascarion, and you won't be the last. At least it wasn't Harking, right?"

"I'm going to have nightmares, Jaycel."

"Oh, if you think *he's* a bad idea, wait until you see my date for tonight! And anyway, you're one to talk about questionable choices, given you're gawking at Rika Nonesuch."

"I'm not gawking." I jerked my eyes back to Jaycel from a certain silver-gowned figure I hadn't even realized they'd been resting on.

"Just keep it to looking." She wagged a finger at me. "Waxing Cloud Moon and waning Cloud Moon don't mix. Truth and lies, darling."

"I don't think you have to worry about that. We're not too fond of each other right now."

That might be an understatement. Though honestly, it wasn't like Rika had wound up in the city jail due to the Echo Key affair—I'd checked, not that I felt bad or anything, but her papers were in order and they'd released her to her guild. Nothing close to the shame and discomfort of waking up on a hard floor under a pile of garbage, with a headache like the Moon's own wounds, panicked over whether the drug she'd slipped me would be bad for Emmi. (It wasn't—Rika was too much of a professional not to take that into account—but *still.*) It had taken me days to get the stink out of my Damn Good Boots. And that wasn't even touching the bone-deep embarrassment of knowing she hadn't meant a thing she'd said to me in the café that day.

Jaycel must have heard something in my tone. She gave me a searching look.

"Something happened between you two, didn't it? Are you all right? Do you need me to punch her?"

I sighed and pushed a loose lock back from my face. I'd tried to put my hair up for the party, but Emmi had cried the whole time I worked on it, so it wound up a bit of a honey-colored mess; I'd left a few tendrils down in the weak hope that people would think I'd been going for "artfully disheveled" rather than "panicked rush job."

"I'm fine. You don't need to punch her. I don't want to talk about it. Or my romantic prospects, for that matter." It sounded brusquer than I meant it to, but Jaycel wasn't the type to read too much into tone. "I had a baby, I'm kind of a mess, and I would like a nice, relaxing, low-pressure night out to…" I trailed off. *To remember who I am* sounded overly dramatic, but really, that was more or less what this was about.

An incredulous noise burst out of Jaycel. "Low pressure! And you came *here*?" She flung an arm over my shoulders. "We're Southside girls, Kembral. Look around you. It's all Hillside aristocrats and rich Tower merchants and bankers. You're at the wrong party."

"Maybe," I allowed ruefully. "Why are *you* here, then?"

"To be seen, of course!" Jaycel gestured expansively. "This is a work night for me. Everyone here is a prospective client. I've got to be entertaining. I've got to make a scene. I've got to *perform*."

"That sounds exhausting."

For a moment, she dropped her sparkling public persona and gave me a look that was three parts tired, one part amused. "You have no idea. I wish I'd had the rockheaded stubbornness to stick with the blink step training like you. You'll *always* have value to them. I have to keep dancing like a trained goat or they'll lose interest, and then I'd better hope my family takes me in, or I'm out on the street."

Jaycel had joined Almarah's class of hopeful apprentices at the same time I had, but like most of the kids there, she liked the *idea* of being able to blink step much more than she liked the reality of dedicating fifteen years of her life to learning it. She'd stayed with it for almost a year out of friendship, which was longer than most of the class managed, and she'd kept walking with me to class for months after she'd dropped out.

I shifted uncomfortably. "Blink stepping is only useful if I can still do my job. It's been a while."

"Bah! You'll be fine. Come on—if you want to enjoy yourself, I'm nearly the only one here who can help you. Try one of the crab puffs, and I'll fill you in on all the gossip from the old neighborhood, since you're all fancy living near the guildhouses now."

I let Jaycel's words wash over me as she chattered about a girl we'd known as kids who was running for the Council of Elders, then launched into a story delighting in the current misfortunes of a boy whose eye she'd blacked for calling me names when we were eight (he'd been rude to an old woman who turned out to be an Echo in disguise and gotten cursed). It was beautiful just to bask in her presence.

It wasn't long before she got distracted by the pair of Butterflies I'd seen earlier, coming to talk to her about fight choreography in their new play. I hesitated, not sure whether I felt up to joining them; I knew swordplay, but I didn't know the Butterflies.

Out beyond the tall windows beside me, something moved in the garden.

I snapped my gaze past the glass in time to spot a figure slipping between the bushes with the swift, furtive motions of someone trying not to be seen. It was there and gone so quickly I wasn't sure whether I'd imagined it.

My senses went alert. I moved closer to the windows, eyes fixed on where the figure had disappeared—if it had been there at all. Sometimes when Emmi really, *really* hadn't been sleeping, I saw stuff like that, and I didn't always trust my senses anymore. No sign of it now.

All right. It was probably nothing, but between the skulking figure and the sparkly mouse (or whatever it had been) and the strange clock, this was starting to get weird.

"Kem. Hey, Kem."

Pearson again, startling the daylights out of me. The man didn't know when to give up—but then, he *was* a Hound, even if more the papers-at-a-desk type than the investigations-and-bodyguarding type.

"This had better not be about that job," I warned him.

"No! No. Well, yes, but no." He pushed on stubbornly, ignoring my best skeptical glower. "I was thinking if you won't take the job, maybe I could just *tell* you about it and you could let me know what you think. Like an advisor. That's not work, right?"

That was damned well work and he knew it. Not least because once I heard about the job, I'd want it—and he knew that, too. But I had to be home in four hours to nurse Emmi, and I refused to waste half the party talking about whatever leaking Echo was causing trouble in the city this time.

"This had better not involve a kid or a dog," I muttered.

"If it did, I would have led with that." Pearson started to laugh, then swallowed it with the guilty wince of a man who suspects he's about to be slapped.

He'd deserve it. "The last lost dog job you gave me took me six Echoes down, Pearson. *Six Echoes.*" One Echo down, fine, that was almost like our Prime layer of reality. Two got strange, three downright surreal—and anything past that descended rapidly through creepy and dangerous into pure nightmare.

Pearson nodded. "The deepest any current Hound has gone and returned alive," he said, with a touch of awe that would have been gratifying if he weren't the one who'd fucking sent me there.

"The river was flowing with *spiders* and the walls were dripping blood," I told him. "I had to run from things with *eyes in their teeth*, Pearson."

"You brought the dog back," he pointed out. "You always bring the dog back, even when anyone else would give up. That's why we send you on those things. But no, this is nothing like that. You shouldn't have to go into an Echo at all. I hope."

"You're right," I said, "I won't. Because I'm not taking the job."

"Right, of course, but here's the thing—"

Whatever else he was going to say got lost in the suddenly raised voice of Dona Vandelle, who was facing off with Harking halfway across the ballroom, her hands jammed in her pockets as if the sleek black velvet of her tailcoat was the only thing holding her back from strangling him.

"Because you're a writhing sack of vermin, that's why!"

Damn, she could project from the diaphragm. The Grand Theater should put her onstage. The whole room went silent and turned with varying degrees of subtlety to watch the show. Pearson gave me a pained, almost apologetic look.

Harking swirled his wine in his glass with an unmistakable air of menace, his eyes hooded, as if Vandelle's shouting bored him to the point of dozing off.

"So impassioned," he drawled into the sudden silence. "It's too bad that the council doesn't vote by volume."

"Half of them do—by volume of the money bags you hand them," she retorted. "You've washed your hands in blood for years and dried them on letters of credit, but that's over now. A reckoning is coming, and you're not going to like it."

Vandelle stormed off. Harking watched her go, a smile teasing the corners of his mouth. The room erupted into excited murmurs, everyone turning to their neighbor with some comment on the public drama. Swirling clusters of supporters enfolded both Harking and Vandelle.

Pearson turned to me with a little grimace. "Politics. Right?"

There was nothing unusual about the exchange—city politics got pretty heated—but combined with Marjorie's comment earlier about being glad I was here plus the figure sneaking around outside, I didn't like it.

"Yeah," I mumbled. "At it again. Good to see you, Pearson."

I slipped away before he could start in on this job of his again. I'd feel bad about shaking him off, except the man had no mercy. When I'd brought Emmi to the guildhouse at three weeks old to pick up some things I'd left there, he'd practically elbowed aside everyone cooing over the baby to try to get me to take on a job investigating the months-old murder of a smuggler.

Besides, I was determined to get a better look out that window. It'd be just like our City Elders to plan a dramatic public assassination to ring in the New Year.

Cold poured off the glass from the wintry outdoors; bushes and bare-branched trees made flat black shapes against the shadow-mottled lawn of the walled garden. No sign of any movement, but that didn't mean anything. Maybe I should talk to Marjorie about her security.

"Oh!" someone cried in alarm nearby, overlapping with an "I say! Did it bite you?"

I whirled from the window in time to spot that same little scurrying thing I'd noticed earlier, fleeing a couple of flustered party guests who brushed at their expensive clothing as if afraid there might be more. The small creature darted under a chair a few paces away, iridescent colors flashing on its back. This time, I got a good enough glimpse to see six scuttling legs.

Huh. Not a mouse, then. Wary and curious, I stalked over to the chair and peeked under.

A large beetle with feathery antennae and a shimmering rainbow carapace skittered off, making a panicked sound like dropped wind chimes.

I froze. That was no beetle. It was an Echo.

It was likely harmless, the whimsical reflection of some common insect, probably from just one layer below our own Prime reality. But it shouldn't be here.

Things from Prime sometimes slipped down through weak spots in the Veil to the Echoes beneath us, but it was less common for things from Echoes to find their way up into Prime—and it was rarely an accident. For an Echo to ascend into Prime, it had to fight the pressure of increased reality. They could come here on purpose, and occasionally in places where the Veil was particularly thin you might get some flotsam from the shallow Echoes washing up—but a mindless bug wouldn't wander up into Dona Marjorie's year-turning party at random.

Someone had sent it here.

I glanced at the pair of guests it had startled, but the musicians had struck up "Under the Flower Moon," and they were heading, laughing, to the dance floor along with half the party. They seemed unharmed and unworried, and the bug had fled like any vermin with no purpose more sinister than a strong desire not to be stepped on. Maybe it was someone's idea of a prank to turn an Echo beetle loose in a party, or maybe it had been smuggled up as an exotic pet and escaped.

Not my problem, I reminded myself. Not my job to figure it out tonight. And neither were strange figures that might or might not be in the garden. I was here to relax, even if apparently all my brain could do was latch on to small things as possible threats.

Still. Couldn't hurt to talk to Marjorie. I started making my way toward where she stood beaming in a cluster of guests, feeling a bit like a thundercloud blowing in to rain on a picnic. Maybe Rika was right about me not knowing how to stop working—not that I'd ever admit it to her.

Before I reached Marjorie, Dona Tarchasia Vandelle slouched up to me, lean and artfully disheveled, her grey hair tousled, dark eyes burning. I'd worked with her a few times before; she hired the Hounds on a regular basis to investigate when she suspected worker accidents or deaths in Dockside might be the result of questionably legal practices of the rich merchants who owned all the warehouses and ships. She was one of the Elders who represented Dockside and had grown up there herself; her staunch loyalty to her people was one of the reasons I liked her.

"Ah, Signa Thorne," she greeted me. "Just the Hound I was looking for."

"Dona Vandelle. Striking fear into the hearts of the rich and powerful again, I take it?"

"Always." She flashed a sharp-toothed grin at me. "Actually, I'm hoping you can help me with that."

Bloody Moon, not another job. "I'm not working right now. I just had a baby."

"Oh, no, of course not!" Vandelle looked genuinely shocked. "Nothing like that. Marjorie told me you had some good dirt on Harking, and I'd *love* to take him down a notch. Care to spill?"

I lifted my hands as if I could physically ward off getting council infighting all over me. "If I had anything concrete, I'd have handed it over to the authorities."

"Of course, of course. But she said you could connect him to the Redgrave Academy scandal." There was something almost like hunger in her eyes.

If Marjorie was spreading *that* rumor around, no wonder Harking had threatened me.

"Don't I wish. I've got no proof, just a series of suspicious coincidences." I shook my head in frustration. "It's a scent, that's all. And I'm not allowed to follow it without a job."

"I'll hire you. I'll hire you right now."

It was a far more tempting job offer than Pearson's. "I'm on leave," I said reluctantly.

"The minute you get back to work, then." Vandelle saw the hesitation in my face and pressed. "Surely you must want to take him down, especially if he's behind Redgrave. All those poor kids abducted and their magical talents auctioned off under the pretense of a charity school for Echoborn orphans—doesn't it make your blood boil?"

"It does," I admitted. "It really, *really* does. I'm just…I haven't decided for certain whether I'm going to take field jobs again when I go back."

"What?" Vandelle snorted a dismissal. "You can't quit, Signa Thorne. I know the work you do. Acantis needs you."

Of course she couldn't resist the chance to poke at my grumpy, contrary, simmering ball of resentment at being told what I should do. Everyone had an opinion.

"Things have been busy," I said. "I haven't had time to sit down and really think it through. I'm not going to quit entirely, but I have to consider whether I'll need to scale back somehow."

The look Vandelle gave me was frankly disbelieving.

I didn't mention the other problem with this particular job of hers. Harking had influence all through the city. I wouldn't hesitate to make him an enemy for my own sake, but there were so many ways he could pull a string here and a string there to ruin Emmi's life. I wasn't going to let him intimidate me into silence, but I couldn't plunge straight into something this politically messy without a thought to the consequences anymore, either. I had to take steps to protect Emmi first.

But that was something Vandelle wouldn't understand. She'd never hesitated a second before standing up for what was right, and to the Void with the consequences. It was something I liked about her, but...things were different now that the stakes I could put on the board weren't all my own.

I sighed. "Look, there's only so much I can say right now, but you can definitely post the job with the Hounds. Whether I'm back on full duty or not...Well, we do help one another out and share leads within the guild."

Vandelle grinned, seeming satisfied. "You can bet I will. Things are going to change in this city, Signa Thorne. I'll take every chance I can get to make sure of it."

She took her leave and strolled off, looking as if she might burst out whistling any minute. I wished I felt half so sure of myself. Nothing was simple anymore.

My gaze fell on Dona Marjorie, talking with Carter near the ballroom doors. *She* had children, and a demanding and potentially risky job, and she'd managed all these years. Maybe I should ask her for advice. Or, given that we'd become friends when she'd hired me to protect her adult son from assassination attempts aimed at rattling her, maybe not.

Wait. I squinted harder at them. Carter seemed agitated, and he was clutching his arm—was that blood? He must've cut himself cleaning up all that broken glass.

On the far side of the ballroom, someone screamed.

I whipped around to see a commotion ripple through the guests, a surge forward and away at the same time, everyone staring at something on the floor. My confused brain jumped to several wild conclusions at once: It was the Echo beetle. Someone had knifed Carter and was now on a rampage. A server had spilled hot soup.

More screams rose up, one of them to an ear-shattering pitch: "He's *dead*!"

Well, shit.

WATCH THE ENTRANCES

I pushed my way toward the disturbance, Pearson converging with me through the crowd to fall in at my side. I couldn't see the body, only the reactions to it: gasps, drawing away, a quick burst of movement as a physicker dashed to the scene. Not much use in that, if someone was really dead, but best to be sure; sometimes people got excited and yelled things prematurely.

My mind buzzed like a kicked hive. Apparently I wasn't being overly jumpy after all. I wondered if I could have stopped this if I were in top form—if my mind hadn't been too foggy with exhaustion to pick up on all the cues—but I cut that line of thinking off quickly. It wasn't helpful.

"Poison," more than one person murmured. "Murder," an old woman's rough voice declared, with the assurance of an experienced sommelier identifying a particular vintage. I didn't doubt she was right.

Too many people clustered around the dead man; I couldn't get close. I opened my mouth to call out *Hound on the scene*, then decided I was *not* up for taking charge of an impromptu murder investigation right now and shut it. Instead, I hopped on a chair and used my vantage point to check the exits for anyone fleeing, then scanned the room for anything out of place.

Pearson cleared his throat, almost apologetically. "Hound on the scene."

I trusted him to check the body, talk to the physicker, ask people what they'd seen. Meanwhile it was my job—not my *job*, damn it, call it a professional courtesy—to spot every anomaly, remember every detail. It was hard to shove my brain into motion, to exercise mental muscles two scant months of motherhood had yanked out of shape—but it felt weirdly *good*, too. Like I was *me* again.

No. Someone was dead. Fun time was over.

I found Rika first; she looked as alarmed as anyone else, craning her head to see what was going on, but that didn't mean anything— she was a professional. Marjorie was weaving her way through the crowd, her cheery face gone grim, her party ruined. I took note of a few guests acting oddly: one with his face in his hands, another slumped against the wall as if in shock, a woman pale and wide-eyed who wasn't staring in the right direction. A waifish child in a smudged apron hovered near the clock, half hidden behind it—what was she even doing here?

A tickly feeling shivered along my skin. The same feeling I sometimes got at the beginning of Echo retrieval missions, just as I approached the place where the lost kid or dog or whoever had fallen through. As if a lightning-laden wind blew gently through the frayed thinness of the Veil between worlds.

This had better not be Echo business. A mundane murder was sad but simple; Echo business was messy, and had a way of spreading. I thought at once of the sparkly beetle and cursed under my breath.

"Who's the victim?" I asked Pearson, pitching my voice low and keeping my eyes up. No use looking at the dead man—he was the only person here pretty much guaranteed not to be a threat at the moment.

"Jarid Enwright. Textile importer." He rose from the dead man's side, leaving him to the physicker for the moment. "Not someone with serious enemies. I don't like it, Kem."

"It would be weird if you did."

"You know what I mean." He wiped his brow, voice going even quieter. "Poison at a big party like this. It's risky."

I knew too well what he meant, and I didn't like it, either. There were so many uncontrolled factors; the killer might have gotten the wrong person. This might not be over.

Marjorie arrived at the scene, Carter firmly but politely clearing a path for her, just as the physicker rose and shook his head.

"It was an Echo poison," he said. "I've seen this before. Several different systems just shut down for no reason, all at once."

Now, *that* was interesting and a bit ominous—not many people had access to Echo poisons—but it was Carter's arm that caught my eye. Tucked protectively against his side, it definitely bore a drying splash of blood.

"Carter," I said sharply. "What happened to your arm? Is that related?"

He hesitated, his curling mustache tilting as he bit his lip. "I don't think so. Some strange lout off the street tried to get in without an invitation. Claimed he was on the list but in disguise. When I stopped him, he pulled this weird glass knife and cut me, then ran away. He looked like—"

He broke off as a sudden fluttering caught our attention. Marjorie swayed on her feet, clutching at her chest.

"She's going to faint!" a doe-eyed young tailcoat cried, stepping up as if he might catch her.

Dona Marjorie wasn't the type to swoon dramatically in a crisis. Her face had gone greyish, her lips purpling—she was in trouble.

I had a Hound's training to stay calm in an emergency, but Marjorie was my *friend*. This was not okay. A bubble of panic tried to rise up in my chest, but I ruthlessly crushed it down.

"Physicker!" I snapped. "Quick!"

She crumpled like a falling soufflé, skirts puffing out around her. Carter half caught her with a cry of alarm, lowering her to the floor.

The crowd drew back with gasps of horror to make room for the physicker, but he didn't move. Blood on the Moon, this was no time to dither. I jumped down off my chair and shook his arm.

"Hurry!"

He only swayed, clutching his own chest, breath coming in hoarse little gasps.

Oh. Oh, shit.

Shrieks rose up around the ballroom in several scattered locations. Right beside me, another guest staggered and fell to his knees.

I whirled on Pearson, the white-hot energy of mortal crisis lancing through my veins.

"We need an antidote! Or a purgative. Do you have anything?" I usually carried an emergency kit on me, but I had nothing, *nothing*, because I wasn't working.

Pearson stared at me, his face blank with shock. *Desk Hound.* I whipped around, looking frantically for some Elder paranoid enough to carry antidotes, or an Echo worker—anyone or anything that could help.

I didn't find help. I found an unfolding nightmare.

All around the room, more party guests tumbled into heaps of puddled finery where they stood. More and more people stumbled and swayed, straining to breathe, to keep their hearts beating, each their own small desperate island in a sea of terror. The companions of the fallen dropped to kneel by them on the floor, crying for help, begging for them to hold on. There were so many of them, so fast, as if a deadly wind swept through the room bowing people like grasses.

My chest tightened. I couldn't tell if it was from fear or if the poison was starting its work on me, too. But I had to keep my head—*had to*—because nobody else was.

The ballroom had already descended into pure chaos: elegantly dressed partygoers screaming, crying, staggering into things. Half the buffet cascaded to the floor. People tripped over one another, tumbling to the ground clutching at their chests and throats. Some of the growing number of fallen moaned and gasped, still struggling; others lay still, blue-tinged faces staring unblinking at the ceiling. *Dead, but don't think about that, think about what to do.*

Marjorie probably kept antidotes somewhere. I could blink step to get them and be back before too many more people succumbed.

I whirled to Carter to ask him, but he was on his knees beside Marjorie, one hand braced on the floor, the other clawing at his throat. *Fuck.*

"Kembral!" Rika shouted at me from twenty feet away, a sea of panicked and poison-stricken people between us, her grey eyes desperate. "You're a Hound—do something!"

"You're a Cat! You work with poisons! Do you have an antidote?" I called back.

"Tried it already! No good. Nothing I have works on Echo poison."

So much for that idea. There had to be something I could do besides wait to feel my own breath cut off, my own death rising up in a black wave. I couldn't die here. *Couldn't.* Emmi needed me.

"Is anyone here an Echo worker?" I called desperately, without much hope that I'd be heard above the clamor.

Rika had threaded the chaos to reach me with the slippery grace of a minnow. She caught my arm, nails digging into my skin.

"Kembral," she said hoarsely. "I need to tell you. About the star diamond incident."

"That doesn't matter now! We've got to find someone who can work Echoes! Wait, you can do a bit of illusion—can you..." I broke off as I got a good look at her face.

She shook her head, desperately trying to speak. I read my name on her lips, again and again. *Kembral. Kembral.*

"Rika!"

I caught her as she collapsed in a swirl of silvery fabric. She was utterly limp in my arms.

My soul seemed to crack open, sure as the face of that clock, a pain sharper than broken glass stabbing through me. No, this couldn't be happening. Cats didn't get poisoned, and Rika Nonesuch was far too good to die like this. She was faking, or messing with me, or...

"Hey. Hey! Rika, quit it!"

I shook her, but she didn't respond. I couldn't tell if she was unconscious and dying or already dead. Fuck. *Fuck.* A great shock of grief twisted my gut with physical pain, as if I'd been run through. I dropped to my knees, cradling her in my arms, my mind making a blank roaring noise that nearly drowned out the screams all around me—not least because the latter were becoming disturbingly sparse.

Pearson crawled up and grabbed my sleeve, his eyes bulging. He drew in a horrid, shaking gasp.

"The convergence," he rasped. "It's *them*."

"Pearson! Not you, too!"

This had to be a nightmare. It *had* to be. It was too grandiosely terrible to be real, and exactly the sort of messed-up thing I'd dream just to ruin whatever sleep-deprived sliver of a nap I'd managed. Any minute now I'd wake up in my chair by the fire, having dozed off nursing Emmi, my neck stuck in some uncomfortable, flopped-over angle and aching.

Any minute. *Come on.*

Pearson collapsed beside me, and I still didn't wake up.

I knelt alone in a sea of the dead and the dying.

Bodies piled thick around me, some still moving weakly and gasping, others utterly still—like Rika, heavy and unresponsive in my arms. Only a scattering of others remained standing: a couple of house staff, pressed against the wall, eyes wide with terror. A furtive movement by the clock—thank the Moon, the little girl was all right. A handful of guests, some frozen in shocked despair, others crying for help. Debris scattered everywhere, as if a storm had blown through: shattered plates and glasses dropped from nerveless fingers, wine splashed across the fallen like blood.

The wine. It must have been in the wine. Everyone had been drinking, because Marjorie always brought up the good stuff from her cellars for the year-turning. Except I couldn't, because I was nursing. Emmi had saved my life.

But I had no power to save anyone else. Pearson, Jaycel, Marjorie, Rika—they were all dying or dead, and there was nothing I could do but sit here with a howl building in my throat that would shake me to pieces when I released it.

Footsteps echoed on the marble floors outside the ballroom. Not rushing in panic to help, but advancing at a steady, inexorable pace.

Someone was coming to check for survivors.

I couldn't see the ballroom doors from where I knelt—there was a table in the way—but I heard them fly open. That end of the ballroom seemed to grow dimmer, as if a thin black smoke blew across the threshold.

"Look at this mess."

The voice was rich and soft, dropping into the awful silence like a knife sinking into flesh. It resonated in a way that set my teeth on edge—not because it was discordant, but because I could feel it in my whole body.

"What were they thinking? There's almost no one left to kill."

The hollow percussion of his boots cut across a quiet broken only by the soft, desperate moans and choking gasps of the dying. The pace was too slow and confident, a casual stroll through a garden of death.

He had to come from an Echo. A deep one, most likely. Pearson's last words whispered a chill into my blood: *It's them.*

I should have taken that mission.

I eased Rika's head gently from my lap to the floor, my whole body tense and ready to move.

"I can't decide whether this is inexcusably sloppy, or a clever masterstroke meant to eliminate us all at once." The terrible voice uttered a musical sigh. "I suppose I'll have to improvise."

His voice deepened, taking on a cold edge like a drawn blade. I surged to my feet, ready to fight.

At the exact same moment, a deep, ominous sound shattered the deathly silence.

BONNNNNNG. The clock shook the whole room, the sound reverberating in my nerves and blood. It pealed only once, long and resonant, but that was enough to set reality itself rippling around me.

What the—

I barely had time to register a single dark figure standing above the carnage. As the bell rang, it drove a great black sword down into a prone body with a sickening crunch. Eyes lifted to meet mine, gleaming an inhuman silver.

The world blurred beyond comprehension. There came a dropping, sucking feeling, like stepping through a trapdoor into murky black water.

I fell through.

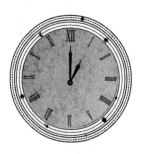

DON'T FALL INTO AN ECHO

The party was in full swing, fever-bright and loud with laughter.

Dancers swirled through the ballroom in flowing gowns of silver and copper and gold, more suited for a Coin Moon than a Sickle Moon. The music kept them moving, quick and fey like a flash of wild lightning. At least half the guests wore glittering, fantastical masks; some had them pushed up on their flushed foreheads or dangling forgotten from a wrist as they laughed with friends. Richly patterned gold silk covered the walls, crystal chandeliers shone with a thousand flickering lights, and the tables overflowed with fanciful bites teased into artful perfection by a master chef. A chocolate fountain burbled in several spectacular tiers at the center of the spread.

I'd be having a lovely time if it weren't for the little fact that I'd just seen all these people die. As it was, every laugh scraped my raw nerves like a fork on glass, and I stared around in numb shock.

Jaycel bantered with a handful of appreciative young tailcoats, cutting the air with her hand as she described some duel; never mind that I'd last seen her sprawled dead across a pile of elderly magistrates. Marjorie twirled on the dance floor with surprising grace, gold lace dripping from her gown, wearing a mask of gilded roses that twined up into her artfully styled iron-grey hair. Rika talked in low, serious tones to an older woman in a silver and violet cat mask, no attention to spare to glare at me. A maskless Pearson stood at the buffet, loading a tiny plate with what looked like stuffed mushrooms.

The clock stood unchanged in the same spot, crack snaking down its face, the sharp tip of its hour hand now pointing precisely at the numeral one. The spears of its other hands ventured forth without hesitation into the second hour, dividing time and conquering it. The other clock, the mundane marble one on the mantel, showed about ten minutes to nine.

What the *fuck*?

I leaned against the wall, steadying myself against a wave of dizziness. My heart was going like someone was trying to kill me—and I couldn't blame it, given that two minutes ago I'd been ready to fight for my life.

Hadn't I? I mean, my brain had been a bit foggy since having Emmi, but that was *memorable*.

Marjorie swirled up to me, breathless and flushed from dancing. "Signa Kembral! I'm so glad you came. How's little Emmelaine? Is she sleeping?"

I stared at her. She was very alive, eyes sparkling beneath her mask, not at all concerned about having died a moment ago. "I . . . she's . . . what?"

Marjorie laughed and patted my cheek fondly. "I'll take that as a no. You look exhausted, dear."

"I . . ." How did you ask a person why she wasn't more upset about being dead when she was unquestionably alive?

Maybe I was dead, too. Maybe we were all dead together.

"Well, enjoy the party, but you might want to get home right after midnight and start out the New Year with some sleep!" She gave my arm a gentle squeeze and swept off.

I stared after her. No one seemed concerned or upset. I must be dreaming after all.

"Kem. Hey, Kem."

It was Pearson, wineglass in hand, clean-shaven in a bronze brocade tailcoat. He certainly hadn't been wearing that before. For that matter, it didn't look like something he'd wear at all.

"Pearson." It wouldn't do to lunge at him and grab him and shake him. "What the Void is happening?"

"Uh...it's a party? The year-turning?"

Had I somehow imagined the whole thing? I wasn't *that* short on sleep.

"You don't remember anything...dramatic happening?"

"Must have missed it. Political drama again?" He rolled his eyes up toward the inexplicably gilded ceiling in dismissal of the city's elite. "Always happens at these things."

"What were you going to tell me? *Them* who?"

Pearson blinked. "Um. I was going to ask if you were having fun at the party?"

"No, not now. When you were..." *When you were dying.* Which he clearly didn't remember. New strategy. "That job you were trying to offer me. When I told you I was on leave."

He laughed, the same nervous laugh as always. "Figured you'd punch me if I offered you a job when you're on leave. Baby and all."

"And you're right. But tell me about the job anyway. Something stirring in the Deep Echoes, you said."

"Right. That's why I thought of you for this one. Echo stuff, you know." He grimaced. "Spooky. Dangerous. Not my specialty."

"And? Is it related to all *this*?" I waved at the transformed ballroom, desperate for him to show even a flicker of understanding that things were seriously not normal.

"To Dona Swift's party? No, I don't think so." He frowned. "Heard some rumors from our Echo contacts. Been talking to them about that murder investigation that's had us stumped for ten months now—you know, the Echo relic smuggler. Turned up dead with some highly dangerous cursed coins stolen from him, and the Fisher Queen was furious. Still hoping you might help with that one—no?" He grimaced at the look on my face. "No. Right. Anyway, the Echoes he was dealing with passed us a warning. Something's got them nervous—some kind of big contest going on in the coming year. Powerful Echoes involved. They called it a crux year, whatever that means. I was hoping you could look into it."

He lifted his glass toward his lips. On a surge of panic, I knocked it out of his hand.

"Hey! What'd you do that for?" He shook out fingers soaked with red wine. The glass lay in shattered gleaming pieces on the floor.

"It's poisoned!" Heads turned toward us; I dropped my voice. "The wine for the whole party. It's poisoned."

But was it? All the food was different, and the decorations, and the outfits. Which made no sense, unless...

The glimmer of a suspicion started to make its way through the haze of my shock.

Pearson's eyebrows climbed his forehead in alarm. "Poisoned?"

Calm, I reminded myself. A Hound stayed calm in emergencies. Whether my suspicion was correct or not, I had to make sure we weren't all about to die again first. I drew in a steadying breath.

"It might be, anyway. We need to find someone to test it, quick."

Pearson frowned, glancing around the ballroom. "I hate to say it, but your best bet to test for poison is a Cat."

"Ugh."

"I know, I know. But Rika Nonesuch and Adelyn Cail are both here."

I knew that name from somewhere, but my brain was soup at the moment, and I couldn't place it. "Adelyn Cail."

"Sure. Higher up in the Cats. One of their Watchers." He must have noticed my glazed look. "Acts as a backup on missions with a high chance of failure—trainees, Cats on probation, particularly difficult missions—in case the primary Cat can't do it. Come to think of it, with her and Rika both here, something big must be going on at this party."

You don't fucking say. "Do you know either of them well enough to ask? I, uh, don't get along with Rika."

"Oh? Oh." Pearson grimaced. "I can imagine, after the Echo Key thing. *And* the star diamond thing. I have a professional acquaintance with Cail. I'll ask her."

He moved off through the crowd, vanishing into the riot of color.

Now what? I could jump up on a table and yell at everyone that the wine was poisoned—but that would start a panic, and it might not be true. Even if I wasn't dreaming—even if time really *had* somehow wound itself backward and undone all those deaths—things had changed. My conversations were playing out differently, not to mention the frankly superior food and outfits.

I glanced at the mantel clock again; the hands had moved, so it wasn't simply stopped at ten minutes of nine. It had reset to the same time it showed when the grandfather clock played its first unsettling music. But Pearson and Marjorie hadn't remembered our conversations from *before* the clock sounded, and they clearly weren't seeing the strangeness of their surroundings—something was messing with their minds as well.

That clock was at the center of this mess. My eyes pulled toward it, hoping for some clue about what under the bloody Moon was going on.

The sad-eyed girl lurked beside it, wearing a plain smock and a grease-smeared apron. She looked around ten years old, a faded wisp of a thing, like a background character from a painting of a street scene. Sandy hair, and the pale skin that meant her ancestors probably immigrated to Acantis from Viger in the big wave at the fall of the republic, like my grandparents had. She seemed oddly familiar, and a little creepy if I was being completely honest.

She was the only person here besides me who looked exactly the same as they had before the clock struck. Everyone else had at least small details changed—new ornaments in their hair, new flashy waistcoats (some of them iridescent, scaly, or feathered), and of course the masks—but she looked identical, and very much out of place at a fancy party. And despite that out-of-place-ness, no one but me seemed to notice her.

This was one of the many things my mentor, Almarah, had told me: *Find the piece that doesn't fit.* I started making my way across the ballroom, giving a wide berth to the dance floor, weaving my way through jarring laughter and too-loud conversations. Everything felt surreal and threatening. I tried not to jump at sudden movements.

The girl could be anything. A servant child wandered in to look at the dancers. An Echo from some deeper layer of reality, casting her curse over us all. An urchin someone had paid to slip poison into the wine. I thought of Emmi, and my heart constricted. No matter what she was, I'd get the girl out of here safely if I could.

When I made it to the clock, she was gone. Of course.

There'd been something in her gaze—she remembered. No one else here did, that much was clear; they were too happy, dancing with too much abandon, faces lit with pleasure. Only the little girl and I knew that nearly everyone here had just died.

Maybe it was because we'd both survived? But no, there had been others who lived, enough that there'd be noticeable signs of distress among the guests and staff if they all remembered. There must be some other reason.

I stared around the ballroom, lost, half expecting to see an expanse of sprawled bodies again. Instead my gaze caught on a full mask like the round face of the Moon, splashed with shadowy blood, its empty dark eyes turned toward me.

I smothered a startled curse. *Creepy bastard.* Everyone else's masks were light, ornamental things of wire or lace or silk, showing half the face or more; this joker was drifting around the party with his blank Moon face and a deep cowled cloak, probably laughing his ass off behind the mask at making people jump.

Or it might not be a mask at all. I wasn't going to make assumptions when something this bizarre was going on.

As for what...I had my suspicions, and an easy way to test if they were true.

Heavy brocade curtains draped the ballroom's tall windows; it was full night, so for the most part they framed only darkness. I moved closer to one, forcing my eyes to look past the bright, enticing reflections of the glittering party into the night beyond. I knew what I should see: a stretch of carefully sculpted garden, the bare cascading branches of a weeping tree, a little fountain, and a stone wall enclosing everything.

There were still a tree and a wall. But the tree looked sculpted from gold, smooth and stylized. The fountain poured out molten metal instead of water, its sullen glow catching reflected sparks in the gleaming bark of the tree. I couldn't make out much of the garden in the darkness, but more sparks of reflected fire suggested that the other plants had been transformed to metal, too.

That settled it. This was an Echo.

I closed my eyes a moment in a giddy mixture of horror and relief. Being in an Echo was bad, but it explained—well, not everything, but a lot. If I'd somehow fallen into an Echo, then nothing around me was quite real. Or rather, it was *very* real, but not from my own Prime reality.

Unless...Maybe the whole ballroom had sunk down into the shallowest Echo, almost like Prime but not quite, and we were all stuck here together.

That would make sense, given the way the whole room had shimmered and melted when that damned clock sounded the hour. Which was bad, because it would be substantially harder to fix than me just finding a way out for myself—but also much, much better than the alternative, because it meant all these people were really here. Their true, Prime selves, and not Echoes.

I could still save them.

Mind you, that wasn't how this worked. Falling into an Echo didn't bring dead people back to life. But barring illusion or shapeshifting, Echoes of people were usually noticeably different from their Prime counterparts; even in the shallowest layers, a person's Echo might have a completely different personality, a different hair color, a third eye. Aside from the new clothes, everyone here seemed to look and act more or less the same.

For whatever reason, they weren't dead, and that was what mattered. That clock was clearly a powerful Echo relic, so I'd chalk up any additional strangeness to its influence and leave the particulars to the Ravens.

I let out a long, shaky breath. I rescued people from shallow Echoes all the time. I should be able to handle this.

A crash of shattering glass made me jerk alert, my knife half out of its sheath, before I realized it was Carter's tray of wineglasses getting knocked over again. I stared, uneasy, as the same drunken tailcoat apologized profusely, and Carter politely waved off his fumbling attempts at help.

They certainly didn't look like they remembered this happening before. Apparently some things were playing out differently, and others just the same.

"Kem. Me again."

I almost jumped, but it was only Pearson, looking puzzled. "Oh. Hi, Pearson."

"The wine's fine. Why'd you think it was poisoned?"

What to tell him? *I watched you die, and everyone else in this room, too. Stood there and watched. Nothing I could do.* I'd sound like I'd been taking hallucinogens. But then, Pearson was no fool.

"Look around you, Pearson," I said. "Notice anything strange?"

He frowned. It was one of the most common tests they gave trainee Hounds, even those destined to sit behind a desk. He turned and gazed around the room, carefully, analytically. His face tensed as if with some inner struggle. "I . . . There's something. Huh. Didn't think I'd had that much to drink, but it's fuzzy."

"Does this look like one of Dona Marjorie's usual parties?"

"Er, no. Bit more . . . lively?" His frown deepened, becoming almost pained. "Ugh, I'm getting a headache."

"You're in an Echo."

"I'm sorry, what?" He blinked at me. "I missed that."

"An Echo. We all fell into a shallow Echo, one slice down."

He cupped a hand behind an ear. "Pardon?"

"AN ECHO." His face remained blank. So the Echo wouldn't let him hear me; sometimes they did that, drawing your mind into their own reality in place of Prime, refusing to let outside interference break the spell. That might be what was messing with his memory, too. "Never mind. Go have fun. But let me know if you see anything strange."

"Sure." He hesitated. "Any chance you'll be coming back to work soon?"

I am working, you asshole. "No. Ask me again in a few months."

As he wandered off, it hit me that my chances of getting paid for this were minimal. Curse it. Not only was I working on leave, I was working for free.

That was definitely Pearson, though, muddled memory and all. Which meant he and everyone else at the party were alive. *Thank the Moon.* I wasn't fool enough to think the danger was past, but I had another chance. With luck, I could get everyone safely back to Prime and get home by one o'clock like I'd promised my sister.

I scanned the room, seeking any trace of whatever hole in reality we'd fallen through. There was usually something: a shimmer in the air, or a place where things didn't quite line up right—the angle of a corner off, the colors of a wall not quite matching, the light too bright or too dim in one spot.

"Kembral Thorne. I didn't believe it when I heard you were coming tonight, but here you are."

Rika. She'd snuck up on me again—annoying in every Echo. Yes, that was definitely annoyance swamping me, and not wild relief that she wasn't dead.

I wanted to spin and grab her, but I forced myself to turn slowly, as if nothing strange and horrible were happening. The sight of her face—*alive*, a healthy warmth to her cheeks, only the light twist of mockery on her lips rather than a final agony—left my knees weak.

"Here I am," I agreed. "Do you know where *here* is?"

She raised an eyebrow. "Dona Swift's estate, in the Tower district. Did you hit your head? Or is this your attempt at philosophy? I honestly can't tell."

"You're close. One Echo off, in fact."

She gave her head a sharp shake, as if a fly was bothering her. "Philosophy, then, because now you're not making sense at all. Leave it to the academics, Thorne. You can't even handle your real world problems."

So she couldn't understand me if I talked about being in an Echo any more than Pearson could, even if I did it obliquely. Ah well, it had been worth a try.

"Never mind. I'm just glad you're not dead." The words fell out of my mouth before I could stop them.

"Why, Kembral, what a morbid thing to say. Are you quite all right? Did someone spike the cider with something experimental?"

"Ha, ha. Look, Rika, I can't play your games right now. I'm dealing with a situation."

"You *are* a situation, Thorne. And why do you think I'm playing games?" She stepped in closer, her voice dropping. "I need to talk to you."

Her grey eyes allowed mine no escape. I swallowed. Was this a feelings talk? I wasn't going to have a feelings talk with Rika Nonesuch, not now. Not ever.

But this was Rika. She didn't talk about feelings, except the one time when it had been a trap. She probably thought I had information she wanted, or else she was distracting me.

"This is urgent," I said. "I'm sorry, I don't have time."

Before I could make things any weirder, I started to walk away. I had a mass Echo retrieval to coordinate.

A cloud of dragonflies swirled in my face, gleaming jewel-bright, and I balked despite myself. Rika stepped in front of me as the insects faded into wisps of mist and vanished: illusions, shadows summoned from an Echo for a brief instant. I *knew* she could do that, but it still startled me every time.

"Too busy for small talk? Fine." Rika pointed one perfectly tapered, silver-painted nail at me. "Don't give me that you-wouldn't-understand act, though. If there's one thing I can't bear, it's condescension. Tell me what this *situation* is that has you all bothered."

She literally *wouldn't* understand, thanks to the Echo, but telling her that was clearly not going to cut it. I had to give her something. And if I could put her on her guard, so much the better. Time to try a new tactic.

"Some murderous Echo is messing with us, so far as I can tell."

Her gaze flickered. She'd understood. Apparently I could talk about Echoes, just not *being* in an Echo. If it could plausibly happen in Prime, they could hear me. *Interesting.*

And more—that startled spark had looked like recognition, or maybe fear. I jumped on it.

"You know something."

"I know lots of things, Thorne." She gave an airy wave of her hand, but it was too late to cover up her reaction.

"About an Echo crashing the party tonight? A powerful one? Is that what you wanted to talk about?"

She didn't meet my eyes. "Do I look like I casually socialize with powerful Echoes?"

"I mean, yes, you sort of do."

It came out without thinking, because Rika was a creature of mystery and beauty and near-ethereal arrogance, and I was tired and not watching my damn mouth. She recoiled as if I'd dropped a snake on her.

"I mean it as a compliment," I amended, not sure what I'd stepped in. "Mostly."

"Why do you think I know her?" Rika's voice had gone taut. "Who is this powerful Echo you're talking about?"

"'Her'?" I hadn't gotten a good look at the silver-eyed figure I'd glimpsed as the clock chimed, but I would have guessed *him*. "Who do *you* think it was?"

"I...no one. Earlier, I thought I felt..." She visibly gathered herself, then waved the question off with false unconcern. "I misunderstood you, that's all."

"Wait. If there are multiple powerful Echoes involved in this mess, I need to know about it." Pearson had said something about a contest, after all.

"I told you, it's nothing." She started to turn away. "Don't let me keep you from your Hound business—it sounds quite dramatic."

Desperate, I grabbed her wrist. "Don't walk away now, you—"

I broke off. Something damp and sticky met my fingers. I let her go at once, shocked to find a smear of red on my hand. For a brief instant, I glimpsed a cut on the side of her hand; then it blurred with the subtle sparkle of illusion and vanished.

"What was that?" I demanded. "Are you all right?"

"Ugh, I'm fine." Rika gave her hair an annoyed toss. "My colleague handed me something surprisingly sharp, if you must know."

"You expect me to believe that? Since when have Cats been careless with knives? First the Echo comment, now this—what are you hiding?"

She laughed; it had a bitter edge. "More than you can imagine."

"Rika—"

"Goodbye, Kembral. Try to stay out of trouble, will you?"

A puff of illusory smoke swirled in my face, and she was gone.

She'd suddenly wanted out of that conversation like I'd brought up her late taxes. For a moment, I hovered on the brink of going after her. I could follow her—see who she went to, what she did, maybe ask her some questions. Find out why she'd looked so haunted for a minute there, as if *she* were the one seeing a roomful of ghosts. Maybe make sure she was all right—subtly, so she wouldn't know I was checking on her.

No. I didn't need to unravel the mysteries of Rika's labyrinthine mind. All I needed was to find a way back to Prime and guide the hundred-odd of Dona Marjorie's party guests and staff through it. *Stay focused on your objective*, Almarah's voice said in my memory.

"Some people make it hard," I muttered.

I headed for the ballroom doors. In theory, this should be simple; I'd done plenty of Echo retrievals. A whole *place* slipping through like this was new to me, though, and a little trickier. I didn't understand how it had happened—that was Raven stuff—but the solution should be the same. Sure, this wasn't the party I'd thought I was going to, but I'd make it home alive with a good story, and in the meantime I could prove I still had what it took to be a Hound.

Assuming I *did* have what it took. I didn't feel nearly as sure of that as I'd like to. But one Echo down wasn't any more dangerous than the worst parts of Acantis; even at less than my best, I should be able to do this.

A small, skittering movement caught the corner of my eye. I whipped around just in time to catch a flash of iridescence as that same damned Echo beetle scuttled under a table.

My heartbeat thudded in my chest—faster than made any sense, given the minimal threat the thing seemed to pose. There was something creepy about it, and even more so about seeing it in almost the same place I had in Prime, right before everything went so very wrong.

All the more reason to get this over with quickly. I couldn't chase after the bug any more than I could chase down Rika, or spend more time trying to analyze that clock. Finding a way home had to be my first priority.

Raised voices cut through my thoughts. Another argument had broken out between Harking and Vandelle; it was already drawing an audience.

"Because you're a writhing sack of vermin, that's why!"

A chill slipped down between my shoulders. Not another argument, but the *same* argument. I didn't like to see events repeating themselves like this, given how things had turned out last time.

I walked a little faster, memories of poison and death harrying my heels.

Beyond the ballroom waited a foyer that was usually marble but now dripped with gold and silver ornamentation like it was the Cathardian royal palace. The mansion's exterior doors stood shut against the winter air, suspiciously untended by Marjorie's staff.

Taking a deep breath to brace myself for what I might find, I flung them open onto a world that was not my own.

READ THE SIGNS

I'd been to the first Echo dozens of times, of course. Probably hundreds. But the thing about Echoes was that they shifted and changed all the time; if in Prime reality was like stone, in the Echoes it was like water. So it didn't matter that I was more familiar with the shallow Echoes than just about anyone in Acantis besides the Echo relic smugglers and their legendary Fisher Queen. A particular Echo might tend to follow certain patterns and currents, but you never knew.

The street before me bore little resemblance to the one I'd stepped in from when I arrived at the party. The buildings looked too old, age-worn stone blocks instead of brick; the people bustling along wore heavy furs and enormous hats, their eyes pale and pupil-less, their fingers long and spidery. One walked a little dog that seemed to have an excessive number of legs. Another had the face of a squirrel, with great round eyes and long elegant lashes. All of them seemed in a hurry. It was even the wrong time of day: It had been dark when I arrived and when I looked out the windows into Marjorie's garden, but out here it was a dull grey afternoon, by the look of it.

Standard Echo stuff, and nothing too dangerous. I let out a nervous breath and stepped into the street.

A misty drizzle beaded my hair, too light to even feel wet. A woman in a silvery fur hood nodded to me without looking up as she passed, cradling a massive black snake tangled in her arms. I nodded back, curling my cut finger into my palm so she wouldn't notice it. You never wanted an Echo to see you bleeding.

All right. The Veil was often thin down by the river. Kids and mudlarkers would comb the banks searching for little bits of Echo flotsam, even though it was often dangerous if something actually came through. The same was true all the way down through the Echoes; it was why *fishers* was slang for relic smugglers. I could head toward the river, and maybe I'd find a way back to Prime before I got there.

I started down the street in the right general direction—a few Echoes deeper and I'd be less sure, but this shallow, things were more or less still in the same places. A smuggler's mark scrawled in red chalk on a rough stone wall confirmed I was going the right way, with the cup that meant *treasure* and some wavy lines for a river over an arrow pointing straight ahead.

The trick was going to be getting everyone out before whatever path to Prime I found closed up again. Soft spots in the Veil might last awhile, or even be permanent, but you couldn't reliably walk straight through those without training. For this many people I needed an actual hole, and those rarely lasted long. I'd have to stabilize it with blood.

Prime was the first and truest reality, the rock-hard shore of stability against which the chaos of the Echoes lapped, the baseline that everything in the murky layers below reflected in their own distorted fashion. Prime blood—the ordinary blood flowing through the veins of everyone at the party—was a powerful anchor in the Echoes. One drop was enough to stabilize a closing gap in the Veil for at least a good twenty minutes; I'd used the trick to buy time on retrievals before. But Prime blood was valuable in the Echoes, and using it would attract attention I didn't want while I was shepherding a large group to safety.

Though there might not be much attention to attract. The street seemed emptier than I'd expect it to be on the year-turning, when

Prime was all stirred up and the Echoes should be reflecting the activity. The few people I saw hurried past quickly, eyes down, as if they were afraid it would start pouring rain any minute.

Another smuggler's mark caught my eye, in fresher chalk: a crude staring skull. *Danger.*

My neck prickled. I stopped where I stood.

There was something odd about the light that poured down from the sky. It had a strange violet cast, glinting off the drizzle. A bad, bad feeling gripped my stomach.

Slowly, almost against my will, I looked up.

"Oh, fuck," I whispered.

A strange blurry hole in the sky hovered directly over Dona Marjorie's house like some kind of great negative cloud, displaying a tattered glimpse of midnight sky speckled with stars.

It didn't fit with the pale overcast, not in any way, and the fact that it showed night instead of a grey indeterminate day was only the beginning. It was too deep and flat at the same time, and it emitted a purple-black not-radiance that hurt my eyes. Those stars winked with the cold, hard brilliance of the Void, piercing straight into my brain through my eyeballs.

"Unnerving, isn't it," said a small dry voice near my elbow.

It was a relief to look down. An ungainly, stork-like bird stood there, one of a few clustered together, their faces serious, shifting from one spindly foot to the other. One wore a lumpy woolen scarf, and another had round spectacles perched on its beak.

Only one Echo down, and we were already at talking birds. What a day.

I cleared my throat. "Do you, ah, know what it is?"

The bird with the scarf shook its massive beak in disapproval. The one with the spectacles made a clicking noise.

"It's a hole," the smallest bird piped up helpfully.

"I can see that. But they don't...I mean, gaps between Echoes don't usually look like that."

"Are you from Prime, then?" the bird with the spectacles asked, its tone pleasant and curious.

"Yes," I admitted, slipping my cut hand into my pocket.

"So you don't *know*." More clicking, and the birds exchanged significant glances.

"No, but you could tell me."

"Oh, if you stick around, you'll see soon enough." The one with a scarf chuckled darkly.

"I wouldn't, though," Spectacles Bird advised. "Stay well clear of that house, young miss, if you know what's good for you."

"Why?"

"It's marked for death," Scarf Bird said.

"More than just death," Spectacles Bird corrected. "*Worse* than death."

"Oh, much." Head bobbing and clicking all around.

Lovely. Even the local poultry knew we were doomed.

"Care to elaborate?"

Beaks wagged emphatically back and forth. "We wouldn't *dare*," piped the small one.

"Look, I need to find the nearest gap that goes to Prime. Do you know where I could find one?"

Spectacles Bird sighed in a sympathetic sort of way. "I'm afraid you're not going anywhere, young miss. Or rather, not anywhere *up*."

Oh, *that* was ominous. "What do you mean?"

Scarf Bird dipped its curving neck toward the doors to Marjorie's house. "It's too late for you. You're already marked."

"You're part of the game," the smallest one added helpfully. "You must have been under *that* thing when it started."

I was liking this less and less. "What game?"

"One with very nasty players." Spectacles Bird's feathers ruffled up and then quickly subsided, like a shudder.

Pearson's Echo contest. I'd bet on it. Lovely. "And these players... They're at the party?"

The small one let out a frightened squeak. Spectacles Bird spread a reassuring wing over its shoulders.

"Goodness, I hope not. We'd want to be *much* farther away if they were. No, rumor has it they're sending agents to play for them. Pieces they can move on the board."

"And how does this game work, exactly?"

"You'll see." Scarf Bird gave the mansion a darkly significant look. "Sooner than you might prefer, I'd wager."

I followed its gaze. I still had a good view of Marjorie's house, thanks to a bend in the road, and a strange shimmer caught my eye on the mansion wall. An iridescent speck—no, several of them—moving slowly up the side of the house. Then another, and another.

That couldn't be good. I started instinctively toward the mansion, my pulse speeding.

"You want to go the other way," Spectacles Bird suggested.

"Can't," I said shortly. "My friends are in there."

"Ah well," Scarf Bird sighed. "It's your funeral, I suppose."

There was something familiar about the sparkle of color in those specks, in the way they moved—more and more of them, scuttling up the side of the building toward the windows. It was that Echo beetle I'd seen in Prime, and a hundred of its friends.

Make that thousands. The scattering of specks swelled suddenly to a wave swarming up the walls. *Bloody Moon.* I broke into a run.

"Good luck!" the smallest bird called cheerily from behind me. "Goodbye!"

The beetles reached the windows and started pouring in through the cracks, and I was still too far away to get there with a blink step. I could maybe make it if I did several in a row, but that would leave me too spent to actually fight. A year ago I would have done it anyway—flung myself recklessly at the threat by any means in my power, and to the Void with the consequences, because my *friends* were in there. But with Emmi waiting for me at home, suddenly it seemed a lot less heroic and a lot more irresponsible to throw my life away like that.

I forced myself to run faster instead, pushing a body still unrecovered from the ravages of pregnancy harder than I'd dared in ages, trying not to think of what those bugs might do to Jaycel and Marjorie and Pearson and Rika. My mind raced with frantic plans—maybe I could set up a fire barrier, or get everyone into the wine cellar and defend that, or...

From within the house, muffled by walls and distance, came the faint high keen of many voices screaming.

Shit. I drew my knife, for all the good it'd do me, ready to slip into the Veil and see how far I could get in a single blink step. But I didn't get the chance.

A sound shook through me: the deep, metallic tolling of the clock. A mortal dread pierced deep into my bones.

The clock struck a second time, and the screaming fell ominously silent.

Not again. No, we weren't doing this again, it wasn't—

The misty street around me smeared into blinding light, and the world fell out from under me.

DO YOUR RESEARCH

Light sparkled all around me. I caught my balance as the world settled into strange, elegant, glittering angles.

Towering panes of clear glass formed three out of four ballroom walls plus the ceiling, with only thin strips of silvery metal holding them together like the bars of a fancy birdcage. Snow drifted down from a clear sky, settling in a sparkling dusting across a winter topiary garden that certainly didn't exist in the Prime version of Dona Marjorie's mansion. The Moon hung dazzlingly bright and full above, with no shadows of old blood spattered across it.

Jagged columns of clear rock crystal stood in corners and on tables, glowing from within with a cold white light; ice sculptures and mirrors and strange glass centerpieces caught sparks of that light from every plane and curve until I had to squint against the dazzle. Shimmery music hung echoing in the air, played on silver chimes and glass flutes. Everyone's clothes had gone white and silver and pale ice blue, with crystals and tiny mirrors sewn into bodices and waistcoats, and diamonds gleaming on throats and in hair. My bright red peacock coat stood out like blood on the snow.

The clock still stood in its spot, unchanged, jarringly out of place in this palace of light and glass, save for the silvery gleam of the crack down its face. The hour hand now pointed to a swirly number two.

What the fuck had just happened?

That had felt like sinking into a deeper Echo. But it was strange enough for a whole building to slip down between worlds once—to do it *twice* was unheard of. No doubt it had to do with that eye-hurting rip in the sky I'd seen when I stepped outside, but that didn't make me feel better.

Not to mention that I hadn't even been *in* the building, or under that Void-cursed sky hole. If the house had fallen down to the second Echo, I should have been left behind in the first. Everything about this went against all the knowledge I'd painstakingly gleaned about Echoes during my ten years of doing missions into them as a Hound.

The bird's voice came back to me: *It's too late for you. You're already marked.*

Great. Just great. Not only were we all pieces in some Echo game now, but we couldn't leave the board without getting pulled back in.

I took a deep, steadying breath, then another. Everyone was alive and well at least, with no sign of whatever those bugs had done to make them scream like that. Maybe they'd just been alarmed at seeing a million beetles pour into the house and nothing bad had happened at all. Sure, I could tell myself that.

Or maybe something truly horrible had happened, but it had once again all been undone.

My eyes pulled to the mantel clock, which had transformed from marble to crystal to match the new aesthetic theme. Just about ten minutes of nine. Again.

This wasn't something as simple (ha!) as a huge hole in the Veil opening up under Marjorie's house and it falling through into the first Echo. Something more complex and sinister was going on. I had to shake the dust off my brain and figure out what.

So. We were stuck in an Echo game, which was bad news. It happened sometimes—powerful Echoes who couldn't meaningfully hurt one another playing out their conflicts through hapless human proxies in some twisted contest. You heard stories. My favorite dumpling place had closed when the owner got drawn into some stupid feud between quarreling Echoes, his life spent with the casual disregard of a chess player sacrificing a pawn. And everyone knew about how the fall of the Sigil Empire began when warring Empyreans—the most powerful Echoes of all—had turned its capital city into a great labyrinth to see whose chosen mortals would make it out alive.

Probably the bugs were the agents of one Echo and the silver-eyed swordsman was the agent of another Echo, and their masters had declared this place their game board and marked everyone here as pieces. But none of that explained why I was the only one who remembered what had happened, or what that great cursed grandfather clock was doing with time. Or how to get us all safely out of this mess.

I needed more information. For starters, I should take advantage of the resources I had—and I'd been underusing one of my best ones.

Time to find Pearson.

It wasn't hard; he was at the buffet, picking through lumpy pale fruit with a frown denting his forehead, as if he couldn't quite figure out why everything looked so strange.

"Hey. Pearson."

He turned, and his face lit up. I felt a bit guilty about brushing him off earlier. "Kem! Didn't expect to see you here, what with you on leave and all."

"I didn't move to another country," I reminded him. "Just had a baby."

"Baby. Right." Another puzzled look crossed his face as he struggled to remember. "Small...potato-shaped human? I heard that somewhere."

"Yeah. From me."

His frown only deepened; he didn't remember.

"Listen, Pearson. You know everyone who's anyone, right?" I tried what I hoped was a flattering sort of smile.

Pearson squinted as if he couldn't make out what had gone wrong with my face. "No? No, not personally. I know *about* everyone, for the job, but they're not inviting me to their weddings or anything."

Desk Hounds were researchers. Fountains of information. And

Pearson was a classic Lantern Moon—planning and knowledge, granting insight and guiding the way. I should have come to him earlier. Almarah always said to do your research first, or regret it later.

"Who at this party would you ask if you had a question about Echoes?"

He peered around the ballroom. "Hmm. Oh, definitely them." He jerked his chin at the lean youth with shaggy black hair I'd noticed earlier, who now plucked curiously at the sparkling white robe they were wearing as if not certain how it had come to be on their body. "Signa Blair. They're a Raven."

The name made it click: *That* was why the kid had looked familiar. "Blair *Morningray*?"

"That's them. Right, you're friends with their sister, aren't you?"

"Last time I saw them they were about three inches shorter and had long scraggly hair." They'd also been emaciated, haunted, and wearing a Redgrave Academy uniform. They looked worlds better now, considering it couldn't have been…huh. The Redgrave job had been the last one I took before finding out I was pregnant, so it'd been about ten months already. It seemed unfair that the world had kept going so fast while my life was paused.

"They were only recently sworn in," Pearson said, "but a Raven is a Raven. No one better to ask about Echo stuff."

"Perfect. Are they an Echo worker? That's exactly what I need." I wasn't sure; I didn't know Blair very well. They were much younger than Jaycel.

"No. Works in their library."

So much for that. Well, it was better than nothing.

"Thanks. Got a theory question for them."

Pearson nodded in an *Echo theory is incredibly boring, please don't tell me about your question* sort of way.

What else should I ask him? I suspected I didn't have unlimited time before everything went to shit again. "Another people question for you. If you knew a fight might break out at this party, who would you want on your side? Besides me."

"Oh, that's easy. Beryl Cascarion."

I barely stopped myself from physically recoiling. *"Beryl?"*

"Yeah. You know, Beryl. Wolf guild mercenary, rugged-looking, sense of humor. You two were…" He grimaced. "Sorry, stepped in that, didn't I."

"Beryl isn't even in Acantis," I said flatly. "He took a mission overseas and said he wasn't coming back." The very day after I'd told him I was pregnant, in fact. "Who would you want on your side who's actually *here?*"

"Oh, right." He chewed his lip a moment, then said decisively, "Rika Nonesuch."

"Besides her," I said through my teeth.

"She's the best choice." He shrugged. "What do you have against her, anyway?"

"She's a Cat."

"Sure, Cats are annoying, but they're not *that* bad. I get along okay with some Cats. *You* get along okay with some Cats."

"Not this one. Not after the star diamond thing."

Pearson blinked. "Oh, come on, Kem, that was just business."

I wasn't about to explain to him how it wasn't *just business* when, at the single most vulnerable time of your life, someone who you really liked pretended to be romantically interested just so she could drug you in order to steal some stupid trinket.

"We handed each other our worst failure," I said instead. "And we both hate to fail. Of course we don't get along."

An odd little smile twisted its way onto Pearson's face.

"What?" I growled.

"Nothing."

"What?"

"Oh, no. I don't want my face punched in." He lifted his hands in surrender. "But if you think something might happen at this party, you should talk to her. Whether you hate her or not, she's good."

Whether I hated her or not wasn't a question I was ready to deal with. "Ugh. You're probably right. I'll go talk to her."

Pearson clapped my shoulder, gingerly and in slow motion, giving me plenty of time to stop him if I saw fit. "Good luck."

"I hate luck. If I do my job right, I shouldn't need it. But thanks."

I spotted Rika right away, standing with that same older woman in the purple dress (now palest lavender)—she must be the other Cat, Adelyn Cail. Rika's face was shuttered and tense; whatever her colleague was telling her, she didn't look happy about it. Now was maybe not a good time to talk to her. Which was fine, because in all honesty I was *not* up for dealing with Rika Nonesuch quite yet.

I made my way to a less crowded spot, where I could see around people to look for Blair (at my height, seeing *over* the crowd was not an option). The dancers streamed off the floor as the musicians took a break, and for a moment I had a clean line of sight to the grandfather clock where it presided over the room in ornate and sinister glory.

It had tolled right before we fell into a new Echo, both times. I *really* needed to ask Marjorie where exactly she'd gotten that thing. Honestly, I should never have touched such an obvious Echo relic—it was sheer luck I didn't wind up cursed.

Something moved just beyond the clock, a flash of pale hair and a drab apron. The little girl.

Her eyes caught mine, widening. I restrained the impulse to chase after her and instead gave her a friendly smile and a little wave. Sometimes you had to build confidence before you approached a potential contact.

She flashed a smile back—brief, hesitant, and heart-meltingly sweet. Then a drunken tailcoat wove in front of me, talking too loudly to a friend who lagged behind him; in the second it took him to pass me, she disappeared.

Wait. That drunken tailcoat was familiar. Sure enough, here came Carter with a tray of glasses balanced on his hand, moving briskly through the crowd.

The inebriated youth tripped and staggered. I dove for him, half catching him and redirecting his momentum toward his friend instead. Carter swerved, a startled exclamation marring his perfect poise.

The drunk stumbled into his friend's steadying grasp. Carter's tray teetered, swayed...and stabilized.

I let out a great breath of relief.

"Whew! Thanks, Signa Thorne!" Carter smiled and mimed wiping away sweat. The young tailcoat apologized, mortified.

"My pleasure." I gave them both a nod and turned away before they could see the disproportionate grin spreading across my face.

I could change things. I could *save* things. The future wasn't written in stone.

As if to confirm my luck was turning, I found Blair. They were staring up at a lamp that hung where a chandelier used to be; it glowed with a soft bluish-white radiance, and little flecks of what appeared to be snow drifted continuously down from it.

I approached and stood next to them, staring at it, too. "Strange lamp."

"Is that what it is? I thought it was a condiment." They fluttered their fingers, imitating the snow-stuff. "I want to lick it, but that's probably a bad idea."

"Probably," I agreed. Now *I* wanted to lick it, damn it. "I'm Kembral, by the way. In case you don't remember. I know when we last met things were... well, complicated."

Blair turned to me, blinking. Their great shaggy fall of black hair obscured one eye; the other peered out a surprisingly deep sapphire blue from a solemn, pale face.

"Oh, I remember. My sister talks about you all the time."

"She talks about you, too." It was true enough, if mostly in the context of affectionate headshakes and eye rolls. "I hear you know a lot about Echoes."

"I don't know about a *lot*." They waved the back of their hand at me, showing their guild tattoo as if that explained everything. "I have more questions than answers. Did you know we're in an Echo right now, for instance?"

"Oh, *finally*, yes! Yes, I do!" It was all I could do not to grab them with both hands. "Do you remember what happened? How we got here?"

"It's the strangest thing," they said dreamily, "but no. I must have been distracted. I just had one of those moments, you know, where you realize you've been staring at something a long time, and you don't know what you were doing before that."

I nodded as if I knew what they were talking about. *Ravens.* Blair must not remember any more than the others, then; they'd just figured out we were in an Echo on their own.

"Do you have any idea how we *could* have gotten here? What sort of circumstances could cause a whole building full of people to fall down to a lower Echo?"

"Oh, it's probably the convergence."

A thrill of recognition tickled my spine. That was what Pearson had said right before he died.

"What's a convergence?"

Blair placed their palms together in a meditative gesture. Then they rotated them in strange directions, making little *Pssshhh! Psshh-eewww! Brooooop!* noises.

Jaycel's eye rolls all began to make sense. "Uh. Signa Blair?"

"Just Blair is fine," they said serenely.

"Fine. Blair. What the Void did that mean?"

"Oh, wasn't it clear?" They seemed genuinely crestfallen.

"I think I may lack the, uh, theoretical grounding to follow you. Can you use . . . words?"

"Hmm." They tilted their head. "Well, it's a bit like how anyone slips through into an Echo, only more so."

"Right. Thin spots in the Veil."

"They're good places for Echo working." Blair sighed. "I can't do it yet. I'm a little nervous about trying, after my teachers were so mean about it at Redgrave. But my mentor in the Ravens tells me that's all right, I should wait until I'm comfortable, and in the meantime I'm still useful to the guild because of my eye."

"Your . . . eye?"

"Yes, it's quite handy." Blair slipped a hand under their thick fall of hair and pushed it back from their face, revealing their other eye: a wild, intense blue like the deepest depths of a lagoon, with a sheen of colors shifting across it as if it bore a thin coating of sun-struck oil.

My breath hitched. "Right. You're Echoborn. I keep forgetting because Jaycel—"

"Isn't, I know. I'm her half brother. Or sibling, I suppose, but I grew up with *brother* and I like it."

I'd known they were Echoborn, of course, even without having seen the eye before. Every kid at Redgrave Academy was. But there was a difference between knowing in the abstract that someone was Echoborn and having a gorgeous, magical, inhuman eye suddenly blinking at you from their face.

Blair let the curtain of hair fall back into place. "It's by way of my grandfather. Both his eyes are like this, and he has pointed ears and a tail. He was always very nice to me when I was little, but he's not allowed to visit anymore after he tried to steal me away on my twelfth birthday." They sounded a little mournful, as if they were sorry he'd failed.

Fascinating as this was, I couldn't wander off track. "So with your Echo eye, you can see this convergence?"

"Sort of. The Echoes are always shifting, always flowing. Like water or mist. The soft spots move around, appear and disappear. But sometimes they line up, temporarily, and that's how people can fall down more than one Echo." They stuck a hand out into the snow falling from the lamp, letting a scattering of flakes collect in their palm. "Two layers lining up happens all the time; three is rarer, and four you only see maybe once a Moon."

"Right. I know about that—I just didn't know the term convergence." Of course the Ravens would have a fancy name for it. "So three layers lined up tonight? With a soft spot big enough for a whole room to fall through?"

"Oh, no. Not three." Blair carefully licked one of the white flecks on their palm. They made a face as if it tasted bad, seemed to give it some thought, and then licked another one.

I had a sinking feeling. "How many? Four? *Five?*"

"Twelve." Awe came into their voice. "Prime reality and all eleven Echoes. It goes all the way down."

Below the last Echo, all that remained was the Void. I thought of that tear in the sky over Marjorie's house, stars glimmering through it, and my blood went cold as ice.

"That sounds...really bad."

Blair seemed to consider. "Well, I think it'll be all right? The layers will shift out of alignment in a few hours."

"Wait. A few hours in whose time? I know it can flow differently from Echo to Echo." Not to mention that it was a bit out of kilter at the moment.

"Oh, everyone's time."

I rubbed my temple. "Explain it to me like I'm a Hound, which I am, and know a lot more about swords than about Echoes, which is also true."

Blair pressed their fingertips together, matching each carefully to its twin and thumb to thumb, and peered at me through the resulting cage with their brilliant blue eye. "The convergence occurs in time as well as space. The points all line up."

Pieces began clicking together in my brain. "So does that mean the convergence starts and ends at the same time in each Echo? And if, for instance, you kept slipping down from one Echo to the next, is it possible you might start at the beginning of the convergence in each layer?"

"You're getting it!" Blair beamed at me.

"Would that actually turn back time, though? Undo everything that happened in the previous Echo?"

"Oh, no. Even an Empyrean can't change things that have already happened. You'd just be arriving at, say, the reflection of ten o'clock in each Echo, the same way you could arrive at the reflection of the Grand Theater. I suppose a really good Echo worker might possibly be able to use that synchronicity to reverse the *effects* of things that happened during the lost time—passing through the Veil is a lovely cleanser, you know, very good for the skin—but it would all still have *happened*."

So everyone *had* died. Someone had reversed the results of the poisoning rather than undoing the event itself. Which seemed to come down to nearly the same thing; my brain felt a bit stretched trying to work it out. Either way, it raised the question of *who*. So far as I knew, no one here had the skills to work Echoes at all, let alone perform a working that powerful.

"I see," I said. "Thank you for explaining."

"Oh, it's my pleasure. It's all very interesting."

I hesitated, then nodded at their finger, where a few flecks of white still clung. "So, what does it taste like?"

They blinked their big blue eyes. Or the one I could see, anyway. "Oh, it's terrible. A bit like grapefruit, I think."

"Grapefruit? That's terrible?"

"It is when you're expecting sugar."

"Fair enough." Something occurred to me then, its unpleasant implications skittering across my thoughts with too many legs. "Wait. If the convergence ends at the same time in every Echo, and you think it'll last a few hours...Does that mean it'll end right around midnight, at the year-turning?"

"Oh, now that you mention it, yes! And the year-turning is a big important event that makes ripples all through the Echoes, so the year won't turn anywhere until it turns *everywhere*."

A crux year, Pearson had said. No wonder there was some kind of Echo power play going on.

"Great," I muttered.

"It really is! We're lucky the convergence happened to occur here. It could have been anywhere."

"It sure is some kind of luck, yeah."

"It's a shame it's so short." They sighed. "I doubt I'll ever get to see another full convergence in my life."

"Ha, well, if you want it to last a little longer, you could bind it in place with..." I trailed off, horrified realization sinking in.

Blair waited expectantly, calm and curious, as if they were used to people's thoughts wandering and leaving sentences unfinished.

"Blood," I whispered. "What if someone stabilized the convergence with a blood seal?"

One drop was enough to keep a normal hole in the Veil open a little longer when I needed to buy time on a retrieval. There were a lot of drops of blood in a human body.

Blair tipped their head, thinking about it. "That would work, though for something this big it might take a death to make it stable. And they'd have to carve the blood seal into every Echo, plus Prime, too. Then the passage would stay open, with the layers pinned in place." Blair made a strained sort of grimace, as if they meant to smile but knew on some level that it wasn't funny. "Of course, no one would do that, because it would require a truly excessive amount of violence."

So that was their game. The silver-eyed nightmare and an unknown number of others were vying to build a tunnel straight through reality to the deepest Echoes. The ones where everything dissolved into madness and darkness, and even I wouldn't go after a lost dog because it would come back with six eyes and bonus tentacles. They were paving a highway in blood that all those incomprehensible horrors could march and slither and ooze up into my reality, my city, my home.

This was so, so much worse than I'd thought.

BE READY FOR ANYTHING

It was hard to enjoy food while contemplating the apocalypse. I forced myself to grab some crab puffs anyway, because I apparently might have to battle horrors from *eleven fucking Echoes down* before the night was over, and I'd need my strength. I gulped down a cup of water for good measure. Liquid victory, Almarah called it.

I wiped my mouth on the back of my forearm, across the stylized silhouette of a running hound tattooed there. *Right*. This had escalated from murder investigation to Echo retrieval to a situation that could destroy Acantis. I couldn't mess this up.

Think, Kembral. If these Echoes were trying to make a blood seal, I had to keep them from killing anyone else. But there had to be more to their goal than simply murdering one person in each layer; too many things didn't add up. And then there was the clock. I still had no idea how it fit into the picture I was building. This game had additional rules I didn't understand, and if I couldn't figure them out soon, more people were going to die.

This was way too big for me to handle alone. I needed to recruit help—which was going to be hard when I couldn't explain what was going on.

There had to be *some* reason I wasn't forgetting like everyone else.

Greater Echo experience, maybe? But that didn't make any sense. Was there something I'd done that no one else here had? Something I ate or touched or . . .

My gaze dragged across the ballroom, to where the grandfather clock loomed above a swirling mass of dancers. That thing was at the center of this mystery—straight from a Deep Echo or I'd eat my socks—and I'd *bled* on it.

The little cut on my finger still hadn't closed, though I supposed it had only been an hour or so (if time even meant anything anymore). I glanced at the thin red line—and froze at what I saw.

Tiny rainbow sparkles gleamed in the cut, mixing with my blood, embedded in my flesh. Dust-sized specks of glass from the face of that Moon-cursed clock.

I was no Raven; I had no idea what that meant. Maybe Blair could explain what would happen if you got little bits of a powerful Echo relic in your veins while also accidentally putting a blood seal on said Echo relic. But if I was looking for what set me apart from everyone else here—well, it seemed like a pretty safe bet.

I curled my wounded fingertip against my palm with its neighbors, making a careful fist. This was creepy, but I could use it.

A startled cry sounded nearby. My head jerked up in time to spot a flash of scuttling iridescence as a couple of richly dressed party guests brushed frantically at their clothing.

"Oh!"

"I say! Did it bite you?"

The beetle was scurrying for the cover of a table. Distant screams echoed in my memory, and my stomach turned over thinking about what might have happened to my friends when thousands of them swarmed into this place.

I took a few quick strides over to the glittering thing and brought my boot down on it, hard.

There was no crunch, just a puff of glittering dust. Echoes always had a strange give to them, as if their reality collapsed in the face of Prime violence. I might feel bad about it if I weren't pretty sure these things had just killed a whole bunch of people in a fashion I didn't want to contemplate.

An insidious thought weaseled into my brain: Could I have stopped it? If I hadn't held back—if the instant I saw those bugs streaming into the mansion I'd done a chain of blink steps to get inside before the screaming started—could I have saved them? Before I had Emmi, I would have tried, without a second's hesitation.

I squashed that line of thought as firmly as I had the bug. Sure, I would have tried, and I probably would have collapsed exhausted on the floor from overextending myself, unable to help anyone. I was more cautious now, yes, but in this case cautious equated to smart. Maybe it always had, and I'd been a young and reckless fool.

No wonder so many Hounds took up desk duty or teaching once they had kids. I doubted I'd be keen anymore to take on the kind of jobs that required a willingness to jump in front of a knife.

Better to realize that now than to hesitate in a crisis. I couldn't afford mistakes tonight—I had to do this right, using every resource and skill I had, if I wanted to make it home alive.

Every resource.

I swallowed my pride and my scruples and whatever else was clogging up the back of my throat and went looking for Rika.

—ɱ—

I found her slinking up to the damned clock, giving it a look like it was a mark she planned to relieve of its cuff links, graceful as always in a silvery variation of that smoke-and-shadows gown.

Time to turn the tables. I moved up behind her as quietly as I could. Her focus seemed intent on the clock, so maybe this once—

She turned. "Why, Kembral Thorne. You weren't trying to sneak up on me, were you?" Her lips pulled to one side, as if the idea were adorable.

"Of course not."

"That's good. Because if you were, I'd tell you to leave it to the professionals."

I jerked my chin at the clock. "Like that thing? You looked like you might have a professional interest in it."

Rika let out a rich, velvety laugh. "It'd be a bit big to slip in my pocket."

The smoother Rika was on the surface, the falser she was underneath. I'd gotten used to a more rough, wry, honest Rika before things went sour, and the cultivated music of that laugh felt like a gut punch. I tried not to let it rattle me.

"What do you know about the clock?" I asked. "It's important."

She eyed me speculatively. "What do *you* know? We could trade information."

"Believe me, I'd love to." This would be so much simpler if the Echo would let me explain what was going on. "All I can say is that something big is happening tonight, something extremely dangerous to all of us, and this clock is at the middle of it."

"Oh, don't get theatrical on me, Thorne." Her polish chipped, an edge of frustration showing through. "If you don't want to tell me, just say so. If you want something in return, ask. I'm not in the mood for games."

"*You're* not in the mood for games? I didn't realize that was even possible."

"It happens," she said curtly. "So tell me what you know about this clock, or shove off."

Whoa, something must be *really* bothering her. A traitorous glimmer of concern welled up in me. There'd been a time when I would have asked her what was wrong. A time when she would have sighed and said *Come on*, and we would have found some private spot—the rooftop, maybe—and she would have told me.

I suddenly hated what I was about to do, and not only because working with her right now would be like sticking a fork in an infected wound. She was clearly not having a great night, and I was about to make it so much worse.

I swallowed. "Can you...Listen, can you just trust me?"

She drew in a sharp breath. I held her gaze, even though my cheeks were burning at my own audacity in asking that of her now, after everything that lay between us. A long moment slid by.

"I can't," she said at last. "Not on this."

"Fair." I rubbed my face. How was I going to get her to do what I needed, if I couldn't explain and she wouldn't trust me?

Oh. Hmm, that might work.

I gave her my most level look. "I can tell you this. If you run your finger along that crack in the clock's face, you'll learn everything I know about it."

"What? Is this some joke, Kembral?"

"I am absolutely, deadly serious."

She frowned. "Are you going to explain?"

"No. You have to try it yourself. I promise, if you do, everything will become clear."

I forced myself to turn without another word and walk away.

Don't look back. Don't look back. I wanted so badly to see if she was going to do it—if she stared after me, frustrated and puzzled, before turning slowly to face the clock—but if I looked back at her, I'd ruin it. I had to walk away with all the supreme confidence of someone with nothing to lose.

Except that I had everything to lose. So did Rika; she just didn't know it.

All right. Ally hopefully acquired. Next: information. Time to ask Dona Marjorie about that clock. If Almarah ever found out I'd waited this long to properly investigate it, she'd put me back in novice training.

I found Marjorie quickly enough, resplendent in acres of puffy white tulle at the center of the party. More of that fake grapefruit snow floated down around her, making her a vision of winter. She was surrounded by guests, but when she saw me, she laughingly disengaged herself from them and swept over to say hello. Flecks of glittering white clung to her elaborate grey braids.

"Signa Kembral! I'm so glad you're here. How's little Emmelaine?"

"Wonderful, thank you." It seemed quicker than getting into the whole not sleeping thing again. "I wanted to ask you—"

She patted my shoulder. "Do you need a private room to deal with your milk? It's not a problem, dear, you can use the blue guest room on the second floor."

"What? No—or yes, I probably will at some point, thank you— but I actually wanted to talk to you about a security concern. I don't mean to alarm you, but there might be some...unfortunate Echo business in play at your party tonight."

Marjorie pressed a hand to her bosom. "Oh dear. They do get unruly sometimes, don't they? I hope it's nothing serious."

Far less surprise flickered in her eyes than I expected. *Huh.* Maybe I could cut straight to the point.

"I'm wondering where you got that clock, actually. There are rumors flying around about it."

Dona Marjorie procured a lovely filigreed fan from her sleeve and spread it before her lips. "Well, I did hope it would be a conversation starter! You know I love to collect interesting antiques, but this one practically fell into my lap. Someone heard I liked that sort of thing and came straight to my door with it, selling it for a song."

"And you weren't worried it was a trap?" It had been a while since I'd done bodyguarding work, but the notion of some stranger offering up an Echo relic to a City Elder gave me hives.

Marjorie laughed. "Oh, of *course* I had it vetted. It's perfectly safe."

Sure it was. "If you had it vetted, what does it do?"

"Why, do you think it might be an Echo relic?" Marjorie made her eyes wide and fluttered her fan, which might have fooled someone who didn't know her as well as I did. "Oh my Moon and stars! What a notion!"

The idea that she could possibly not realize that it was an Echo relic was absurd, of course—*Emmi* could probably tell that was an Echo relic. If she was reluctant to admit it, that probably meant she'd gotten it through the black market, like half the city's elite did. Fine; I could ask her more later, when we weren't surrounded by a crowd of people who might be in range to overhear.

"Let me be clearer. The reason I'm asking is that the unfortunate Echo business I was talking about is mass murder."

Marjorie's eyes widened a fraction. *That* had surprised her.

"I know your security pretty well," I continued, "and I want to talk to your people and make sure every magical, physical, and human protection possible is in place."

Marjorie nodded, all serious now. "You know I trust your judgment, after all you've done for my family. I'll send Carter to talk to you, and I'll go see if I can scare up a useful Echo relic or two—you never know what I might find in the attic!"

"Thank you. That's perfect." I glanced around and dropped my voice to a low murmur (Marjorie couldn't hear whispers, because they were too high-pitched for her aging ears). "With that context, I hope you can see why I'm concerned about the clock. Are you sure there's nothing you can tell me?"

A spark of understanding kindled in her dark eyes. "I suppose it's fair to say that I got a tip things might get *interesting* at my little party tonight—though I didn't realize they might mean *lethally* interesting— and someone I trust told me the clock might help."

"Forgive me, but are you being vague on purpose to protect their identity, or was your source vague when they passed you this information?"

She laughed as if I'd made some witty joke. "Oh, Kembral. A little of each, my dear, a little of each. If I had any more real information, rest assured I'd give it to you. I must say I'm very glad to have you here tonight!"

I sighed. "I'm glad I'm here, too. I wouldn't want you to have to deal with this on your own."

She swept off to find Carter. I watched her go, mulling my next steps as the familiar sound of Dona Vandelle calling Harking a writh-ing sack of vermin rose above the noise of the party. If Vandelle kept using that line in each Echo, did that mean she'd rehearsed it in advance? I couldn't suppress a chuckle at the thought.

"Signa Thorne. May I have a moment of your time?"

I turned and took in dark hair barely streaked with silver, a shim-mering gown of palest purple, and eyes hard as agates. It was the woman I'd seen Rika talking to earlier: Adelyn Cail, the Watcher. Damned Cats, always sneaking up behind a person.

"Signa Cail," I greeted her. "Of course."

"Forgive my bluntness, but what exactly is your relationship to Rika Nonesuch?"

I blinked. "Pardon?"

"You're not on duty. You're therefore not relevant to her job. And yet she's been watching you all night, to the detriment of her work. I need to know whether she's compromised. What is your relationship?"

My eyes must have been bugging right out of my head. I wasn't sure what was more unbelievable—that Rika could be watching me (*to the detriment of her work*, no less!), or that her superior in the Cats would come straight out and admit to a Hound that they were working a job tonight in order to pry into my personal life.

"This is a very strange thing to ask," I said carefully.

"These are strange times. Answer the question, Hound."

Aha. I leaped on that. "Strange how?"

"If you don't know, I'm not about to discuss it with you. Now answer me. What is your relationship with Rika Nonesuch?"

How was she a senior Cat if she was this unsubtle? Or maybe she was up to something tricky and complicated. Maybe she didn't care about the information and was just looking to rattle me—in which case it had worked. But she seemed to expect a reply.

I felt a slow smile tugging at my mouth.

"If you don't know," I said, "I'm not about to discuss it with you."

"This is important, Signa Thorne."

"Care to explain it, then?"

She gave me a look of mute frustration. I dipped my head to her in what was almost a bow.

"I'm happy to reciprocate when you are. Until then, have a lovely evening, Signa Cail."

Maybe it wasn't a good idea to alienate a senior guild member when I needed all the allies I could get. But between this and that whole bit with the sharp object earlier, I was starting to suspect *she* might be the reason Rika was so rattled. If Cail was messing with Rika...well, it was none of my business, but still: fuck her. Anyway, I had a lot more important things to do than add details to some Cat guild dossier on me.

I was saved from any possibility of a response from Cail by a sudden squealing stream of people rushing toward the dance floor between us. The musicians were back and had struck up "Under the Flower Moon," which judging by the general reaction must be the season's big popular song. Stars, even I'd heard it, and I'd been practically living under a rock.

I heard someone coming up behind me and turned to find Harking, not so sneaky as a Cat but just as dangerous, his dark eyes dancing.

Jaycel's bad decisions notwithstanding, there was no denying Harking's outside was less objectionable than his inside: tall and lean, with handsomely silvered temples to match the buttons on a tailcoat that this Echo had turned to pale grey brocade. He had a long face and the sort of deep vertical grooves beside his mouth that seemed to exist to bracket sardonic smiles delivered to enemies just before their destruction.

"Signa Thorne. So lovely to see you here tonight."

After our last conversation, I certainly wouldn't have expected him to apply the word *lovely* in my general vicinity. But there was no sign of a threat in his demeanor this time.

"Dona Harking," I greeted him warily.

"I'll admit I was surprised when I heard you were coming, but I'm glad to see you back in the game." He lifted his glass to me; I strove not to show my surprise at a sentiment so opposite the one he'd expressed in Prime. "I was hoping to hire you, once you're back at work. I always have use for a competent professional such as yourself."

"You can post a job with the Hounds anytime. We're all competent professionals."

"Of course. But one hears such good things about you, Signa Thorne. Your diligence. Your discretion. You are a particularly skilled bodyguard, are you not?"

What was he up to? Earlier he'd been flat-out threatening me if I came back to work, and now suddenly he was flattering me and offering a job. It was like he was a different person. He'd even greeted me differently—back in Prime, he'd said he was surprised to see me, but this time he'd said he was surprised to *hear I was coming.* Which was strange in and of itself—I hadn't known my sister could take Emmi until two days ago, so how the news could have made it to

76   MELISSA CARUSO

him was a mystery—but it was an even stranger thing to lie about. Why pretend to be surprised if he knew I'd be here?

Unless it wasn't a lie. There was one way he could both have known I was coming *and* be surprised to see me: If he didn't expect me to make it here successfully.

Or alive.

Harking was waiting expectantly for my reply. I struggled not to show any sign of the sudden chill gripping me, plastering a smile on my face instead. I couldn't let my suspicion show; either I was wrong, which would be embarrassing, or I was right, and I needed to squeeze every drop of information out of him that I could if I wanted to live.

"I don't do bodyguarding anymore. Why, are you worried about assassins tonight?"

He let out a false little laugh. "One must always watch out for assassins, of course, as a City Elder. But no. I'm concerned about... other threats. Ones you might be uniquely suited to deal with."

There was a subtle tension beneath his voice. Maybe from hiding his animosity toward me, but I didn't think so. The way he glanced around from beneath those heavy lids, the tight set of his shoulders— Harking was afraid. This wasn't just a setup. Which meant he might know something about what was happening here tonight.

"I'm uniquely suited to deal with it, huh? I can't think why you'd need a bodyguard who can blink step. Did you run afoul of an Echo?" I let the question drop casually, almost a joke.

"Not precisely," he said evasively. "I suppose you might call the problem... Echo-adjacent."

Oh, he was in this up to his eyebrows. "Do tell."

"I'd have to hire you to tell. To be sure everything would be protected under your guild's client confidentiality rules."

Ah. So that was his angle. Whatever he was afraid I'd find out— whatever secrets or evidence he'd threatened me to keep me away from—if he hired me and told me about them, I could never tell anyone. Even if I found out the same information on my own in another job, it would be protected, and I'd be bound into silence. Clever.

"Alas, I'm not taking jobs now," I said.

"I could make it worth your while."

Let's see if I could startle some truth out of him. "I'm *especially* not taking jobs from people who want me dead."

His eyes narrowed. "Signa Thorne, you greatly exceed your—"

Over his shoulder there suddenly loomed a sinister and alien face, round and shining and spattered with darkness.

Harking's back arched with sudden impact. The tip of a sword sprouted from his chest like a bloodstained miracle.

The cloaked figure in the Moon mask had run him through from behind.

NO MERCY FOR MONSTERS

Without stopping to think, I slipped out of space and time.

It was like holding your breath. That shift that comes when you fill your lungs, up and outward. Except my breath wasn't the only thing that paused; everything did.

The world went golden and blurry, as if I'd plunged into a vat of honey. Harking froze in mid-stagger, blood drops hanging in the air, wineglass stopped in mid-fall, hand clawing for the dagger at his hip.

The figure behind him stood braced to pull the sword back out of his body, shoulders bunched strangely beneath that concealing cloak, tarnished silver mask tilted as if in contemplation. Up close there was something unnatural about the angle of the head, the clawlike shape of the gloved hand on the sword hilt. *An Echo.*

I drew my knife and launched into motion.

I could only remain in the Veil briefly, but I didn't need long. One quick pivoting step to close from the side, and I angled my blade up under the mask's chin—against a throat I could now see was too thin, too lumpy, inhuman.

I let go, and color and motion rushed back into the world.

This was no time to hold back, and the thing would re-form from the stuff of Echoes later anyway. I slashed the creature's throat. My blade met the strange lack of resistance that came when you cut an Echo, a sudden yielding as if its flesh gave up pretending to substance.

The Echo collapsed in a jumble of angles and pooling cloth. A puff of greyish smoke rose up; the tarnished mask clattered empty against the white marble floor. I stood over it, heart pounding, blood singing with the fear-edged thrill of the fight in a way it hadn't in almost a year.

I hadn't needed to think. I'd just *moved*. I could still do this.

A slight trembling strain started in my muscles, the kind I normally wouldn't feel until I'd fought for a couple of hours straight. *Already? Really?!* Apparently I could do this, but maybe not for as long as I might hope.

Cries of alarm rose around me. Harking knelt on the floor, coughing blood and gurgling; one glance confirmed he was beyond my help. Marjorie let out a startled gasp and hurried toward us, picking up her majestic skirts to sweep a swifter path.

"That was too easy," I muttered, nerves still sizzling with the uneven energy of surprise emergency violence.

"Physicker!" Marjorie called out to the stunned ballroom. "Oh my Moon and stars! Hurry, please!"

The same hapless physicker who'd tried to treat the poison ran over and dropped to his knees beside Harking, talking to him in a soothing voice even as his eyes went wide at the quantity of blood spreading startlingly red against the pale grey brocade. I hoped he could save him, even if I held no love for Harking. I didn't want him *dead*—and besides, we couldn't let them establish a blood seal.

Marjorie held her closed fan like a weapon, eyes hard and narrow, all pretense of fluttery vapors gone.

"Signa Kembral, I believe you wanted to talk about security."

"Do you have guards on duty?" I pitched my voice as low as I could and still be sure she'd hear me over the agitated cries of the party guests.

A grim nod. "Some."

Her serving staff were already moving, dropping trays and pulling blades in their place. Their purpose stood out against the panic of the crowd. But so did something else.

More cloaked figures with awkward angles and tarnished silver masks converged toward us. Their cloaks showed dark against the pale clothes of the guests and the sparkling white of the furnishings. *Here we go.*

I snatched the Echo's bloody sword off the floor and gave it a quick wipe on its empty cloak, picking out my targets: one, two, five, fuck-ing *twelve*, all over the ballroom. Not great odds, even with help from the guards and the hundred or so guests. Echoes were often far more dangerous opponents than humans.

Emmi needs you, a small voice said inside me. *She needs you alive. Get out of here while you can. Run home and make sure she's safe.*

No. I was still a Hound, damn it, and these people needed my help.

I cut the air a few times as a space cleared around me, trying to get the feel and balance of the sword. Not bad, though the hilt was wrapped thicker than I liked, fit for a large man's hand (or a long spindly claw).

A dozen silver masks turned toward me. A soft chittering arose from them, necks tilting those blank faces too far. *Twelve of them, oof.* This was going to be rough, especially with my endurance apparently shot. I couldn't let it go too long.

As one, the Echoes cast off their concealing cloaks. The dark mantled shrouds fluttered to the ground, revealing skinny limbs in close-fitting black as the creatures drew bright steel. There was a deep *wrongness* about them. Joints folded backward, limbs stretched too long, heads tilted at extreme angles, extra fingers gripping sword hilts.

One of them drew not a sword, but a weird glass dagger, oddly curved and with a green tint to it. Huh—this must be the strange party-crasher who'd cut Carter back in Prime. Looked like this Echo game had a third player, besides the bugs and Silver Eyes.

Most of the guests pressed back against the walls with shrieks and gasps, but some were frozen with shock or less mobile. The masked figures moved after them, limbs flexing in sickening directions. One knocked over a glowing crystal lamp with careless violence; it shat-tered into a thousand shining pieces, skittering among the feet of the frightened guests.

Another lifted a sword to strike down Blair, who stood staring with dreamy puzzlement and not nearly enough alarm, as if the Echoes were pigeons who had somehow got into the ballroom. Jaycel had her sword out and was sprinting toward them, fear in her eyes, but she wasn't going to make it in time.

Luckily, I could make it there *outside* of time.

I stepped once more into the golden border of realities, where time froze like bubbles in the air and space was an illusion I created for my own sanity, and sprinted across the room. I passed straight through the blurry shadows of panicked guests as if they were phantoms. My feet didn't touch the floor—didn't touch anything. There was nothing to touch, no air to breathe, no sound but a profound muffling silence. A pressure built and built inside me for one heartbeat, two.

I reached Blair and brought my sword up to meet the one coming down at them, slipping back into reality just in time for metal to clash against metal, swatting the Echo's blade aside. Noise hit my ears in a sudden roar, feeling jarring back into arms that had been merely notional half a heartbeat ago—but I had trained all my life for this.

The creature hadn't. It recoiled in shock at my sudden appearance, uttering a skittering insectile shriek; I ran it through before it had time to realize what was happening.

Blair's eyes widened, their mouth shaping an O. Before they could speak, before the creature could puff into smoke, I slipped out of space again, my bones aching with the effort.

A quick scan showed me some masked figures still advancing, others engaged with guards, Rika slipping a stiletto into an Echo's back as it slashed in confusion at a whirl of illusory leaves, Cail stabbing another in the gut—*there*. Three were converging on the oblivious physicker as he closed Harking's eyes; Marjorie stood over him, her fan brandished before her. One sword slashed at her side, frozen in the amber of the timeless Veil between Echoes.

Time to put a stop to *that*.

I crossed the distance between us and flung myself back into reality blade first, knocking the creature attacking Marjorie into its fellow as

I stabbed it. Echo smoke exploded in my face, and a tarnished mask clunked off my shoulder. The second one staggered, too-long limbs flailing for balance; I shook my blade free of the collapsing cloak of the first and slashed it in two before it could recover.

My breath came hard as I whirled to face the last one, legs weak already. Three blink steps in a row was draining at the best of times, and I was wrecked by months of pregnancy and lack of sleep.

Only a puddle of cloak topped with a staring empty mask remained of the third. Marjorie stood above it, fan spread and ready like a shield.

You did not mess with Dona Marjorie.

All right, four down—seven counting the ones Rika, Cail, and Carter had just finished. Maybe we could handle this after all.

The ballroom doors flew open with a bang.

A cold, shuddering wind blew through the room, setting the chandeliers to tinkling and the false snow to swirling. The crowd instinctively stilled and pulled back, like an indrawn breath.

Into that tense waiting moment strode a man who was anything but human.

The cloak caught my attention first. It floated behind him like half-substantial black fog, its edges shifting and blurring, ends trailing ragged into thin air. Stars shone from within it, as if he'd ripped off a piece of night sky and pinned it to his shoulders.

His eyes gleamed like mirrors in a too-smooth face, a pale mockery of youth that contrasted jarringly with the ancient cruelty that radiated from him. Black horns curled from his brow, holding back a mane of silver hair. He wore midnight armor that fit him close as leather and flowed like water despite its hard metallic sheen.

It was the Echo I'd glimpsed earlier. I didn't feel any better getting a good look at him—anything that looked like *that* was very, very bad news.

The remaining Moon masks seemed to know it. They drew together in a sudden clump, chittering in awe or fear.

He surveyed the scene—the wounded, the dying, the few masks scattered empty on the floor—and his mouth twisted in disgust. In a long, slow motion, he drew a sword like a great jagged shard of black glass.

"This is a mess. None of these were your targets. Are you truly the best your master can field?"

Jaycel stepped forward into the moment as if it were made for her, a bloodless slash in one snow-white sleeve, and pointed her blade at him. Her face shone with glorious intent. Ever since we were children rattling around the Southside streets, she'd loved nothing better than standing up to a bully.

"If this is *your* mess," she said, "you have a lot to account for, darling."

A strange expression flickered across his alien face as he regarded her. "More than you can imagine. When you're in this far, all you can do is keep going. But no, this one isn't mine."

"Then whose is it? I normally avoid bills come due, but this one I'm eager to collect."

She'd gotten him talking. I didn't hold much hope that we could turn this into a negotiation and sort out our differences peacefully, but I'd take a distraction where I could get it.

"Much as I like the idea, I fear you might find that difficult." His silver gaze flicked suddenly to the grandfather clock, as if he'd heard something. "Ah. *That's* what's bringing them back. Clever. The poisoner must have known—a bold move. I must admit, I admire it."

Movement behind the Echo caught my eye—Carter, holding a shortsword in place of a serving tray, sneaking up quietly with determination in the set of his mustache. Oh, he did *not* want to do that. Carter was brave and game for anything, but he had no guild tricks to let him stand up to an Echo this powerful.

A few paces away, the Moon-masked Echo with the glass dagger lifted it in Carter's direction. A greenish light kindled within it, and the creature emitted an excited hiss.

I started to move—to wave him off, to defend him, *something*—but the silver-eyed Echo whirled on him with terrifying speed.

With a great arcing stroke, he buried his black sword in the angle of Carter's neck.

It was too fast for me to blink step, too fast even to react. I froze halfway through my instinctive lunge forward, catching in a sharp, awful breath.

"Good try," he said to the Moon-masked creature. "But you're too slow."

Carter went down in a bloody tumble.

There was no way he could have survived that. The Echo stood over him, blood on his sword. My gut twisted with sick grief; Jaycel let out a blistering curse, all showmanship banished by shock.

"You could never have won," Silver Eyes murmured to Carter's body, "but I admire that you were willing to play."

The deep, brassy note of the grandfather clock crashed through the ballroom, startling the panicked crowd into silence. Once, twice, three times, shattering us all with its heart-stopping thunder.

The Echo's face—bemused, almost sad—was the last thing I saw before the world melted, walls dripping into ruin around me as if it were all a watercolor painting in a heavy rain.

GATHER YOUR ALLIES

The point of a dagger pricked my back.

"What. The. *Fuck*," Rika hissed from behind me.

"So you remember this time," I greeted her without turning.

The party swirled giddily, mad with baroque splendor. Cascades of golden leaves and clustering grapes dripped from the corners, sculpted to such perfection I couldn't be sure they weren't real, edged with a faint black dusting of rot. Heavy curtains shimmered with rich colors, layered one atop another in artfully contrasting shades, until only a tiny square of window peered out onto the night sky from each massive frame of nested decadence; mildew faintly speckled these as well. A cloying scent of wilting roses and dust lay on the air. Cobwebs draped the massive twelve-tiered chandeliers in grand swaths, with all the pride of fine lace; the candles set there and in the walls flickered with a sickly greenish hue, dimming and brightening as if they could barely sustain themselves.

The dancers had changed to match. Too much powder whitened their faces, and too much kohl blackened their eyes. Gowns trailed sumptuous trains of ragged, moldering lace, and magnificent swallowtail coats with tarnished silver buttons bore the depredations of nibbling moths.

Only Rika remained unchanged, her perfume light and spicy as it had ever been, her gown of smoke and silver back to its original form as I glanced over my shoulder at her. Rika and me.

"*This* time? You mean to say there's been—oh. Oh, shit." The dagger eased away from my back. I dared to turn, facing a Rika gone haunted and hard-eyed. I couldn't help a stab of sympathy at the horror straining her face. I'd been there pretty recently, after all.

"This is an Echo, isn't it?" she demanded, glancing around as if her steely eyes could slash this false reality to ribbons. "I *hate* Echoes."

"You and me both."

"What's going on here, Kembral?" She brandished her bloody finger at me. "It's because of *this*, isn't it? You did this to me!"

"No." I caught her wrist just as she started to shimmer with illusion around the edges; I couldn't let her disappear now. "Rika, listen to me, or we're both screwed."

"What have you pulled me into? Is this your idea of payback?"

"I didn't do this. Do you remember an Echo with black armor and horns? And a bunch of others with Moon masks?"

"How in the Void could I forget them? They came storming in here and attacked us!"

"That wasn't the first time. It's some kind of Echo murder game with a new round in each layer of reality, and we've been drawn into it."

"That's fascinating, and this party's been lovely, but I'm afraid I can't stay any longer in this *cycling Echo death trap*. So if you'll just be so kind as to point me on my way—"

"Were you listening? They're *killing* people, Rika. I need you to help me stop them."

"No, no, no." She shook her head, black hair swishing around her jawline. "Don't mistake me for one of your Hounds. I'm a Cat. I don't fight Echoes. When things get dangerous, we run away, like anyone sensible should."

She extricated her wrist from my grip with a neat twist and started to go, that silvery dress flowing around her.

"If you walk out of here, you could get lost in this Echo forever,"

I called after her. It wasn't quite true—she'd get pulled into the next one—but I had to stop her, and that would take too long to explain.

Rika froze. "How far down are we?"

"Three Echoes down."

"Blood on the Moon." Her throat jumped. "*Three Echoes.* I've only ever been down one, and that was horrid."

I refrained from pointing out that I'd gone down six, thanks to fucking Pearson and his lost dog job.

"The only way we make it back home is to solve this, and I can't do it alone. I don't like it, either. But we've got no choice."

She raked trembling fingers through her hair. "You don't understand. I need to get back to Prime, *now.* I can't be here."

"None of us want to be here. The only way out is if we stop this Echo bastard and his pals from filling out their murder collection. We're tied into the game—we can't leave until we figure out how to flip the board."

Rika gave me a long, hard stare. At last, a gusty sigh burst from her painted lips. "*Fine.* If it's the only way, I'll help you."

"Great." Some of the tension left my shoulders. Rika might not be the person I'd have picked to work with, but it sure beat trying to do this alone.

"So how do we get out of this mess and back to Prime as quickly as possible?" She crossed her arms, making a tight bundle of herself.

"We need to stop them from completing a blood seal in any one Echo. So far as I can tell, that should end the game and let us escape." I frowned. "It looked like they were after a specific target last Echo, so it may be that they can't kill just anyone to make the seal."

"The man with the delightful mustache, you mean? That glass knife glowed when they pointed it at him."

"Carter. Yeah, maybe, though I don't know what's special about him." Something about that didn't feel quite right. "They seem to enjoy some indiscriminate killing along the way, too. I can't make sense of the rules yet."

Rika frowned. "Do we *need* to know the rules? We want them to stop murdering people. I don't much care how that affects their score."

"Good point."

"Leave it to a Hound to overcomplicate things." Her grey eyes swept the ballroom. They still showed some frightened white around the edges, but having a problem to work on seemed to be helping. I supposed that was one of the few ways we were alike. "I don't see any Echoes now. Do they always come in from outside?"

"So far as I can tell. I see where you're going—if we can keep them out of the building, they can't kill anyone." I liked that; securing buildings was something I knew how to do. "It's going to be tricky. That silver-eyed Echo seems powerful enough to overcome most guards, and one of the players is a bunch of beetles—it'd be impossible to seal every crack in this big old place tight enough to keep them out."

Rika's brow twitched. "How many—"

"You don't want to know."

She made a disgusted face. "You owe me for this, Kembral. Ugh. It's a shame we're not in Prime; an invitation ward would do the trick. But I don't exactly have one in my pocket."

I straightened. "Now, *this* is why I wanted you on my side. That's not a bad idea."

Rika was giving me a strange look. "Did you think I *wasn't* on your side?"

"You know what I mean. Those wards keep out anyone without an invitation, right? Serious Raven stuff."

"Echo stuff, actually. The only source I know for them is the Fisher Queen." She was still eyeing me dubiously. "I've had to try to get past them once or twice, and I regret to report they're unbreakable. Plus they work on any Echo, no matter how powerful, all the way up to an Empyrean."

"That makes sense. Echoes are pretty susceptible to stuff like hospitality rules. This might just work, if we can get our hands on one." I snapped my fingers. "If the Fisher Queen sells them, that means you can get them in the shallow Echoes."

"Are you suggesting we can just...*buy* one?"

"That's exactly what I'm saying."

Rika's brows climbed her forehead. "Do they have shops in the Echoes?"

"Sure. What they sell gets weirder as you go down, mind you, but that might work to our advantage." What they took in payment also got weirder, which I wasn't happy about—but if it came down to it, there was one coin almost any Echo shop would accept.

She glared at me suspiciously. "I thought you said that if we leave this room, we're lost in the Echo forever."

"I said *you* would be. *I* know my way around Echoes. Come on."

—⟐—

On the way out, I stole a curtain tieback cord (to hang my newly acquired sword at my hip) and gulped down some kind of spicy-fruity meat roll thing and some water (to help steady legs still trembling from my little burst of violent Veil-hopping activity). You wouldn't think so, but usually it was safe enough to eat and drink in Echoes, though I had to scout a bit for something that didn't look moldy. I absolutely hated how insecure the bare blade felt dangling at my side, like it'd slip out or foul my legs at any moment, but with murders happening on a recurring schedule it beat having no sword at all.

I was clearly going to have to get used to how every effort, both physical and mental, was this weird mix of both harder and easier than I expected. Easier without the baby; harder than before. I was getting tapped out faster than a cheap wine keg, but I was so used to pushing on through exhaustion now that it was second nature, so it wasn't slowing me down much. But coming home tonight to a sleepless, hungry baby was going to be rough—and having to continue caring for that sleepless, hungry baby tomorrow instead of sleeping half the day and groaning about my sore muscles was going to be rougher.

When I went back to work—*if* I went back to work—this would be my new reality. *Damn.* Maybe they'd let me take naps at the guildhouse.

We passed Jaycel chatting with a pair of waifish tailcoats, and for one fleeting moment I thought about telling her to go cut her finger on the clock so I could get more reinforcements. But then a breath-taking collage of memories of Jaycel making terrible life choices flashed before my eyes—challenging people to duels, jumping into the harbor, taking various ill-advised scoundrels to her bed, vandalizing the doors of city hall, stealing a horse, crashing a carriage...and actually, no. She was a good friend and a good fighter, but this situation was messy enough without contributing her wild impulses to it.

Rika eyed the door that led to the street as if it might bite her. Three Echoes down, that was a valid concern.

"Here we go," I breathed, and pushed it open.

The city we stepped out into had changed dramatically. Of course it had—but still, I couldn't help standing there blinking for a moment or two, struggling to map what I saw now onto the Acantis I knew.

"Shit," Rika whispered. "Oh, I don't like this."

"You get used to it," I said, which was absolutely a lie.

All right. Ignore the copper-green glow of the sky, sullen and stormy. That giant twisting spike of filigreed brass with a stylized eye set into its apex was probably the clock tower. The immense birdcage looming over the rooftops several blocks away, full of disturbingly large birds with bright plumage and cruel eyes, was in the right general location and shape to be the Grand Theater. Which meant the tilting castle covered in needle-thin towers must be city hall. Best not to ask what that irregular black lump was clinging to the tallest spire.

"I think I've got it," I muttered.

Rika was staring around wide-eyed at what had once been a stately Tower district street lined with the elegant brick townhouses and city mansions of the wealthy. In this Echo they lay in ruins, bricks and stone crumbled into the street, twisted bones of iron poking into the air. Some held rooms half-intact and open to the air like a doll's house, with furniture and threadbare wall hangings still in place, cheery fires laid in the hearths. Fluttery dark things circled overhead; they could have been bats or crows or something in between.

"I've spent my whole life trying to stay out of Echoes, and now you drag me into one." Rika wrapped her bare arms around herself and shivered. To be fair, that dress didn't look warm.

"*I* didn't drag you anywhere. *I* came here to relax and enjoy myself on my one and only night out in the past two months, which is now ruined, thanks." I eyed her sidelong. "Why have you been trying to stay out of Echoes your whole life?"

Not that they were a great place to visit, but it was an odd thing to say. Stumbling into Echoes wasn't all that common.

Her lips pressed tight, as if she'd realized she'd said too much. Finally, she let out a dramatic sigh. "I had a bad experience once, all right?"

"With an Echo?"

"With an Empyrean."

"Holy fuck."

I stopped in the ruined street and stared at her. A scuttling clockwork ant the size of a small dog ran past, making an ominous humming sound, and I didn't so much as glance at it.

"Yes," she said in a clipped tone, as if that closed the matter.

"Oh, come on. You can't just say you had a bad experience with an *Empyrean* and then not elaborate."

"I can, actually." She gestured pointedly down the street. "Lead the way, Kembral."

Well, now I was desperately curious. The Empyreans were the strongest Echoes, divine monarchs among the strange lords of elsewhere, born of the mingled blood of the Moon herself and the Void that wounded her where it splashed down at the sundering of reality. I'd maybe, *maybe* crossed paths with one indirectly a couple of times before, and it had been terrifying.

The only person I knew who'd actually *met* an Empyrean was Almarah, in her youth, and she didn't like talking about it because she'd lost a friend and wound up cursed until the year-turning. Which might be an indication of why Rika didn't want to talk about it either, but *still*. That was like saying you'd had a torrid affair with the Moon or you'd picnicked in the Void once but refusing to go into detail.

"Fine," I mumbled, tearing my eyes away from Rika's strained face. This was no time to get sidetracked, anyway; I could hunt down gossip when we weren't in mortal peril.

The only smuggler's marks I spotted were old and just standard stuff: cups pointing the way to the river, scales to the shops, and skulls warning not to go toward the graveyard or the docks. Only the bravest and most experienced of the Fisher Queen's lot would venture three Echoes down, so you didn't find a lot of fresh marks this deep. I gave the street a good look, up and down, checking for subtle dangers. Cobblestones looked solid, trees and buildings weren't moving, no sinister noises...ah. My reflection in Marjorie's windows was backward. And there was a faint, bewitching scent of lilac that I probably shouldn't think about too hard. Well, that wasn't so bad.

It occurred to me belatedly that *inside* the mansion hadn't had nearly the level of weirdness I'd expect from three Echoes down. Maybe it was an effect of the convergence, or maybe Dona Marjorie had some kind of protections on her mansion; either way, it was a relief that I probably didn't have to worry about people getting eaten by the chandeliers or something while we were out.

"Let's see...This way, I think. Keep close and don't touch anything. Oh, and don't let anyone see you bleeding."

Rika's hand twitched; her fingertip sparkled briefly, and then the cut was gone, covered up by illusion. "Will Echoes really attack you if they scent blood?"

"Not usually. It's like...flaunting your wealth when you're walking through a dangerous neighborhood."

I started in the direction of Clocktower Street. It had a long strip of fancy shops in Prime, and its shallow Echoes usually had shops as well, selling to locals and Echo relic smugglers alike. It was easy enough—if a bit disconcerting—to head for the obvious spire of the tower with its great glaring eye.

I glanced back at Marjorie's mansion to get my bearings for the return trip...and stumbled midstep at what I saw.

Her house looked more like it did in Prime than most, at least from the outside; the shape of it was the same, even if the stonework was more ornate and weathered. But coils of brass grew all over it like vines, with clockwork gears hanging off them in place of fruit.

Sure, she'd vetted that clock. About as much as she'd vetted my *ass*.

That wasn't what had made me trip over my own feet, though. No, that would be the eye-watering hole in reality that still hovered over the house, a tear in the sky bleeding stars and the purple-black light of the Void. *The convergence.* That thing was beyond creepy. It hurt my mind in deep places just to look at it.

At least it wouldn't be hard to find our way back. Rika seemed shaken enough already, so I didn't point it out to her.

I set as quick a pace as I dared, stretching my legs to lengthen my stride. It was a tricky balance—we had to get the ward before the party could get attacked again, but you couldn't charge around recklessly in an Echo. I skirted a small puddle in an unwholesome shade of green, then a deep crack in a wall from which a cluster of three shiny eyes blinked out at me. Rika stayed close, glancing nervously down every alley.

It was awkward, being alone in an Echo with her. The silence grew until it became a heavy thing. I kept flicking quick looks at her—to make sure she wasn't spooked enough to do something rash, I told myself, but really it was just so strange to see her face unguarded and vulnerable like this.

It occurred to me that despite our long and varyingly close acquaintance, there was a lot I still didn't know about Rika Nonesuch. She'd never mentioned any family. I didn't even know what quarter of Acantis she came from, which was pretty unusual in a city where Hillside, Tower, Southside, and Dockside each had their own unique and competitive flavors of intense neighborhood pride. As a Cat, she could sound like she came from anywhere, switching up accents and local slang and diction based on whom she was talking to; I'd always vaguely assumed she was a Tower girl, given how fashionably she dressed, but that was probably yet another mask. Her fine, golden-brown features suggested her ancestors had always lived in Acantis or one of the other League Cities, rather than descending from the pale, freckled, hawk-faced Vigers like me, or from the Cathardians with their dark brown skin and beautifully sculpted cheekbones like Marjorie and Almarah. But her grey eyes were an enigma, and she could pass for carrying a little ancestry of anywhere. Trying to figure her out was like trying to hold the shape of fire in your mind.

It didn't matter now anyway. Out in an Echo, all that mattered was whether I could trust her at my back. A year ago I would have said yes, unhesitatingly. Now...I still wanted to say yes. Damn, I was a fool.

"So," Rika said at last, her voice a bit uneven, "is that clock actually resetting time?"

Thank the Moon, she wanted to talk about the job. That was easy.

"I think it's just resetting people. Their memories and their physical condition. That silver-eyed Echo seemed to think the clock was responsible for bringing back the dead." I swerved around a door lantern that was swinging a little too far in our direction and burning a little too eagerly.

"Wait...what time is it in Prime, then?" Her voice rose in alarm. "How long has this been going on? Have I lost hours? *Days?*"

"No, no. From what Blair said, we're doing the same few hours over again in each new Echo. I think the game ends at midnight, so we probably won't get there until it's over, one way or another." Which was a good thing, because my sister would be furious if I came home late.

"Then how long do we have until the Echoes kick in the door again?" Rika glanced back at the mansion. "Because—Bloody Moon!"

"Don't look at it."

"What in the Void is that?!"

What in the Void was probably all too accurate. "A convergence of thin spots in the Veil. It's why this mess is happening." I didn't want her to lose her composure thinking too hard about that, so I pushed on. "And I'm not sure how long until the next round of murders happens. Maybe an hour? But time doesn't operate normally in Echoes. How long it *seems* to be has definitely varied so far."

"So we need to hurry." She started walking faster, with the staccato rhythm of fear.

"Yes, but—" I caught her arm, jerking her to a halt. "We have to be careful."

She yanked out of my grip as if my touch burned. "Don't—"

"Sorry. Look." I pointed at the cobbles a few feet in front of her.

"Oh! Oh, *ugh.*"

The dry little corpses of flies blanketed a patch of road about three feet wide. Or something like flies—their wings had a reddish sheen, and the number of eyes and legs varied.

"I don't know what killed them, and I don't particularly want to find out. Best to give that spot a wide berth."

Rika nodded, lips pressed together. She let me go half a step ahead of her, which only made me more tense. Sure, I'd been to the third Echo dozens of times, but not recently—I was bound to make mistakes, and now it was my job to keep her safe.

Which would be easier if she wasn't holding back crucial information.

"Listen," I said gruffly. "We need to share everything we've got. You're clearly interested in that clock, and you *must* have some job related to it. What do you know about it?"

"You know I can't talk about my jobs," she protested.

"Make an exception."

"Funny, you don't *look* like my guildmistress, and she's the only one who can authorize that."

"Be reasonable, Rika. I don't like you and I don't trust you—"

"Why, Kembral, you flatterer."

"—but we've got to work together if we don't want everyone to wind up dead. I know you're hiding things."

"Of course I'm hiding things. I was born in a waning Cloud Moon, and I'm a Cat. I live and breathe secrets."

I didn't mention that I was a waxing Cloud Moon, supposedly honest as dirt and a seeker of truth. Jaycel's voice came back to me, warning me that we would make a terrible couple.

I already damn well knew that, given how our one arguably romantic venture had ended.

"I don't have the patience to tease secrets out of you," I said. "I haven't had more than three consecutive hours of sleep in two months, and before tonight the only adult conversation I've had most days is to thank the dairy woman when she delivers the milk. If you're looking for some kind of subtle repartee from me, I regret to inform you that I don't have that in my pockets tonight."

"Right. I keep forgetting you had a baby." She gave me a strange look, her voice losing some of its edge. "Stars, that's weird."

"People have babies all the time. *This* is weird." I gestured up at half a ruined townhouse, its side open to the street. An emaciated-looking woman played melancholy, halting music on an untuned pianoforte, her grey hair trailing two stories down into her garden. The music followed us as we tramped along the street; crumpled paper blew past, and an exceptionally tall person in a long hooded cloak hurried by. I couldn't see a face inside the hood and didn't look too hard.

"What's she like? The baby." There was something oddly wistful in Rika's question.

"Her name is Emmelaine—Emmi for short. She's...pretty great, actually." She was distracting me, of course, but it was working.

"Cute?"

Cute didn't begin to describe Emmi. The delicate tracery of tiny veins in her eyelids when she was sleeping, the tiny perfection of her nose, the soft fuzz of her hair. The way her eyes lit up whenever she saw my face, or the dreamy paralysis that stole over me when I cuddled her in my arms. I didn't have words for her.

"Yeah," I said instead. "Really exhausting, though."

"You love her a lot, I can tell." An odd smile hovered on Rika's lips. She tipped her chin down, her hair falling in a curtain across her face. "Lucky baby. It must be nice to have a mother who loves you."

I grimaced. "I'm sorry. I knew the Cats took in orphans sometimes, but I didn't realize—"

"Oh, my mother is alive."

Her tone was flat as an iced-over pond. I didn't dare ask, even though curiosity was burning me up. My imagination painted an emotionally distant Hillside aristocrat, or maybe a cruel Dockside crime lord.

Now things had gone deadly awkward again. What could I say to that? Why were we even talking about personal things like babies and mothers, when we were enemies now? Or at least not friends.

Maybe if we were talking about this stuff, that meant we could fix things, if we wanted to.

I rolled the idea of being Rika's friend again around in my head, in the dusty places where I'd left my feelings for her. All I got were sharp aching pangs as it bumped up against memories. Rika slipping me a wicked wink as she pickpocketed a Hillside landlord while I blocked him from harassing my Dockside client (it had been so hard to keep a straight face). Rika unexpectedly dangling out a window in the night to toss me a pilfered rose (I'd fumbled it, cursing and cutting myself on the thorns, but kept it in a vase until its battered petals all fell off). Rika glaring at me in exasperation when I opened a door she'd been working on, having blink stepped inside the building like a "dirty cheater" (it had been a rare joint Cat-and-Hound mission, to rescue a rich banker's kidnapped son).

I wanted it all back so badly. But her lies in that café had gone well beyond the line of rivalry or business. She *knew* Beryl had just dumped me. She *knew* what a vulnerable mess I was, alone and pregnant and unwanted. She'd listened sympathetically while I poured out my heart to her over tea, and then she'd stabbed me in the exact vital spot I'd just showed her.

Rika spoke into the painful silence, bright and false. "Anyway, the baby sounds marvelous, but you should really get out more, Kembral. Sometime when there's *not* an apocalyptic murder game going on."

It was too close to what she'd said to get me to join her at the café that awful day. It had been a trap then, and it was hard not to suspect it of being a trap now. Just an attempt to get me to stop prying after her secrets—a hollow surface kindness with nothing beneath.

"I don't know why you still pretend to care." I tried to throttle the words, but they slipped out of my throat anyway.

Rika slowed, her brows lowering. "What?"

My face burned. "Never mind. I didn't say anything."

"No." She put a hand on my arm, fingers hard as steel, stopping me in the road. "What was that?"

I gave a half-angry, half-embarrassed sort of shrug, feeling like a fool. "I *know* you don't care about me. After the star diamond thing.

Or at least, I don't see how you could. So it's just...weird, when you pretend."

I couldn't look at her. The silence stretched awkwardly on. Something sinuous slithered up the wall of the building opposite and disappeared into a hole in the mortar; I wished I could do the same. Void take me, I shouldn't have said anything.

Finally, in a frosty tone, Rika said, "I see."

I couldn't help glancing at her. To my shock, instead of remote and disdainful, her face was—flushed. Something very like anger shone in her eyes.

"Rika...?"

"You don't have the faintest idea what you're talking about, Thorne."

"Look, forget it. We need to—"

"No, you listen." She jabbed a sharp-nailed finger at me. "You don't get to say that to me. I'm here *because of you*. I'm in this mess *because of you*."

A spark of irrational anger ignited in my chest, as if Rika's fury were catching. "I'm sorry, all right? I needed help, and I picked you because you were the most competent person in the room. Clearly I should have let you continue in ignorant bliss and just watched you die again."

She threw up her hands. "That's not what I'm talking about! You don't even know—"

"I don't know because you're not telling me anything!" This was a terrible place for this argument, but all my bottled-up anger and fear was overflowing at last, and I couldn't stop it. "We're all going to *die* because you can't let go of your precious little secrets!"

"It's my job not to divulge secrets! You of all people should understand that!"

"Well, *you* should understand—"

"Hullo," said a deep gravelly voice.

We were not alone.

DON'T BARGAIN WITH AN ECHO

I pivoted, heart jumping. Rika didn't quite suppress a strangled little shriek.

In the road in front of us stood a stocky man with a ragged coat, an excessively tall hat, and a truly enormous sack over his shoulder. An extra pair of eyes blinked in his forehead, all four of them fixed on us in curiosity. His sack squirmed subtly, shadows shifting on it in the greenish light.

"Hello," I said cautiously.

"You're from Prime." His cheerful voice was rough as a bag of rusty nails.

"Yes," I admitted. You never wanted to give anything to an Echo for free, even information, but it hadn't been a question.

"Having an argument, are you? Carry on, carry on." He blinked, one set of eyes and then the other. "Don't let me stop you."

I cleared my throat. "Actually, we're looking for a shop that might sell invitation wards."

"Oh, aye. I got one in the sack." He hefted it suggestively on his shoulder; it bounced as if it were full of nothing heavier than crumpled paper, making a rustle and then an angry hissing noise.

"Do you," Rika said faintly. "How lovely."

"You could just…" He wiggled his eyebrows suggestively. "Reach into the sack and take it, like. Would open it up for you and everything."

"Oh, fuck no," Rika breathed. "No thank you."

"That does sound a bit like a trap," I apologized, as politely as possible.

The man laughed, a booming sound that drew angry cries from the bird things fluttering around the ruins. "Oh, aye. That it is. Absolutely a trap. If you reach into the sack, he'll eat you, he will."

I didn't ask for a clarification as to whether the sack itself or something inside it would eat us, much as I both wanted and didn't want to know. "If there's a shop that might sell them, though…"

"Oh, I'll sell it to you, if you don't want to reach in and get it." He waggled his eyebrows again. "Lots of good stuff in there, though, if you change your mind and want to just stick your arm in and feel around for it. Treasures, trinkets, your heart's desire."

"No, that's all right, thanks." Right now my heart's desire was a nice long nap, and I sure wasn't taking *that* three Echoes down. "How much for the invitation ward?"

"Oh, well." He seemed to think it over. "You got a really good memory you want to part with? Or your firstborn child? I'd throw in your heart's desire for that."

I stifled the sudden irrational urge to grab his neck in my hands and snap it. "My firstborn child isn't for sale," I said through my teeth. "No memories, no people, no names. No personal qualities, talents, abilities, or virtues. How about a lock of hair?"

He eyed mine skeptically. "You don't take good care of it, do you? You should use a nice conditioning tonic, you should."

"He's not wrong," Rika murmured.

I noticed she wasn't making any offers herself. There was always blood—it was a near universal currency in the Echoes—but you never knew how much they'd ask for, and I suspected I'd need to be parsimonious in my spending of that particular coin tonight.

"How about a truth I've never told anyone before?" I asked, getting desperate.

His eyes lit up. "Oh, aye! I do like a story. Tell me, and I'll give you the ward."

"I won't forget it or not be able to tell it anymore or anything like that, will I? I just tell you this once, and there are no additional effects, and that's the whole of our transaction?"

"Aye, aye. I'm not one of those tricksters. Well, unless you want to reach in my bag." He hefted it suggestively again; the hissing intensified.

"No, that's all right. You swear it three times?"

"Aye." He placed a hand over his belly—which might be where he kept his heart, or he could be hungry. "The whole of our transaction, no tricks. I swear it, I swear it again, and once more I swear it." He brightened. "Now, what've you got?"

"Let's see." I combed through my memory for something harmless that couldn't possibly be used against me, even if the information found its way back to some seriously malevolent Echo. Nothing about Emmi, for certain. "How about the real reason I learned to blink step?"

"I always wondered about that," Rika said, smooth and buttery, playing up the value of what I had to offer. "You have to start the training when you're a small child, right?"

"Yes. It's why so few people learn. You have to start while your grasp on reality is still loose enough to drift a bit out of Prime, but you also have to keep at it for years before you see any progress. Not a lot of kids have the dedication for that." I eyed the Echo with the sack, who looked so eager he was nearly salivating. "Do you want to hear what made me so resolved that I stuck with it?"

"Oh, aye!"

"Fine." I closed my eyes. "There was a little girl. When I was maybe five years old. She must have lived near our apartment in Southside, because we met up in the plaza out front a few times to play pretend games together. But then one time she started fading."

"Ah," the man with the sack said knowingly. "That happens to your little ones, sometimes. We find them in the oddest places."

Rika muttered something rude under her breath.

"Right. Her imagination must have been too strong, and we'd stumbled on a thin spot, and she started slipping away into an Echo." I could still see her face after all these years, framed by a tangled mane of brown curls. The desperate fear in those wide dark eyes, and a kind of sad resignation, as if she knew she was already lost. That was what had driven me to do it—I couldn't bear that she'd given up already. "I grabbed her hand before she faded all the way out. They tell kids not to do that, because you can get pulled through to the Echo, too. But I'm stubborn as a rock; I grounded us both and pulled her back."

I opened my eyes; the Echo was looking at me strangely, his head tilted, his eyes bright. "We played together a few more times, and I caught her from fading once more. Earlier, because I was watching for it. But after another week or two, I never saw her again." Damn, now my throat was tight—I thought I'd gotten over this kid ages ago, but apparently not. "I was so worried about her—it haunted me, thinking that maybe she'd slipped into an Echo and I hadn't been there to save her. So I decided that I would learn to blink step and become a Hound, so I could go into the Echoes and find her, and even if she started to slip out of this reality, I could catch her in the Veil."

"And did you?" The Echo's bright eyes fixed on me. "Did you ever find her?"

"No." A strange pang twisted my chest. "No, I looked for her, but I never did."

He laughed that great booming laugh again, and he set his sack down. "Oh, that's a funny story. I do like that one. Oh, it's too perfect. Right, you earned it, you can have the ward."

I didn't think it was funny at all, but fine. Echoes were strange. I tried not to look annoyed. "You're sure this thing works?"

"I guarantee it. Swear on my name. Do you want to reach into the sack and get it yourself?"

"I think we've been over this."

"Oh, aye, but I had to try. All right, all right. Easy in there." He addressed this last to his sack, which was hissing and writhing. "I'm going in. Now don't bite me, you hear? It's me."

He reached into the sack; it clamped shut around his arm and started working up to his shoulder, its burlap edges fluttering hungrily. He groped around in it, scolding it absently.

"Ah, ah, what did I tell you? Down, lad, easy, or you'll get no supper. Ah, there it is."

He pulled out a withered bundle of bones and black herbs. The sack drooped and went still, slumping as if disappointed that his arm came out intact.

I glanced at Rika. "Does that look right to you?"

She was watching me strangely, as if I might be an impostor. It took her a moment to examine the bundle; her grey eyes kept trying to pull back to me.

"Yes," she said, sounding subdued. "I told you, I've had to get past them before, so I know them. It's real."

I frowned. "Wait, I thought you said you *couldn't* get past them."

She raised an elegant brow. "I said they were unbreakable. I can get past anything." At my glare, she added, "I had to get an invitation from someone inside. There's no other way, once you hang pieces of that bundle on every door and window. They only last for a day, but that should be more than enough time."

"Perfect." I took the bundle from the Echo, offering him a little bow. "Thanks."

"Oh, I think I came out the better in this deal." He chuckled. "Now, you'd better get back. Big night, you know. Can't miss the year-turning." He winked, as if we were in on some joke with him, and then winked again in case we'd missed it.

"Right," I agreed. "Ha ha. Can't miss it."

He heaved his sack back onto his shoulder, waved to us, and walked away whistling. I turned to Rika, the ward tucked in the crook of my arm.

"I should have asked if he had a sword to sell," I realized once he was gone. "I don't like the grip on this one."

"Oh, no," Rika said, her voice a little strained. "I think that was quite enough, thank you. Now, let's get back before any inanimate objects eat us."

As we headed back toward the mansion, Rika jumped at every shadow—which was fair, because one of the shadows tried to grab her skirt and another had about forty-seven blinking eyes glowing in it. Still, I'd have to be pretty oblivious not to notice that she seemed to have more than the usual, sensible dose of apprehension.

Once the man with the sack was well out of earshot, she gave me a strange, sidelong look.

"You're really such a softhearted fool that you spent all those years learning to blink step just because of some little girl you played with a few times? And then you never even found her?"

"I know, I'm a sucker *and* a failure. I don't want to hear about it, all right?"

Remembering the girl had left me grumpy. Now that I was a parent, I couldn't bear to think of kids getting lost. Blood on the Moon, it was going to be tough doing retrieval runs into Echoes after missing children when I went back to work. But if I saw one on the board, there was no way I'd be able to turn it down.

"You're a grouch, Kembral Thorne. But you're much softer on the inside than you like to act. I guess you're not all work and no feelings after all."

There was a faint hint of warmth in her voice, as if she didn't despise me. As if maybe everything wasn't irrevocably broken between us. It was absolutely terrifying. It meant I could still fuck this up.

Or it meant she'd decided I was still useful and worth putting on the charm for. I'd almost rather believe that—it was safer.

There was nothing in the churn of words trying to escape me that I wouldn't regret later. Not now, while my emotions were a hot, tangled mess—my sister had warned me not to make any major social decisions for the first few months.

I kept my mouth shut and grunted something like *Hmph*.

A pack of young locals hurried by, shooting nervous glances at the eye-aching void of the convergence in the distance, as if it were ominous weather that could break on them any second. I eyed them warily; they looked like they might be heading off to a party of their own, dressed in shimmering scraps of snakeskin and dragonfly wings, whispering and giggling to one another through sharp teeth.

When they were almost past us, one of them slowed and turned.

"You're bleeding," she hissed, her forked tongue flicking out.

Shit. I instinctively made a fist of my cut finger and kept walking, pretending I hadn't heard her.

Lizard-quick, she darted in front of us, blocking our way. Her grin spread wide, almost to her ears, showing multiple rows of sharp fangs.

"Smells like Prime blood to me." She held out a hand like a beggar asking for change. "Just a drop. Come on, you've got plenty."

Her friends were behind us now, which I didn't like at all. Rika's hand slid inconspicuously toward a dagger. I didn't reach for mine, because I didn't want to start anything.

"I'm keeping it inside my veins, thanks," I said evenly.

"No you're not." Her tongue flicked the air again. "You're dripping it around, wasting it. Might as well give it to me. Just a spoonful. Come on. A cup or two."

I could feel her friends closing in behind us, sure as if I were watching them. Rika slid closer to me, angling so we were back-to-back.

"You don't want to start this fight." I kept my tone calm and even, my weight balanced and ready to move. I relaxed my mind just a little, like slightly unfocusing your eyes, right on the cusp of sliding into the Veil.

"Hey," said one of her friends suddenly. "Hey, Ixi, she's right. Look closer. They're marked."

Ixi scowled, her extended hand dropping. "Ugh. You're right."

"They're part of the year-naming rite." Her friend's voice got insistent, even scared. "I'm not touching that."

Ixi tossed her head, with a shimmer of blue hair. "Fine. I'm not getting on some Empyrean's bad side. Let's go."

The young Echoes moved off. Rika whirled, her breath catching high in her throat. "Empyrean? Wait, what do you mean?"

The Echoes didn't answer, or even glance back. They were getting out of here like we were cursed and they were afraid it might be contagious—which was probably more or less true. Rika took half a step after them, but I shook my head.

"Let them go. We've got to get back and put this ward up."

"But they said—"

"I know. I'm not thrilled about it, either. But they probably don't know anything, and they're just kids. We can't waste time chasing after them and beating them up."

"They were going to beat *us* up!" Rika protested.

"They thought they were." I gave her a fierce little smile. "You and I know they were wrong."

The smile felt suddenly strange on my face, something from the old days. I turned away from her before I could see her reaction, in case I couldn't bear it.

"Anyway, we've got to get back. Come on."

I started walking. Rika hurried to catch up—half a step behind, to let me find whatever traps the Echo might have laid for us, but close enough that she'd run into me if I stopped suddenly. It should have made me twitchy to have her at my back—she'd proved herself plenty treacherous—but somehow it made me feel safer instead.

I must be losing my mind.

I couldn't waste more time thinking about Rika Nonesuch, no matter how close her warm and spice-scented presence was at my side. We'd gotten lucky finding the ward so fast, but time was slipping away from us.

The bundle securely under my arm, I made myself hurry faster than I really would have preferred toward the terrible rip in the sky.

FIND YOUR TRUE TARGET

One of the first things I noticed when we got back was an iridescent beetle skittering up a moldy lace curtain. *Well, shit.* I supposed it would be too much to hope that things hadn't advanced while we were gone.

I jerked my chin at it, pointing it out to Rika. "The Echoes are on the move already. We're going to have to hurry."

"Right." She visibly steadied herself, shaking off all lingering vulnerability and going clipped and businesslike. "Who are we bringing in next?"

I frowned. "What?"

"Like you did to me." She held up a finger, the cut still cloaked in illusion. "Much as I'm charmed to be working with you, this job is too big for just two of us."

She was right. There was no reason I should feel a strange reluctance to get anyone else involved; they were already involved, like it or not. Ignorance wouldn't save them. Though we had to be careful about who we brought in—I'd seen what could happen when random people without any training involved themselves in a dangerous job, and it wasn't pretty.

"Hmm. More guild members would make the most sense, so probably either Pearson or Signa Cail."

Rika stilled some expression before it could quite reach her face. "Adelyn Cail is..." She hesitated.

"A bitch?" I supplied helpfully.

"Ha! No, you and I can handle a bitch." Amusement flickered across her lips and then was gone. "It's more that she's...very focused on her job today. I'm not entirely certain she wouldn't have a conflict of interest."

"Do *you* have a conflict of interest?"

"I'm handling it," she said curtly. "Anyway, Signa Pearson would be better. Why don't you go ruin his night, and I'll get Dona Swift and her staff to help hang the ward."

"Can't we just put it up ourselves?"

"We could hang the anchor wishbone on the front door easily enough, but every single door, window, and fireplace in the entire building also needs a twig or a bone over it. There've got to be well over a hundred windows in this place. Dona Swift's staff will know where they are much better than we will."

"Makes sense. I'll go talk to Pearson. We should keep an eye on Carter, too, since they might target him."

I started to move, but Rika put a hand on my arm. Her touch and the sudden intensity of her gaze froze me in place.

"Just tell Pearson the truth. Don't trick him like you did to me."

"Of course I won't trick him," I retorted, stung. "He'll want to help voluntarily, because he's not an asshole."

Rika's hand left my sleeve. "Good for him. Maybe he can teach you."

She softened it with a wink. I had no idea what to do with that.

Rika took the ward bundle from my suddenly numb hands and moved off without hesitation, all the slinky Cat grace of her usual walk focused into a stride as direct and ruthless as the thrust of a knife.

I had to admire her ability to shake off emotion and uncertainty to focus on the task. I was struggling with that myself right now. I hoped it was just a passing side effect of having a baby, and I wasn't going to be a big mess of feelings for the rest of my life—I could just see myself bawling my eyes out all through any retrieval mission involving a kid, which would be great fun when I had to fight off Echo monsters while half-blinded by tears.

A flicker of iridescence caught the corner of my eye as I set off to locate Pearson. A beetle scuttled across floor tiles painted with coiling grape vines, heading toward a familiar pair of not-yet-bitten party guests in elegant clothes.

I veered out of my path to stomp on it.

I found Pearson lingering at the wine table, dubiously sniffing the glass he'd just picked up. Given the moldering state of everything else in the mansion, I couldn't blame him. He glanced up as I approached, breaking into a broad smile. Probably one of joyous anticipation at the thought of giving me a job.

"Oh, hey, Kem! Didn't expect to see you here."

"That's me. Surprising everyone, over and over, all night long. Listen, Pearson, we have a problem."

"The kinds of things you think are problems tend to be absurdly dangerous, Kem."

"Yes. That is an accurate description of this situation. Come with me."

"Come with you...*away* from the danger? Because I'm a desk Hound." Pearson grimaced. "Not really the danger-facing type. Outside my area of expertise."

"I regret to tell you that there *is* no *away from the danger* at this time." I clapped his shoulder. "I want you to do something for me."

His brow furrowed. "This a prank? You're not still mad about that job with the dog, are you? Look, I'm really sorry, they told me it was three Echoes down."

"This isn't about the dog. Come look at this clock."

Pearson's shoulders relaxed a little. "Raven stuff if I ever saw it. Sure, can't hurt to look."

That was debatable, but I led him to the clock anyway.

Its phantasmagorical face remained unchanged, the crack snaking down it like the elusive borderland of the Veil. I hesitated as we stood before it together. Rika had a point about not tricking him; I hadn't lied to her, but I hadn't been completely honest with her, either. With Pearson, I should do this right and make sure he understood what he was getting into. Well, as best as I could manage without being able to explain that he was in an Echo, anyway.

"Pearson. If something big were going on, something really dangerous that threatened the lives of everyone here, would you want to know about it?"

"You're not making me feel better about this, Kem."

"But would you?"

"Of course." He shrugged sheepishly. "Might not be tough like you, but I'm still a Hound. I'd want to help."

"I figured you might." I took a deep breath. "Well, surprise, there *is* something like that, but there's Echo nonsense involved. I can't explain it to you properly unless you swipe your finger down the crack on that clockface."

Pearson gave the clock a dubious look. "That's an Echo relic."

"Pretty obviously, yeah."

"It's going to do something to me?"

"It's already doing something to you. This will free you. I think."

Across the room I glimpsed the little girl in the smock, peering at me from behind a tarnished statue. She caught my gaze and shook her head urgently, eyes wide. My insides lurched with sudden apprehension.

"Like this?" Pearson asked.

"Wait! Maybe we should—"

"Ow!" He shook out a bloody finger. "I thought you said you weren't mad about the dog job! Bloody Moon, Kem, why did you…" Pearson trailed off, staring around the ballroom. "This…isn't Dona Swift's house."

Well, what was done was done. I'd better hope this wasn't a mistake.

"You can see it now?"

"Are we…" He swallowed. "Is this an Echo?"

"Yes."

"Oh, no." His eyes got wider and wider; his shoulders started to tremble. "No, must be dreaming. Got to—"

"Pearson, listen to me." I grabbed his shoulders. "We don't have time for you to fall apart. Remember your Hound training; do it later."

He nodded, eyes still white and round. "Okay. Training. Right."

"I'll explain everything, but I need you to stay calm. This is all related to that job you were thinking about offering me. The Echo game you heard rumors about—I think we're in it."

"The job?" He shook his head. "This is part of *that*? Oh, we're all going to die."

"Pearson."

"Right." He squeezed his eyes shut. "Stay calm. I don't know how you do this, Kem."

"Practice. You're doing great. Now, do you remember anything about that job? There was a contest. Something about a crux year. What else? Give me the briefing."

I glanced around the room, nerves on edge, watching for Echoes. Guests danced and laughed in their tattered tailcoats and rotting ball-gowns, oblivious to danger. Carter seemed safe; he was hurrying from window to window along with the rest of Dona Marjorie's staff, hanging warding sticks and bones. Vandelle and Harking had faced off in their usual argument. Rika . . . She was in a corner with Cail, who handed her some small object. Rika took it with clear reluctance, her fingers seeming to shrink from its touch before they closed around it and she made it disappear. *Huh.*

"So. Mission briefing." Pearson took a deep, steadying breath. "There's not much more than you said. Except I got the impression it was going to be going on all year, not specifically on the year-turning."

"Let's hope that was a misunderstanding. Did they say anything about a year-naming rite?"

"Yes! Now that you bring it up, they did mention a naming thing. Said they'd know better how bad the year was going to be after they saw how that went. No idea what it is, though."

"How about an Empyrean? Did they say anything about Empyreans being involved?" I tried to sound casual, and to not betray the dread those kids had set in me with their parting line.

His eyes widened. "You don't think *they're* behind this?!"

"No, of course not. Just eliminating possibilities. You didn't hear anything, then?"

"I mean, I didn't talk to our Echo contacts directly, just compiled the reports of the people who did. But I'd remember if anyone had mentioned an Empyrean. Sort of thing that sticks in your mind."

That might not mean anything. Some Echoes were reluctant to speak of the Empyreans, for fear it would draw their attention. Still, it was a relief.

"Thanks, Pearson. Let me know if you think of anything else." I squeezed his shoulders and let him go; he winced. "All right, come with me, and I'll tell you everything while we help hang some bones."

———※———

On the way to join up with Rika, I spotted another glittering rainbow carapace, but it skittered under a cabinet before I could step on it. All three of us got sticks and bones from Carter, and then Rika stomped on *another* beetle on the way to the row of ballroom windows he'd assigned us.

Lovely—they were everywhere. I kept glancing around for more as I pinned a bone on one of the tall glass doors that let out onto the garden. In this Echo, dust rimmed each pane and cracks webbed the glass, but those shouldn't matter; it was the symbolism of the barrier that counted, not its physical integrity. In the darkness beyond, a tangle of wild grapevines smothered the lawn, heavy with fruit in disregard of the season, making strange and twisted shapes.

As I started to turn away from the door, a pale flicker of movement in the garden caught my eye. I snapped my gaze back, straining to catch it.

Nothing. Everything was still. There wasn't even a breeze to stir the dreary skeletal branches of the weeping tree. Except—wait, there was a pale oval in the deeper shadows out by the wall. I peered closer, nose almost touching the grimy window glass, trying to tell whether it was a face or just a spot of moonlight.

A great cheer rose up behind me as the musicians struck up "Under the Flower Moon." I glanced toward the sound in instinctive dread. Everyone looked disturbingly happy, flushed from dancing and drink, enjoying the party as if nothing terrible had ever happened here. Suppressing a shiver, I turned back toward the window.

A face stared back at me, mere inches away on the other side of the glass.

I gave out a strangled yelp, barely stopping myself from blink stepping halfway across the ballroom. A cloaked figure with a Moon mask stood there motionless, its staring eyes dark and unreadable.

It lifted a gloved claw and scraped it down the window, uttering a low hissing moan.

My heart pounded. "No, you can't come in. Go away."

It kept staring from that unnerving mask. More figures emerged out of the darkness, their oval masks splotched with shadow, drifting closer.

I whirled to face the ballroom, searching for masks inside, but didn't see any. Only swirling tattered skirts and tarnished brocade, wide laughing mouths, deep purple wine, all of it lit by the greenish flicker of the cobweb-draped chandeliers.

More and more masked faces gathered forlornly at the windows, staring in. Two windows down, Rika jumped and swore; Pearson scrambled backward, barely managing not to drop his ward bones.

"Can they get in?" I asked Rika, hand on my sword hilt.

"Through any portal without a ward, yes."

Our eyes met with a grim realization: We were only about halfway done. There was no way we could finish before they found a way inside.

A nearby servant's door banged open, startling me halfway into drawing my sword. Carter burst through it, eyes wild, mustache working with agitation.

"Signa Thorne! We went down to do the cellars and they're already there! Thousands of them!"

Shit. "We've got to seal off this room and defend it. Carter—"

I broke off. From the dusky corridor behind him came a horrible chittering surge of noise. And *movement*.

Iridescent backs sparkled in the dim lamplight, so many that they ceased being *bugs* and instead became a single horrid, writhing mass. Legs and feelers flailed at the crest of a knee-deep advancing wave. They poured through the hallway like water from a burst dam, no end to them in sight, glittering and swarming, the terrible sound of chitin against chitin rising to a thunder.

My breath stopped in my lungs. Moon save us all—this wasn't something I could fight with a sword.

Carter slammed the door behind him and leaned against it, eyes wide with horror. "The others... They couldn't..."

I didn't wait for him to finish. "We need to seal that door! Cram tablecloths into the cracks! Anything!"

I yanked a cloth off a nearby drink table, sending glasses and bottles crashing to the ground in a cascade of shattering glass. Others moved to help, and Carter—

Carter lurched to his knees, crying out in terror.

Beetles poured under the crack in the door, swarming over him. His legs vanished in a sparkling wave; more scuttled up his body, quick as lightning. He screamed, and they poured into his mouth.

I grabbed a candle off a table in one hand and a broken-necked carafe of some boozy-smelling cocktail in the other in the vague, desperate hope that I could make a fire barrier to keep the beetles at bay. I couldn't make myself look at Carter. There were just too many beetles—I couldn't save him—but his choking screams ripped through my ears and into my heart.

Motions jerky with panic, I cast streams of liquor in an arc at the beetles, holding my candle ready. It was a laughable effort, and I knew it. We were all going to die horribly, swarmed under and *inside* by millions of scuttling iridescent legs.

Something moved past me like a black wind. A chill pierced my bones, and a flutter of stars swirled in front of my face.

The Echo with the horns and the silver hair stood between the beetles and the rest of the party, his jagged black sword in hand.

With one brutal stroke, he silenced poor Carter's screams. My whole body flinched.

"No." His voice was deep and deadly soft. "You won the second round, but I won't give you this one. You've lost. Go home."

For a fraction of a second I wasn't sure who he was talking to. Then the Echo beetles surged away from him as if he were death itself. A high, panicked chiming noise rose from them, drowning out the hissing scuttle of legs and wings and carapaces. They swarmed over one another in their desperation to flee, bunching up into a writhing mountain before the narrow gap under the door. As rapidly as they'd burst into the room, they flowed out if it, like a tide receding.

They left Carter still and ruined on the floor behind them.

I shouldn't have looked, but I did, for one brief instant—and by the Moon, I wished I hadn't. He was a bloody wreck, full of holes, his legs stripped down to the bones. Something about the way he lay on his face made it all too clear there was no life in him. My stomach twisted.

I braced myself for reality to collapse around me. But the clock bell didn't ring. The awful moment kept unfolding, time continuing on its way.

All around me, people screamed; some tried to flee, pressing back against the walls. Others stood frozen, afraid to move and draw attention to themselves.

"Is he helping us?" Pearson whispered hopefully. "Are we saved?"

"No. We are not." I drew my sword.

The silver-haired Echo turned slowly around. His cloak of starry sky furled behind him; his black armor gleamed in the wavering greenish light. Mirror eyes swept the room, ignoring me, searching for something—and finding it.

His boots rang hard against the floor as he strode toward his quarry with the inexorability of nightfall. The crowd melted away before him.

I loosened up my sword arm and stalked after him, ignoring Rika's warning hiss of "*Kembral, you idiot!*"

His target waited, wineglass in hand, with a calm that had to be feigned. *Harking.* He stood by one of the tall glass doors to the garden, past which a dozen Moon-masked figures waited in a silent, impassive line.

"That was impressive, with the bugs," Harking said conversationally, as if the silver-haired Echo were sipping brandy with him rather than stalking up with death in his hands. "Well done."

I couldn't tell if he was bluffing or if he actually had some reason to think he was safe. Either way, the Echo didn't slow his murderous advance.

"I have no interest in your approval." His fluid voice held that unearthly resonance. "The one thing you can give me that I care about is already mine to claim."

Harking's fingertips went white on his glass. "Surely...surely there's no need for..." His throat jumped, trying to regurgitate more charming words and failing as his death bore down on him.

Of all the people in this building, Harking was the one I least wanted to risk my life to save. If I weighed his stained soul against Emmi's chance to grow up with a mother, there was no question which side the balance came down on.

But damn it, I was a Hound. And more, I was *me*—I didn't have it in me to stand aside and watch while someone got skewered if there was something I could do about it. Even someone who might want me dead. I closed my eyes for the briefest instant. *Kembral Thorne, you really are the worst kind of fool.*

"*Hey*," I called out, opening my eyes again.

The Echo stopped, his starry cloak undulating in an unreal breeze.

"Why are you doing this?" Anger burned away the remnants of my caution. "What's so important about your cruel little game that you're willing to murder people again and again for it?"

He turned his silver eyes to mine.

There was a look in them I'd seen before, on the faces of my fellow Hounds when it had been a long, dangerous night. I'd seen it in the mirror. A ragged exhilaration that would crash into complete exhaustion the moment you stopped moving.

He was *tired*. Beneath the murderous triumph, he was tired, and that frightened me more than the terrible sword he carried.

He lifted it to me as if in salute, still dripping with poor Carter's blood.

"Because to turn *this* year is to hold the next hundred in your hand."

Pieces fit together in my brain. The year-naming rite. A crux year. The convergence, hovering over Dona Marjorie's year-turning party. It all poised on the verge of forming a clear picture, of making dazzling and perfect sense.

The Echo turned back toward Harking.

Pearson stood inexplicably between them. *Pearson*, for love of the Moon. Revelation lit his face—maybe the same one I'd had. He held up his hands.

"Wait! I have questions!" His eyes shone with the eagerness of a Hound on the scent. "Can you tell me—"

"I am not here to dispense information for mortals."

With no more warning than that, the Echo swept his great black sword in a lethal arc at Pearson's neck.

This time, I was ready. I slipped into the Veil the instant he moved, the air around me gone thick and gold as honey. I sprinted past Rika, straight through a table and some chairs and the Butterfly with the painted eyes, who was caught in the amber of time with his hands halfway to his mouth in horror.

All of it blurred past, insubstantial; I focused only on Pearson. He hadn't even raised a hand to defend himself. Shock and fear had barely begun to register on his face. Protective fury boiled in my veins—he was so entirely harmless. There was no damned reason to hurt him.

The sword hovered a bare inch away from his neck, its deadly arc arrested but unstoppable. There was no room to slip my blade in for a parry. So I tackled Pearson instead, flinging myself at his middle and jolting back into reality right before I hit.

The wind of the sword sliced over my head. Sound slammed into my ears: the screaming of partygoers, Pearson's cry of pain. We went down in a tangle.

Ignoring jabs of pain from new bruises and twinges of protest from abdominal muscles barely back in place after pregnancy, I rolled off Pearson and to my feet—just in time to catch the Echo's blade on mine as it descended toward us. Impact jarred up my arm, and silver eyes fixed on me. This close, I could see that his pupils were rectangular, like a goat's.

"Well, well." The Echo's sword scraped off mine. He stepped back, considering. "A mortal player. Interesting."

I risked a quick, desperate glance at Pearson; his head was still attached, thank the Moon, and his skull looked intact, but a nasty cut near his crown was bleeding heavily as he tried to roll over.

The Echo's gaze hadn't wavered. "Do you seek to challenge me, Kembral Thorne?"

He knew my name. And he'd called me a player, too. Dread slipped down into my stomach like swallowed ice.

"I'm not going to stand by and let you murder people, if that's what you mean."

"I'm intrigued. You, however, are not the one I need to kill."

The silver eyes slid past me to Harking, who I'd almost forgotten about in my rush to save Pearson. Harking, who was reaching for the door handle with the slow stealth of someone intending to slip out the back while no one was looking—clearly unable to see the line of masked monstrosities staring and clawing at the doors.

"Stop!" I called in alarm. "They'll kill you!"

Harking didn't listen. He flung the door open and hurled himself at it—straight onto the glowing blade of the green glass knife.

The silver-haired Echo emitted a frustrated hiss. Harking staggered backward, clutching at the terrible wound in his chest, eyes wide with shock. The glass knife slid out of him, the light within it glowing faintly red now.

A wild, bitter fury surged up in me all at once—at being made a pawn in their stupid games, at their disregard for human life, at having my one night out ruined. I was sick of feeling helpless.

On a sudden impulse, half inspiration and half spite, I lunged forward and brought the pommel of my sword crashing against the glass blade of the bloody knife as hard as I could.

Green glass shattered with an intensely satisfying crunch and tinkle; shards nicked my hand as they flew out from the impact. The creature holding the blade screamed in agonized horror. Light blazed from the broken remains of the hilt in a brief, intense flash and died.

The Moon-mask Echo kept screaming, holding up the broken hilt and staring at it through its mask-hole eyes. All the others started screaming, too, some of them clutching their heads or bellies as if in absolute, wrenching despair.

Harking slipped to the floor with a hoarse, awful moan. With hostile Echoes standing all around, no one dared move to try to help him, or Pearson, either. I kept my guard up, breathing hard.

The silver-haired Echo threw back his head and laughed in apparent delight. "Oh, very clever! I see it now. The *dagger* was a player, wasn't it? That way you could pass it among yourselves and keep your master in the game if some or even all of you died. But that didn't work out well for you in the end, did it?" He nudged Harking with one booted toe; Harking let out an agonized gasp, clutching his bloody chest with both hands. "You won this round, but you lost the game."

The Echo turned those mirror eyes on me. Their impact hit me like twin spears.

"You destroyed their player," he said, seeming to relish each word. "You don't even understand what you've done. You, a mortal, have knocked their master out of the running."

A thrill lanced through me at the words. I hadn't realized it was possible to eliminate players. This changed everything.

I had enough sense not to utter some foolish threat out of sheer bravado. But I settled into a more precise stance, evening out my breath, shifting my feet and the angle of my blade to face him and him alone. As I met his gaze, in that one clear moment of pure focus, it was without fear.

He approached, his sword down at his side, boots ringing cold and hard on the floor. Offering me no violence, but staring at me with eyes full of a hungry light.

"If you challenge me," he said softly, almost gently, "you should know that I always win."

The clock began to toll, its jarring notes crashing through my body. Slowly, Harking's hands slid away from his still chest, uncovering the deep crimson stain drenching his waistcoat.

The Echo stood within my range, his gaze locked onto mine, pale face still and expectant, waiting.

I had no clever retort. I didn't want to be in this fight. I didn't want to be here at all. But I was still angry as the wounded Moon, so I brought my sword up in a vicious arc toward that pretty face.

Before the blow could land, the clock struck a fourth time, and the world turned to water.

MISTAKES HAVE CONSEQUENCES

The world resolved into exquisitely symmetrical brass filigree, with a purple depth of twinkling night sky above. The ballroom had gone round, with high windows that let in a sickly golden light that gave the lie to the stars glimmering in its dome. Dancers in brass buttons and warm colors moved in slow, stately patterns to equally slow, stately music on a dance floor inlaid with an intricate compass rose. Everything was ordered and precise.

Except for Pearson, struggling to rise from the floor. Shining wetness soaked his dark hair, and he couldn't get past one elbow because he kept slipping in his own blood.

My heart wrung itself tight like a washcloth. I yelled for the physicker, grabbed a handful of napkins off a table, and dropped to my knees at his side.

"Hold still, damn it!"

He kept trying to get up, his movements weakening rapidly. "Sorry, Kem. Just a minute...sorry..."

"For Moon's sake, don't apologize!" I grabbed his head and crammed the napkins against the gash in his scalp. "Lie down. Holy Void, you're bleeding everywhere."

It wasn't the reassuring sort of thing you were supposed to say when someone was hurt, but this was too much blood, and it slipped out before I could stop it. The bunch of napkins dampened rapidly beneath my fingers. *Shit.*

Rika bent over us. "Why isn't he better? Everyone else got better! Dona Harking is fine, and he was *dead!*" The panic in her voice matched what rose in my own gut.

"I don't—*oh.* Fuck." I *did* know. The knowledge sank in like I'd swallowed a brick.

The clock. The cuts on our fingers hadn't healed, either, and our clothes didn't change with each Echo. It was the clock that reset everyone's bodies as well as their memories, and I'd severed that protection from all three of us. The little girl had tried to warn me.

This was my fault, for bringing Pearson in.

The physicker arrived—the poor man had no idea how hard he'd already worked tonight—and I quickly yielded my position to him. A crowd of anxious onlookers surrounded us, murmuring with alarm. *What happened? Did you see? How did he get hurt?*

I rose, hands red with blood. Pearson's eyes were drifting shut as he murmured incoherent answers to the physicker's calm questions. Dona Marjorie swept up, fan aflutter, offering a private room and all her resources for her guest; Carter appeared with a basket of medical supplies, mustache jumping with concern. Words caught my ears like barbed hooks: *Too much blood. Have to stitch this up quickly. Might need a Raven.*

Rika shook my arm. "Kembral. Get that look off your face and answer me."

I tore my gaze away from Pearson. "I...It's because he did what we did." I held up a bloody fingertip. "Look at us, Rika. We haven't changed like everyone else. When we cut ourselves out of whatever enchantment is clouding everyone's memories, we stopped resetting in time, too."

She went very still. "So he can die now. *We* can die."

"Yes." I forced the next words out past a lump of queasy guilt. "I didn't know. I'm sorry."

Rika shook her head. "No, you'd have botched this up without me. It's good that you brought me in. But poor Signa Pearson. He didn't deserve that."

"No, he didn't."

The physicker had finished bandaging Pearson's head. Carter and another of Marjorie's staff were carefully lifting him, the physicker gathering up his tools and hovering close. Pearson mumbled weakly to them, something about needing to be well enough to work tomorrow. My throat burned with unsaid things as I watched them carry him off to some more comfortable and private place to get stitched up.

I tried to swallow it all down to deal with later, like a good Hound, with mixed success. "Later" was racking up enough debt to fill the Void.

"So." My voice came out uneven. "I guess we're not bringing anyone else into this."

"No," Rika said, subdued. "No, I suppose we shouldn't."

"It's just you and me."

She raised troubled grey eyes to mine, and for a moment, there was something true and vulnerable there. But then it was gone, quick as if I'd imagined it.

"Moon help us, yes. Ugh." Eyeing my bloodstained hands, she grabbed a pitcher of water and a pristine pile of gold-embroidered napkins off a table. "Here, get cleaned up. I'm going to go talk to Dona Swift to make sure the house gets fully warded and her people are on alert. You use your vaunted Hound investigation skills to figure out what's going on and fix everything."

"That's some division of labor."

"I have faith in you, Thorne." She thrust the pitcher and napkins into my hands and turned to go. She was being sarcastic, of course. At least, I was pretty sure.

"Rika..."

She paused. Her smoky skirts shimmered with inexplicable movement—her hands were trembling at her sides.

"What?" Her voice held an edge, but it wasn't the hostility I needed it to be. It was the brittle sharpness of someone barely holding herself together.

In that moment, all I could think of was how she'd looked, dying in my arms. Of how rock-bottom wretched it'd be if she got killed tonight, with a hot, tangled mess of betrayal and anger unresolved between us.

"Just...be careful."

She shook her head. "I'm a Cat. I'm always careful. You're the one who needs to learn to guard your back."

I snorted. "Against *you*."

"You'll never be good enough to do *that*. Get your paws clean, dog."

She slipped away, the smoke-and-silver gown flowing behind her, equilibrium restored to the universe with her final, confident taunt.

I had to shake her off like a haunting.

I dutifully scrubbed my hands, but I couldn't forget that it was Pearson's blood on them. He was a desk Hound, curse it. I should never have put him in danger. Rika had tasked me with fixing everything, but this was one thing I couldn't repair.

I had to wipe awkwardly at my eyes with my forearm because my hands still weren't clean. Damn it, he'd better not die.

"Kembral darling!"

It was Jaycel, striding up with her arms spread wide. Generous white sleeves fluttered from them, and a belt of gold medallions girdled her hips over impossibly tight breeches. I hastily wiped the last of the blood off and stuffed the stained napkins behind the water pitcher on a nearby table to avoid awkward explanations.

"Jaycel." I couldn't quite muster a smile.

She clasped my shoulders, somehow managing not to spill her drink on me in the process. I wondered distractedly if her general level of inebriation got reset when the clock chimed, or if she was going to get increasingly sloshed as the night progressed, all the while thinking she was only a few drinks in. Probably the former, given that everyone had recovered from the poison, which was just as well for her already challenged liver.

"You look good! Tired, but good."

"Thanks. Listen, Jaycel—"

"Except for that belt. Good heavens, what is it, a curtain tie?"

"Well, actually, yes, but—"

"Don't worry. Whatever dire threat has forced you to don a poorly accessorized sword, I stand fashionably ready to meet it." She patted her own exquisitely sculpted sword hilt fondly.

"I desperately hope that won't be necessary, but—"

"Necessary! When have I ever gotten in a fight because it was *necessary?*" She slid her arm comfortably through mine. "Come on, you're stiff as a board. I swear those aren't muscles in your shoulders, they're just giant tension knots. Have a drink or several with me."

"I can't." I made a vague gesture. "It'll go into my milk."

"Then get the baby drunk! It'll be good for her. Maybe she'll sleep better." Jaycel finished off her own drink as if to demonstrate, then with breathtakingly flawless precision reached back without looking to swap her glass for a full one from a passing tray. "You could use some more bad ideas. You and Blair . . ." She trailed off, the sauciness fading from her stance, her eyes latching on to Blair across the room. They were gazing out a circular window ringed with brass filigree at a velvet starry sky that seemed far too low and close.

"I suppose Blair has their own kind of bad ideas," she murmured, watching them. "I don't know, Kembral. They're doing all right, really, given how bad Redgrave Academy was. But I worry about them anyway. I can't always be there to protect them."

A pang went through me, and I put a hand on her shoulder. "The Ravens will take care of them. The guilds protect their own."

"I suppose so." A wistful smile pulled at her lips. "I'm so proud of them, you know. My baby brother, a Raven! We all dreamed of joining a guild when we grew up, remember?"

"Of course I do." Every kid in Southside did. It was a way that anyone could move up in the world, no matter who their parents were or how little money their family had. "You couldn't decide whether you wanted to be a Wolf, a Hound, or a Butterfly. You'd change three times mid-game."

"And you always wanted to be a Hound, because you're dreadfully boring." She elbowed me and grinned. "Look at you now. You got what you wanted. I think nearly everyone in our old crew tried out for one guild or another at some point, but you were the only one who made it."

I shrugged, a little uncomfortably. "Not through any special talent. I was just too stubborn to quit."

"Bah! You'd be a Hound even if you'd never learned to blink step. You're everything they look for. Stubborn, yes, but also smart, loyal, and determined—you never give up, even when anyone else would go home and go back to bed, and you get things done. Not to mention nosy, interfering, bossy, stodgy..."

I laughed despite everything. "All right, now *that's* me. What about you? You could still be a Butterfly for sure, you know. You're damned good with a blade, and I don't know anyone who's half as quick with witty quips or heroic couplets."

"Oh, no. I've seen how hard you work." She waved a hand. "I don't want that anymore. As for what I *do* want, well...it changes minute by minute, so I get it a fair percentage of the time. And what I want right *now* is to get you to relax and have a drink with me. Tea, if you must."

"Stars, I'd love to, Jaycel." I rubbed my face. "I'm dealing with a bit of an emergency. Tell you what—when I wrap this up, we can get tea together."

"I'll hold you to that." She flipped me a jaunty salute. "Good luck with your emergency. If you need anyone dramatically stabbed or poetically eviscerated, let me know."

"Always."

She swaggered away, off to find more trouble. I stared after her, feeling inexplicably bolstered, as if Jaycel's easy confidence in me had rubbed off.

Figure out what was going on and fix everything, huh? I'd see what I could do. I smoothed out my bunched-up brain like a blanket and tried to lay things out neatly.

So. I'd eliminated a player. If the Moon masks were out, that left Silver Eyes and the bugs...plus whoever had poisoned the wine back in Prime. I couldn't see the beetles managing it, and the Moon masks had to make their kills with that dagger. Given that Silver Eyes had seemed surprised, we must have a fourth, secret player. Very possibly one with a human accomplice to administer the poison, since I hadn't seen any other Echoes lurking around.

I didn't like that at all.

There was also the matter of the masters the silver-eyed Echo had mentioned. If these Echoes were only pieces on the board, that begged the question of who was moving them. That Echo kid who'd almost mugged us had mentioned Empyreans—which might explain some things, but not in a *yay, I figured it out* kind of way. More of a *we are seriously fucked* way.

This was no petty Echo power game. The crux year, the year-naming rite, the convergence—everything had a terrible ancient grandeur to it. This was deep stuff, running cold and awful through all the bones of reality, deadly as the white fire of the stars that glimmered in the Void itself. Far, *far* beyond anything a Hound was equipped to deal with.

But I wasn't powerless. I'd taken out one player, and that meant I could take out more.

"Oh!"

"I say! Did it bite you?"

I whirled toward the familiar sound. This time, I was close enough to see when the panicked lift of a silky skirt revealed a tiny spot of blood on an ankle. The beetle had left its mark.

A few quick strides brought me to the startled guests before they finished brushing off the beetle's imaginary friends from their clothes. I caught a glimpse of glimmering carapace and stomped on it, then had a thought and turned to the small cluster of Hillside aristocrats tutting over the bite.

"There's more of them," I advised. "Keep an eye out, and step on them if you see them."

"Oh, how horrid!"

"*Crush* those nasty things."

"Vengeance for Penelope!"

They raised their glasses in salute and immediately began searching around for more.

The beetles' strength was their numbers. I'd seen Echoes like them before; they were likely all one creature, a living swarm. You couldn't fight something like that. But if Rika and Carter got the invitation ward finished—and I could see them running around hanging sticks and bones even now—then we'd only have to deal with the ones already in the building. For those less-than-apocalyptic quantities, we just might be able to finish them off if I recruited enough boots to help.

Time to talk to Marjorie. I moved through the ballroom, watching for the slightest glimmer of iridescence, catching the attention of one group of guests after another for a quick warning. *Beetles loosed in the ballroom, probably a prank, definitely biting people. Keep an eye out, and stomp on them if you see them.* Based on the startled exclamations in my wake, that warning would spread itself just fine. I spotted a beetle myself and didn't even get to it before someone else crushed it.

I found Marjorie in the middle of a conversation with Dona Vandelle. I hovered a few steps back, not wanting to intrude on council business, but Marjorie waved me over.

"Harking just called the people who died in that recent warehouse collapse *poor Dockside scum*," Vandelle was saying, her hands jammed into her tailcoat pockets as if she hoped she could punch through them and find weapons on the far side. "He and his cronies are the reason I couldn't get the worker protections passed that would have saved them! He's killing people, and he doesn't care. I'm *done* playing nice."

"Oh my Moon and stars." Marjorie placed a hand on her bosom. "How absolutely wretched of him! What will you do?"

For a moment, fire flared in Vandelle's eyes. She seemed poised on the brink of some wild and brilliant answer, ready to utter words that would change the world. Then she sighed, running a hand through her hair to dishevel it even more, and it was gone, replaced only by weariness.

"Maybe I'll quit. I can't take this job. All the way to the Council of Elders from Dockside, and I still have no power to see justice done."

"Oh, don't do that!" Marjorie put an earnest hand on Vandelle's shoulder. "The city needs you, dear. Even when you don't win, you usually manage to wring some concessions from them."

"I'm damned tired, Marjorie." Vandelle looked it. Disillusionment had settled into jaded lines around her eyes. "Playing the game all these years has done me little good. Some days I want to flip the table, but I'm afraid all that would do is scatter the pieces and make a mess."

Dona Marjorie patted her arm. "There's always a way forward, dear. Even a man like Ryvard Harking has his weaknesses. Why don't you talk to Signa Thorne about him? I suspect she might know a few."

"I what?" I protested, startled.

Vandelle straightened, her dark eyes sharpening. "You have dirt on him? Blood on the Moon, tell me!"

"I actually wanted to talk to you about an urgent security concern," I said to Marjorie, with an apologetic grimace for Vandelle. "Sorry, Dona. Maybe another time, though—he really is the worst."

Vandelle sighed. "Ah, I'll excuse myself then. But I'll hold you to that, Signa Thorne."

Marjorie deployed her fan with an alarmed fluttering snap as Vandelle slouched off. "Oh my, another one? Signa Nonesuch already has my staff running all over the house putting up wards!"

"I'm afraid so." I explained about the bug situation, framing it as an Echo invasion of nebulous and undefined purpose.

Marjorie's gaze went razor-sharp. "I'll have Carter get everyone to scour the place for them at once."

"Sorry to make you worry at your party."

"Not at all, dear." She waved the idea away. "I'm worrying much *less* because you're here."

"Well, thanks." It'd be nice if I felt nearly as competent as everyone else seemed to expect me to be. "Oh, and do you happen to have a sword with a real sheath and belt I could borrow?" I gestured to the one at my hip with a grimace.

"I'm certain we can round something up for you, dear." She patted my arm fondly. "Is there anything else you need?"

I laughed, a bit hollowly. "Not unless you've found a good substitute for a few days' rest."

Her brown eyes filled with sympathy. "Newborns are so exhausting, aren't they? But it does get better. I found I actually had more energy after I went back to work—it's just so draining not having a moment to yourself."

I hesitated. I needed to move on to the next task, but I couldn't resist asking the question burning in my mind. "Did you... How was it for you? Going back to work?"

"Well, sometimes I wore my babies in a sling on the council floor, nursing in my office and everything, and let me tell you, that wasn't easy! But I had aides and such, and they were delighted to occasionally play with a baby instead of fetching me paperwork. And it made my opponents underestimate me." Her eyes twinkled. "Most of the time, my husband took them. If you do decide you want to stay home with her for a few years, don't let that guild bully you into coming back before you're ready! I took two years off with my first."

"You did? I ..." This was not the time for this conversation. I blinked back something that felt suspiciously like tears. "Thanks, Dona Marjorie. I'll keep that in mind."

Marjorie swept off to talk to Carter. I'd barely finished reining in my unruly feelings when Rika glided up to me, wearing a faint frown. I composed myself as best I could, feeling like I was sweeping dirt under the rug as guests walked in the door.

"The ward is up," Rika reported, all business. "Carter has people double-checking every possible entrance. I checked on Pearson, too, and talked to the physicker. He's stable but unconscious—Dona Marjorie gave him some kind of Echo salve. She must really like him, to use something that rare on him."

"Is he going to be all right?"

Rika shrugged. "I've certainly seen people survive worse."

"Good." My shoulders sagged with relief. "Thank the Moon."

"So..." She hesitated, her face uncertain. "It wasn't Carter after all? Their target. It was Dona Harking this time."

"Yeah, I think so. Nothing happened when they killed Carter, and that glass dagger glowed for Harking. Maybe they can't use the same person for a blood seal twice."

"What under the Moon do Carter and Dona Harking have in common? They're practically opposites."

"I have no idea. Maybe they touched something, like we did. Maybe they have a rare kind of blood or something." I shoved both hands up into my hairline, further accelerating the straggling disarray of my hair. "Maybe it's random, like the location of the convergence was random, and they're marked somehow. I wish I knew who the other previous targets were, but the poison got almost everyone in Prime and I wasn't in the building for the first Echo. We need more information."

"So what now?"

"If you got the ward up, hopefully that's most of the battle. I'm working on enlisting everyone at the party to help us hunt down the remaining bugs that are already inside. I talked to Dona Marjorie, but we should spread the word to anyone competent—Jaycel, Vandelle..." I cocked an eyebrow. "Signa Cail?"

Rika sighed. "Yes, Cail. She's trustworthy. She's just...Look, today has been strange. Even before we fell into an Echo."

I went alert at the clear distress pinching the edges of her face. "Something wrong?"

She let out a strained little laugh. "What *isn't* wrong right now?"

It was the sort of brush-off you gave a colleague when they got close to something too full of raw feelings for casual discussion, an easy out to divert from a messy topic. An acquaintance would take that grace and shift the subject back to the task at hand. A friend might not.

I had no business trying to be Rika's friend right now. We weren't friends. We had to work together to prevent some kind of cosmic disaster, that was all.

Which would be easier if I weren't choking on six different conflicting emotions every time I looked at her.

I let out a long breath, feeling like I was letting go of something I'd been clutching tight in my fist. Maybe something precious, or maybe just some stupid rock I'd been carrying around for no reason.

"Look, I can tell you're not all right. Something's bothering you, beyond all the many obvious things. You don't have to tell me what's going on, but…if you want to, well." I shrugged, feeling gruff and ruffled and awkward.

Her eyes flicked away, avoiding mine. "It's nothing. There was a… little incident right when I arrived. Something I had to take care of. It started the party off on the wrong note, so I've been on edge ever since."

I chuckled to try to ease the tension radiating off her. "You make it sound like you murdered someone."

Silence. She still didn't meet my eyes.

"Holy shit, Rika. You murdered someone?"

"I didn't say that."

"You can't just…" I clamped my mouth shut, trying to wrestle my shock under control.

This was Rika. Sure, she'd done some things that had hurt me pretty deeply, and yes, she was a Cat, but she didn't just haul off and murder people for no reason. So either it was Cat business, which I needed to damn well keep my nose out of no matter how little I liked it, or it was…something else. Something harrowing and personal enough to leave her shaken.

I remembered how she'd looked flushed when she said hello back in Prime. Like she'd been dancing—or like she'd been in a fight.

"Did someone *attack* you on your way in here?" I asked, incredulous.

"Something like that." She waved it off. "I don't want to talk about it."

"I…All right. Fair."

She met my eyes at last, and hers were unexpectedly full of pain. Like she wanted to say something, or like she wanted *me* to say something, and instead we were standing here locked in our own separate worlds, three feet of aching silence between us.

She didn't move. We stared at each other, the silence growing thorns. Funny things were happening in my chest, all the unspoken, snarled-up tension between us tightening into a crushing pain until I *had* to say something, but I didn't know what or how.

"Do you..." I cleared my throat. "Do you need help?"

She blinked, as if that were the last thing she'd thought I would say. Her gaze softened a little. "No. But...thanks."

"Listen, I...I don't actually mind working with you."

Her mouth crooked. "Why, Kembral. Such flattery."

"Oh, shut up. The point is, I'm messed up today, too. So if I'm an asshole, just...ignore it."

A sparkle came into her eyes. "I try. Sometimes you make it hard, Thorne."

"You're no paragon of compassion yourself," I grumbled. "Look, we should get moving on those bugs before it's too late."

"Of course. Why don't we..." She broke off, staring past me with a suddenly very neutral expression.

Adelyn Cail swept up to us like a winter breeze. Constellations mapped the bodice of her flowing gown, its skirts the deep purple of a midnight sky. The gaze she turned on Rika was hard as a tomb door.

"Enjoying yourself?" Her icy tone suggested that perhaps Rika should instead be working.

I bristled instinctively but forced myself to smile. "Signa Cail. It's a party. We're all here to enjoy ourselves. Aren't we?"

"Of course." Her eyes barely flicked to me, dismissing me. "Excuse us, Signa Thorne. Rika and I have matters to discuss."

Rika seemed almost to wilt. That couldn't be right—Rika None-such, looking miserable as a wet cat? I'd never seen her...no.

I had, once. The look she'd given me when I turned her over to the guards after she fell into my trap during the Echo Key affair. Well, now I felt cruddy. And, strangely, all the more protective.

"Rika and I are having a conversation." My tone was too chilly for speaking to a senior member of a rival guild, especially since she wouldn't remember our earlier conversation when she'd been rude to me first, but I didn't care. I was out of the capacity to worry about politeness or appearances, and it was immensely liberating. "Sorry, Signa Cail, but you'll have to wait."

"No, it's all right." Rika attempted something that was probably supposed to be a smile, but didn't quite achieve it. "This'll only be a moment. I'll catch up with you later."

"You're sure?"

"Yes. I'm a grown-up, Kembral. I'll manage on my own."

I couldn't help staring after them as they started off across the ballroom. No matter what she said, Rika didn't look too happy.

Well. She *was* a grown-up, and I had a lot to do. Rika could take care of herself; she didn't need a Hound stalking after her, looming ominously and staring at her guild superior, much as that might be personally satisfying for reasons I wasn't going to examine right now.

She could take care of herself so well, in fact, that she'd apparently killed someone on her way to the party. Or gotten in a tussle. Or *something*. I couldn't feel entirely easy about that. I knew we drew lines at different places, but still... I really hoped that whatever had happened, it had been a matter of self-defense.

Shouts broke me out of my reverie—not of alarm or fear, thank the Moon, just Vandelle's usual argument with Harking. *Right.* Time to get back to work. I climbed up on a chair to scan the ballroom for beetles.

I didn't see a glimmer of iridescence anywhere. What I *did* see instead warmed my heart.

All across the ballroom, a sea of heads looked down, searching for bugs. Little scattered islands of commotion broke out here and there, briefly, as someone called "There's one!" or a couple of people engaged in a burst of gleeful, vigorous stomping. Everyone was laughing and smiling, bringing surprisingly joyful energy to the task.

"Oh, good job!" Marjorie called, from where she stood on another chair over by the musicians. "Well done! Another point for you! Who's in the lead?"

She'd turned it into a party game. *Brilliant.*

A flicker of hope warmed my chest. The elite of Acantis were merchants; they were nothing if not competitive. At this rate, they'd wipe out the bugs in no time, and that would be another player eliminated—the only one inside the invitation ward, so far as I could tell. Our plans were working. We could *do* this.

My gaze snagged on a familiar figure over by the grandfather clock. Blond hair unbrushed, eyes huge, apron smudged with grease—watching me.

Now *there* was someone who probably had some answers I was looking for. She'd been skulking around that clock since the beginning, and she clearly knew what was happening.

It was time for us to have a talk.

CULTIVATE YOUR CONTACTS

I pretended not to see the little girl as I hopped down from the chair and strolled in a direction that would take me past her, my eyes fixed on some imaginary goal across the room. When I got close, I pivoted to face her. She took a step back in alarm.

"Wait! Don't vanish. I just want to say hello."

She hesitated, frozen like a deer at the edge of a clearing. I gave her a reassuring smile, trying to make myself small and harmless, and took a careful step closer.

"I saw you earlier, and I wanted to make sure you were okay. I'm Kembral Thorne."

She jerked her head in a quick nod, big eyes fixed on my face. "I know."

Well, that wasn't alarming at all. "Right. Well, I'm glad to meet you, ah..." I trailed off, inviting her to fill in the blank.

She hesitated. "The Clockmaker. I'm the Clockmaker, so you can call me that."

An Echo, then, unless they'd started passing out grandiose titles to schoolchildren. I forced myself to stay relaxed. One thing you learned early as a Hound was that you had to always treat people as *people*, not just as leads—not only was it the right thing to do, but they were much more likely to talk to you.

I glanced at the clock with a suitably impressed look. "Did you make this one, then?"

She gave a tight little nod.

"It's amazing. You do incredible work."

A real smile flashed across her face at that, and she nodded again, more enthusiastically.

"Did you sell it to Dona Marjorie? Back in Prime?"

Yet another nod, this one wary.

"She's lucky to have such a well-designed clock."

The Clockmaker said in a very small voice, "It had to be here."

"Oh?" Sometimes just looking expectant and interested was enough to draw out answers.

"To keep awful things from happening." Her small hands twisted her apron.

"Well, if that's what it's for, it's very much needed." I dropped my voice from its cheerful, friendly tones to something more serious. "If I understand right, you saved a lot of lives tonight. Thank you."

"It won't save yours anymore, though." Her eyes had gone damp and shiny. "You cut yourself out of the enchantment, and now you don't have an Echo shield around you like the others do. It can't reset you to how you were. Please be careful."

"Thanks for the warning. How about you? Will you be safe?"

Inexplicably, she turned pink, a blush creeping over her face. "I'm protected."

"Because this game seems really dangerous, and if you're a player—"

"I'm not!" She shook her head vehemently. "I wouldn't. I don't want any part of the year-naming. I'm just here to help . . ." She trailed off into a murmur. "People."

That was a relief. Of all the enemies I'd faced in my career, the one I absolutely could not handle would be a little kid.

"I really appreciate the help. It must have taken a lot of effort to create such a powerful artifact."

"Oh, I found a way to make it easier!" Her whole face lit up, like the sun coming out from behind a cloud on a brilliant spring day. "It uses energy from the creation of the blood seals. They release a lot of power—pinning the entire Echo to the convergence *and* the crux year so forcefully it knocks the whole house down through the Veil." She punched her palm to demonstrate, or maybe just out of enthusiasm. "That sets off my clock, which harnesses the extra energy and uses it to reset everyone to how they were when the convergence began in Prime. There's enough left over to refresh the shield on the house, too!"

"Shield on the— Ah. That's why there are gears all over the outside of the mansion?"

She nodded vigorously. "It's to keep everyone safe as the Echoes get deeper, so it doesn't get too dangerous inside. Otherwise if we got more than about nine Echoes down, you'd all die."

"You really thought this through. I'm impressed." It wasn't just flattery; this kid would put most Ravens to shame. "I don't suppose you built in a way for us all to get safely back to Prime?"

"I…Yes, but…" She clutched her apron in distress; I noticed tools poking out of the pockets. "The year-naming rite has to finish first, one way or another, or it'll keep pulling you all back in. At midnight, either someone will complete the rite and name the year, or if they haven't made all twelve blood seals, the year will just turn normally. Either way, my clock can use the resonance of the year-turning to bring this place and all of you back to Prime— everything going back to where it started, like the year beginning anew."

"That's brilliant." My praise seemed to ease her anxiety; she tentatively returned my smile. "I'm relieved we're not going to be stranded in the Deepest Echo, I'll be honest. Do you know what happens if they *do* finish the ritual and name the year?"

"I'm too young to remember the last one, but I've heard stories." She bit her lip. "I think whoever wins gets to decide what the year will be like, and it reflects through all layers of reality. So we care about it down in the Echoes, too. We're really hoping you can stop them."

Lovely. My responsibility on my night off had escalated from saving one houseful of people, to the entire city, to *every single layer of all reality.*

"I'll try," I promised. "So how do they win? Is it whoever makes the most blood seals?"

She bit her lip, half closing her eyes, as if she were trying to remember. "Making a seal gives the player more power over the year *if* they're the one to name it in the end. But I think any player still in the game can name it in the final Echo."

"Do you know how they stay in the game? It'd be great if I had some easier way to eliminate them besides killing them."

Her pale brows pinched together. "I think...I think she said that to stay in the game, a player has to make a blood sacrifice in every layer of reality, to bind themselves to the convergence. So in each Echo, only one player can make the actual seal by taking a specific life—I don't know how they determine that—but every player needs to make a sacrifice, which can be any Prime blood."

"Ah!" That explained some things. "That's why all the Echoes seem so eager to stab or bite people who aren't their target. They've got to shed blood whether they personally make the seal or not."

"Yes. Which makes it really dangerous to be here." Her eyes had gone wide and solemn. "The sacrifice doesn't have to be a death, but most of them don't care, so with several players times eleven Echoes plus Prime..."

"It turns into a bloodbath," I finished. That was some frightening math, but there was another detail I didn't want to let escape. "Also...*she* said? Who is *she*?"

The Clockmaker's face went ghost pale. Her lips pressed together.

"Were you not supposed to mention her?"

She shook her head, miserable.

"It's all right. I'm a Hound; we get passed information all the time from people who can't tell us their sources. Either because they're protecting someone, or because they're scared." I let that dangle, watching her face to try to figure out which one it was.

The Clockmaker nodded vigorously. Hard to tell, but if I had to guess, I'd go with fear. A protective urge kindled in my heart, buried but intensely violent. I could see it sure was going to be fun going back to work and wanting to dismember anyone who ever threatened a kid.

"I won't ask who it was. I'll just assume somebody tipped you off that this game was going to happen and told you how it works." Who and why were certainly some burning questions, but I wasn't going to push her when she was scared. "Is that how you knew to build the clock? I'll bet you didn't throw *that* together in a day."

The tension in the girl's face eased, and her smile came out again. "Two days," she said proudly. "It was my own idea. I don't want you to think I work for her! She warned me that...that people would be in danger, and she told me about the convergence and the year-naming. But I made the clock all on my own, and convinced the lady who lives here to buy it."

"Everyone is very lucky you did. I hope this doesn't put you in any danger, interfering in a powerful Echo game like this."

"I...No." She ducked her head. "It helps them, too, if people keep coming back to life—they don't run out of victims that way. So they don't mind. But that's not why I made the clock!"

"Of course not. I'm glad you're not in danger. Keep safe." I gave her a big smile. She might be an Echo—she might be ten thousand years old, for all I knew—but she was helping us. The least I could do was show her some friendship and gratitude. If it turned out in the end that she was doing all this so she could eat us or something... Well, it still wouldn't hurt to be nice to her now.

She smiled back, an odd wistfulness in it. "I will."

The first familiar notes of "Under the Flower Moon" teased my ears. My whole body went instinctively tense.

The girl's eyes flicked past me, widening with alarm. "He's here," she breathed.

I turned to see who was approaching, but all I saw was a great migration toward the dance floor. When I glanced back, the Clockmaker was gone.

"Who's here?" I murmured to the empty air, the uneasy feeling in my belly yawning wider.

Screams of raw terror erupted near the ballroom doors. I whirled, hand on my sword.

I don't know what I expected. The black-armored Echo cleaving a path through the guests, I suppose, possibly followed by more of those Moon-masked creatures.

I did not expect a *giant fucking spider.*

NEVER UNDERESTIMATE YOUR OPPONENT

Let me make something clear. I *hate* spiders. Absolutely fucking hate them. The legs, the way they move—everything about them starts up a raw, primal scream deep in some old, scared, animal part of my brain.

What burst in through the doors wasn't quite a spider, but close enough: a many-legged monster of brass and iron, all scything razor-edged limbs and no face. The silver-haired Echo rode its back, the ragged tendrils of his night-sky cape streaming as the thing reared back onto half its legs to strike with deadly accuracy at fleeing guests with the others. It pierced through one man's chest with curving brass blades as long as my whole body, then slashed open another woman's side. Blood spread across their finery and splashed the monster's brass claws.

There are some things training can't really prepare you for. Going in the space of about two seconds from a peaceful conversation to a huge deadly monster gorily murdering people in front of you is one of them.

What *can* prepare you for that, sort of, is ten years of experience doing Echo missions.

Before my brain recovered from its initial horrified shock, I'd already drawn my sword and was closing on the monster in a tight, fast arc that would put me out of the Echo's line of sight. I didn't have to make a conscious decision, which was good, because what passed for my conscious mind in that instant was still stuck wordlessly screaming. By the time rational thought kicked in, I was almost in range, and at that point... Well, someone had to deal with this thing, and everyone else was far too busy panicking.

I darted in *much* closer than I wanted to, the thing looming massive and deadly over me, and hacked at one of those awful scythe-blade legs.

My sword chipped a chunk out of it, but its armor was tough, and the strike didn't get through. The impact almost wrenched that too-big grip from my hand, and it certainly didn't do the blade any favors. The spider reared and struck at me in response; I threw myself out of the way. Its leg punched a hole in the marble floor where I'd been.

Right. The joints, then. Another leg spiked down at me, and as I ducked it I slashed at one of its horrible angles.

This time, my sword caught for one brief moment, then met the strange liquid yielding of Echo flesh and sheared straight through. A surge of wild, fierce satisfaction surged through me. *Yes.* The joints were vulnerable.

Unfortunately, it turns out that when you have eight legs, losing half of one is really not a big deal.

Now the thing was mad. Its remaining seven legs came for me with a horrifying scuttling speed, huge and sharp and deadly, slicing the air and spearing down at me. Raw adrenaline flooded my veins, all my nerves awake and singing.

I had to fight the urge to blink step out of there. But I could only do it a few times in a row, and with seven legs and one malevolent silver-eyed Echo left, it was way too early in this fight to start wasting my most precious resource. So I dodged, one leg slamming down close enough that it caught the edge of my peacock-tail skirt and nearly pinned me. Another sent chips of marble flying up to sting my arm and cheek.

Now I was under its belly, in the metallic looming shade of it, beneath the cage of its legs. I stabbed up into a crease between its awful insectile chest plates, hoping to reach whatever cold lump of malice this creature used for a heart.

It *hissed*, the sound steaming from its joints in lieu of a mouth, and reared up in pain. The motion yanked that uncomfortable hilt out of my grasp. *Shit.*

I scrambled out from beneath it, dodging limbs that flailed in agony. The crowd fled as far away from it as they could, crying out in terror, half the party hiding in back rooms or under tables. A few brave souls stayed to fight the spider, slashing ineffectively at its other legs: Dona Marjorie's guards and a handful of others, including Jaycel. Vandelle glared at the Echo with her fists at her sides as if he'd offended her personally, yelling something about a murdering bastard.

The silver-haired Echo didn't much seem to care. Up atop the spider, he rode its writhing back with grace and ease, his mirrored gaze sweeping the crowd, searching for something.

I hesitated just out of range of the thing's deadly flailing legs, frustrated and swordless. All I had left was my belt knife, more for utility than monster-slaying.

"Kembral!"

Fifty feet away, Marjorie held up a sheathed sword one of her staff had just passed her, waving it in the air like a signal flag. I could have kissed her.

The Echo looked toward the movement, and an ominous grin spread across his face. "There's one at last. Perfect."

The wounded spider gave one final rear and suddenly came back under absolute control, advancing on its remaining legs toward Dona Marjorie with terrible, murderous purpose.

Oh, no you don't. I stepped out of time and space, like slipping through the narrow gap of a closing door.

The world went to honey and amber. I sprinted straight through everything and everyone in my path: a man stopped in mid-scream, a woman halfway through stumbling over a chair in her haste to escape, a dropped wineglass that hung fixed in midair with ruby droplets scattered like jewels across the timeless instant.

I burst back into color and noise before Marjorie, who was still holding the sword up to signal to where I'd been across the room. It looked Echo-touched, its swept hilt glittering with red-gold curves like a stylized swirling flame—probably one of her "antiques." I hoped it still had an edge. I grabbed the hilt and ripped the blade free of the sheath in Marjorie's hand before she'd realized I was there.

"Oh! Hello!" She gave a little jump of shock, fumbling the scabbard.

I couldn't so much as acknowledge her; the brass monster was bearing down on us, its legs spearing into the gleaming patterned wood of the dance floor. I spun to face it, no time to get a feel for the blade in my hand beyond a vague impression that it was light and well-balanced but a touch on the short side.

I drew my knife in my off hand and stepped between the charging monster and Marjorie, desperately searching the gleaming arcs of the beast for any sign of a weak point, but it was like a bunch of curving knives fused together. No eyes, no organs, no brain. I could go for the joints again, or I could go after the Echo on its back.

Taking out legs one at a time would be too slow. I knew who the true head of this monster was.

I plunged once more into the golden liquid silence of the Veil.

A quick sprint took me close enough to bound up one of those vicious curving legs. I could technically have run up the air itself, since the floor was no more real or solid here, but it was much easier to move when you maintained the illusions that made it all seem natural.

I reached the thing's back, heart pounding from the strain as I strove to hold myself out of space and time a little longer. The Echo sat astride the spider creature's narrow middle, his grin of triumph revealing pointed teeth.

I launched myself at him, sword arcing for his neck, ready to let go and blink into existence to let the strike land before he even knew I was there.

His goat-pupiled eyes flicked to mine.

In that timeless non-space where everything else was still and frozen, he *moved*. One gleaming black bracer swung up to block my blade.

Oh *fuck*.

Equilibrium shattered, I stumbled, starting to slip back into reality, my sense of space warping, feet not remotely placed for reentry—

He caught my arm. The golden world steadied around me, everything else still frozen in place, only the two of us loosed in time. This close, I could see the tightness around those mirror eyes and his grinning mouth, as if beneath his exultation he was in pain.

Hello, Kembral Thorne, he said.

I didn't hear it; there was no sound in the Veil. But the words reverberated through me, deeper and more profound than any mere noise.

Fuck fuck fuck. This shouldn't be happening. I'd blink stepped against Echoes many times before; none of them could do this. Almarah had taught me that Echoes could no more come here without years of training than humans could, and they didn't have the secret techniques that the Hounds guarded so closely.

He shouldn't be able to move here, to talk here, to stare into my eyes with such bitter-edged mockery. This was impossible.

He could have killed me easily in my moment of shock. All he'd have to do was let me slide back into the world and stab me like I'd been about to do to him. My lungs burned and my head pounded with the urgent need for reality, more vital than air; I couldn't have stayed here any longer on my own.

But he was holding me in the Veil, like pushing down on a drowning swimmer's head to keep them underwater.

Who are you? I tried to ask. What I wanted to say was *Let me go*, but that would be the surest way to make sure he never did.

He inclined his head in a taunting bow. *You may call me Rai, little dog.*

My pulse burned through my whole body. I strained desperately to plunge back into the world, starved for time and space, feeling as if my soul would shake apart any minute. Almarah had warned me never to push past my limit and stay more than a few heartbeats. I couldn't exist here for long; nothing could.

Except for one thing.

The Empyreans were older than space and time, and not bound by their petty rules. An Empyrean was formed of celestial ichor and divine essence, not flesh and blood, and could probably stay in the Veil indefinitely without the slightest discomfort.

Oh, I was *completely fucked.*

With the desperate energy of panic, I swung the pommel of my off-hand blade at those mirror eyes to make him blink, then wrenched my arm free of his grip.

At once I was breathing again, color in my eyes and chaos in my ears. The air whooshed past me as I fell from the monster's back, its razor-sharp legs stabbing down all around me.

I tried to slip back into the Veil out of pure panicked instinct, a reflex trained into me whenever I was falling. Blinding pain stabbed through my head, and the world only flickered gold for a brief instant.

It was enough to swing my legs down more or less under me. I landed in a tumbling mess, barely managing not to stab myself with my own blades as I rolled across the floor. Everything hurt like the wounded Moon. I was dry and gasping as a fish out of water, my whole body shaking with the stress of spending so long in the Veil.

Never mind that overdoing a blink step normally landed me on my back for several full minutes. I couldn't be incapacitated now. I hurled myself toward my feet, missed, and staggered to my knees instead. My head felt like a saber was embedded through my skull, but I threw myself forward on my unsteady limbs again, blinking sense and shape into the madness around me . . .

Just in time to see a great curving brass blade stab down into Dona Marjorie's neck, driving through half her body and pinning her to the floor.

"No!" I screamed, my voice raw, all my calm shattered. "No, wait, no, *damn it!*"

An amused voice drifted down from the cluster of massive

knife-legs above me, somehow slicing through the wails and cries of fear and despair.

"I'm not going to make this easy for you, dog. I don't let people win."

Rika came bursting through the crowd, gown flowing around her like smoke, face stricken for one brief moment as she saw Marjorie before the shutters closed, and she met my gaze with a grim, professional mask.

The clock struck, making reality shudder. A wave of pain to dwarf the previous ones crashed through my head. The world fell away, but what I plunged into wasn't gold—only darkness.

THERE'S ALWAYS A WAY

Kembral. Damn you, Kembral, wake up. This is no time to take a nap. *Kembral Thorne!*"

It was Rika's voice, distant and frustrated. I tried to explain to her that I wasn't taking a nap, I was *unconscious* because some fucking Empyrean had held me in the Veil until I nearly drowned. Or suffocated. Or something else there wasn't even a word for, because only a handful of people in the world could go to that place at all, but apparently the Empyreans could just lounge around there anytime having tea and cookies.

A nap would have been nice, though. Blood on the Moon, I could use a nap.

Something ice cold splashed in my face.

I woke up gasping and sputtering, taking a swing at my attacker. Rika was already out of reach, grey eyes calculating, empty glass in her hand.

"Oh, good," she said.

"What the fuck, Rika! What did you do that for?"

She gave an elegant shrug. "I thought about slapping you, but this seemed safer. Did you mess up your blink step somehow, or are you just that sleep-deprived?"

I was dimly aware that something smelled nice, and there were soft colors all around me, and I was sitting in a chair in an out-of-the-way corner of the transformed ballroom. Right now, I was entirely fixed on Rika, all my leftover jittery fear and anger overflowing.

"I didn't *mess up* my blink step, for Void's sake." I lurched to my feet, still a bit unsteady; my headache flared, and I couldn't help a wince. "I got *attacked in the Veil* by a fucking Empyrean!"

Rika went deathly still. "What?"

"Yes!" My body still thought I should be fighting; I had to pace in tight little arcs to work it off, legs trembling. "Our friend with the horns? Apparently his name is Rai, and he's an Empyrean. He didn't just send Echoes to be his pawns in this death game like the others—he came himself."

"Blood on the Moon," she whispered, on a bare thread of breath. I took a vicious satisfaction in the fear harrowing her face; it was the same terrible, hollow feeling in my own gut. "Are you sure?"

"Yes." I said it through my teeth.

"Then we're doomed." She hooked the chair out from behind me with a graceful movement and eased into it, glassy-eyed. "We can't win against an Empyrean, Kembral. They're as far beyond normal Echoes as a mountain is beyond a pebble. They're *divine celestial beings as old as life itself.*"

I couldn't take her being scared and vulnerable anymore. I wanted her competent and fearless so that *I* could lose my courage, because holy Void, I was absolutely terrified. I had no business going up against an Empyrean, no business being here at all. I should be home with Emmi, holding her safe and warm in my arms, completely oblivious to whatever deadly cosmic bullshit was unfolding in this room tonight.

"I know." My voice cracked. I could feel myself unraveling, right here in front of Rika. "Believe me, I know. I don't want to be here, Rika. I can't do this. I just want to go home."

Rika stared at me as if I'd spoken in Old Viger. "What?"

"You heard me." My face burned, but it was too late to walk it back, so I plunged in further. "I'm not up for this. I just had a baby, for Moon's sake. I couldn't handle an Empyrean at my prime, and now..."

"Oh, don't be ridiculous." Rika waved a hand at me. "You're Kembral Thorne, pride of the Hounds, insufferably competent and annoyingly duty-bound. So what if you're not in top form? If I had to pick one person in Acantis to take on an Empyrean, it'd still be you."

"That's very flattering, but—"

"Don't let it go to your head." Her mouth quirked. "Maybe I meant because you're the one I'd miss the least when he inevitably destroys you."

"Thanks. That's exactly what I'm concerned about. The inevitable destruction." I sagged against a table, since Rika had stolen my chair. "I've got Emmi now, Rika. I can't throw my life away for the job like it's nothing."

A sudden fury flushed her face. She surged to her feet, grabbed the collar of my coat, and twisted it in her fist, yanking me close to her. We were only inches apart, her angry grey eyes burning into mine.

"This is what's wrong with you," she hissed. "This is why I hate you. Your life was *always* worth something, you insufferable fool."

Her honey-and-clove perfume enfolded me. This close, the faint shimmer of illusion showed in the perfect sweeping lines and smoky hues of her makeup. The air between us felt soft, permeable, as if it could vanish in an instant.

All I could do was stare at her. My brain kept flipping uselessly between *I hate you* and *your life was always worth something*, unable to untangle the knot, stunned into panicked blankness.

Rika leaned in even closer, and for one terrifying, heady moment I had the wild thought she was going to kiss me. But instead she closed her eyes for half a breath, muttered some word I couldn't hear, and gave me a little shake.

"Now stop it. You're not going to die. You're going to come up with some clever plan and figure out how to get us all out of this. And I'm going to help you."

I struggled to recover a shred of composure. "It's not that easy."

"Of course it's not easy. You never do anything easy. If it *were* easy, you'd figure out a way to make it hard."

She let me go with a strange, awkward jerk as if she'd only just realized she had ahold of me. She stepped back at once, brushing the offending hand through her hair. An odd little shudder passed through me—too many feelings, all of them riled up and unable to settle. I took a deep breath, trying to summon the calm I desperately needed.

"Fine. I'll do this, because I have to, but you're expecting too much." Everyone kept doing that, myself included. "I came into this party with nothing left. It was supposed to be *rejuvenating*, for fuck's sake. How am I supposed to fight an Empyrean? They're immortal, and they can shape Echoes to their will. It's not like I can just stab him and expect him to die. And...bloody Moon, I can't even do that, because I lost my sword again."

"I saved it for you." Rika waved toward the wall. "I even grabbed the scabbard off the floor right before the last bell. Are you going to thank me?"

I blinked. "You did? I take back everything bad I've said about you for the past fifteen minutes."

For the first time since waking up with Rika's drink in my face, I looked around.

It was as if the ballroom and a jungle had tried to eat each other alive. Whispery silver-edged grass covered the floor, dotted with vibrant sprays of flowers. Vines heavy with purple and red blooms dripped from a glass ceiling, their tendrils slowly curling and uncurling, groping the air as if searching for something. A verdant perfume smothered the air. Moss covered the walls, dotted with a pattern of tiny starry blooms.

The Echo sword Marjorie had lent me stood propped against the wall, the tip of its scabbard nestled in the grass, flame-swept hilt bright against patterns of grey and green lichen. I scooped it to my chest, an eager spark of hope kindling in my heart despite myself. I hadn't really gotten the chance to use it, but it had felt much better in my hand than the last one.

"That was a magnificent act. Thank you." I untied the ridiculous curtain cord from my waist and buckled on the sword belt conveniently threaded through the scabbard fastenings. Oh, this was *much* better. The sword rode angled properly behind my hip; no more worrying about it tangling my legs.

"You're right, though," Rika said. "You can't stab him. You can't do anything to him. We can't fight an Empyrean." She hugged her arms, strain showing around her eyes. "That's why I need you to stop the defeatist talk, Kembral. Maybe you're not at your best, but you're still the best we've got. So tell me what to do."

She was so scared. A protective instinct prickled in me for a moment before I squashed it. I let out a long, ragged breath.

"All right. Let me think."

She suppressed a little smile. "Don't hurt yourself."

The gears of my mind started turning, grinding into motion through my headache, slow and rusty with weariness and disuse. I had to push aside the unpleasant shock of having been so helpless in the Veil, of realizing I was a speck before an inferno. Raw power wasn't everything. Almarah had taught me early that your opponent's strength meant nothing if you didn't let them bring it to bear.

"We can't fight him, true," I said slowly. "But we shouldn't *have* to fight him. The Clockmaker told me—"

"Wait, who?" Rika's brows flew up.

"The little girl in the apron. You must have seen her lurking around the clock. Looks maybe ten years old, blond hair. Really out of place." There was still no comprehension in Rika's eyes. "Have you not noticed her?"

"No, and I assure you I've been paying *particular* attention to who's coming and going around the clock. I'd ask if you were feverish, but I think we're well past that point, so I assume she's an Echo?"

"You guessed it." I filled her in on the basics of what the Clockmaker had told me, skipping the part about her mysterious information source; if she needed to keep that secret, well, she presumably had her reasons, and Hounds protected their allies.

"So," I concluded, "if they don't get their mystery special target by midnight in any Echo, this wretched game is over, and we all go back to Prime. And if this ward works, that means we literally don't have to do *anything*, because even an Empyrean can't get inside to make the...oh. Oh, shit."

Rika's eyes narrowed. "I don't like it when you say things like that, Kembral."

"Rika." It was all I could do not to grab her. "You said the invitation ward was up. Are you sure?"

"Yes, of course. It—*oh*. Bloody Moon. He came right in through the front door. He has an invitation."

"What does that mean?" I demanded. "Can we *un*invite him?"

"Only the person who issued the invitation can retract it." She pressed a trembling hand to her temple. "It could have been almost anyone. The ward recognizes everyone with a valid invitation as belonging inside: people on the guest list, people with standing invitations to the mansion, people who live or work here. And anyone who belongs can invite guests."

The implications of that spread through me like a bloodstain. "So it was someone here, at the party."

"Almost certainly," Rika said grimly. "They may have been tricked into it, or not realized his intent...or they could be working with him deliberately. In which case—"

"One of us is a traitor."

PAY ATTENTION TO DETAILS

We decided to divide up our various distressingly urgent tasks based on expertise: Rika, skilled in espionage, would try to discover the traitor, and I'd work on bolstering our defenses. While she circulated the party, sifting through rumor and overheard conversation and all the subtle cues of face and body, I quickly checked on Pearson—who was stable but unconscious—and then navigated trailing vines and tangling blooms to find Dona Marjorie.

There she was, talking to Harking, in a glorious pale gold gown trimmed with champagne-colored roses. As soon as she saw me, she broke off her conversation with him—Harking stared at me like he was trying to do murder with his eyes—and swept to meet me, fan aflutter. My heart lurched, remembering her pierced by that wicked brass spider leg and soaked in blood—but she was all right. Everyone was all right. I just had to keep them that way.

It did beg the question of why the Empyrean had targeted her. He'd seemed almost to recognize her, or something in her—something Carter and Harking must also have had. Maybe it was a personal quality, like determination or charisma. It was hard to imagine what could unite the three of them, though.

"Signa Kembral!"

"Dona Marjorie. Good to see you looking well."

"And you, I'm happy to say." She eyed me critically. "Are you all right? It was so dramatic when you fainted! I'd expect that from one of Jaycel Morningray's shows perhaps, but if it's *you* swooning, I have to assume you're on the verge of death."

I blinked. "I fainted?"

"Yes, it was quite alarming! Don't you remember?" Her fan whirred faster as she peered into my face. "Signa Nonesuch seemed rather concerned. She caught you and settled you in a chair and fussed over you. I would have stayed to make sure you were all right, but she asked me to help cover for her and make it seem like you were just resting, since she thought you wouldn't want to attract any notice. But you look well now! I'm so glad."

Blood on the Moon. The thought of Rika catching me and *fussing* over me set a strange uneasy flutter in my stomach. I'd have expected her to step back and let me hit the floor, then maybe kick me awake.

"I'm fine," I said, my voice coming out gruff. "I just...you know how it is, when you're nursing and you're tired and sometimes everything just..."

"Oh, I know, believe me." She tapped my shoulder with her fan in gentle sympathy. "You should get off your feet and rest. You have to take good care of yourself if you want to take good care of little Emmelaine."

"You're not wrong. I'll rest soon. First I need to talk to you about security threats."

I filled her in once more about the threat of Echo attack and the invitation wards and so on. The last thing I wanted was some industrious servant pulling the bones and sticks off the windows as unsightly trash.

Halfway through, I spied Carter making his way across the ballroom with a tray of drinks; I called him over to join us just as a certain drunken tailcoat staggered past, and he swerved unwittingly out of the path of destruction. *Ha.* I'd take that as a good omen.

"This Echo attack will have a specific target," I told Marjorie once she'd sent Carter off to brief her staff, "but I'm not sure who yet. Once we do know, I'd love to get them somewhere defensible. Do you still have that warded safe room we used back when I was doing security for your son?" The protections on the room wouldn't keep out an Empyrean, but maybe they'd let us hold him off until midnight.

"Of course, and you're welcome to use it. I'm so glad you're here to help with this situation, my dear! We're lucky you had an invitation ward handy, too." There was a sparkle of curiosity in her eyes, though she was too polite to ask *why* exactly we'd had one.

"Speaking of that ward, I want to make sure there's no way to circumvent it. You don't have any standing invitations issued to Echoes, do you?"

She hesitated for the smallest instant, but it was enough to make my brows crawl up my forehead. Marjorie noticed, and deployed her fan to daintily cover a laugh.

"Oh my stars! Well, you never know. When you're as old as I am, you've done a lot of things and met a lot of people."

I didn't know why I was surprised; this was simply how my night was going. She could have invited every single Empyrean and all their favorite Echoes to come have tea anytime. She probably played tiles with them on Tuesdays.

I rubbed my temple. "Can you declare some kind of blanket disinvitation for them or something?" She looked uncertain, so I added, "Maybe a temporary one? I wouldn't want to ask you to do anything that might offend them."

"Of course!" She beamed at me. "I think it should be well within proper etiquette to disinvite everyone until the first dawn of the New Year. Echoes do that sort of thing all the time. Will that be enough?"

"I think so. Thank you." Interesting that she knew that, though. "Maybe you could ask any of your guests who you think are the sort to deal with Echoes to do the same."

"Should I make a general announcement, perhaps?"

I thought it over. "No. That would let everyone in the party know that we've got the invitation ward up, and I think the Echoes haven't realized that yet. If they *do* have agents inside the ward, they could easily sabotage it. Better to exercise control over who we tell."

Marjorie chuckled. "I like the way you think, Kembral. Well! I'd best go deal with all of that, then! Do make sure you take care of yourself, dear."

I smiled and waved as she swept off, but didn't answer. I was pretty sure that the opportunity to take care of myself wouldn't arise tonight, and I didn't like lying to Dona Marjorie.

I glanced at the mantel clock: nine thirty. Rai seemed to usually show up sometime between ten and eleven o'clock. Hopefully I still had time to help Rika search for our culprit before everything went straight to the Void.

Something caught my eye. The shimmering back of a lonely beetle, scurrying toward the usual cluster of Hillside aristocrats.

I strode quickly over, cutting it off from its prey. This one looked different—it was a little bigger than the others, and a stylized opalescent eye stared up from its back. It veered away from me, scuttling under a table.

I dove beneath the tablecloth with complete abandon. There it was, a lightning glimmer trying to dart away between some chair legs.

"Oh, no you don't," I muttered.

I brought my bare fist down on it as hard as I could.

A chiming *crunch* reverberated through my hand. The beetle puffed into pearlescent, faintly glowing smoke, its touch chill and oily on my skin. The smoke dissipated, and it was gone.

I let out a breath. Was that it? The last one?

I had a feeling I might have just knocked another player out of the game. I couldn't help grinning as I climbed back out from under the table, drawing startled looks from people nearby.

What I saw when I emerged stopped me where I stood.

I'd come out near the great grandfather clock. Beyond it, farther from it than I'd ever seen her, was the Clockmaker—and there was Blair, talking to her. Not just talking; both of them were smiling and animated, hands waving, eyes shining.

At the sight of the kid's smile, a sudden wave of missing Emmi came over me. I wanted more than anything to hold her and know she was safe—which made absolutely no sense, since *I* was the one who was in danger. *She* was fine, home in my sister's capable hands. I tried to push her from my mind before my milk could let down, feeling weirdly guilty about having not thought about her for a bit. *No.* There was no reason to feel guilty. Emmi was where she needed to be—and so was I, trying to keep all these people safe. And getting outside the damned house. And holding a sword instead of a baby for a little while. On a night where everything was going terribly wrong, me being here—if not entirely great for me personally—was one thing gone right.

The Clockmaker gave Blair a little parting wave and headed back toward her clock, still grinning. She noticed me watching and gave me a big, dazzling smile and an even more enthusiastic wave; my heart squeezed in my chest as I waved back. She swerved out of her course to meet me without hesitation.

"Hi," I greeted her. "I see you were talking to Blair."

"Yes. They're really nice."

"That they are. It's good to see you looking happy."

She flushed a little. "I'm excited you're doing so well. You got the beetles!"

"Did I? Oh, good! I was hoping that was the last one." Relief flooded me. Another one down, though that left the hardest still to go. "Listen, you don't happen to know who invited Rai, do you? The Empyrean with the horns?"

She shook her head solemnly. "He hasn't talked to me. I've been hiding from all the players."

"That's smart of you. Stay safe."

"You too!"

She gave me one last imploring look before hurrying off to her clock, as if my safety were of utmost urgency. There was something so *familiar* about her, but I just couldn't place it.

The crowd flowed between us, and she was gone. *Right.* That had been delightfully wholesome, but all things considered, it was maybe time to have a quick word with Blair about talking to strange Echoes.

"Signa Blair," I greeted them as I approached. "I couldn't help but notice you had an interesting conversation partner a moment ago."

"Oh, yes." Blair gave me a dreamy smile. "She's very nice."

"I don't think everyone can see her—at least, not unless she wants them to—but I suppose I shouldn't be surprised that you can."

"She *is* a bit shy. But Echoes tend to come and say hi to me when they're around—I suppose because I'm Echoborn. It always made my parents rather nervous in shops."

I jumped on the opening. "About that. We have reason to believe there's a hostile Echo trying to get into this mansion, but he needs permission. Just in case you accidentally said something to him at some point that could be construed as an invitation, would you mind..."

"Certainly. I understand." Blair cupped their hands around their mouth and *hollered*. "HEY! ECHOES!"

Every head in the ballroom turned to stare at us. I tried to look calm and reassuring and not at all like I wanted to crawl under a table.

Blair forged ahead at full volume, undaunted. "If I invited anyone to this party, it was a mistake! Especially if you're an Echo! It's not a real invite! I revoke your invitation, I uninvite you, three times I uninvite you!"

"Good job with the three times," I murmured.

Blair dropped their hands and said conversationally, "Well, I *am* a Raven."

"That you are. So what were you talking about with the Clockmaker?"

"Oh, I was telling her how much I liked her clock."

"That's lovely." I should have figured it would be something sweet and wholesome, not mysterious at all. An idea struck me. "Hey, you probably read a lot of arcane tomes and stuff in your spare time, don't you?"

Blair brightened. "Oh, yes, I do love a good arcane tome! Yesterday I found one in the guild library about cooking with Echo ingredients. I wanted to try, but Jaycel says I'm a hopeless cook. I think she's wrong, though. The food comes out fine. It's more of a setting-things-on-fire kind of issue."

"Right." Someday, I really needed to talk to Blair when there wasn't a dire crisis and I had time to spin off into all of their weird tangents with them properly. "So, ah... in your reading, have you ever come across anything about naming the year? Some kind of Echo rite?"

"I think so. A couple of times." They blinked. "I'm a bit worried that you're asking. It doesn't sound very nice."

"I have a bad habit of asking people questions about worrying things. What can you tell me about it?"

"Well, one of the books was a very old one, and it was supposed to be a history, but really it was only a history of the Raven who wrote it, who thought he was very good at Echo working. I didn't like it, but my teacher made me read it because he really *did* know a lot about Echo theory, if you could pick those bits out. While he was rambling on about how amazing he was as a child, he said that the year he turned twelve had been named the Year of Hunger by an Empyrean called Teeth Within the Smoke. Apparently all the crops withered and the people were starving and terrible beasts roamed around eating people."

Well, that didn't sound good. "Let's hope he was exaggerating. What about the other one?"

"That book was much more interesting! It was about Empyreans, and it gave the year-naming as an example of one of their contests. It said that not all years get named, but those that do rarely go well for mortals. Apparently the third Cathardian War started during the Year of Strife, and the coup that destroyed the Viger Republic happened in the Year of Ambition, and the Umbral Scourge that finally finished off the Sigil Empire was in the Year of Curiosity. Which you'd think would be good! But I suppose they meddled with Echoes too much and unleashed something unfortunate."

My heart sank. They'd just rattled off three of the most terrible historical events of the past hundred and fifty years.

"That's... educational," I said weakly. "Thank you."

"I suppose we'd better hope no one names *this* year!" Blair lifted up onto their toes as if this were an exciting idea. "If I had to name a year, I might name it the Year of Moths, because everyone likes moths."

I made a mental note to never let Blair name any years. "Thank you, Blair. You really are incredibly helpful."

"Am I?" They looked surprised. "Oh, that's good. I thought I was fairly useless."

I was suddenly ready to fight someone. "No, not at all. Who told you that?"

"Well, my teachers at Redgrave, but Jaycel says I shouldn't listen to anything they said."

"I don't say this often," I told Blair with great gravity, "but Jaycel is absolutely right. Also, your teachers from Redgrave are in prison now, so clearly they weren't the best judges of character."

Blair broke out in a wide, wondering smile. "I suppose you're right."

I left them contentedly examining a lightning-blue flower the size of their face and went to find Rika, unease swirling my thoughts. Every time I thought I understood how bad this situation was, it turned out to be even worse.

I glanced around, trying to pick the shimmery smoke of Rika's dress out of the riot of color from the verdant growth that had consumed the ballroom. It was gorgeous, really—everything from texture to scent to the layered depth of leaves and vines and blossoms all enticing and soothing senses that really needed to be on high alert. Hillside aristocrats could only dream of decorations this breathtaking for their Flower Moon parties.

Something itched in the back of my brain. Hadn't I thought something similar about the first Echo? Everyone's transformed metallic fashions and the gold and silver opulence dripping everywhere had made it look like a high-end Coin Moon gala.

I chased the idea down, trying to think whether any of the other Echoes might have had Moon themes. The second Echo would certainly have put any Snow Moon festival I'd ever seen to shame. The third Echo...it could be a waning aspect twist on a Wine Moon theme, all rotting decadence and spoiled bounty. The fourth one had had compass roses and brass circles and celestial navigation everywhere, so maybe a Compass Moon.

The Echoes were mirroring the year, one Moon at a time.

Not in the usual year order, though, and not everywhere; the themes hadn't extended outside when I stepped through the doors into the street. Only in Marjorie's mansion, under the convergence. I wasn't sure yet how this knowledge could help us, but surely it must be significant. I had to tell Rika.

I spotted her across the ballroom—and all my excitement immediately curdled.

She was sidling up to the grandfather clock, her professional face on, blank and focused. Her fingers ran down the back of it, light and nimble, searching for something.

After everything we'd been through, she was *still* messing with the clock.

I'd been so good about not prying into her Cat business, so willing to trust her despite everything up to what amounted to a murder confession. But I'd apparently been a fool to think she cared less about that damned job than she did about keeping everyone here alive. Well, I was done looking the other way.

A storm seething in my chest, I strode up to confront her.

KNOW YOUR ENEMIES

Rika saw me coming and stepped fluidly away from the clock as if she'd just been passing by, greeting me with a dazzlingly false smile.

"Why, hello, Kembral. My, you look grumpy."

"I thought we were past this, Rika."

She forced a brittle laugh. "I don't know what you're talking about."

"Yes, you do." I caught her arm and lowered my voice. "I don't care what your job is. You *have* to leave that clock alone."

Pain twisted across her face. I dropped her arm at once, wondering if I'd somehow squeezed too hard, but that only made it worse.

"Of course I know that," she hissed. "But damn it, I…"

Her eyes had gone wet. Rika Nonesuch didn't cry, ever. All my anger collapsed like a card house.

"What the Void is going on? Something's clearly wrong. Rika, *tell me*." My hand lifted on its own, hanging a fraction of an inch from gently touching her shoulder. I snatched it back.

"Yes, something is wrong. Because of *you*. This is all *your* fault." Fury infused every shaking syllable of her whisper.

I stared at her. "What are you talking about?"

"I'm on *probation*, you idiot." She dug a single long nail into the top of my sternum, just under the hollow of my throat. "Adelyn Cail told me that because I bungled the Echo Key job so badly, this mission with the clock is my last chance to redeem myself. If I don't do it, my career as a Cat is over."

"You didn't bungle the Echo Key heist," I objected, stunned. "I spent *weeks* setting up that trap, with all the resources of three Elders at my disposal, and you evaded every piece of it. You were smart enough to leave when you saw how it was, and you would have gotten away clean if I hadn't blink stepped after you to cut off your escape."

"I'm *well aware* of that," she said through clenched teeth. "Apparently my superiors don't care. I won't get another chance."

"That doesn't make sense. Your guildmistress is a fool if she'd punish her best Cat over something like that. Is there some way you can—"

"No. Never mind. It's none of your business anyway." She shook her head, not meeting my eyes. "Fine; you're right. I shouldn't mess with the clock. It's over."

"That doesn't—"

"Shut up, Kembral. Let's talk about how we get out of this alive and get back to Prime, and forget about my career. All right?" She flashed a vengeful ghost of her charming smile. "You can rest happy knowing you destroyed it, and I won't be a menace to the peace of the city any longer."

"That's not what I wanted," I said roughly. "That was never what I wanted, no matter how mad I was."

"I know." Her voice was wound tight almost to breaking. "I know that, or I wouldn't have come tonight. And then I wouldn't have run into Cail, and I probably still wouldn't know I was on probation at all. Which makes it even more your fault—and yes, I know that's irrational, but indulge me. I've had a trying day."

"Why...why wouldn't you have come tonight?" It didn't make any sense. Unless she'd been hoping to see me, which was a thought that started a dangerous and complex fluttering in my stomach.

"Because I have better places to be on the year-turning." Rika drew in a long, shuddery breath. "I only came here because I got a tip that you would be here—and that you'd be in danger."

"Wait, *what*?"

"Don't ask any more," she snapped. "I can't tell you. I shouldn't have even told you that much. But you keep going all sullen when I say I'm here because of you, and I got tired of waiting for you to figure it out."

"How in the Void was I supposed to guess that?" I threw up my hands in frustration. "And more importantly, how can you tell me *that* and then say not to ask any questions? I swear you'd keep the color of your eyes a secret if they weren't right there on your face!"

She flinched as if I'd hit her. The look she gave me, Moon's wounds—her eyes went huge and shimmering. She blinked furiously, and that wet glimmer overflowed.

I'd made her cry.

"Wait, don't cry. *Fuck*. What did I say?" Panic surged through me, the desperate desire to fix whatever I'd broken. "I don't understand."

"No." She laughed, a sound that made me wince for how much it clearly hurt her. "No, I suppose you don't."

"Hey..." I became monstrously aware that I had hands, and no idea what in the Void to do with them. "Look, I won't ask questions. I'm sorry."

"You're absolutely maddening, did you know that?" She ground the tears from her eyes with brutal efficiency. "Never mind. You have no idea, and that's good. We can pretend this didn't happen. Bloody Moon, I can never keep it together around you. Where were we?"

We were at the part where she told me she was on probation. But I couldn't say that. I could barely *think* it. It didn't make sense. Nothing she'd said made any sense, but that least of all.

She was one of the best Cats in Acantis, and certainly one of the finest burglars and spies in the city. Her illusion magic was extremely rare outside the Ravens, who hoarded most knowledge of Echo working. She was far too valuable for them to want to lose over something so silly as failing to pull off an impossibly difficult heist. They shouldn't have sent her on that job in the first place; they should have canceled it once they heard about the target hiring a Hound, since that meant they knew someone was going to try to steal it.

Something else must be going on here. Internal Cat politics, maybe. A setup; an effort to discredit Rika by her rivals or enemies.

I didn't owe it to her to figure it out. I had too much to do just trying to save our lives; I couldn't afford to take up precious time trying to unravel some mess of guild backstabbing. The memory of tears filling those grey eyes should make absolutely no difference.

"Rika," I began unsteadily, "I—"

I broke off. Adelyn Cail was heading toward us, face remote and severe, weaving sleekly between the masses of circulating guests. In this Echo, she wore a lavender velvet gown with a cascade of orchids across the bodice; another orchid pinned back one side of her silver-streaked dark hair.

Rika spotted her and let out a soft little sound between a sigh and a moan. "Here she comes again. Every time we reset, I have to sit through another lecture about how I'm on probation and this mission is my last chance."

"Ugh. That sounds horrid. I'm…" I stopped myself. I wouldn't apologize. If she wanted me to let her go when I caught her, well, she shouldn't drug me and leave me in a garbage pile. "It doesn't make sense. Someone must have it in for you."

"Entirely possible." She shrugged, setting her smoke-and-silver gown to shimmering. "When you're the best, you do accumulate rivals and enemies. Not that you'd know about that."

I snorted. "I'll have rivals when we get another active-duty Hound in the city who can blink step. I could use a nice rival, honestly. Someone else to take the hard and dangerous jobs. Sounds nice."

Cail swept up to Rika before she could retort. Disdain glittered in her dark eyes. "Excuse me, Signa Thorne. I need a word with Signa Nonesuch."

Rika winced.

Screw this. We didn't have time to lose twenty minutes to her getting scolded every cycle. Besides, this whole situation was suspicious.

"I'm sorry, Signa Cail, but we've got an emergency that has to take priority."

"A Hound cannot dictate priorities for a Cat," Cail said coldly.

"No, but common sense can." Void take it, I might as well give it a try. "You may have noticed that we've slipped into an Echo."

Cail glanced around with no more interest than if this were city hall. "Of course. That changes nothing. This matter takes precedence."

My attention sharpened to a razor's edge. "Wait. So you understand that we're in an Echo?"

"Yes, and that's a matter of concern that I trust you're dealing with, as the Hound on the scene."

She knew. Which meant that either she'd touched the clock as well, or something else strange was going on. I checked her fingers but didn't see any telltale cuts.

"Not the only Hound," I pointed out, trying another angle. "My colleague Pearson spoke to you about the wine, remember?"

She waved it off. "Yes, of course. The point, Hound, is that this is none of your business. Rika?"

I tried to give Rika a meaningful look. She was frowning, eyeing Cail uncertainly.

"Signa Cail, with all respect," she said carefully, "if you understand our current situation, I'd much appreciate any knowledge you can share about it. Signa Thorne and I are working together to try to stop any more deaths from occurring. It's a matter of *utmost* importance." She made a gesture with her left hand, a questioning sort of twist with certain fingers extended.

She might as well have yelled *This is a code word and here is my secret hand signal*. But given how intently Rika was watching Cail's face, subtlety wasn't what she was trying for this time.

Cail shook her head. "Later, perhaps. First we need to talk, Rika."

Rika took a half step back. I read volumes into the small motion. I let my hand rest on my belt, near my sword.

"If you remember the previous Echoes, Signa Cail, why do we need to have this conversation every time?" Rika asked, her voice tight.

Cail's lip curled. "Because you aren't making any progress, girl. You've had several chances to do what I asked, and you keep stalling."

Rika drew herself up. "No. If that clock is what's bringing people back from the dead, sabotaging it could doom everyone here. I can't risk it."

Cail seemed almost to swell, like a shadow growing at sunset. "Remember, this is your last chance! If you refuse this mission, you're done, child. Your career in the Cats is over."

"No, it's not," I said, certain of it now. "Because she's not on probation. She never was. And you're not Adelyn Cail."

I let my hand rest on my sword hilt in a clear, obvious threat. Cail didn't so much as blink.

In fact, come to think of it, she hadn't been blinking at all, the entire time we'd been talking to her.

Cail looked back and forth between us and sighed. "I'd hoped not to have to do this."

She rippled with a heat-shimmer blur and *changed*.

Long wicked claws sprouted from her fingers. Her teeth sharpened to fangs, and her eyes grew wide and unearthly green. A shiver of sheer *No* swarmed up my spine, and I took an involuntary step back; it was one thing to suspect the person you were talking to was an Echo, and another when they turned into a monster right in front of you.

She lashed out at Rika, sudden and vicious.

If she'd hoped to take advantage of the shock of her transformation, she hadn't reckoned with Rika Nonesuch; a swirl of illusory petals blinded her at once. Rika dodged to the side, drawing her own knife, spitting out curses.

"It pains me to shed the cloak of seeming my lady gave me, but you've forced my hand, rebellious child," Cail hissed at her. "I'll spill your blood myself and mark this Echo for my liege."

I generally liked to solve problems without violence. More often than not, even once people had weapons drawn you could figure out some other way to get everyone what they needed. But that line was a lot mushier with Echoes, since they didn't die like humans did; if you could kill them with plain steel at all, they'd just reform in a day or two anyway, so long as whatever they were an Echo of was alive or remembered. And once they were trying to eviscerate people, it was definitely time to take steps.

So I stabbed her.

She was fast; my blade slid along her ribs rather than between them as she spun to face me. But I was fast, too, and the claws that came whipping at my face as she whirled caught only air.

I had the range advantage, so I backed up to keep it, slashing at her torso for good measure. The thing that wasn't Cail didn't come ravening after me like I expected, though. She reeled back instead, trailing smoke from the cut in her side.

She clutched at the wound as more wisps of violet mist rose from it, glancing around with her inhuman eyes narrowed. The crowd surged and shouted around us, startled by the sudden eruption of combat.

Her gaze locked on Rika. "So be it, ungrateful whelp. I'll give my lady your regards."

Rika's breath hitched, and she drew back as if the Echo had burst into flame.

I took advantage of Cail's distraction, lunging in again—and almost speared that same damned drunk kid in the tailcoat as he stumbled between us, shoved by some friend or enemy in the chaos.

Shit. I pulled my blade up in time; the tailcoat uttered a yelp and fled, but Cail was already gone.

"Do you see her?" I called to Rika.

Only a vanishing flutter of smoke and silver answered me. She was already after Not-Cail at a run. The crowd parted for her, drawing back with gasps from her knife. I followed, sword low to avoid accidentally impaling anyone.

"Signa Kembral!" Dona Marjorie demanded as I ran past. "What's going on?"

"An Echo attacking your guests!" What the Void, why not—I raised my voice to the full-out bay of a Hound in pursuit. "Stop that Echo!"

Gratifyingly, other voices took up the cry. I plunged onward after the shadowy flicker of Rika's gown, straight into an open space—the kind that formed when people made room for an unfolding spectacle.

Rika had stopped. Cail had stopped. A woman with a flower-bedecked duelist's cloak slung off one shoulder and glorious slashed sleeves was facing her down, sword drawn, teeth flashing.

"I don't know who you are, but if you're bringing violence to the party, you simply *must* allow me to return the gift."

Jaycel Morningray, playing this scene to the *hilt*. I should have seen this coming.

Cail launched at her with speed and fury, claws slashing, and for a moment I was worried that Jaycel might be too tipsy to deal with such a fast opponent. But no one had yet invented a liquor that could keep Jaycel from the flawless execution of a bad idea. Her blade moved in quick little slashes, her wrist supple as ever. Cail had to leap back and circle her, snarling, to look for an opening.

I itched to come up behind the Echo and stab her. Jaycel would be really mad, but I should probably do it anyway.

Rika, untrammeled by any fleeting sympathy for Jaycel's sense of drama, didn't hesitate. She flicked her fingers at Cail like she was done with her, and half a dozen smoky silver serpents suddenly reared up in her face, hissing. Cail recoiled, giving Jaycel a clean opening to strike.

She didn't take it. I could have told Rika she wouldn't. Jaycel always did insist that no matter how she debased her personal life, her public duels had to be honorable. She struck a damned *pose* instead.

"I'm afraid you picked the wrong party to crash," she declared. It was her familiar rhythm, feeding her opponent an easy line so they could respond with something they thought was clever, and then she could escalate her wit and destroy them.

Cail, however, glanced from Jaycel to Rika to me—taking in the hostile crowd along the way—and seemed to conclude that Jaycel's quip was pure truth. She bolted for the door without bothering to deliver the retort Jaycel was waiting for, disappointing her crowd like a total churl.

Rika chased after with the driving fury of someone who'd been wrestling with a massive burden of shame all night for no reason. I followed them across the ballroom and into a foyer covered in tiny flower mosaics, several steps behind.

Cail never slowed down; she reached the mansion doors, slammed them wide open, and flew through them, Rika on her tail. In a heartbeat, they were both out in the street.

Or whatever passed for a street, five Echoes down.

"Fuck," I breathed, and sprinted after.

FOUR IS THE LIMIT

Almarah had taught me some good and simple rules about going into Echoes on retrieval missions.

One Echo down, if you kept your wits sharp, you'd be fine. Two and three, all right, there was some real danger, and you'd better be careful.

Four... four was the limit. That was where even the most daring and legendary smugglers stopped. No one with any sense should go past four without a damned good reason.

More than four Echoes down, you could die without ever knowing why. The ground might open up beneath you, the rain might burn holes straight through you with each drop, a passing sparrow might open its beak wider than a mother's patience and swallow you whole. Being smart, being careful, being able to blink step weren't enough to save you when the world went so arbitrary and dangerous. Almarah herself had never gone more than five Echoes down, even if it meant giving up some poor soul for lost. When she'd heard I'd gone down six after that dog, she cursed me up one side and down the other until my ears shriveled.

Five fucking Echoes down, and Rika just ran out there after Cail with zero preparation. And here I was, the biggest jackass in the world, going after her.

I stepped out the door to face a murky dark street dotted with intermittent ruddy lights—and immediately flattened myself against the comforting stone of the mansion wall, heart racing.

Beyond the mansion's front steps, a sheer edge plunged into darkness. A swirling wind rose from the depths, stinging my cheeks and setting the lanterns that flanked the mansion doors to guttering. The doors and rows of windows opposite peeked not from a building, but from the face of a cliff.

Dona Marjorie's mansion was now embedded in one wall of a chasm, its face nearly flush with an endless, stomach-churning drop.

Windows peppered the chasm faces on both sides, some dark and empty, others glowing with lamplight, framed in age-crumbled brick. Narrow, rickety ladders descended and climbed the sheer walls to weathered doors, all of them locked and barred and chained. Brass lamps hung over the windows and doors, creaking and swinging gently in a cold breeze exhaled from the deeps.

It all went down and down and down, windows and lamps and ladders fading into a bottomless darkness. The chasm walls rose up above as well, bracketing a wide strip of star-studded sky and a leering yellow Moon. A large black shape flapped across its face on leathery wings.

My heart thudded so hard I could feel it reverberating into the stone wall through my back. It was too easy to imagine Rika running straight off the edge into that terrible, bottomless darkness.

"Rika?" I called, knowing too well it was a fool's play to draw attention to myself.

Faint, mocking echoes floated up from the darkest reaches of the pit below, in a voice not my own. *Rika? Rika? Rika?*

I deserved that, I guessed.

I closed my eyes, breathing hard. The wind pulled at me, tugging me toward the brink. It occurred to me that I could just turn around and walk back into the mansion. There was nothing stopping me. I could make sure I lived to save the others, and to raise my daughter. I could quit this stupid job with all its terrifying risks, never set foot in an Echo again, and focus on Emmi.

Something strange bubbled up in my chest—a wild laughter, trying to make it loose.

Nah. Screw that. I owed Emmi nothing less than my true self. And this—standing on the very brink of oblivion, wind whipping yet more strands of my hair loose from its poor mangled arrangement, five Echoes down with a clear and perilous mission stretching before me—this made me feel *alive.* This was the thing I'd trained for, the thing I was good at. I'd missed it.

There was definitely something wrong with me. But whatever that was had brought dozens of people and the occasional dog back from the Echoes safe and sound, so maybe it was a good thing.

Right. Time to add Rika to that count of successful retrievals. First, look for signs of which way they'd gone.

Just beyond the safe island of the front steps, a slim ladder climbed the face of the mansion, reaching up past three floors of windows and continuing toward the clifftop above. There was no other obvious escape route, so unless the Cail-Echo had hurled herself into the abyss, they must have gone up.

I took a careful step toward the ladder, feeling the stone with my toe. Seemed solid enough. A few more steps, and I was as close to the edge as I could make myself go. The ladder hung tantalizingly near, maybe a foot beyond where the stone ended and the empty air began. If there were floor beneath it instead of endless nothingness, it'd be the easiest thing in the world to grab it and start climbing.

I drew in a steadying breath and reached.

The ladder came suddenly alive, squirming like it was made of snakes.

My undignified yelp rang off the chasm walls as I flung myself back against the safety of stone. Echoes ricocheted up from below, sounding like laughter. Great, now anything that had somehow missed me calling for Rika knew I was here.

Fine. Fine. I shook out my jittery limbs, glaring. There was no time to try to finesse this; I'd have to force it. My cut from the clock was still slowly oozing blood, a ruby bead clinging to my fingertip. It would do.

I jabbed at the writhing ladder, smearing it with that tiny drop of blood.

"You're a *ladder*," I told it firmly. "Good for climbing. You're sturdy and stable and easy to grip."

It went still immediately. That was the power of Prime blood; it could stabilize Echoes, forcing them to stop changing or to adhere to Prime reality. You could wield it like a cudgel in a pinch. But that meant that every denizen of the Echoes wanted it for its power to shape their world, and leaving a trail of blood behind you in a Deep Echo was not a great idea.

This time when I grabbed the ladder, the wood felt smooth and strong, fitting my hand perfectly. I swung out onto it and started climbing; it didn't so much as wobble. Given that my cut was continuing to leave tiny bits of blood on it, this was going to be the best damned ladder in the world by the time I reached the top.

Climbing felt good at first. It had been so long since my body did something physical like this, loose and limber, rather than curling and contorting protectively around the baby. Well, aside from the times tonight when I'd been fighting for my life, but then I'd been too focused on survival to enjoy the pure sensation of moving freely. The only problem was that I'd last nursed on the left side, and oof, lifting my arms up over my head *definitely* reminded me that it had been a while for the right one.

I tried to focus on those physical sensations—the uncomfortable fullness, the strangely pleasing ache of hard use in my arms and shoulders—because it sure beat thinking about all the nothingness beneath me. The wind teased the back of my neck, stirred the tail of my coat, ran fingers through my hair. I passed one flickering lantern and another, shifting from light to shadow to light again. The ladder kept going up.

Far above, the leathery-winged creature let out a mournful wail like a peacock's. Some deep animal part of my brain apparently decided that this sounded like Emmi's cry. A fierce yearning for her went through me like a knife, and my milk let down all at once.

"Great," I muttered in despair, as warm wetness soaked into the absorbent padding I'd stuffed into my bodice for exactly this reason. "Just what I needed. Great."

My arms were getting tired. I'd drawn even with a wide stone ledge beneath a shuttered window; it looked like a good place to rest. I poked it with my toe a few times, then stepped off the ladder onto it, shaking my arms to get the blood back into them. The top looked a lot closer; at least I wasn't stuck on some infinite climb, which was definitely a concern in some Echoes.

The shutters on the window beside me cracked open. A round, glowing yellow eye with a diamond-shaped pupil regarded me through the gap.

I made a stifled noise and grabbed the ladder.

"Hey," a voice croaked from within. "What are you doing on my ledge?"

"Sorry." I grimaced. "Sorry, I'll just get back on the, uh..."

I trailed off as several thin red tentacles seethed out of the gap, groping toward me.

"Wait. You're from Prime. You're bleeding—I can smell it."

Oh, I *really* didn't want to have to fight on this ledge. I stepped half onto the ladder, ready to start climbing again. "You can't have it. Sorry."

"Wait! I'll buy it." The eye pressed up to the gap, more tentacles boiling greedily out to grasp the shutters and haul the creature within closer. "What do you want? Information? You're chasing those others who went by earlier, aren't you?"

I paused. "Yes," I admitted reluctantly. "Do you know where they went?"

"Maybe I do. Maybe I'll tell you, for one drop of blood."

"Maybe you don't, and you're lying."

The Echo's voice deepened to a guttural growl. "Maybe I'll take it by force."

"I don't recommend that," I said sharply. "Have you ever seen someone from Prime here before?"

"No." The hunger in its voice was palpable.

"Ask yourself what kind of person travels five Echoes down from Prime. Ask yourself if you really want to fight that person."

The tentacles withdrew a little, knotting together. "One drop. One drop, and you can use my ledge as long as you like, and I'll tell you what I saw."

I hesitated. "You'd better not just tell me they went up. I can figure *that* out on my own."

"No. I promise. I swear it. Three times I swear it."

I was already leaving a blood trail. I sighed and squeezed my finger until one bright red drop welled up at the tip. "Fine, but you'd better not—whoops."

I'd squeezed too hard. The drop of blood fell from my finger and over the edge, vanishing down into the void.

A strangled gasp sounded through the window. "What have you *done*?!"

The tentacles all withdrew, fast as slurped-up noodles. The eye recoiled from the gap in horror.

"Wait! Do you still want the deal?"

"No! You fool, you've probably awakened them!"

The shutters banged shut. There came a rattling of chains and a slamming of bolts.

Oh, I *really* didn't like the sound of that. Cursing, I started climbing again, as fast as I could.

The darkness pressed in around me, palpable, hostile. The ruddy golden light from the flickering lanterns on their swinging chains seemed downright homelike by comparison, but I knew none of those doors or windows would be open to me now. More chains rattled behind other doors as I climbed, and the lights in some windows blew suddenly out.

If I could reach the top before whatever was in the pit finished waking up, I'd be all right. At least, I was going to keep telling myself that.

"Rika!" I called desperately. "Are you up there?"

Rika? Rika? The echoes laughed from the pit. *Who's Rika?*

The cold wind walked up my spine. I kept climbing, weighing the risks of a reply. Ignoring an Echo was usually a bad idea—except in the cases where it was the only thing that would save you. If I made the wrong choice, falling off the ladder could be the least of my worries.

"Someone I'm looking for," I muttered.

Someone I'm looking for. Who's Rika? Rika? More laughter; the flames in the hanging lanterns danced.

Is she your friend?

My arms were trembling from the strain of climbing, but I kept going, pulse racing. I had no desire to answer that question, but whatever was down there, I suspected things would go very poorly for me if it decided I was boring and our game was over.

"It's . . . complicated," I said carefully.

Complicated. Complicated.

"Have you seen her?" I tried. Anything that kept the things down there talking instead of eating me—and maybe they'd answer. "I'm worried she might be in trouble."

Trouble. Trouble. She's trouble. More laughing, like I was absolutely the most hilarious thing the voices had heard in weeks. Which might be true, because I didn't see a lot of very funny stuff happening in the immediate vicinity.

The wind had gotten colder. My ladder ended suddenly at an iron door, set into the wall and wrapped in thick chains. Another ladder started a few feet to the side. I clung to mine as tightly as I could and reached out toward it.

The new ladder started crumbling around the edges as my hand got near, shedding sawdust into the abyss. A rain of pale specks swirled down into the darkness a dizzyingly long way and vanished, my hope of making it to the top disintegrating with it.

It was suddenly too much, one more bad thing in a night with far too many. The emotional distance I'd been carefully maintaining evaporated, and for a moment a tightness pressed at my throat as I fought off tears.

I lunged for the lowest remaining rung, barely grabbing it with my cut hand before it could fall apart completely. "You're a ladder! You're a ladder, you're strong and stable and really good for climbing! Super well constructed and sturdy!"

It went from splintery and weak under my grip to rock solid in an instant. I leaned precariously over the drop, one hand on each ladder, one foot on a rung and the other hanging over depths bottomless as the Void itself. My breath was coming too high and fast, and I had no clever answer for whatever waited hungrily in the bottomless darkness below.

"All right," I whispered to myself. "All right, let's go."

Go. Go. Wait—DON'T GO!

The voices strengthened, weaving around one another, a spine-chilling hissing rising beneath them. Deep, deep in the chasm, something massive stirred, scales grinding against scales with the weight of millstones. More window lights immediately went dark; shutters slammed in fear.

"Blood on the Moon," I breathed, too softly for echoes.

I swung over to the new ladder and clung there, wrapping myself tightly onto it, heart pounding. Silently praying that nothing was going to rise from the deeps and pluck me off the wall like a berry from the bush.

Seen her, the voices hissed. *We've seen her. Tell us. Is she your friend? It's complicated. Complicated.*

I sure as the Void did not want to hang here on a ladder in the dark over a bottomless pit talking about my feelings to some terrifyingly enormous monster. I could keep climbing, save my self-reflection for the Mirror Moon festival, and find Rika on my own. But being rude to something that sounded big enough to eat Marjorie's mansion in about six bites was not a great idea, either.

Was Rika my friend? Damned if I knew. Was that what you called it when you couldn't stop thinking about someone, like they were a pebble in your boot? When their presence felt as familiar as an old shirt, complete with all the places where the seams sometimes galled you? Did friends drug you and leave you under a pile of trash in a tenement cellar, and then refuse to apologize for it?

Maybe not that last one. But when enemies did that sort of thing, it didn't hurt so much.

I squeezed my eyes shut, trying not to think about the drop and what waited in it, and trying not to think too hard about Rika, either.

"She *was* my friend. And then I thought maybe we might be getting romantically involved, and then she betrayed me and we were definitely *not* friends for a while, and now..."

Now? Now?

Fucking abyssal horrors, eager for gossip.

"If I'd given up on her, I wouldn't be out here doing something this stupid to try to rescue her."

A terrible noise like the squeal of an ancient rusty gate scraped up from the darkness below.

Wouldn't be out here. You like her.

"Fine. Yes. We're friends. I like her."

Like her, the echoes whispered and murmured, overlapping and bouncing around between the windowed walls until half of those *likes* sounded like *love.*

"Hey!" I protested. "I never said—"

Never said, the echoes agreed, sounding far too amused. *Never said. Love her.*

The voices pulled together, smoothing into one great, deep voice that made the ladder shake beneath my grip. I whispered curses and clung on as tight as I could.

You gave us an offering of blood. In return we will not harm you, and we grant you this: Climb to the top, and then go toward the Moon. She went that way, pursuing the other.

The problem with Echoes was that sometimes when you passed their little tests, they granted you what you sought, and other times, there never was a test at all and they were just messing with you. Not to mention all the times they flat-out wanted to eat you. I didn't survive so many trips into the Echoes by being rude to monsters, however, so I just said thank you and started climbing again.

My shoulders ached, but I had more than enough motivation to ignore it and go as fast as I could manage. Relief gave me a nice extra burst of energy—that they weren't going to eat me, that I was almost to the top, but more than anything that Rika was alive. Thank the Moon, she hadn't fallen.

It seemed like only seconds later that I hauled myself up over the edge, gasping, onto blessedly solid and horizontal ground. I wanted to just lie there, hugging it and recovering, but five Echoes down you did not have the luxury of rest. So I rose to a wary crouch, looking around to get my bearings.

I was on a sort of causeway, broad and smooth, stretching off into the distance. Chasms plunged down on either side of the road, the warm light of lanterns seeping up from below. More causeways ran parallel to mine or intersected in the distance; a chill wind blew across them. Light marked their edges, some brighter and some dimmer, forming a strange maze.

A maze I knew well. It was still Acantis, but inverted. That vibrant glow rising up from a crack in the distance must be the theater; the grand open space ringed with great metal spears probably marked the city hall. Scents of cooking food and distant voices and music wafted up from the abyss on the far side of my causeway, where perhaps no monsters dwelled and people dared make a little more noise. Everything was just...upside down.

Shapes with burning eyes prowled the other paths at the top of the maze, far enough away to be a mystery and close enough to be a worry. The moonlight shone through their empty bones. It was hard to tell in the darkness, but I'd bet cold money they had a nonstandard number of heads, tails, and legs.

I might have been safer in the pit.

I started walking toward the Moon. It was hard to force myself to take it slowly and carefully; Rika had been out here alone for far too long, and I knew too many awful things that could have happened to her. My imagination kept trying to pull terrible details out of the shadows on the road ahead: a splash of blood, a mangled corpse.

Voices echoed strangely down the dark road before me, ricocheting along the chasms full of shuttered windows, carried to my ears by the teasing wind.

One was Rika's, and the other, Cail's.

WATCH YOUR STEP

The spear of relief that went through me at the sound of Rika's voice was so intense it nearly dropped me to my knees. I missed the first half of what she was saying.

"...this clear to her: I'm not her tool or her toy. And I'm never coming back."

Cail uttered a throaty laugh in response. "Child, you never left. You are hers. You'll *always* be hers. She has been watching you all your life. You cannot escape her."

I took a second to steady myself, stuffing down the unexpected surge of emotion, and crept closer. I stayed low in hopes that they wouldn't see me any more than I could make them out in the darkness ahead. Eavesdropping on such a private exchange didn't feel great, but giving up the advantage of surprise against Cail would be foolish.

"I've escaped her just fine for almost twenty years, until now," Rika snapped. "Curse you for stumbling across me tonight and ruining everything."

"My lady sent me, and she does not *stumble*. The others might fling themselves at the prize with no preparation, but she has laid her plans well for this night. You were a part of them long before you set foot in that place."

"So she wants to name the year." Strain roughened Rika's voice. "She's already so powerful—why does she care? What does she hope to gain from this?"

"Oh, wayward child." Cail's voice grew soft, but I was getting close enough to hear her anyway. "It's for you. It's all for you."

An awful chill unfurled within me.

I could just barely make them out in the darkness on the causeway ahead now. The light shining up from below had gone dim, as if this neighborhood were empty or asleep, and the shadows were deep and plentiful. No bone creatures prowled this area—which, knowing Echoes, was probably actually a bad sign, but for the moment it worked to my advantage. I could get a little closer and then—

Sudden screams shattered the quiet.

I drew my sword and sprinted ahead, heart leaping up my throat.

Something pale and shimmering thrashed in the road ahead. It swore with ear-sizzling virulence. Yeah, that was her. I ran faster.

"Rika!"

"Kembral! Watch out!"

You didn't ignore a warning like that five Echoes down, no matter who was in trouble. I slowed my headlong charge.

Just in time, too. Rika and Cail both struggled in the road ahead, grappling with something dark and amorphous—and some kind of oily puddle lay in the road before me. I flung myself to the side, straining to make sure no part of my boot touched its dark stain.

It reared up, letting out an angry burbling roar as it formed whip-like liquid limbs and reached for me.

I veered wide to dodge them, cursing; they stretched after me, elongating like dark shining rivulets of animate ink. An endless drop gaped beside me, too close, a cold breeze reaching up from it to tug at my coat. My gap to squeeze through and get to Rika was rapidly vanishing.

I slashed at the tendrils of wet shadow; some recoiled, and others lost their tips. It bought me just enough room to lunge past and strike at the one attacking Rika.

Black coils wrapped around her legs and one arm; I didn't dare try to cut them off with her struggling so violently against it, so I stabbed the mass of shadow where all its appendages met and pooled in the road. It let out the same awful noise the other one had, furious as a seething kettle, and shied away.

Rika tore free of the writhing ragged ends of shadow, giving the thing a good cut with her daggers on the way out, and fell in by my side.

"*There* you are," she gasped. "You're too slow."

She was moving fine, with no blood or curse marks on her, and there was plenty of vigor in her voice. She was all right. *Thank the Moon.* My knees tried to go to water with relief; I had to steady myself.

"At least I didn't run off into a Deep Echo like a fool. You're going to turn my hair grey."

"I'll admit it wasn't my best idea."

The shadows regathered themselves and began writhing in our direction. I angled my blade to offer a little cover to Rika, too, and braced my back foot to be ready to lunge into action.

A terrible animal cry shredded the air. It came from Cail.

It was too dark to make out exactly what the shadow-thing did to her. There was a sudden violent motion—a clench of rippling darkness—and a bad crunching sound. One moment she was there, solid and real, snarling and fighting; the next, she exploded into a puff of smoke that drifted up toward the swollen orange Moon.

My stomach dropped. She was my enemy, but it didn't feel like a victory.

"Shit," Rika whispered.

Undulating like wind-rippled sails, all three shadows moved toward us. Tendrils of darkness reached from them, ends streaming into the velvet night like whips of fire. They formed a curving line that closed in on us, blocking the road back toward Dona Marjorie's house and safety. We fell back before them, side by side.

Three was bad. Three was especially bad given that one of them had popped a reasonably strong and clever Echo like an overripe fruit. I wasn't at all sure how to kill them, since a thrust to the center hadn't done the job.

I steadied my breathing and eased my mind toward the exact point of equilibrium that would let me slide a knife between one layer of reality and the next and wiggle through.

"Get ready to run," I murmured.

Rika stared at the three shadows, the ruddy moonlight gilding the curves of her face.

"I'm going to try something," she breathed.

By the haunted look in her eyes, I didn't like the sound of that. "What?"

In answer, she burst into brilliant silvery light.

Vast shining wings sprouted from her shoulders, an exultant explosion of ethereal feathers, unfurling across the entire causeway. She *glowed* all over, but especially her eyes, which blazed a searing red—I had to wince away from them, they were so bright. A wind I couldn't feel stirred her dress and lifted her hair, which suddenly grew from its jaw-length cut, floating out around her in a streaming nimbus of Void-black glory. She rose a few inches off the ground.

What the *fuck*—oh. Right. Illusion.

The shadows cowered back from her, making high-pitched keening noises, a fluttering ripple of apparent terror shuddering through them. One thing every crawling nightmare in the Deep Echoes knew: There's always a bigger monster.

"Fools!" Rika's voice thundered through the darkness like the peal of the great bells in the city clock tower. "You dare assault me? You *dare?*"

Damn, she was good. I'd never heard of a Raven illusionist doing something like this—I had to wonder if she was at least a little bit Echo-born, which might explain some things. Beauty and power rolled off her in terrible glory.

Rika spread her arms. "You will suffer for this blasphemy! Prepare to feel my wrath!"

The Echo creatures broke. One after another, they fled off down the causeway in long, sudden streaks, quick as if they were true shadows cast away by her light.

Rika dropped her arms, and her glow faded. Strain tautened

her face. I knew I shouldn't stare at her, but I couldn't pull my eyes away.

"We'd better hurry back to the mansion," she said, sounding inexplicably subdued. "In case anything smarter, braver, or more powerful noticed that."

"I'm sure they did. It wasn't exactly subtle."

She turned to face the road, avoiding my eyes. "Then let's go."

"Rika..."

She flinched, as if the sound of her own name was a weapon.

I swallowed. "I'm really glad you're all right."

She looked up then, her face full of some desperate, exhausted emotion. "Me too."

All the worry and terror and relief I'd tried to shove in a box came rushing out all at once. Before I could think better of it, I caught her in a quick, fierce hug.

"Please don't run off like that again," I murmured. "I thought you... It was a long way down."

She was stiff with tension, her shoulders like rocks; I let her go at once. Her eyes had gone deep and dark, full of murky unknown things I couldn't understand.

"Sorry." I grimaced. "I shouldn't have... Sorry."

"No, it's all right." She wrapped her arms around herself as if she were cold, but with far more gentleness than the other times I'd seen her make the gesture. "I was just surprised. Nobody ever..." She shook her head, sharply. "We should go."

Far above us, the great flying creature let out its mournful peacock call in the empty night sky. It sounded closer now.

"You're right. Let's move quickly."

We set off at a brisk pace, walking close enough together that our hands almost touched. Rika wasn't the only one shying from shadows this time, which was unfortunate because there were a lot of shadows. I knew I had to focus on getting us back safely, but there was something I really should say.

I cleared my throat. "I, uh, heard some things back there."

For one blazing instant, the look Rika shot me was one of pure panic. Then her expression shuttered surely as the windows in the chasms flanking us.

"Did you, now."

"I have no idea what any of it meant, and it was none of my business," I said gruffly. "Keep your secrets if you like. They're yours."

She let out a shuddery breath. Our feet hit the strange smooth surface of the causeway, walking fast but not running—never running, because that marked you as prey. The wind teased the edges of her night-black hair.

"I told you I had a bad experience with an Empyrean once," she blurted in a rush. "She…stole me when I was a kid. Maybe ten or twelve. Only for a few days, but it was…bad."

There were plenty of stories about people who attracted the attention of an Empyrean. The proud fisherwoman, the boy who wandered in the woods and sang too sweetly, the hapless tinker, the lonely widow. Every story started with the Empyrean lavishing their chosen mortal with gifts, aid, health, love, riches—whatever a human heart might yearn for—and ended with the mortal broken and ruined at best, and more often dead.

"I'm sorry," I said, at a loss for anything more profound.

"I thought she'd forgotten about me, so this is…" She let out a breathless, hopeless laugh. "I'm going to try not to think about it."

"I won't tell anyone," I assured her, because I sure as the Void couldn't fix this, but in that moment I had a burning need to promise her *something*. Something true and solid and reasonable in a night of Echoes and pain and chaos.

The sidelong look she gave me was full to bursting with some deep, heavy emotion I couldn't parse. Like she was showing me the truth in all its terrible glory, but I was too illiterate in her mysteries to read it.

"I know."

She slowed. For one wild, heart-pounding moment, she reached tentatively out toward my face across the unsteady distance that separated us.

I missed a step. The ground vanished beneath my feet, my belly lurching—but no. I hadn't stumbled; the world had.

A jarring clang echoed across the sky, and the Moon itself rippled with the force of it.

"No," Rika protested. "No, it's not fair, we haven't—"

Reality cared nothing for fairness. It shredded away, shivered apart by the metallic toll of the distant clock.

WORDS WIN MORE ANSWERS
THAN STEEL

The clock still echoed in my ears, its brassy chime reverberating through my bones. Its final toll shuddered through me, warning that time was passing, our chances dwindling, the Void rushing up to meet us.

The scent hit first: the unique musty smell of old books, all leather and aging paper, dusty and strangely sweet. The ballroom had transformed to a great airy library walled with books, with more on a balcony level that ran all the way around the room beneath a high, arched ceiling. No windows let in light, but they didn't need to; dozens of glowing golden orbs floated in the air, balls of soft, faintly flickering radiance the color of a candle flame. Their warm light, the gleaming wood, and the books all around us gave this Echo an inviting, homey feel that was downright surreal, given the sheer amount of murder that had happened here tonight.

No one was dead. No one was screaming. Everyone milled and made conversation, and some people sat in corners reading books they'd pulled off the shelves, sometimes aloud to one another. It was... *nice*. It felt like a place I could sit down for one stolen minute and catch my breath.

Rika glanced around, looking as shocked as I felt, standing close to my side as if for protection against this strange, pleasant near-normalcy. I couldn't help remembering the taut muscles of her shoulders within the circle of my arms; the distance between us felt dangerously slim.

"I don't see Cail," she breathed. "Is she gone? Was she ever here in the first place?"

"I don't think the real Signa Cail was ever here. I think that Echo was a reflection of her, not just disguised as her." She'd still looked like Cail after she dropped the illusion—a monstrous Cail, granted, but recognizable—and she knew too much. "Let me guess: She met up with you here at the party, maybe unexpectedly. You had no inkling about supposedly being on probation until tonight, and she gave you the clock mission verbally on the spot."

"Right on all counts. I came here on my own, and then Cail showed up to ruin my night." She rubbed her arms as if they ached. "Why would she do that? Why send her here to tell me something so cruel? Would she really go to all that effort just to mess with me?"

It took me a second to realize she wasn't talking about Cail's Echo anymore. "That Empyrean you mentioned, from your childhood. Cail's lady. She's got to be involved in this year-naming game. She was probably trying to use you to help her win it."

"It's so lovely to know that every time I think this is the absolute most terrible situation I could possibly imagine, it can still keep getting worse and worse." Rika straightened, shedding vulnerability like water. "But you're right. She likes manipulating things from afar without getting her hands dirty. Recruiting an Echo of Cail to set me up to do her bidding is exactly the sort of thing she'd do. Layers of remove to make it harder for other Empyreans to figure out she's playing the game."

"What exactly did Cail's Echo want you to do to the clock?"

"I was supposed to get into its innards and then cast the contents of this into it." From some hidden pocket in her dangling split sleeves she pulled out a small black velvet pouch.

"Have you peeked?"

"No, of course not!"

I stared at her in disbelief. "What? How could you not peek?"

"The parameters of the mission. I was instructed not to open it until it was time to use it." She glared at me. "I thought I was on probation, remember? There was no way I was going to mess it up. Now that I know it's not a real job..."

She undid the knot of the drawstring and teased the neck of the pouch open. Inside I glimpsed something silvery and soft-looking, with faint sparkling lights scattered through it.

"Ugh." Rika tugged the drawstrings closed. Her lips pressed together.

"What *is* that?" I almost reached for the pouch, but Rika was already tucking it away. "Should we have Signa Blair look at it?"

"No. I've seen something like it before." Rika's voice was tight and unhappy.

I waited, but she didn't say any more. "If it's a secret, maybe you can at least give me the vague version."

"It's not a secret. It's just...a bad memory." She looked away, her hair falling to curtain her face. "I don't know exactly what it does, but it's definitely *hers*. She uses...webs. Nets like this. To influence, imprison, or control." Her throat jumped, and in that moment I was ready to go find this Empyrean and punch her in the face.

Rika must be barely holding it together. First whatever scuffle she'd had on arrival, then thinking she was on probation, then getting stuck in this Echo game, then finding out the Empyrean she clearly had nightmares about was back in her life. I had a sudden urge to hold her again, like I had for that brief moment on the causeway—to shield her from the world and let it pass her by unharmed.

There was so much hurt still unresolved between us. But with the many layers of reality pressing down on us with all their combined importance, with the divine lords of starlight bent on our destruction, a little personal betrayal seemed like a much smaller thing.

"Hey," I muttered. "You've really been having a bad day. Do you want to sit down or something?"

She gave me a strange look. "We don't have time to sit down."

"No, I suppose not. Never mind." I lifted a weary hand to my temple and came up against the hopeless wreck of my hair. "Fuck it. Time to simplify."

"What?"

I ruthlessly pulled my hair down from its remaining pins, thinking aloud. "All right. Cail's Echo was working for this Empyrean of yours."

"She's not *mine*. But yes."

"So with Cail out of the picture, has she lost her agent in the game? Is she out?"

"I wouldn't assume so. She's always got plans within plans." Rika's face was solemn. "It's *bad* that she's involved, Kembral. Not just for me, but for all of us. She's not just powerful—she's *smart*, and she usually gets her way."

"It's not great," I agreed. I twirled my hair into a basic twist, snarls and all—not exactly elegant, but this should keep it out of my face. "She clearly knew about the clock from the start, given that she wanted you to mess with it. But Rai didn't—he was surprised when it restored everyone. How did she know it would be here?"

"She's an *Empyrean*. She knows all kinds of things. You saw how Rai could just look at someone and know they were a target, or how he knew your name—they've got the insight of the Moon and stars, looking down and seeing the whole world laid bare. They still have to know what to ask or where to look, but it's hard to keep secrets from them." A brief shudder rippled through Rika, but she suppressed it quickly. "Cail definitely knew more about the clock than she shared with me. I was trying to weasel more out of her."

A thought hit me just as I fixed the last pin in place, and I froze with my hands still up in my hair.

"The Clockmaker said *she*," I whispered.

Rika raised an eyebrow. "You're being cryptic, Thorne. That's my job."

"Someone told the Clockmaker about the convergence and the year-naming. That it would be here, and that it would be dangerous. That's how she knew enough to make the clock. She promised not to say who told her, but she let slip that it was a she."

Rika's eyes widened in comprehension. "Arhsta didn't just know about the clock in advance. She's the reason it's here in the first place."

"Arhsta? Is that the Empyrean's name?"

"No. It's...something she told me to call her." Rika worked her jaw like she wanted to get the taste of the name out of her mouth. "So she told the Clockmaker about the year-naming to manipulate her into making the clock. Why did she want it here? It couldn't be just so I could tamper with it—that's a bit convoluted even for her."

"The Clockmaker mentioned that the clock actually helps the Empyreans, too, by making sure they don't kill off all their possible victims before the game is done. In fact—*that's it.*" An ill-fitting piece that had been bothering me all night finally clicked into place. "The poisoning back in Prime didn't make any sense if the poisoner didn't know about the clock, because if everyone died in Prime there'd be no one left to kill to make the blood seals in all the Echoes. Rai said something about it being a clever move, trying to eliminate the competition all at once—if she wiped out everyone at the party before any other players could make their own blood sacrifice in Prime, she'd be the only player left to continue down to the final Echo. She'd win the game when it had barely begun."

Rika let out a low whistle of grudging appreciation. "That does sound like something she'd do. Strike first and hardest, before her opponents have even found their footing."

"Could the Echo of Cail have done the poisoning?"

Rika studied her nails in an evasive sort of way. "I don't remember the poisoning, of course, but her Echo was acting sufficiently like Cail that I'd say yes, that sounds like something she'd be qualified to accomplish."

"I'd bet cold money it worked, too." I felt the urge to pace, to use up the energy of all the sparks connecting in my brain. "It makes no sense that just a handful of Empyreans would be interested in the year-naming when it's clearly such a big deal. She probably knocked at least a dozen other players out of the game in her opening move. The only ones still in were the ones who shed blood early. Even Rai barely got his sacrifice in after the bell, just before we dropped to the next Echo. *Damn.*"

"I told you she was dangerous," Rika said quietly.

"But we took out Cail—her player. That has to be a huge setback, even if we don't dare count her out of the game. And we've got the invitation ward up." I took a deep, steadying breath. "We've got one definite player left—Rai. We can keep our security tight, and we can keep trying to figure out what backup plans Arhsta may have, but our first priority has to be getting Rai's invitation revoked."

"Right." Rika let out a strained little laugh. "That's what we were doing before Cail pulled her little transformation trick. Stars, it feels like it's been days."

I glanced at the mantel clock; it was barely nine. Still plenty of time. "I hate to tell you, but it technically hasn't even been a minute. How did things go with your snooping? Any idea who might have given the invite?"

"Hmm, well, no solid leads, but definitely some thoughts and suspicions." She hesitated a moment, then took a deep, bolstering breath and plunged on. "Empyreans like to involve themselves with people who they think have great promise, especially if it hasn't yet been fully realized. A boring mortal has nothing to offer them in a bargain."

I glanced around at all the stolid bankers and merchants around us. An elderly woman's booming voice floated over the crowd, going on with great confidence about something to do with currency exchange.

"That does narrow it down a bit."

"Add to that someone who *wants* something badly enough to make a deal, and combine it with the gossip of the night, and I have a short list of top possibilities. But before I tell you mine, I want to hear yours." She raised a hand. "And don't give me all your diligent Hound 'not enough evidence' nonsense. We don't have time for that. I want your gut instinct."

I snorted. "My gut instinct is Harking, but I don't trust my gut in this case because I already don't like him."

"My gut agrees with your gut."

"It could be anyone with a stake in city politics—this stinks of a council power play to me—but Harking seems most likely."

Rika tipped her head, pensive. "I wish we could solve this by killing him. That would be much simpler. But if it *is* him, we need him alive to revoke his invitation."

"I'm a little concerned by how quickly you jumped to murder, but...yes. It does make it harder." I rubbed my forehead. "I'm not sure I could convince him to uninvite Rai, or to confess for that matter. I think he might want me dead."

"Really. Whatever gave you that impression?"

I couldn't honestly tell if she was being sarcastic. "Call it a hunch. Anyway, nothing I say is going to sway him. You, on the other hand, are a Cat. Skilled in the subtle arts of manipulation. A master con artist. A virtuoso in the symphony of lies. A—"

"I get it, Thorne. Fine. I'll see if I can talk him into it. And you?"

"He's hardly the only suspect. I'm going to talk to the close second on my list," I said. "Dona Tarchasia Vandelle."

—⁓—

It was easy to find Vandelle; she was in full form yelling at Harking.

"Because you're a writhing sack of vermin, that's why!"

"So impassioned," came Harking's usual retort. "It's too bad that the council doesn't vote by volume."

"Half of them do—by volume of the bags of money you hand them! You've washed your hands in blood for years and dried them on letters of credit, but that's over now. A reckoning is coming, and you're not going to like it!"

Vandelle's closing line rang a little differently after my chat with Blair about coups and wars. The uneasy feeling settled deeper into me, all the way to my bones.

I recalled the vector at which Vandelle usually stomped away from her fight with Harking and moved to intercept her. She spotted me and veered in my direction, evading a few supporters who tried to converge on her.

"Signa Thorne! Perfect. Just the Hound I was looking for. Marjorie tells me you've got dirt on that wretch Harking."

I opened my mouth to give some evasive answer, ready to steer us to the question of Echoes instead. But at the last second, I changed my mind.

"You know what? Yes. Yes, I do."

Sure, I couldn't prove any of it yet, and Hounds had to be politically neutral—but the fate of the world was at stake, and this—this was *leverage*. I could spend all night trying to get a reliable, honest answer out of a City Elder, even a down-to-earth one like Vandelle. When you had something to trade, however, suddenly everyone in Acantis remembered how to deliver the goods.

Besides, fuck Harking.

Vandelle rubbed her hands. "Oh, excellent. Spill it, if you please!"

"I will, but you've got to promise to answer one question fully and truthfully when I'm done."

Wariness dimmed the excitement in Vandelle's eyes. "That's a dangerous promise to make in Acantis."

"Only if you've got something to hide."

She seemed to struggle with that for a moment, then grinned wolfishly. "Well, whatever I've got to hide, it can't be as bad as what Harking has. I promise, so long as you tell me everything!"

"Oh, I will. You know the Redgrave Academy scandal?"

Vandelle nodded. "I know the basics."

Redgrave Academy had seemed like a good idea: a charity school for lost, orphaned, and unwanted Echoborn youth. There were lots of those, unfortunately, since Echo parents often didn't claim their half-human offspring, and Echoborn were at the highest risk of slipping away through the Veil. But Echoborn often had unique magical talents, which made them valuable, and Redgrave hadn't always waited until kids got lost or orphaned—which was how Blair had come to be there. The academy had covered their tracks well enough that until my investigation exposed the kidnapping scheme, nobody suspected them of foul play.

"On paper, Harking was just one of their many donors," I said. "He claimed to be duped like the others, but he was in it up to his eyeballs. I couldn't investigate him directly, but his name kept coming up again and again. It wouldn't be hard to find the trail—there'll be payments, communications, all of that if you just dig a little."

Vandelle's eyes had gone bright as jewels. "Oh, that's good stuff."

"There's more." The fires of old anger stoked in my belly just thinking about it. "I was hired to find some of the missing kids. The reason it took me so long to trace them back to Redgrave was that time and again, the people who might have seen something or known something kept turning up dead. Including some of the kids' families."

Vandelle frowned. "You'd think a string of murders would have gotten attention."

"They didn't look like murders. No sign of violence—no clear cause of death. They all just didn't wake up one morning." My jaw tightened. "Besides, they were just a scattering of poor Dockside and Southside folks—no one important."

Vandelle's mouth twisted as if the words tasted as sour to her as they did to me. "Of course. That's how it always is. That rotten bastard. Can you connect the deaths to Harking?"

"Not yet. But there's one more thing. You remember how the headmistress, Camille Redgrave, confessed to being the mastermind behind the kidnappings?"

"Of course. It's why they didn't investigate any further."

"Well, it got hushed up, but shortly afterward, she wound up conveniently dead of a sleeping draught overdose. Except that was just the physicker's best guess, because there was no clear cause of death. She just... didn't wake up one morning."

Vandelle's eyes narrowed. "Are you saying that—"

"I'm not saying anything. We're not having this conversation. But it's worth investigating. The death of a Hillside scion like Camille Redgrave leaves more of a trail."

"I see. Thank you." Vandelle shook her head. "All this—the murders, the kidnappings—it's just sick. You can't come back from that. And this monster is in our *government*, damn it."

"My feelings exactly." I'd been infuriated enough at the time, but now that I had Emmi, the idea that Harking had been involved in *stealing children* was enough to make my vision go red.

Much as I agreed with Vandelle, however, I had to admit she

seemed ripe for an Echo's manipulations. If some tentacled horror crawled out of the river right now and offered to consume Harking for her, she'd probably ask if it wanted some honey sauce to sweeten him up. I might just pass it a fork myself.

"Thank you," Vandelle said. "I hope I can use this to bring him down. If I can't—well, knowing this makes my priorities clear. He's got to go, one way or another."

"He does," I agreed. "Now, if you don't mind, I'm dealing with an emergency, and I really do need an answer to that question I mentioned."

"Of course. If it's for an emergency, you could have just asked."

"It's important enough that I wanted to be sure." I held her gaze. "Dona Vandelle. There's an Echo planning even now to storm this party and murder people. Someone gave him an invitation, possibly without understanding his true intent. Was it you?"

"What? No, I don't..." Her brow creased. "I mean, I don't *think* so."

"Is there any chance you could have given him permission to be here, even by implication?" I pressed. "Lives are at stake."

"I certainly would never ask an Echo to come to Marjorie's house and murder people! As for whether I might have said something that someone could take advantage of..." Doubt entered her eyes. "Echoes are known for being devious about this sort of thing, aren't they?"

My interest sharpened to razor focus. "They are. Have you been dealing with one?"

"I haven't *made* a deal, no, but... Well, you have to understand that as a City Elder, it's inevitable that sometimes we have to interact with those from other realities." She bit her lip. "Let me think about this."

"We don't have time for you to think about it. He could show up any—"

I broke off, a cold wave of dread passing over me, as strains of familiar music rose up from the dance floor. "Under the Flower Moon." We were out of time.

A movement past Vandelle's shoulder caught my eye. Perhaps

thirty feet away, a man who'd been reading at a little table lowered his massive black leatherbound book.

Silver goat-pupiled eyes stared into mine. Rai grinned, showing pointed teeth, and beckoned me as if I were a dog.

All my insides turned to ice.

"One moment," I murmured to Vandelle. "Hold that thought."

Some invitations you couldn't refuse, no matter how much you wanted to.

Hand resting less than casually on my sword hilt, I went to meet the Empyrean.

NEVER TALK TO AN EMPYREAN

Rai gestured to the chair opposite him. "Come now, dog. And stop fondling that sword; we've established that you can't win against me with violence. Sit, and let's talk."

A year ago, I'd have succumbed to bravado and retorted that I couldn't be sure unless I kept trying. But I'd be a fool not to hear what he had to say—and most likely a dead one. So I dragged out a chair and sat, arms folded to keep my hands out of trouble, heart pounding like I'd gone ahead and started the fight.

"Frankly, I'm curious why you want to talk to me at all. I'd expect you to consider me beneath your notice."

"It's unwise to discount mortals. You live with limited time, and you know how to get things done." He eyed me speculatively. "You've set yourself against me, of course, but it doesn't have to be that way."

"Doesn't it? You seem pretty set on murdering people, and I'm not inclined to stand aside and let you do that." A deep pit of pure terror waited beneath my surface defiance, but I had to keep skating if I didn't want to fall through.

"You haven't shown any ability to stop me, so that's hardly a concern."

"And yet there must be something you want from me, or we wouldn't be having this conversation."

"Must there? What if I simply enjoy the pleasure of your company?" He pulled a bottle and two glasses from thin air and poured a fizzing silvery liquid into both. It was disturbingly opaque.

"I'm not drinking that," I said flatly.

"I never said one of these was for you." He raised one to me in a toast, wicked eyes laughing, and took a sip. "But no, of course you're right. There *are* some mortals I would seek out for their company, and some I would seek out for... other qualities. But you don't have what I need." There was that exhaustion around those alien eyes again. "You lack ambition, Hound. You are content to serve."

Something about the way he said it made me very glad indeed that I didn't have what he was seeking. He sounded... hungry. No— *starving*. As if whatever it was he needed, the lack of it was slowly killing him.

"So if I'm not a threat, I'm not fun, and I'm not useful, why are we talking?"

"I'm talking to you because you've established yourself as a player in this game, and I don't think you realize what you've done."

"This is because I touched that clock, isn't it." I curled my cut finger into my palm.

"Yes and no. If you don't know the rules, I'm certainly not going to explain them. You're more useful to me if you're involved but have no chance of winning."

I grabbed the second glass just to have something in my hands, rolling its stem between my fingers. "There's only one reason to want someone in a game if they're not on your side. To waste your opponents' resources."

"And you've done an admirable job at that. First you eliminated Wounds Reflected in Water from the game by breaking that dagger. Now you've knocked out Glimmering in the Swarm as well."

"And isn't that convenient for you."

"Oh, come now. You wanted them gone, too." He sipped his silvery drink. "Have you figured out who else is left?"

Cail's lady, of course—Arhsta. I racked my brain trying to think whether I'd seen any signs of others. There could still be some hidden player I hadn't discovered...

Oh.

"You don't know," I realized. "You're up against someone subtler than you, and you're hoping I stop *them* instead of you, or at least flush them out."

"You Hounds are investigators, are you not?" He shrugged, his close-fitting armor moving with a fluidity metal could never achieve. "I've lived long enough to know my own limitations; uncovering information I cannot simply *know* is not a skill I possess. Given the amount of power I hold, it's in your interest to help me."

"What makes you think I'd work for you, after all the murder you've done tonight?"

One silver eyebrow lifted. "I've done less than you seem to think. Regardless, it hardly counts. That quaint little clock has kept any of it from sticking."

He leaned forward, his eyes narrowing, and I felt the full force of his attention coming to bear on me. The pressure of it nearly crushed the air from my chest, and the room seemed to grow slightly darker.

"Of course," he said, "it *will* stick if you stop me."

My shoulders tensed. "What do you mean?"

The pressure in the air eased. He knew he had me. Satisfaction glittered in those mirror eyes.

"You must have noticed that interesting little clock returns these mortals to their previous state whenever one of us wins a round. Whenever *you* fail." He ran a finger around the rim of his glass, coaxing a high eerie chime from it.

"When you make the blood seal, you mean."

"Yes. And if no one succeeds in carving a blood seal into a given Echo, the convergence falls apart, the year-naming can't happen— and the clock's work is done. It will remain silent, with nothing to power its restorative magic. Whatever state all these people are in will be permanent."

Shit. That made this a lot more complicated. I had to not only stop him—and any other Empyreans still in the game—but I had to do it without casualties.

Whatever he saw in my face seemed to please him. His mouth curved into a smile. "You see now, don't you? If you help me, I'm content to limit myself to killing only the one person I need in each Echo to make the seal. Which means that only one person will *truly* die, in the final Echo when my success is complete."

"I've seen jobs with lousy payment before, but 'I'll only murder one person' sets a new record."

"You're not in a position to negotiate a better offer, Hound. Will you take it?"

Every kid in the League Cities grew up hearing stories about what happened to people who made deals with an Empyrean. Sure, they could get you what you wanted—*anything* you wanted—but they only did it to serve themselves, and whatever strange obsessions drove them. In the end you'd be used up, ruined, cast aside, and likely everything you cared about would lie broken in that heap with you.

Maybe Rika would have said yes, and found some way to milk him for information while wriggling out of the deal. Maybe she would have given him Arhsta's name, whatever it really was, in retaliation for kidnapping her—but I didn't know enough to do that safely, only enough to point him at Rika like a loaded crossbow. Maybe a Raven like Blair would know how to shape a contract that would place careful limits on the bargain, buying clemency without committing to anything they didn't intend to do anyway.

I was a Hound, and a waxing Cloud Moon on top of it. I didn't do that kind of slippery stuff. I just had to hope being straightforward wasn't about to get me killed.

"No." I set my glass down, the silvery liquid in it untouched. "Even if I worked for murderers, which I don't, or for free, which I try very hard not to . . . I'm on leave."

"You're certain?"

"I'm afraid so."

"I see." He finished his own glass, taking his time, and set it down with a regretful air. "In that case, Kembral Thorne, it's in my best interest to make sure you have an incentive for me to win."

Oh, that sounded ominous. I tensed, ready to spring into motion.

The light changed.

Shadows raced across the Empyrean's face as the soft warm gold of the floating lanterns turned greenish and began swarming madly above the ballroom. Everyone looked up, me included, as they danced around like a cloud of suddenly agitated bees. Rai leaned back in his chair and steepled his fingers.

Dread settled into my stomach. "What are you doing?"

"Winning."

I turned from him with a curse, looking for any clue as to what awful thing was about to happen and how I could stop it. A sea of faces stared up at the whirling lights, confusion and anticipation warring in their expressions, clearly wondering if this was some entertainment. I couldn't shake the horrible, growing suspicion that they were all about to die.

Rika slithered through the crowd toward me, grey eyes grim. I didn't want her to have to come face to face with Rai, so I left him with a final glare and hurried to meet her.

"I saw who you were talking to." Rika sounded downright accusatory. "Is this your fault? Did you make him angry?"

"No! He's just an asshole!" I checked the windows and doors, in case the lights were a distraction and monsters were about to attack or something. "All I have is a sword, and I don't think stabbing something is going to help here. Do you have any—"

I didn't get to finish. One of the lights dove suddenly into the crowd, like a stooping hawk. I braced myself for screams, but only a startled yelp rose up from where it had struck.

Another light swooped down, and another, and another. One struck Vandelle, standing not far away, right in the chest; she let out a startled cry, her hands flying up to cover her heart, but it had vanished into her.

She pivoted, her gaze raking the crowd. "Who did this? If this is some prank by a bored, rich brat playing with an Echo relic, I swear I'm going to have their pampered ass arrested."

"I'm afraid we're not so lucky." I watched her for signs of distress, heart pounding, all too aware that calamity couldn't be more than a few breaths away. "How do you feel?"

"Fine, but—" She broke off as her gaze lit on Rai, some twenty feet away, leaning back in his chair and grinning. "What the... Is *he* doing this?"

A commotion broke out before I could reply. Halfway across the ballroom, near where the first light had gone down, a young man was climbing up on a chair—no.

He was floating.

Little lights swarmed under his skin like fireflies, green-gold specks glowing from within his hands and face. His mouth worked silently, his arms stretching wide as he lifted up off the ground, tailcoat stirring as if in a soft breeze.

His friends tried to pull him down, but he kept rising gracefully upward. More tiny lights emerged from his straining mouth to swirl around him, zipping in graceful arcs like sparrows harrying an eagle.

"Oh, that bastard," Vandelle whispered hoarsely, her eyes going wide. "He wouldn't have. That *bastard*."

"Do you know him?" I demanded, pouncing on her words. "What did he do?"

She looked as if she might answer, ire sharpening her gaze. But instead she let out a sudden gasp and pulled back her sleeve, lifting her arm to stare at it in horror.

Tiny green-gold lights danced under her skin. They spread from her elbow toward her wrist as we watched. She opened and closed her trembling hand.

"Oh no," she whispered. "Oh no."

The floating man hung in the air above the crowd as if pinned there, back arched. His eyes had begun to glow, and more tiny lights drifted from them, whirling around him like snow on the wind. For a moment, a thick silence blanketed the ballroom, everyone staring at him in fascinated horror, unsure what to do.

Then it shattered into chaos as more lanterns swooped down at people in the crowd, plunging into their torsos as they ran and screamed and cowered. Tables crashed to the floor, people fell, but no one was fast enough to evade the diving lights.

"Stop this!" I yelled at Rai, sure he heard me even across half a room of mayhem. "You've made your point, you grandstanding Voidspawn!"

He lifted his glass to me in mocking salute.

More people began to rise up in the air, lights racing under their skin and circling around them, backs arched and bodies straining in apparent transcendence or agony. And here I stood, seething with frustrated rage, hands clenched so hard into fists my knuckles ached, with not a single damned thing I could do about it.

Unless I gave in and took his bargain. The *fucker*.

"Kembral!" Rika cried, and gave me a vicious shove.

I staggered, and a glowing sphere of green-gold light zoomed past me, ruffling my hair.

I barely had time to think *Oh shit* before it swerved with the abrupt precision of a pendulum changing direction and came right back at me, speeding toward my chest.

It was too fast for anything more than my most instinctive panic reaction. I threw up my hands in front of me with an undignified yelp. Its glow filling my vision, I drew in my existence like a breath and dodged out and *away* into the Veil.

Abrupt silence fell. In the molten non-space between Echoes, the globe of light about to crash into me inverted to a seething ball of darkness.

I flung myself away from it, passing through the shade of Dona Vandelle frozen as she began to lift off the ground, her arms outflung, face tilted up to release a few sparks of the darkness that swarmed beneath her skin. Rika still reached for me, lips parted to shout my name, black hair frozen in mid-swirl.

If that attack ball was going to follow me, I couldn't lead it toward anyone else. I sprinted across the ballroom: one heartbeat, two, toward the knowing mirror eyes that moved to track my approach.

I erupted back into the world beside the Empyrean.

"Leave them alone!" I demanded. "You said you only need one person."

More and more people were rising into the air, lifting up slowly above the crowd, surrounded by swirling lights. I recognized Jaycel, Carter, so many others. Few of the luminaries remained aloft.

"I only *need* one," Rai agreed. "But if I take more, it's insurance. You wouldn't want *this* to be the reality that sticks, would you?"

A sudden shower of sparks burst from the first man who had risen, motes of greenish gold twinkling in the air in glory, leaving him devoid of lights.

He fell limp and empty fifteen feet to the floor, landing with a hard, sickening thud.

I braced for the clock to toll, but it didn't. The moment stretched, and still, the chime didn't sound.

Another eerily floating guest went up like a green-gold firework, sparks spraying from them in a sudden, lovely burst, and dropped as a dead husk. *Crunch.*

He was killing them for effect. To make a grandiose point. Rage flooded me in a tremendous wave; there was murder in my hands.

Calm. I forced myself into the fragile, temporary calm Almarah had taught me, smooth as glass and far more brittle, shoving my maelstrom of emotions in a box to be unpacked later. Not now. Now I needed to be under perfect control.

"You're only creating enough chaos to cover whatever your opponent is doing," I said coldly. "It's a sloppy move, and it could cost you the game."

Rai's brows twitched down. I tried not to look as more lights exploded over the ballroom, shedding glowing motes of radiance. But I still heard the awful thuds and crashes, the cries of fear and grief. I couldn't suppress a flinch each time.

"You have a point," the Empyrean allowed. "Take my offer, then. Find my opponent, learn their plans, and I'll keep the killing *and* the chaos to a minimum, so you can do your work."

"There is no way under the Moon or in the Void that I'll ever work for you."

"Then you'll die," he said, with great indifference, and looked meaningfully at my hand.

I'd noticed somewhere, in the back of my head, that my fingertips were tingling. I glanced down at them, following his gaze.

Golden sparks seethed under my skin, all the way down to the middle knuckles.

Fuck. Fear leaped up my throat, the deep primal dread of death. I stared at the sparks, frozen as if someone else had slipped into the Veil and caught me there.

Rai was beside me, too close, whispering in my ear, his breath tickling my hair.

"Your daughter needs you alive."

That was it. Of all the things he could have said, that one snapped something inside me like a bit of brittle kindling. My mind went white with fury.

I drew my sword and stabbed him.

It was so easy, like stepping off a cliff, trust-falling into the arms of a beloved bad idea. My sword leaped from its sheath like a shout of wild gladness, and I rammed it up under his shining black breastplate.

There was no resistance whatsoever, as if his armor were hollow.

A very bad feeling shivered through me.

BONNNNNG, clanged the clock, reality shuddering, people rising and glowing, bodies falling like overripe fruit to the floor. BONNNNNG.

Rai laughed. He *laughed*, and closed cold fingers around my wrist. He pushed my blade deeper into his chest, grinning, never breaking my gaze.

"I am born of the blood of the Moon," he whispered caressingly. "I am born of the blood of the Void. You cannot hurt me, little dog. What is older than death cannot die."

He cast my arm contemptuously aside as the clock's deep bell rang out again. My blade passed through him as if he weren't even there; I barely managed to hang on to it, a sick feeling growing in my chest. I hadn't so much as scratched his armor.

BONNNNNG.

His starry cloak unfurled into great black wings, spreading out of nothingness from his shoulders. With a few quick beats that blasted icy wind into my face, he was up in the air with the dying.

"Come, you can do better than that," he called, spreading his hands wide. "Find my enemy for me, Kembral. Find them before it's too late."

FINISH THE JOB BEFORE IT FINISHES YOU

My fingers had gone from tingling to aching. The glowing lights remained within them as the world blurred and flowed from one Echo to the next, though their dance slowed to a placid swirl. Reality rippled, and everyone was mingling and laughing and talking again—alive and well, the flush of health in their cheeks. No one was dead, no one was floating, and no one had lights glowing like burrowing fireflies beneath their skin.

Except me. *Fuck.*

The walls had turned to mirrored glass. I stood near one; the scene it reflected back didn't quite match reality. In the glass, most of the party guests were skeletons, still clad in the same finery, dancing and laughing and pouring wine through their empty jaws. My own reflection looked at me with hollowed eyes, and the fingers I held up in stricken shock showed bare bone protruding from the receding meat of my hand.

I tucked my hand away, trying not to panic. Seven fucking Echoes down, deeper than I'd ever gone, and I was under some strange curse. If I could get back to Prime, it *might* stay behind—a lot of the time making it back to Prime alive was all it took to undo whatever horrors the Echoes wrought upon you, as Prime's version of reality proved stronger. I'd returned from almost this deep before; I had the skills and the knowledge to get out of here, go find a weak spot that *wasn't* compromised by some awful blood ritual, and climb my way from Echo to Echo, thin spot to thin spot, until I came out back home. But that would mean leaving Rika and Pearson and Marjorie and Jaycel and Blair and all the rest to be lost here forever.

I couldn't do that. I always brought the dog back.

Someone was waving urgently at me across the room. The Clockmaker, her smudged apron askew, beckoning me with apparent distress from behind her clock.

That couldn't be good.

I made my way across the room as quickly as I could without drawing attention to myself. I hadn't spotted Rika yet, and I didn't want her to see me like this. My reflection slid along the mirrors I passed, sometimes fairly normal, sometimes ghostly or glowing, once dripping a trail of blood. I tried not to look. I couldn't help but notice that my pulse quickened more than it should from such mild activity, and I felt a bit light-headed.

Lovely. Just so long as my toes didn't start lifting off the floor. I clenched my light-infested fist in my pocket.

"You're hurt," the Clockmaker greeted me, her eyes big and round with apparent distress. "I didn't want you to be hurt."

"It's all right," I assured her. "I'm going to get this all sorted out, and I'm sure it'll clear up when I get back to Prime."

"There's not enough time." She wrung her hands together; I couldn't help but notice her nails were bitten down, like mine. "Please, I want to help you. Let me reestablish your link to the clock. Then it can turn you back to how you were, and keep you safe."

"That's very kind of you to offer. But if I link to the clock, I won't remember previous Echoes, will I?"

She reluctantly shook her head. "With each reset, you'd forget everything from the start of the convergence completely, and things would be blurry for a little while before that, too, to soften the transition. But you'd be safe! *Please.*"

It was tempting. I could ensure that I'd live. I could be done with this nightmare, all memory of my friends dying over and over wiped from my mind. Maybe Rika could muddle through on her own and save everyone without my help.

Ha. Rika would kick my ass if I ditched her with this mess, and I'd deserve it.

"I can't," I said regretfully. "It's kind of you to offer, but I can't."

The Clockmaker's eyes filled with tears, but she nodded. "I knew you'd say that."

"Why do you care so much?" There was something *so familiar* about her, as if her face had been carved on my heart in some forgotten past. "Do I know you?"

She hesitated, then shook her head. "We've never met."

"But you know me, somehow."

"You..." She bit her lip a moment. "What you Prime folk do ripples down through all the Echoes. My Echo is very dangerous, but I've always been safe. Because of you."

I blinked. "Me?"

"You don't know it, but you've protected me all my life." Her small voice had gone very soft. "So when I heard you'd be in danger, I wanted to help you."

She was the third person who seemed to have known that I'd be here and in danger, after Rika and Harking. Someone had been spreading that little tidbit around, and I doubted very much it was out of any wish for my continued health.

A tear trickled down the Clockmaker's cheek, her expression pure misery. A sudden gush of protective instinct flooded me out of nowhere.

Blood on the Moon. *That* was how I knew her.

"Emmi," I whispered. "You're an Echo of Emmi."

Every Echo was different from the Prime person they were a reflection of, in large ways or small. Age could be one of those ways. I'd once met an Echo of a young friend of mine that appeared as an old man, and Almarah had told me she'd met a reflection of the founder of Acantis with the guise of a child. Time flowed strangely in Echoes anyway. I should have realized before—but how could I? Emmi was a newborn. This girl looked almost nothing like her, except perhaps in the shape of the eyes.

The Clockmaker nodded guiltily, as if I'd caught her at something. "Yes."

"How am I protecting you? Sure, what we do in Prime trickles down, but nearly everyone in Prime has got parents. Wouldn't most Echoes have that kind of protection?"

She shook her head. "No one but Emmelaine has a parent who carried her into the Veil."

My heart sank. "I talked to *six* Ravens, and they *all* said it should be okay to blink step while pregnant so long as I didn't stay in too long. They said so long as *I* was safe, the baby should be safe—"

"She is! She was!" The Clockmaker waved her hands, eyes wide. "Not her. It didn't change her. It changed *us*. All of her Echoes— we're all...special. It's why I could make the clock."

"Of course you are." A strange rush of pride swamped me, chasing out the fear. "And you built it all by yourself! *Damn*. That's my girl."

She blushed. "I'm not—you're not my mother, but I—" She swallowed, her eyes shining. "Thank you. I'm really proud of it."

Of course I wasn't her mother. Echoes didn't have mothers. Usually they were pretty different from their Prime counterparts, especially in the Deep Echoes where this girl probably came from. But still, if anyone said one cruel word to her at this party, I was going to punch them through a wall.

"Because you carried her to the Veil, the connection is stronger, too," the Clockmaker said softly. "Your will to protect her resonates down to us *much* more strongly. You keep us all safe. So I don't want you to get hurt. None of us do."

I reached out and very gently touched her soft, pale hair. "I'm glad," I told her. "I'm really glad I keep you safe. Don't worry about me. I'll keep *myself* safe. I'm a Hound; sometimes I have to put myself within danger's reach to defeat it. You keep doing the amazing work you're doing helping to save everyone at this party, and *I'll* handle saving me."

"You should go," the Clockmaker said, through fingers raised to hide her spreading smile at my praise. "She's looking for you."

Rika. I didn't turn yet; I reached out my good hand, offering it to the Clockmaker. "Thank you."

She clasped my hand in both of her small ones and squeezed it tight. "Hurry," she whispered.

I nodded, gave her an encouraging smile, and went to find Rika Nonesuch.

The reflection that walked beside me was a skeleton now, with green-gold sparks swirling through its empty rib cage. Rai's remembered voice whispered in my ear, insidious. *Your daughter needs you alive.*

"Fuck you," I whispered.

"Nice to see you, too, Kembral. It's good to know that motherhood hasn't affected your exquisite manners."

I whirled. Rika stood there in her smoke-and-silver gown, brows lifted. The mirror hadn't shown her at all.

I curled in my firefly fingers and jammed that hand in my pocket. "I wasn't talking to you."

"Good to know that motherhood hasn't affected your razor-sharp and rock-steady mind either, then."

"Are you all right?" I asked, a bit grudgingly. "None of those lights got you?"

"No, thank the Moon," Rika said. "You?"

"I'm fine." The lie came as a knee-jerk instinct.

"Oh, good. That was a close call." She let out a long, delicate sort of sigh, barely a breath. "Another Echo down. This isn't good, Kembral. What did the Empyrean want to talk to you about? Did you learn anything?"

"I learned he's worried about the competition." I flexed my hand in my pocket. The prickling ache of it was distracting. "He offered to spare everyone else besides his specific targets if I gave him his competitor's name. I'm pretty sure the one he wanted was Arhsta. Do you think we should—"

"No!"

I stared at Rika, taken aback. She smoothed her hair from her face as if I'd caught her disarrayed.

"No," she said again, in a more normal voice. "She'd know I was the one who told you, and she'd retaliate. Besides, it's to our advantage if she doesn't realize we know she's involved."

"You'd let more people die just to cover your own ass?"

"Don't be dramatic. It hasn't come to that. If we wind up in a situation where that's the clear-cut choice, I'll decide then." She glared at me. "Some of us don't like suffering if we don't have to. That's not actually a character flaw, you know."

I could think of a dozen arguments to that, but now wasn't the time.

"Did you talk to Harking?" I asked instead.

"Yes, and I think he's guilty as the Void itself."

"In general, or of inviting Rai here?"

"Both." She frowned. "I can't be completely sure, because the lights started getting aggressive before I could confirm. But I did manage to get him to admit he'd made some bad Echo-related choice, and now he's worried that it's going to come due in a potentially lethal way. It was a classic 'rich man distressed to learn his actions actually can have consequences' moment."

"Huh. That does sound pretty guilty. Though my conversation with Vandelle *also* was starting to sound like she might be the one we're looking for. Damn it, now we've got to figure out which one of them it is—or if it's both." By the tingling pain that had spread to consume my fingers now, I might not have much time to do it.

"Since we landed in this Echo, I've checked on Signa Pearson—he's still out, but stable—and gave Dona Swift the usual warnings. I saw you talking to the Clockmaker just now. What did she want? Yet more bad news?"

"No. Just... personal stuff."

"*Personal stuff?*" Rika's brows rose. "You lead a more interesting personal life than I thought if it involves time-bending Echoes."

A whole mess of strangely tender feelings were still flopping around in my chest like fish stranded by the tide. The Clockmaker was Emmi's Echo. Emmi's Echoes were special. The Ravens I'd consulted apparently didn't know a damn thing about maternity and hand-waved me the clearance they thought I wanted, because of course they did. None of this was remotely useful in dealing with the pressing crisis of impending cosmic catastrophe, general murder, and my own rapidly approaching death by creepy floating lights, but it was hard to clear it all away to focus on more urgent things. For that matter, the increasing light-headedness was making it harder to focus at all.

I pressed my fingers to my temples as if I could forcibly squeeze a plan out of my brain. "We've got to solve this before Rai kicks in the door. Apply whatever pressure we have to, pull out all our tricks. We can't lose another Echo."

"Then we should— Hey!"

My legs had gone a little wobbly under me. I caught myself on Rika's arm, embarrassed.

"Sorry," I said gruffly. "Still haven't fully come back from childbirth, I suppose. It takes a lot out of you."

I regained my balance and quickly let go, but Rika grabbed my forearm.

"What the fuck is this, Kembral?"

"I told you, I'm—oh." I swallowed. "That."

She held my arm up between us like evidence. Tiny lights traced graceful swirling paths beneath the skin of my entire hand. My fingernails glowed faintly.

Rika's grip dug into my arm hard enough to hurt. A furious light came into her grey eyes, until they were nearly glowing themselves.

"Yes, *that*. What in the *fucking Void* is this? Don't you dare tell me that lantern got you, because I saw you blink step away from it."

"I wasn't quite fast enough. It barely touched my fingers, and I guess that was sufficient." I tried to sound nonchalant, as if I weren't sick thinking about it myself. I broke her hold with a quick twist and shoved my hand in my pocket. "It's nothing to worry about right now."

Rika grabbed my shoulders, her face incandescent. "Of *course* it's something to worry about, you idiot! You're going to *die* if we don't do something about it!"

People were staring. I dropped my voice. "Look, it's moving much more slowly for me than it did for the others—Rai wants to pressure me to work for him, and I can't do that if I'm dead. We need to get him uninvited before we do anything else. After that, we can—"

She shook me, hard. "*Fuck* that!" Now half the ballroom was staring, and muttering rose up from the crowd. "Moon above, you're the most maddening person who ever lived. No, we are going to get your hand fixed first, and *then* we can deal with all our other problems."

"It's less important than—"

She drew a knife. "You're the one who knows Echoes. Tell me how we fix it or I cut it off before it spreads."

"What is *wrong* with you?" I hissed, moving to try to block the sight of her knife from the increasingly interested crowd. I had to get her to calm down. "Fine, *fine*! I know someone who might be able to help, but it's absurdly dangerous to go out there right now. We're *seven Echoes down*. You wait here, and I'll go."

"No," she snapped. "You can't go alone. You just almost collapsed."

"Not remotely! I got a little unsteady for a moment, that's all." I glared at her. "You're terrified of Echoes. You can't go out there."

"Watch me." She strode toward the main door, her smoky gown swirling behind her.

"Wait!" I hurried after her; I felt a little dizzy and weary, as if I'd done a few blink steps in a row. "You don't even know where you're going."

"Then you'd better show me. Come on." She grabbed my good arm and wrenched it as if she were dragging along some criminal urchin who'd just tried to pick her pocket. "We're going to get this done and get back here in time for me to snap that Empyrean's horns off and stab them into his eyes."

DON'T LOOK BEHIND YOU

I was braced for the world outside. I knew the Deep Echoes. Rika, on the other hand, clearly hadn't mentally prepared herself.

"Oh, *fuck* this," she whispered, freezing half a step through the mansion doors. "No, absolutely not, Moon be my witness."

"I warned you. You can still go back inside and—"

"Fuck you, too, Kembral."

The sky had gone the color of blood. A heavy wet scent like damp moss filled the air, underscored with a metallic tang. A row of stately trees lined the street, their bark a deep, fuzzy emerald. All of their many branches ended in human hands. Their green fingers groped the air, searching for something. A moaning floated on the wind, faint and deep and vaguely musical, like a wailing dirge sung by a hundred distant voices.

It was the buildings, I suspected, that put it over the line. The mansions and townhouses seemed almost normal—narrower and taller than in Prime, with strange angles and a texture like cracked eggshell. But their round windows had become mouths ringed with fleshy pale lips and sharp, gnashing teeth.

A scrap of trash blew down the street, looking like balled-up paper until it came near us. It unfolded six legs to stop its tumbling and skittered under a tree, rustling angrily.

One of the thousand velvety hands shot down, grabbed it, and crushed it.

"So far so good," I murmured, every muscle tense.

"This is *good*?"

"Nothing's trying to kill us yet, so yes."

I strained my senses, carefully analyzing the air I breathed (left a weird metallic taste in the back of my mouth, but didn't seem poisonous), the feel of the wind on my skin (fairly normal), the harmonics of that distant moan (unpleasant, but not driving me mad yet, so far as I could tell). With a cautionary arm in front of Rika—she didn't seem at all inclined to push past me, but after her stunt a couple of Echoes ago I was taking no chances—I pulled a loose hair from my head and dropped it onto the cobbled street.

It smoldered on contact, letting off a nasty burnt-hair smell and a bit of black smoke.

Well, that wouldn't do. I squeezed a drop of blood from my finger, letting it fall near the hair. I really hated to leave a blood trail straight out the door in a Deep Echo, but the other alternative was climbing up to the rooftops to see if it was safer up there, and given that the buildings had mouths, I wasn't keen on that.

"You're a road," I muttered as the drop hit. "You're for travel. You're *not* scorching hot, and you're safe to walk on."

"Do you have to talk to it like that?" Rika asked, her voice barely above a whisper. "I thought Prime blood just made things stable. It's not like you can shape the Echo with your will, like an Empyrean."

"Look, it makes me feel better, all right? And it can't hurt. Now, stay close behind me, and be careful."

I took a slow, cautious step onto the street. It felt warm through my soles, but my Damn Good Boots didn't start smoking, thank goodness.

The area around Dona Marjorie's house was quiet; even this deep, the locals were avoiding the starry dark rift of the convergence. A couple of human-sized things with too many legs scuttled down side streets, odd bulges showing beneath their ragged trailing cloaks, hurrying along with their heads down. The moaning rose and ebbed; they didn't react to it, like it was weather they'd grown used to.

We walked in the middle of the street to avoid the reaching hands that strained toward us from the trees. That worked fine for a block or so, and then the road started getting hotter again, steam rising up from the cracks between the cobbles. I let another drop of blood fall, whispering to the road this time so Rika wouldn't make fun of me. My nerves were jumping and sizzling with the expectation we'd need to run or fight at any minute.

"How far do we have to go?" Rika asked, sticking so close to me she could practically be my shadow. She hadn't put her knife away.

"I don't know."

"What? Don't you know where you're going?"

"We're seven Echoes down. Things are in constant flux. Space and time are negotiable at best."

I scanned the rooftops. The clock tower was easy enough to spot, though a massive bloodshot yellow eye had replaced the clock. It didn't seem to be looking at us, thank the Moon. The dome of the Grand Theater seemed almost normal, except that it was covered in a forest of sharp iron spikes that impaled irregular lumps. From this distance, I could almost tell myself they weren't corpses. That meant city hall must be the massive, irregular mound over there, which...huh.

"Oh," I said softly.

Rika whirled. "What? *What?!*"

"Nothing."

Whatever city hall was, it was alive, and scaly, with a ridge of massive spines down its back and what looked like folded wings. Rika followed my gaze and let out a string of curses.

"At least it's asleep," I offered.

"Please tell me we're not going that way."

"Not directly at it, no. More toward the tower."

"Which is *also* a horror. This whole place is bullshit, Kembral."

"You could go back to the—"

She raised her knife. "If you suggest that again, I swear I'm going to take your hand off right now to be safe."

I hid my aching hand behind a fold of my coat. The lights had crept past my wrist now, languidly swirling up into my forearm. My fingers still seemed to move all right, which was the important thing; I couldn't afford to be fighting with my off hand now.

A cluster of several cloaked figures approached us in the street, moving with an odd swaying gait and emitting a low hiss.

"Shit," Rika whispered.

"Stay calm. This could be fine." I angled my sword for easy draw, though, because it also might be very not fine at all.

We drew closer. A forked tongue flickered from one of the hoods.

"Evening," I said gruffly.

Hissing swelled in response. The figures slowed, and one hood tilted, emitting a sniffing sound. I closed my fist around my bleeding fingertip, barely daring to breathe.

They passed us by. I didn't try to look in their deep hoods, but glimpsed scales and the gleam of eyes in strange places. Rika let out a soft whimpering noise.

Ahead, the road leaped up in a graceful arch, becoming a bridge. The river flowed sluggish beneath it, red as the bloody sky but murkier, bubbling and steaming. I stopped and swore.

"Lovely," Rika said faintly. "A river of boiling blood."

"That's not the problem." I lifted my gaze to the rooftops, searching for the clock tower and its vast bulging eye. "We shouldn't be anywhere near the river. Everything *moved*. Come on, we've got to go this way."

We took a side street into a neighborhood with fewer trees and fewer windows; in fact, the buildings had been replaced by endless rows of doors in all different architectural styles, stacked three stories high in ornate stone doorframes. All their handles were polished to a high shine and gleamed invitingly.

"This is nicer," Rika said. "I almost want to try one, to see where it goes."

A figure in a long hooded coat with a beak projecting from it stomped up to a door with the familiarity of long use and turned the handle, opening it. A massive tongue shot out, wrapped around him, and yanked him inside; the slamming door cut off his despairing cry.

"Or not," Rika amended. "Fuck this place."

We walked in tense silence. The seething feeling beneath my skin crept its way up my arm. I couldn't help thinking some bad thoughts, deeply scary truths that coiled around my heart with a cold and slippery grip.

At last, I swallowed. "Rika. Listen, I know we don't always get along, but you're all I've got right now."

"You're a real charmer, Kembral. Did you know that?"

I plunged ahead. This was too important to get sidetracked. "I have a favor to ask you. A big one. It's not fair, and I'm sorry."

"Stop," she snapped. "This is going to be some 'If I die' bullshit, I can tell. Stuff it. You're going to live, so it doesn't matter."

I clenched my light-spangled hand. "I'm trying to be realistic here."

"Not interested in your realism. We left realism back up in Prime."

"Blood on the Moon, Rika, I'm serious. I need to make sure someone takes care of Emmi."

She froze. Something in her gaze softened a little. "Emmi. You want *me* to take care of your baby."

"I mean, I want *someone* to take care of my baby, and you're who I've got standing here right now. My sister will take her in, but I just need—" A fear that had nothing to do with my own impending death almost choked me. "I need to know someone will make sure she's okay."

Rika reached out and gently touched my cheek, her eyes damp.

"Fuck you, Kembral Thorne," she said, and slapped me hard across the face.

"Ow! What the—"

"Take care of Emmi yourself," she hissed furiously. "You're going to live, you hear me? Moon above, maybe I should take care of *you* instead, since you give up on yourself so damn easily."

"Rika—"

An odd, lonesome, shuddery howl rose up behind us—not close, but far closer than I'd like. Every hair on my body stood up in response. It drove all thoughts of mortality from my mind—at least, mortality further out than the next five minutes.

"I knew this quiet was too good to be true," I breathed. "We'd better hurry."

I stopped myself from reaching for Rika's hand. She glanced behind us, wide-eyed, as we started off at a brisk walk.

"Should we run?" she asked.

"Never run in a Deep Echo. It tells them you're prey. If you have to run, it's already too late."

I tried to keep us headed for the tower as we picked up the pace, but a thick white fog began to rise, bringing that odd metallic smell with it. The howl sounded again, closer and from the right this time. Which could mean the creature was passing us by, or it could mean there was more than one of them. I strove to keep my face calm and not show Rika the electric cocktail of fear and combat-readiness that pulsed through my veins.

It was hard not to draw my sword. But one of the rules for surviving the Deep Echoes was that you didn't show aggression until you had no other option. There were plenty of things down here that would leave you alone if you left them alone, and it was best to keep it that way.

We passed a vaguely familiar graveyard. A transparent specter of an old man in a ratty hat leaned against a memorial obelisk, smoking an insubstantial pipe. A humming sound came from the graves, which I tried not to think too hard about. Rika pressed close enough to me that she was practically in my pocket.

"We're almost there," I told Rika. "I recognize this place."

"Where are we going, anyway?"

"A shop. I know the shopkeeper; she's helped me before."

"Fine, but—"

The specter leaning on the grave lifted his head. Red eyes smoldered like coals beneath the ragged brim of his hat.

"Prime blood," he rasped. "You've wandered too deep, children."

The ground beneath our feet shifted suddenly, giving and rattling with a texture like loose, light gravel. Bones—the whole road was now a flood of tiny animal bones, piled in drifts like macabre snow. The small, delicate bones of birds and mice mixed with curving ribs and staring skulls from what could have been weasels or foxes. I sank in up to my ankles at once; there was no bottom to it.

The specter straightened from his obelisk and took a measured step toward us. The bones at our feet began to move, shifting and rustling on their own, like a meal you've only begun to realize has worms in it. I swore and tried to take an involuntarily lunging step, but my legs wouldn't move.

"Kembral!" Rika called, panic a raw foundation beneath her voice. "I'm stuck!"

"I know," I said through my teeth. I turned to the glowing-eyed ghost. "What do you want?"

"Your blood, your bones." He took another step closer. "All the life that runs through you. All the fire of your soul. To drink it down and be alive again."

Oh, that was *not* a good place to start negotiations. The baleful burning sparks of his eyes fixed hungrily on mine.

Another howl rose up, closer than before. My heart pounded hard enough to burst out of my chest. I had to get us free *now*, or something much worse was going to catch us. I could blink step out of the bones easily enough, but that wouldn't save Rika.

"You don't want us," I said desperately, holding up my hand to show him the lights swarming under my skin. "I'm cursed by an Empyrean. You consume me, you get *this*."

The black void of his mouth opened in a hiss. He recoiled, and the bones prisoning us trickled away into fine white sand.

"Poisoned meat," he groaned. "Poisoned soul!"

This time, I did grab Rika's hand. Her fingers clenched hard around mine.

"Let's go," I breathed. "Walk as fast as you can without running."

Another howl rose up, almost on top of us. I knew that sound. I'd been trying to tell myself I didn't, but I did. *Deepwolves.* There was no fighting them. I only knew of one defense against them, and it wasn't reliable.

"Whatever you do," I said in as normal a voice as I could manage, "keep looking straight ahead. Don't look behind you. If you don't see them, they might not be able to hurt you."

Rika's throat jumped. "And if we *do* see them?"

"Then we're probably both dead. Come on—there's the shop."

An inviting green door waited near the end of the street, its brass handle gleaming, promising safety. We walked so fast it only wasn't a run by the barest of technicalities. Claws scraped after us on the cobbles, too close. *Don't look, don't look, don't look.*

"Kembral," Rika breathed, her voice too high. "There's another one."

I followed her gaze, like an idiot. Down a dark side street, a massive shadow loomed, bristle-edged. Twin pools of swirling blue fire hovered at second-story height. As soon as I glimpsed it, a piercing howl of triumph reverberated through the city, turning my bones to ice.

"*Run!*" I yelled. Tightening my grip on Rika, I broke at last into a flat-out sprint. Claws tore up the cobblestones behind me, hot breath blasting my back, the scent of blood and a baleful blue glow enfolding us. I dove the final yards to the door.

The cool brass handle hit my palm like the Moon's own benediction. We hurled ourselves through just in time. Heart pounding like it would shake my ribs to ribbons, I slammed the door behind us on a street grown dark as night.

"Welcome, travelers," said a calm and crinkled voice, "to Laemura's Curious Tea Emporium."

WHEN IN DOUBT, TEA

Laemura's Curious Tea Emporium was a fixture of Acantis that extended from Prime through every Echo I'd traveled to. It got weirder and more magical the deeper you went, but it started pretty weird and magical at the top. Laemura herself was most definitely part of that, and one rule remained constant in every Echo: Her shop was safe for paying customers. Nobody messed with it. I'd seen a glowing river-haunt three stories tall chase a man into the shop, pause at her door, shy away in fearful respect, and move on. I had no idea if it was because there was some Empyrean compact that protected it because everyone liked her tea, or if they feared Laemura herself.

As always, the first thing that hit me was the smell of thousands of herbs and flowers, a dry, green, enticing smell that got into my lungs and soothed the world away, mortal peril forgotten. A warm light bathed the place, shining from several living octopus-looking creatures tangled in the ceiling beams. Rows and rows of hundreds of little tins and jars lined the walls, all of them labeled in Laemura's spidery handwriting: APPLE MINT INNOCENCE. LAVENDER REGRET. SMOKY CINNAMON VENGEANCE. DOOMED FOREKNOWLEDGE WITH TOASTED WALNUT AND SAGE.

Laemura was scooping a glittering violet powder from a jar into a tea canister when we walked in. All three of her eyes swiveled to greet us (in Prime she only had two, that I knew of), and she blew a puff of breath up past her tusks (also not there in Prime) to shift a loose strand of wild grey hair from her face.

"Ah, Signa Thorne. Come in, come in. Bar the door, there's a good girl; there's all sorts of mischief abroad for the year-turning." She bustled out from behind her counter, smoothing her soft white apron with taloned fingers. "And Signa Nonesuch! I believe you visited my shop once in Prime."

Rika hung behind me, glancing around the shop. "It was a bit different there. I'm delighted to meet this Echo of you."

That was another strange thing about Laemura: Every version of her seemed aware of every other version, as if they shared memories. She was probably Echoborn, but no one I knew had ever been rude or daring enough to ask.

"Well now, what are you looking for today?" Laemura beamed at both of us. "I have a nice blend of Uncomfortable Truth with Bitter Orange. Or perhaps some Chocolate Rosehip Reconciliation? Or how about a cup of nice soothing Chamomile Serenity?"

"The chamomile sounds nice," Rika muttered.

"Actually, I'm hoping for a medicinal blend," I said apologetically. "Again."

"Oh, Signa Thorne." Laemura sighed and shook her head, as if I'd disappointed her. "You should take better care of yourself."

"Sorry."

"What did you do this time?" She put her hands on her hips. "Let me see."

I showed her my hand, feeling for all the world like a guilty child. Laemura pushed back my sleeve, tutting at the progress of the swirling lights past my elbow.

"Well," she said, "it'll have to come off."

"*What?!*" I yelped, yanking my arm back.

"I told you," Rika hissed.

"Oh, calm down, I'm just kidding, dear." Laemura patted my shoulder. "Cutting it off wouldn't help."

I shot Rika a vindicated glance. She only shrugged.

"So do you have something that could cure it?" I asked, trying to sound relaxed.

"This is an Empyrean's curse," Laemura said sternly, all three eyes giving me a look that suggested it was my own fault for getting entangled in Empyrean business in the first place, which I felt was a bit unfair. "No one can remove it save another Empyrean."

My heart plunged. "How about returning to Prime?"

She shook her head. "No, no. That won't undo an Empyrean's work. They're not mere Echoes like me; they're divine beings, born from celestial ichor. They came into being when the Moon was wounded, in the instant before the shattering of reality, so they're part of Prime itself as well as all eleven Echoes. Prime offers no escape from their power, I'm afraid."

Rika's voice went high and strained. "So she needs an Empyrean? Or she'll *die*?"

My insides roiled at the idea. I'd lived my whole life with the fierce belief that I could make myself into whatever I wanted, do whatever I wanted, so long as I tried hard enough and didn't give up. Sure, I wouldn't always succeed at everything—I'd fail, get defeated, make mistakes, maybe die trying. But I'd do it through my own skills and stubbornness, or with help from my friends. The idea that my continued existence could depend entirely on the whims of an Empyrean was repugnant.

A year ago, I might have said *screw it* and just let the curse kill me rather than give in to Rai's demands. But Rai was right about one thing: Emmi needed me. He *had* me, and I hated it.

Laemura was already pulling down tins from high shelves in the back of the shop, straining to reach some with dust on the lids. "I'm going to brew you up a little something to slow it down, at least, to give you a bit more time to find a solution. If the curse reaches your heart, it's too late, and it'll be there in fifteen minutes at this rate."

I clamped a hand over my own bicep as if I could stop the progress of the lights with my fingers. "How much time can you buy me?"

"Time is a poor way to measure things in the Deep Echoes, dear."

Laemura slipped me a sly sort of grin, cheery wrinkles creasing her face. "Let's see...some Vanilla Clemency, Peach Hope, a touch of Almond Resolution, and clover honey for luck."

"That sounds delicious." I slumped into a chair at one of the delicate little tables in her shop, fighting a strange, tingling dizziness. Rika glanced back and forth between me and Laemura, biting her lip.

"She still needs an Empyrean, though," she said, her voice unsteady.

"Well, you're in luck, because there's one not far from here who might be inclined to help you just to meddle with the whole year-turning business." Laemura plunked the packet of tea she'd made for me into a cup, took a kettle off a brazier that burned with a perpetual lick of greenish flame, and carefully poured steaming water over it. "Tilting Toward Oblivion."

"Excuse me?"

"Their name." Rika sank into the chair opposite me as if she were also having trouble remaining upright. "Empyreans always have names like that."

"So would Rai be short for something?"

Laemura tutted again. "Is he the one who cursed you? Most likely Laughing As He Rises, then, but I suppose it could be Rider in the Dark. All of them come here, in one Echo or another, when they need good tea."

"Why do they have names like that?" I asked, to distract myself from my impending doom.

"To reflect their equilibrium." Laemura stirred my tea, peering into it critically. "They're inherently unstable, of course. When the Moon and the Void fought, the blood of the Void scattered across the heavens and became stars, and the blood of the Moon fell to Earth and became life and all creation. But in a very few places where their blood mingled, the Empyreans were born." She shook her head critically. "And of *course* those two divine ichors didn't mix well—two such strong and opposing flavors would make a miserable tea. It wouldn't harmonize."

She scooped the tea packet out of my cup with a slotted spoon, giving a satisfied nod. I eyed it with new suspicion, given that she'd seemed serious about the idea of celestial blood as a tea ingredient.

"If they'd had me there, I could have brewed them up a little something to help stabilize them," she continued with a sigh, "but they didn't. The Empyreans who leaned too far to chaos became stars; those who leaned too far toward order became some part of creation, like a tree or a crystal. The ones still around to cause mischief are here because they found a strand that granted them equilibrium. A direction, a path they could follow—much like how a hoop can stay upright so long as it keeps rolling. But like a rolling wheel, it's a precarious business. Every one of them is a complete mess, perpetually balanced on the brink of destruction from the beginning of time to its inevitable end."

I remembered the weariness lurking beneath Rai's gaze. Eternity was a long, long time to not be able to rest.

Rika's hands clenched on the table. "So why do they always mess with us? If they each have this purpose, why can't they go pursue it and leave humans alone?"

Laemura spooned honey into my cup, clicking her tongue. "My dear, they're far too hopeless to manage on their own. The poor divine wretches were born in the very moment reality shattered into Echoes, and they shattered, too. They exist through all Echoes at once, but they need an anchor in Prime to stay stable. Because they're so powerful and complex, only a strong, complex anchor will do. Or several, ideally."

"Humans," I guessed. "Is that why they make bargains? To form a connection that can anchor them to Prime?"

"Bargains can help. But what they really need is a Prime mortal who they can use as an anchor for their equilibrium thread. Someone who's a good match for their core drive, who they can propel along their path whether they like it or not. That's what you should watch out for, dear; a little side deal won't hurt you, or at least not much, but becoming an Empyrean's anchor will ruin your whole life."

Rika moaned and put her face in her hands.

"Anything a human can do about that?" I asked, with a sideways glance at her.

"Wait until they get tired of you and the connection fades, then pick up the pieces, I suppose." Laemura tapped her spoon on the edge of my teacup and brought it to our table, beaming with satisfaction. "Or send them to me for a nice cup of tea instead. I have special blends for most of them, tailored to their particular equilibrium threads. Some of them taste quite nice."

Rika straightened, pushing back her hair, smoothing composure over herself like a mantle.

"Laemura," she said, her voice all sweet, sultry music once more, "I'd been thinking I might like some of that chamomile, but I've changed my mind. Once you're done with Kembral's tea, do you suppose you could get me some of that?"

She pointed to a canister on a shelf labeled BOURBON CARAMEL RESOLVE.

Laemura chuckled. "Of course, my dear. Good choice. Now, relax and take a moment for a nice cup of tea. It really does fix nearly everything."

—⟁—

Go where the fog is thickest, Laemura had said as she claimed her price—five drops of blood for my tea and two for Rika's. *Down toward the river. You'll find the Empyrean there.*

"That's all?" Rika had whispered as we left, after I forced all seven ruby-red drops out of my poor abused finger into a little crystal vial Laemura proffered. "Just a few drops? I thought it would be gorier, after all the stories."

"Prime blood is rare and powerful in the Echoes, especially this deep. You know how everything shifts?" I waved my hand around the street we stepped out onto. The buildings looked completely different than when we'd gone in, all shiny dark glass now; the fog remained, thick and white and faintly luminescent. "Prime is stability. A drop of our blood on the threshold locks a door in place so your house doesn't move to somewhere dangerous or merely inconvenient.

One in each room keeps the house itself stable, so you don't wake up inside some giant creature's maw one day. A drop over an Echo's heart will keep their own form from changing, which can be a concern this deep down."

Rika shivered. "Remind me never to move to an Echo. No wonder they'll take blood as universal payment."

"It's also why so many things down here will try to hurt or kill us."

Rika sidled a bit closer to me at that. The fog hid everything more than a few paces away, especially as we moved deeper into it, so I couldn't scan for trouble. My ears strained for the slightest scuffle of a claw on rock, the huff of bestial breath, the flap of wings, distant growls or howls or chitters. The odd metallic scent of the fog filled my senses. I hoped it was safe to breathe. I was feeling a bit off, but given the lights swirling under my skin, that was probably unrelated.

It felt like ages since we'd left Marjorie's house. Had Rai burst in and killed half the party again? Had the ballroom dropped down to the next Echo and left us here? We'd been gathered up with everyone else the other times we'd been outside the mansion when it fell, but we were much farther away now.

Time is a poor way to measure things in the Deep Echoes, dear. It'd happen when it happened, I supposed, and there was no use fretting about it.

I was bad at not fretting.

"Rika." My voice barely came out above a whisper. I cleared my throat. "I think this might be a terrible idea."

She gave me an incredulous look. "Of course it's a terrible idea. We're seven Echoes down. I'm sure the only reason we haven't been eaten is that we're getting close to the Empyrean, and everything besides us is smart enough to stay away."

"Well, exactly. Dealing with one Empyrean to escape another doesn't seem like an improvement." I massaged my arm as if I could squeeze the lights out of it. "Maybe I should just...call his bluff. Let this run its course."

"Empyreans don't bluff. They don't need to. You'd *die*. Once you're dead, you get no more chances to be clever or brave or whatever other

Hound nonsense you might have in your head." She let out a shaky breath. "I'm terrified, Kembral. I hate this. But if you need an Empyrean to remove your curse, well, we don't have a lot of options."

It was true enough. I'd thought it through over and over, turning the problem in my head like an old letter worn near to falling apart at the creases. Sure, I could give Rai what he wanted, but I had no illusions that he'd actually lift the curse if I proved it was such a good tool for controlling me. The only other Empyrean I knew enough about to guess she might be willing to break the curse just to annoy Rai was Arhsta, and Rika would probably knife me and leave me in a ditch if I suggested that.

I was at the mercy of creatures with far more power than me, with whom I had no leverage whatsoever, and I hated it.

"Kembral," Rika said sharply, tugging on my arm.

"What?" I tried to turn to her, but I swayed and almost fell—not down, but *up*. My knees buckled, suddenly weak, but I didn't drop; my head whirled, and my toes scrabbled for purchase on cobblestones that tried to slip out from under my feet. *Shit.*

I caught my balance, pressing my soles to the ground, thinking heavy thoughts, heart pounding. Rika didn't seem to notice; she was staring off into the fog.

"Do you hear that?" Her voice was strained, head tilted.

"I don't hear— Wait. Yes." A woman singing, distant and beautiful and oddly familiar. Strange music in the Deep Echoes was *never* good.

Rika froze, her face gone suddenly blank with terror. "It's *her*," she breathed. "Laemura said it wasn't her, but that's her voice. I've got to get out of here."

She whirled as if she might run; I caught her gauzy dangling sleeve.

"Rika! If you run off in this fog in a Deep Echo, I absolutely *guarantee* you're going to get lost. Also probably killed."

She jerked out of my hold, eyes wild. "I don't care! I can't let her see me, no matter what. She'll—"

"There you are, little one," said a throaty, rich, gorgeous voice. "I've been looking for you."

KNOW YOUR WEAKNESSES

Out of the fog stepped a woman with an endless fall of fine Moon-colored hair that trailed behind her like a cloak, glowing with a soft radiance. Her gown was spun of something pale and silky, with shimmering white lights scattered through it; her skin was black as the night sky itself, letting no light escape save where more tiny flecks of luminescence dusted her cheeks and arms like freckles. Her eyes shone with milky light, and her smile turned my legs to water with its brilliance.

"No," Rika whimpered, and fell to her knees.

"Come to me," the woman said, reaching out hands like elegantly shaped holes in existence. "I've missed you."

Rika shook her head, panic in her eyes, mouth working soundlessly.

"Come." The musical voice grew stern. "Your throne awaits you."

Hair-thin lines of black shadow spread from the hem of her gown, reaching toward Rika, tracing a weblike pattern along the ground. Rika recoiled from them with an incoherent cry of fear.

I stepped forward, heart pounding, hand on my sword hilt despite the utter futility of the gesture. "Leave her alone."

Rika whirled on me, eyes wide with panic. "Kembral, stay out of this!"

"Sorry, but I can't do that. Rika..."

I trailed off, a confusion of unspent energy snarling in my chest. The woman was fading like a shadow in the sun, arms still extended. The hair on my neck rose.

The mist swirled through her, and she was gone.

"Did she..." Rika rose haltingly to her feet. "Was that real?"

"I don't know." I kept my voice quiet, still on high alert. "Something's happening, and it's bound to be dangerous. Be careful."

That could have been Arhsta sending an image of herself as a message to Rika. It could have been the fog showing us our worst fears in an attempt to get us to run off a cliff into the mouth of a waiting monster. It could have been anything, because we were in a Deep Echo, and all the rules of reality were getting rewritten every ten minutes.

Rika swallowed. "Do you think she—"

"Hey, sharpstuff," interrupted one of the last voices I expected or wanted to hear right now. "Lookin' good."

I spun, my hands suddenly unsure whether to form into fists or wave hello.

"Beryl?!"

There he was: Beryl Cascarion, all roguish grin and messy brown ponytail, wearing his favorite patched and faded blue linen shirt. He ruffled the back of his head in the self-conscious way he always did when he knew he should apologize but wasn't going to.

"Fighting an Empyrean without me, I see. Hey, if anyone could do it, it's you. How's the kid?"

"*Your* kid, you mean?" I retorted, taking half an angry step toward him before it sank in that no, this made no sense. We were in a Deep Echo, and there'd been an Empyrean here a second ago, equally improbably. "Wait. You're not real."

He cocked his head, still grinning. "A smart lady told me once everything's real in an Echo. Real enough to stab you, and that's what counts, right?"

"Real enough to *be* stabbed, too, if you give me trouble," I growled.

He laughed, showing his good teeth and that one cheeky dimple. "Wouldn't dream of it, sharpstuff. You'd kick my ass through a wall."

That had always been one of the good things about Beryl. It never bothered him that I was better than he was; he respected me, genuinely and without envy, and that was hard to find. Stars, he was downright supportive—about everything except the baby.

Rika put her hands on her hips, eyeing him critically. "So this is him? The one who dumped you?"

"Yeah."

She sniffed. "Not in your league."

Beryl winced. "Hey. That hurts."

He disappeared in a sudden swirl of fog, as if her words had banished him. Barely faster than the real one had once I'd told him the news.

"Right," I said through my teeth. "So this mist is showing us things from our own minds. Classic Deep Echo stuff. We can probably ignore it and keep going, so long as we're careful. Unless it turns out we have to resolve it to proceed."

Rika frowned. "Resolve it? How?"

"I have no idea." I couldn't keep my frustration from leaking through. "Might be that we have to delve deep into our own hearts to confront the unhealed wounds we've carried with us in secret. Might be that we have to say their names backward, or just close our eyes and they'll go away. Echoes never make any damned sense."

Rika made a face. "We'd *better* not have to confront our unhealed wounds, or I'm leaving you to die."

"You shouldn't have come this far in the first place. This isn't your fight. You don't owe me anything."

She looked away. "You don't know when to stay quiet, do you?"

"No. Never did." I let out a rueful little laugh. "Speaking of which... What did she mean, your *throne*? Are you some secret princess or something?"

"No. She... When she stole me, she made me sit on a throne she'd shaped for me in a shallow Echo. She made me a whole castle and everything." Rika shuddered.

"That doesn't sound too bad," I said warily.

"It wasn't. Until I tried to leave." Rika hugged herself as if against the cold, in that same way I'd seen her do before when thinking about her encounter with the Empyrean, rubbing her arms.

This time, the eerie diffuse light of the fog caught something I'd never noticed before. Faint scars all across the bare skin of her arms— probably invisible in the light of Prime. Some formed pieces of a weblike pattern, and others tiny dots like freckles, as if impossibly slender filaments had pierced deep into her flesh in a hundred places.

I remembered the fine black web that had reached for Rika from the Empyrean's shadow, and my gut went queasy with fury.

"Shit," I breathed.

"I'd rather not talk about it. Come on. Let's find this Empyrean of Laemura's before anyone else shows up from our fun memory closets."

I picked the direction where the fog seemed thickest, and we pressed on. My steps felt strange and light, my knees trembling; I had to grab Rika's shoulder at one point and take rapid breaths to keep my feet on the ground. She tolerated this familiarity with tight-pressed lips, looking away from me.

"Sorry," I muttered.

"Just don't die, all right? It'd be too depressing to have to go back to the party and tell your friends over and over."

Another hazy figure approached us through the fog, her stride martial but with a slight arthritic hitch to it. I'd know that walk any-where. I straightened up, even knowing she wasn't real; I couldn't help it.

"Kembral," grunted Almarah, stepping out of the mist and raking me with a glance. "You haven't been practicing."

"I just had a baby," I pointed out.

"And here you are, fighting for your life. Be easier if you were in practice, wouldn't it?"

"Yes, Almarah."

Rika had straightened up, too, even though she'd never met my teacher before; Almarah had that effect on people. She was nearly six feet of lean dark brown muscle in worn leather, her body and blade both cared for with the precise loving attention of someone who knew the value of a well-maintained weapon. Her cascade of braids had already gone grey before I met her as a child; I'd still bet on her against almost any fighter in the city, despite the nests of wrinkles framing those deep-set brown eyes and the swelling of her knuckles.

Almarah jabbed a finger at me. "Children make you tough. Parents are hard as rock formed in the heart of a volcano. You've got no excuse slipping out of form. Keep your mind on the mission, Kembral."

"Yes, Almarah."

She grunted again with a mix of satisfaction and skepticism as her imposing form grew transparent and drifted apart.

Rika gave me a strange look. For a moment, I was sure she was going to make fun of me for talking to this image of my mentor as if she were real; it was silly, but I couldn't help myself. What if Almarah *knew*, somehow, how I'd treated this reflection of her? She'd come out of retirement just to kick my ass.

"You care about her a lot, don't you," Rika said quietly.

"Yeah, I guess. She's a great teacher."

"Must be nice." The corner of her mouth quirked a little. "I respect my teachers in the Cats, but they don't get close to their students."

"You know why, Rika Nonesuch," said a familiar voice. "Because we can't let sentimentality hold us back when you make mistakes."

It was Adelyn Cail, slipped up far too close behind us, her face stern and forbidding. Rika whirled to face her, fists balled at her sides.

"That's *not* why. That's not how it works. Ugh, you're going to make Kembral think we're a bunch of coldhearted, abusive criminals."

"She's given me that impression tonight, yeah," I admitted.

Rika gestured at Cail with liquid frustration. "This isn't what she's normally like! I should have known you were false from the beginning. The *real* Cail would never compromise the mission by undermining a fellow Cat's confidence in the middle of a job."

"You bluster very nicely, Rika, but you and I know that no matter whether I'm real or not, you *are* a failure." Cail crossed her arms. "Echoes can speak the truth. Signa Thorne *caught* you. Not just stopped you, but *caught* you, like some novice on her first assignment."

"Hey." I stepped up closer, too angry to care whether she was real. "I didn't catch her because she made mistakes. She did everything right. She was *perfect*."

Cail regarded me coldly. "Why are you defending her? She betrayed you. She's a liar, a thief, and a spy, and she proved in the star diamond incident that you mean nothing to her."

A few hours ago, I'd believed that. Except she was out here, in a place that absolutely terrified her, looking for a type of being that frightened her even more, in a desperate attempt to save my life. It went far beyond whatever friendly rivalry we'd had before we ruined things between us.

But that didn't matter right now. What mattered was Rika's eyes on me, narrowed to hide the hurt in the back of them, waiting to hear how I'd answer.

"I'm defending her because if I'd known what a big ridiculous deal you'd make of it, I'd have let her go. Stars, I should have let her go anyway. I was angry." I looked at Rika. I was still too stubbornly bitter to do a good job of this, but I forced the word out anyway as a half-swallowed mumble. "Sorry."

Rika stared at me as if the word I'd spoken was in some unfamiliar language. Cail sneered and vanished in a sudden puff of cloud.

I cleared my throat. "Anyway. She's wrong *and* not real. End of story."

"Hmm." Rika stood with arms crossed, fingernails drumming, considering me. What did she want? I'd apologized. For doing my job.

Light footsteps sounded in the mist, striking the cobbles at a pattering run.

Something about them struck deep into my heart with an ominous chill, as if fate itself were charging at us on small, nimble feet. My breath quickened. We both turned toward the sound.

A little girl of about five years old ran up to us out of the mist, with tumbled curling hair and wide brown eyes and a pointed little chin. She saw me and flashed a quick, mischievous grin before running past us into the fog.

I made an involuntary noise in my throat and started after her.

This time it was Rika who grabbed *my* sleeve. "Kembral. She's not real."

"That's *her*," I protested. "That's the little girl. The one I used to play with—the one I saved from slipping into an Echo. The one who disappeared."

"I know. She's not real. Let her go."

"But I looked for her for so long. What if she *is* real?" It was the sort of trick an Echo would play. Give you lies and then truth; twist time on itself and throw back something you'd lost long ago in your face. My throat went tight and hot. "What if I find her now, after all this time, right before I die? I can't just let her go."

"You're not going to die," Rika said sharply, "and that isn't her."

"How do you know?"

She drew in a hitching breath. "Because she's me."

I could only stare at her. She might as well have run me through with a spear. She stared back, annoyance struggling on her delicate features with something older, deeper, more vulnerable.

"You can't be," I said, feeling stupid. "You don't look anything like her. Your eyes are grey, and your hair is straight and black, and—"

"I'm an *illusionist*. My eyes are whatever color I want them to be." They shifted as she spoke, from pale silvery grey through brilliant sapphire blue and piercing sun-dappled green to a warm deep brown.

I could see the resemblance now. Her eyes and hair were different, and her face was nearly a quarter century older—but she had the same pointed chin, the same warm golden-brown skin, the same fineness to her features and stubborn strength at the base of her jaw.

All my life, worry for that kid had been sitting somewhere buried deep in my stomach like undigested poison, and she'd been right in front of me. Rika fucking Nonesuch.

It was too much. All of it—two months of terrible sleep, two months drowning alone in an ocean of powerful feelings; then this night of absolute horror, fighting for our lives, and an Empyrean's curse, and now *this*. It was all too much to keep inside me anymore.

I burst into big, wet, messy tears like a child.

"Kembral, what the—"

"You're all right." I choked on the words, my face already a mess. "Fuck you, Rika, I thought you'd fallen into an Echo."

"I did," she said, her voice careful and subdued. "But several years later. Not when you—not then. I just had to move to a new neighborhood unexpectedly. I didn't know you were looking for me, all right?"

I wiped savagely at my eyes. I was making a fool out of myself. "You were my friend."

"I..." She swallowed. "You were my friend, too."

"And you grew up into *such* an asshole."

Rika threw up her hands. "I give up! You're completely hopeless, did you know that? Here I thought you were finally allowing yourself a shred of genuine feeling, and—"

It started with a stumble, my feet trying to lift off the ground again, and I grabbed at her in panic. But somehow our arms went around each other, holding tight in a surge of desperation. My tears dampened her hair.

"I found you," I whispered. "I finally found you. You're okay."

"Don't let it go to your head," she said, but her voice was rough and thick. "I recognized you the moment I saw you, years ago on the first mission where our paths crossed. I thought you'd forgotten me."

All this time. Over all these years, with every look and glance I'd given Rika, feeling some connection there, she'd known this. I'd had *dreams* about her face fading out of reality, reaching in desperation to catch her and having her fingers slip insubstantial through mine—and she'd been right there. Waiting for me to figure it out, or resigned that I never would.

Well, I'd caught her now. It might be too late to keep her from slipping into an Echo, but damned if I wanted to let go.

A startling staccato sound burst into the moment, shattering it. *Clapping.*

"Oh, very nice," said a child's voice. "But that's only the beginning, isn't it?"

We whirled apart, but there was no one there—only more fog, dense and directionless.

"Do you know that kid?" I asked Rika.

She shook her head, tense and wide-eyed.

"There's more in there." Delight colored the high, piping voice. "What about *this* bit?"

The mists parted to reveal two people sitting at a fancy wrought iron café table, leaning close together across it, staring into each other's eyes as they talked with sparkling animation. Anyone would have thought they were falling in love.

This gullible fool certainly had.

One was Rika, dressed in a practical but stylish silver-grey tunic and black leather bodice, a wide belt settled at her hips with her usual assortment of knives and pouches. Her hair had been longer then, swept back behind her shoulders in a glossy liquid fall. The other... well, she wasn't quite me. She looked too fit and vibrant, too confident and charismatic, her hair a shining deep gold instead of a honey-brown mess, her skin too perfect.

"Who is—" Rika frowned at the pair. "That's not how you see me, is it?"

She looked normal to me. I didn't dare say anything. Was this how Rika saw me, then? Damn, she thought I looked *good.*

Not-Me let out a deep and tremulous sigh of a sort I hoped I'd never made in my life.

"I'm so glad I can open up to you like this, Rika," she said in a voice far too musical to be mine. "It's hard to trust someone after Beryl cruelly left me the moment he found out I was pregnant. That utter cad."

"I never said that," I protested. "I never said anything like that."

"It's true, though." Rika gave a solemn nod. "Beryl *is* a cad."

Not-Rika shook back the river of her hair, a smile curving her full lips. "It's all right, Kembral," she said in a voice thick with compassion. She reached out and laid an elegant hand over the one with nails too smooth and even to be mine. "I'm about to betray you, too, just like he did."

"Hey!" Rika flinched. "I *definitely* never said *that!*"

"But it's true, too."

It wasn't me who said it. I'd *thought* it, sure, but I'd kept my mouth shut for once.

The voice that had uttered my thought out loud came from something that looked more or less like a six-year-old child. Their curling hair was a dull ashy grey, with the curved points of horns sticking up from it; instead of a face, they had a smooth white porcelain mask with great black holes for eyes and no mouth. Their head tilted a little too far, hands clasped behind their back; their ragged grey clothes fluttered in the mist in a way that left me dubious there was anything beneath them.

All right, fine, they didn't look like a child so much as like a creepy child-shaped thing out of a half-remembered nightmare.

"Who are you?" Rika demanded, with the pure unthinking fury of humiliation.

"You can call me Ylti."

Ylti. Tilty. Tilting Toward Oblivion. The Empyrean we'd come to find.

Of *course* they turned out to be just as cruel as all the others.

The too-perfect copies of us were fading. A grin stretched out of nothing on Ylti's mask—not where a mouth should be, but along the curving bottom edge of it, full of needle-sharp teeth. Rika stepped away from them, her breath catching.

"We've been looking for you," I said, keeping my tone polite to the point of deference. "I was hoping—"

"I know why you sought me out, Kembral Thorne." The round black holes in their mask stayed fixed on Rika; instead of glancing at me, they *opened a new eye in their temple*, peering through their grey hair with a bulging dark iris. It blinked at me in dismissal before disappearing beneath their curls again.

I forced myself to continue past a suddenly dry throat. "All right, then you know—"

"Tell her," they said to Rika, ignoring me. "Tell her why you did it."

Rika took a step back. "I'm not telling her anything!"

I couldn't deny I wanted to know. But I also didn't want this nightmarish brat sticking their nose into anyone's private feelings. They might be kid-sized, but they were older than time, so I didn't have to be nice to them.

Except for the part where I had to butter them up so I didn't die.

"Oh, leave her alone," I snapped. "If you're going to help me, help me for some sensible reason like wanting to stick it to your fellow Empyreans or wanting to put an end to their little murder party, not out of some sick desire to mess with us."

Maybe I was bad at buttering people up.

Ylti laughed, and it was a child's laugh, innocent and a little unhinged. "See, she's still defending you, even after what you did. Tell her, Rika Nonesuch. Before it's too late."

I was done with their mind games. I opened my mouth to tell them where they could stuff that.

Instead of words, a green-gold spark flew out of my mouth. *Oh shit.*

An effervescent lightness swept through me, draining the strength from my muscles. *Not yet, not now*—but my body wasn't listening to my panicked efforts to exert my will on it. I fell in a loose giddy swoon, the world going vague and distant around me.

Except I didn't fall. The air cradled me gently, like a dead bird.

My boots lifted off the ground, and I rose.

TRUTH WILL OUT

I tried to curse, but it came out as more lights. They swirled around me like concerned flies, bathing me in a greenish-gold radiance. Everything was dim and distant, as if the universe pressed a pillow gently but firmly over my face.

Rika's cold hand caught mine, trying to keep me from rising farther, her grip like iron. "Kembral! Get down here, damn it! Don't do this to me!"

I would have liked very much to get down. This wasn't how I wanted to die at all. But nothing seemed to care what I wanted, my own body least of all. It stayed upsettingly loose and relaxed even as I struggled to move, and the world kept drifting farther away.

I tried to cling to Rika's hand, my insides burning and my skin tingling as more lights seeped from me. *Don't panic, don't panic, there's got to be something you can do, some favor you can call in, it can't be too late . . .*

I rose up into the fog. Rika strained to hold me, but her grip on my hand was slipping. Her eyes seemed huge and shining; those couldn't be tears, surely. More illusion, and now it was too late to even ask her whether their true color was grey or brown or something else entirely.

"Tell her," Ylti coaxed, their voice sweet as a child begging for candy. "Do it. I'll even give you privacy."

Just like that, the Empyrean was gone, and I could breathe again.

The ground was gone, too, and the fog-shrouded shadows of the buildings. Rika and I floated together in the mist, surrounded by swirling lights, her hand still crushing mine. It would have been an ethereal, beautiful moment if I weren't so terrified.

"Fine." Desperate fury roughened Rika's voice. "*Fine*. I'm breaking sacred Cat law and there'll be the Void to pay, but fine."

"You don't have to do that," I croaked, and this time it came out as words.

"No, let's do this." Rika glared at me as if I were the absolute worst person ever, but she didn't let go of my hand. "You keep going on about what I did to you during the star diamond job. Well, I did it to save your life."

"What?"

"Yes. And you've been a complete bitch about it, too, I might add."

I stared at her, floating in the fog, shifting green light playing across our faces. For a moment, I almost forgot I was dying. My world struggled to invert to match her words, but it didn't make any *sense*.

"How in the Void does drugging me and piling garbage on top of me *save my life*?"

She closed her eyes. That was definitely moisture clinging to her lashes, and it was hard to tell myself they were fog droplets. The mist swirled around us, buoying us like water; Rika's hair lifted, her dress floating around her, and my peacock coat flared like a scarlet sail.

"One of the first rules they teach you as a Cat is that you can't use anything you learn during guild jobs for your own ends." Her voice was a wisp of itself, frayed almost to nothing. "We have to be completely trustworthy."

"We have the same rule in the Hounds." In the course of my work I'd learned a ton of dirty secrets, not to mention the security measures of half the important people and places in the city. "What does that have to do with—"

"Shut up. You're too much of a Hound, Kembral—you ask too

many questions. I shouldn't be telling you this. I should just let you die." She let out a shuddery sigh. "Swear you'll treat it like a guild job. Don't tell anyone, and don't act on it."

We were rotating slowly now, hair and clothes drifting in a lazy arc, firefly lights wreathing us both in a gentle whirling maelstrom. Nothing hurt, but I felt so light and empty—a bit like being in the Veil, as if my substance were meaningless. Maybe the Empyrean had scooped us up out of space and time in some different way, or maybe this was just what it felt like when you were about to explode into a shower of sparks and die.

I should have been desperate for her to finish. I should have shut up and let her talk, let her say whatever she needed for Ylti to decide they'd been sufficiently amused to save me. But Rika was right; I was too much of a Hound not to ask questions.

"Why?" That was the thing I couldn't understand. "We don't know each other *that* well. More rivals than friends, even before the star diamond and the Echo Key. Why would you break a guild oath for me?"

"Because you saved me." She opened her eyes, and they flickered from grey to brown and back to grey again, as if she couldn't decide who she was. "Because nobody gave a shit about me when I was an abandoned kid running around on the streets. Nobody ever, until you did. And I thought maybe you were my protector, some special friend sent by the Moon to watch over me." She let out a bitter laugh. "I didn't know you well enough back then to realize you'd do it for anybody. That I wasn't anyone special to you."

"Rika, I spent *fifteen years* training to blink step because I wanted to find you." I grabbed her shoulders, giving her a little shake. "Do you have any idea how *hard* that is?"

Years of frustration and boredom, meditating forty-seven different ways, trying to touch the Veil for a brief flicker of an instant. Years more getting the balance right to stay there for even one heartbeat without bouncing back to Prime or punching through to an Echo. Years after *that* to be able to move without breaking through the Veil, or floundering around in uncomprehending confusion at the lack of space or time. All for a girl I'd known so briefly, in one of those whirlwind childhood friendships that sticks deep into the shallow earth of a young heart and forms the kind of strong roots you can't rip up without destroying parts of who you are.

"I cared about you *so fucking much*," I whispered. "I had dreams about the look on your face when you were slipping away from Prime. Sure, I'd do that for anyone now, but I'd do it for anyone *because of you*. All those kids I've rescued were because I wanted to save *you*."

"You are *such* an idiot." She was crying. Tears left crystal trails down her cheeks, and her eyes had gone pink. "Why are you like this? Why do I..." She couldn't finish.

There was a roughness in my throat I couldn't clear with a swallow. "Damned if I know."

She reached up and tapped the tip of my nose, the touch quick and light as a cat's semi-affectionate swat. The tears kept flowing.

"Listen. About the star diamond. I'm going to try to do this without technically breaking my oath, so use your tiny Hound brain and see if you can figure it out."

"I'm listening."

"Did you ever wonder why you were given the star diamond job in the first place? Guard duty on such an unimportant bauble, when you're a senior Hound who can blink step? It never made any sense." Her gaze bored into mine, willing me to understand.

"I assumed it was because I was pregnant," I mumbled, strangely uncomfortable under her scrutiny. "They were giving me easy stuff. Jobs I could do in my sleep."

"Was the Echo Key protection job easy, then?" Bitterness edged her words.

"No. Bloody Moon, no." Physically easy, but I needed every day of all my years of experience to come up with those traps. "I guess you're right. I never thought of it, but it didn't make sense."

"There was a reason." She glared at me. "Think about it."

"Someone wanted me for the job? Someone with the clout to call in a favor and get a specific Hound assigned? Maybe someone who wanted a senior Hound involved to bolster their own reputation or something." The rich and powerful of Acantis could be like that.

"You're such a trusting little dog." She shook her head in frustration. "How are you still alive?"

"Give me a few more minutes and I might not be," I said wryly.

"Kembral—"

"Fine, no, let me think." I turned the few pieces I had around in my mind, trying new angles. When I found one that fit, I stopped breathing.

It was a setup.

Rika was watching my face; she saw when I got there. "Yes."

"Someone wanted me there, in a specific place at a specific time, so they could... what?"

"Think," she whispered.

I remembered a cultured Hillside voice saying *I'm surprised to see you here*. "Oh. Oh, it was Harking, wasn't it? He was trying to fucking kill me."

"I couldn't comment."

"That *bastard*." One of the richest and most powerful people in Acantis had planned out my death and gone to great lengths to set it up, and I'd never known. A shiver ran down through my core.

Rika gave a small shrug, a shimmer of silver. "So perhaps you can see why, if someone hypothetically knew you'd be killed if you went to a certain place at a certain time, she might theoretically take steps to make sure you didn't arrive there."

"Wait. If you knew about it— He had a contract with the *Cats*?" I laid a hand over my belly, as if I could somehow retroactively protect Emmi from Harking's malice. "How am I still alive?"

"I wouldn't have interfered if it were a proper contract," Rika said sharply. "I wouldn't do that for *anyone*. Guild oaths are sacred. But occasionally, some fool gets it into their head to try to bypass the strict rules the Cats have about what blood work we'll take. Very rarely, someone might even have the money and connections to fake proof of all the necessary criteria and approvals and authorizations and get a sketchy job onto the guild lists. Possibly Echo magic might have been involved, muddling certain minds."

"Oh wow, he must *really* want me dead." You didn't mess around with the guilds like that. "I need to go back over the evidence I turned up in the Redgrave Academy case to see if I have more dirt on him than I realize."

"You need to guard your damn back," Rika snapped. "When I arrived at this party, I had to quietly take out an unguilded street tough before he put a knife in your kidneys. That's why I came in the first place—I got the tip that you'd be here and Harking was still after you, and I knew I'd have to protect you, since you clearly didn't have the sense to keep lying low. But that's beside the point."

Blood on the Moon, Rika was good—I'd never noticed *any* of that, beyond a little flush in her cheeks. She'd killed a man and sailed right into the party looking fabulous afterward, all for me. *Damn.*

Still. I could do the math, and the numbers were getting better, but they weren't yet adding up.

"If it wasn't a legitimate contract, couldn't you have just...warned me? Instead of knocking me out and sticking me under a pile of garbage?" The sheer humiliation of that still hurt.

"It takes time to get a contract investigated and taken off the list, and I only found out about that one by chance at the last minute." She shook her head. "I didn't know who'd taken the job, and I couldn't interfere directly because it was still on the books as a real contract."

"So the job to guard the star diamond—"

"Was a feint from the beginning. To put you in a spot they'd trapped to the Void and back with Echo relics to try to counteract your blink step."

"Blood on the Moon," I breathed.

"I bribed the junior Cat who'd taken the star diamond theft contract to give it to me instead. So I'd have a guild-approved excuse to knock you out before you could turn up for duty."

I squinted at her dubiously. "And the garbage?"

"What did you want me to do? Just leave your unconscious body where a senior Cat assassin could find it?" She crossed her arms. "I'm a professional. I know how other professionals think. You had to be somewhere they'd never look. Sure, you had to take a bath afterward, but you're alive, all right?"

"So is there still a Cat assassin—"

"No. I got it cleared up. The individual responsible has been banned from hiring any Cat at any guildhouse in any city ever again."

"That's got to hurt the shady old fucker," I said, with satisfaction.

"Hmph. He's rich enough to go through intermediaries, so it probably won't hold him back much, but I'm sure it's only made him madder at you."

"Well... thank you." The words seemed inadequate in the face of everything I'd just learned. I felt queasy thinking of all of Harking's preparations to kill me. But I didn't know what else to say. "This is a lot to take in."

Rika let out a pent-up breath. "Anyway, that's it. That's the reason I did that to you."

She waited expectantly, glancing around the featureless void of mist in which we floated. I waited, too. The lights danced around us; the moment felt stretched and delicate, as if I could blow away into dust on the slightest breeze.

Time seemed to pass, except that it probably didn't.

"Um," I said, after the silence became awkward.

Rika threw up her hands, glaring into the fog. "I told her! What more do you want?"

Silence.

"Did you... leave anything out?" I asked uncertainly.

"No!" A flush crept across her cheeks. She folded her arms, glaring at me. "That's it! I practically wrote you an essay. That's the whole reason! No hidden motivations whatsoever!"

More silence. Rika's face got redder and redder. It was the most extraordinary thing, and I couldn't for the life of me think—oh.

"Ah." Now suddenly *my* face was hot, too.

"Fuck! No!" Rika waved her hands at me, eyes widening with mortification. "No, no, no! It's not what you're thinking!"

"You meant it. When you... when we had tea at the café, before..." I swallowed. "It wasn't just a trap."

"Ugh, *fine*." She scowled at me like I'd said something vile. "No, I asked you for tea entirely sincerely before any of this happened, and it was just *convenient* to make it a trap."

I didn't know if this made things better or worse. She hadn't been leading me along and using me. None of it had been a lie—we'd had a real date, and I hadn't even known it.

Which meant she was perfectly willing to knock a person out on a real date, with sufficient motivation.

I shook my head. "You're such a Cat. You don't *do* things like that."

"I *am* a Cat, and I certainly do."

Something strange and uncomfortable started happening beneath my skin, a hot sizzle sweeping through me in a sharp, painful wave. I doubled over, dimly aware of Rika's alarm.

"No," I gasped, holding up a hand. "No, I think this is...good."

The searing wave of magic fried my lungs, and I coughed, startled; one last spark flew out between my lips.

A dizzying, dropping feeling swept up through me. All at once, my feet touched damp-slick cobbles. I'd never been so happy to have my weight settle onto my legs in the usual, proper fashion. The buildings around us reappeared, this time wreathed in intricate pale stonework. The mist began to thin in patches. Something large swooped over-head, letting out a deep, mournful cry.

I felt as normal as I could reasonably expect, given that we were in a Deep Echo. Like I was going to live, assuming I could get out of this accursed place. A giddy wave of relief swept through me. I barely smothered an inarticulate noise, halfway between a sob and a laugh.

Ylti floated there, hands on their hips like some runty conqueror, ratty grey robe fluttering around them. "There! That wasn't so hard, was it?"

The jittery energy of nearly dying and abruptly getting to live after all teetered on the brink of turning straight into anger, and suddenly I wanted to punch this interfering little wretch right in the middle of their creepy mouthless mask-face.

"Thanks," I forced through my teeth instead.

"And thus it is sealed." They pressed their stubby fingertips together, solemn and pleased.

"Whoa, whoa, wait a minute! I never said I was making a deal with you!"

"A deal?" Their head tilted too far, and then *way* too far, until my neck hurt just looking at them. "I only want you to follow the course you've already set yourself. That's not much to ask in return for your life, surely?"

"Depends." A suspicion started to crawl over me, and I didn't like it one bit.

"Oh, this one is easy. I only want you to disrupt the machinations of Laughing As He Rises and Stars Tangled in Her Web."

Rika's hand flew to her mouth as if she were a prissy old lady and they'd said something obscene. "I can't go up against her!"

"You won't have to." It was an easy promise for me to make; if we directly confronted another Empyrean, all we'd accomplish was getting ourselves annihilated. I turned to Ylti, struggling to sound calm and reasonable. "Look, if by disrupting their machinations you mean stop them from making a blood seal and naming the year, yes, I'm already working on it. If you want me to succeed, instead of extracting promises from me to do what I'd do anyway, how about if you give me some information?"

"I don't need your promises. It's already sealed." That curving line of needle teeth showed at the lower edge of their mask again, and a chill crept through me. Oh, I *definitely* didn't like this.

Rika glanced between the two of us in alarm, then forced a glittering smile. "Well, then! You've got no reason *not* to tell her everything. Right?"

"Right!" Ylti chirped. They put their head on straight again. "Absolutely! What do you want to know?"

Blood on the Moon, an Empyrean being helpful. Mark this day on the fucking calendar.

Of course, it had to be a trap. If the stories were true, just about every aspect of every interaction with an Empyrean was a trap, whether they meant it that way or not. But I was so far in, and we needed so much help, that I might as well squeeze what juice I could out of my momentary advantage. Future me could regret it when the bill came due.

"Why are all of you so invested in naming the year?" It was the first question that leaped to mind, and I didn't want to waste my opportunity hemming and hawing. "I know it's a crux year, but what does that do for you?"

"Always, all we want is to preserve our equilibrium." Ylti drifted through the mist, trailing stubby fingers contemplatively along the intricate ivory stonework of a nearby building. The stone swirled behind their touch, transforming in a jagged scar to mirrored glass. "Naming a year colors the whole year and everything that grows from it, like ink in water. Naming a *crux* year, however...if an Empyrean can give a crux year a name that feeds their equilibrium, they'll likely be able to remain stable for quite some time."

I thought of the exhausted hunger in Rai's face. If I had been striving nonstop to stay alive for thousands upon thousands of years, I might do just about anything for a break. Stars, I'd do almost anything for one now, after two short months with the baby.

Ylti let out a wistful noise between a sigh and a whistle, which was odd coming from a face that currently had no apparent mouth. "If I were a player, which I'm not, I'd try to name it the Year of Chaos. I suspect Laughing As He Rises would name it the Year of Conquest. I'm not sure about the other—she keeps her secrets too close."

Foreboding settled over me like a damp cloak. "So if Rai named it the Year of Conquest, we'd get what? Wars, coups, invasions?"

"Oh, certainly. But it would reach to smaller things as well—individual lives as well as nations. Many more people would turn to violence to solve their problems, or even just for fun, or without knowing why at all. Any victory of any kind would tend to be more absolute, more crushing to the loser."

I exchanged a grim look with Rika. "Is this year-naming something only an Empyrean can do?"

"Not at all. *You* could name it." The mask-hole eyes blinked, which was unsettling given their complete lack of lids. "That would be very exciting. You should try."

I shuddered. "It sounds like more responsibility than I want to shoulder, thanks."

"Oh, certainly. It'd be almost bound to go wrong for you, even

if you picked the most positive name you could think of." They
sounded exceptionally pleased at the idea. "For instance, if I named it
the Year of Success, *every* plan would be more likely to succeed—not
just mine, but my enemies' as well."

"Got it." *Note to self: Do not name the year under any circumstances.*

"I've been dreadfully helpful," Ylti pointed out.

"I suppose you have," I agreed warily.

"You might think you owe me something."

Here it came. There was no way to dodge this; they'd saved my
life. Now they were going to claim some twisted price, and there
wasn't much I could do about it. I swallowed to wet my dry throat.

Ylti drifted nearer. There was nothing in those black eye holes; no
spark of light, no sense of depth, nothing but the pure black emptiness of the Void.

"You don't owe me anything," they whispered, in their child's
voice. "It's a gift. It was all a gift."

Oh, that was worse. I backed up, lifting my hands. "Wait. I don't
want gifts."

That curving, awful arc of razor-sharp teeth spread along the bottom edge of their mask.

"You don't get a choice."

My heart flopped around like a landed fish. Rika swooped in at
my side, drawing herself up regally, and somehow gave Ylti a quell-
ing look.

"She's not yours," she growled.

Ylti let out an eerie, echoing child's laugh. "Is she yours, then,
Rika Nonesuch?"

Rika froze as if they'd threatened her. "I . . ."

A strange sense of doom shivered through me, cutting off whatever I might have said. Ylti cocked their head, seeming to listen.

"Do you feel it?" they said. "You've lost another one."

I *did* feel it, a deepening dread and a faint vibration in my bones—
as if far away, well beyond hearing, a great clock chimed.

I whirled to face Rika. "We took too long. Someone's dead."

Alarm widened her eyes. Inexplicably, she reached toward me, as if worried that I'd start rising away from her again. Her hand hung in the air, slim and elegant, halfway between us. Unsupported, like an unfinished question, tentative and brave.

I reached out and took it. Just like I had decades ago, to hold her in Prime when she'd started to fade away. She stared into my face, her expression strangely open, helpless, stricken. Our hands clasped tight, the one firm and solid thing as reality began to dissolve.

We slid from one world to the next together.

NO PLAN IS PERFECT

The clock's unheard chime still reverberated through my bones as the new Echo took shape around me.

Brilliant panels of shining cloth fluttered everywhere like sails, catching light and shadow from a hidden sun. The ballroom had become something between a tent and a maze, colorful silk hangings divvying it up into a labyrinth of little odd-shaped pieces. Giggles and shrieks and lively chatter rose from shadows moving behind the translucent shifting walls.

Rika and I were alone in an alcove of dusky purple and pink curtains, the light shifting in breezy patterns across our faces. Silk Moon, then—manipulations and machinations, patterns and connections, the ties that bind people together.

Rika cleared her throat. I realized I was still holding her hand and dropped it like an unexpected fish.

"Right. So." I swallowed.

Suddenly I had no idea how to deal with Rika. It was easier when she was an opponent, infuriating and taunting and elusive—that was simple. Even better when she was an ally, someone I could trust to execute her part of the plan competently. But we'd had a *confirmed date.* Now, as she looked at me from guarded grey eyes, vulnerability lurking at the corners of her mouth, I didn't know what the rules were between us anymore.

"Glad to see you on the ground again." She nodded toward my hand, which looked refreshingly normal. "You're far too practical to go floating around like that."

"And yet somehow I keep winding up in situations like this." I shook my head; I couldn't even feel relief with so much still threatening us. "I hope to the Moon I didn't just wind up as that Empyrean's anchor. Some of the things they said..."

"What's done is done." Rika said it with the air of someone clicking a padlock firmly shut on a closet full of mold and spiders. "You can join me in my select and fascinating club of people desperately hoping the Empyrean in their lives has forgotten about them and moved on. Right now you're the only other member."

"Sounds lovely. Listen, Rika..." Everything I'd learned about her in the fog welled up in my chest, as if I were once again full to bursting with firefly sparks.

She laid two fingers against my lips. "Shh. Don't say it. I can see you trying to express a feeling. You're no good at it, Kembral." Her voice softened. "Just look at me. That's enough."

"Okay." My mouth moved against her fingertips. I looked into her eyes and felt I could fall into them, deeper and deeper, until I reached the bottom at last and found their true color there, dark and wonderful.

Her lids closed, as if I were too bright to behold.

"Tonight has been so awful," she whispered. "Just terrible. But here we are, eight Echoes down, and we're still alive. Somehow, we're alive, and we're together."

Her fingers still lay against my mouth. Rika had always been one of the few people whose touch felt entirely comfortable—whose presence in my carefully guarded space didn't feel like an invasion, if sometimes a welcome one. But this went beyond my prickly instincts tolerating her; Rika's skin against my lips felt...nice.

No, I was absolutely not going to do this. I couldn't risk another Beryl—not now, when my emotions were such a mess. Besides, I didn't have the time or energy to so much as daydream about a relationship right now; Emmi left no room for anyone else in my life or my heart.

Damned if it didn't feel like Rika was sneaking in on her light burglar's feet, though.

Her hand slid to cup my cheek. She opened her eyes again, their devouring grey seeking something in my face, deep and troubled.

I gazed into them, searching for secret flecks of telltale brown—but if their color was an illusion, it was perfect.

"You were my anchor." Rika let out a little self-conscious huff of a laugh. "When I was a little girl. I kept slipping away, starting to fall through the Veil—but every time, I imagined you holding my hand. Even when you weren't there. You were so stable, so stubborn, so ordinary... You grounded me. And now here you are, getting me through the Echoes safely again."

"It's a bit early to be sure of that." I reached up to her hand where it lay on my cheek—it was warm for a change, and I had a moment of fluttery panic at the thought that maybe this could become a role I had in life: the woman who warmed Rika's cold fingers. "I'll do my best, though."

"I'm just glad you're not angry at me anymore." Her tone shifted, sharpening. "You were such a complete pain in the ass about it."

Oh, thank the Moon, were we done being soft? I couldn't take it anymore.

I tried a grin. "Damned right. I'm not going to be a *partial* pain in the ass, after all. And... thanks. For saving my life and everything."

She let out the softest breath of a laugh—a disbelieving sound.

"A bit late, but all right." Her hand slipped away, its warmth lingering on my cheek. "You're welcome."

The moment teetered on its edge. We could plunge all the way off into awkward tenderness, heedless of what sort of spiky rocks might or might not wait at the bottom, or I could yank us back onto solid ground right now.

The situation was *far* too urgent for romance, so it surely couldn't be cowardice to step back from the brink. I cleared my throat in a sanity-restoring sort of way.

"I know that was...intense, but...we should get moving. We lost a whole Echo there. No more dawdling."

Rika's left eyebrow flew up. "Keeping you from dying is hardly dawdling."

"Ha. We were just sitting around, drinking tea and talking about the past."

She looked ready to strangle me, which was frankly a relief after all that face touching.

I forged ahead. "So we've got our suspicions about Harking and Vandelle. Who do you want to go after first?"

Her gaze narrowed. "Harking. He's hiding unsavory Echo business, something's got him spooked, and the man positively reeks of culpability. Besides, Rai's killed Vandelle, and he's never killed Harking."

I frowned, thinking back. "I suppose you're right. But Rai was *going* to kill him in that Echo where he seemed to be the target."

"Was he, though? He was walking purposefully up to him, but Harking didn't seem too worried."

"That's not how you walk when you're going to have a nice conversation with someone."

Rika shrugged. "Even if he *was* going to kill him, he knew the clock would bring him back, and Harking was the target for that Echo. He may have felt it was worth it. Empyreans aren't known for putting too much value on the lives of their allies."

I pressed my fingertips to my temples as if I could push answers into my skull. "Do we know there's only one target per Echo? If it was Harking in the Wine Moon Echo, and Carter in the Snow Moon Echo—"

"Wait, what are you talking about?" Rika glanced around, realization dawning on her face. "Shit, you're right. They're not in order, but...Silk Moon, Mirror Moon, Flower Moon, Wine Moon, Compass Moon. The Echoes match up. What does that mean?"

"I think something about the convergence being on the year-turning is making the Echoes align with the year at the convergence point. So you get one Moon matched up with each Echo. The

Clockmaker said something about the blood seals not only stabilizing the convergence, but also pinning the convergence to the year, so…" I trailed off, the full significance of the words I was saying catching up to me at last.

"Kembral?"

"Compass Moon," I breathed. "Marjorie is a Compass Moon. That's the pattern."

"What have I told you about saying cryptic…" Rika trailed off, her eyes widening. "*Oh.* She was Rai's target in the Compass Moon Echo, wasn't she? Is Harking a Wine Moon?"

"I don't know for certain, but a Wine Moon is bounty and plenty, and its waning aspect is corruption and excess. So I'd say that fits for a corrupt, rich Hillside aristocrat, wouldn't you?"

"So you think they need to kill someone born under the matching Moon to properly seal the Echo to the year?"

"I'm no Raven, but wouldn't it make sense? Let's see… Carter was the target in the Snow Moon Echo. They threw a birthday party for him when I was protecting Marjorie's son. I'm trying to remember…" I closed my eyes for a moment, then snapped them open. "Yes! It was a few weeks after the year-turning—still a Snow Moon. That's it!" All but vibrating with excitement, I glanced around the gently shifting tentlike silks as if I could see through them to the party guests beyond. "Who's a Silk Moon? If we can protect them all, we can stop Rai from making a seal."

"How am I supposed to know? *He's* the one who can apparently tell your Moon sign just by looking at you!"

"Maybe we can make an announcement. Ask all the Silk Moons to go to the safe room. Though that might cause a panic." A memory struck me of Marjorie standing on a chair by the musicians, cheerfully organizing her guests to crush the beetles and thus defeat the agent of an Empyrean. "A party game! It makes perfect sense—we can ask Marjorie to pretend it's a party game for the year-turning."

"That's a good idea, but we've *got* to move on Harking immediately. I give us much better odds at getting Rai's invitation revoked than I do at fighting him off."

"You're right." I glanced at the mantel clock. It was already after nine. "All right, you talk to Marjorie and set up the party game thing. I'll get Harking to uninvite him."

"Have you lost your wits? We've been over this before. He's trying to kill you!"

"I know," I said. "That's how we can catch him. I'm the perfect bait."

—⧟—

I navigated the maze of silk to a large open area around the dance floor and the clock, where I spotted Harking at last. He was over by a table heaped with spun-sugar dainties, talking to... *shit.* He was talking to Blair.

There was no good reason whatsoever why that snake should ever talk to a former Redgrave student, and at least half a dozen bad ones. I advanced on their conversation with a suppressed growl in my throat.

Blair's robe fluttered with layers of cerulean silk as they arranged the littlest sweets in pretty patterns, making vague noises back at Harking in the absent way of someone not particularly listening. Harking gestured expansively with his wineglass, standing a little too close in his exquisite tailcoat of green-black silk embroidered with subtle web patterns.

Blair was nodding way too much. *Don't agree to anything he says, you fool, he'll treat it as a binding contract.*

I needed to make sure I approached this just right. My plan was a bit vague, and more than a little dangerous; if I moved too quickly or without a clear angle, I could ruin everything. So I started loading miniature spun-sugar nests onto my plate—they had little sugar spiders in the center, or at least I *hoped* they were sugar—and worked my way closer, listening, pretending not to notice Harking was there. Rika would probably have considered it painfully obvious, but I did my best.

"...should come work for me," Harking was saying, his voice all dark honey. "I could use a person of your talents."

"But I work for the Ravens." Blair's gaze barely flicked up from the pattern they were building. "You can't have another job when you're in a guild. They explained it to me very nicely when I told them about wanting to be one of the people who sell fried bread at the horse races. I think they thought I was serious—which I almost was, because they get lovely red hats and free fried bread, except I'd be terrible at it."

"I could compensate you far better than the Ravens do." The edge of frustration sharpening Harking's voice was music to my ears. Maybe Blair had this in hand after all.

"Oh, I couldn't leave the Ravens. I have the tattoo and everything." They showed it, smiling. "You must have dealings with the Ravens all the time, don't you? I can see the magic on you."

"No, I— What?" Harking went still. I did, too, poised to drop a sugar nest onto my plate. *Interesting.*

Blair waved a vague hand. "Most rich people have some, from Echo relics. My teacher grumbles about the Fisher Queen being too good at smuggling them up from the shallow Echoes, and not all the people she sells to taking adequate safety precautions."

"Is that so?" Harking took a step closer, and now the menace in his posture was clear. "That eye of yours sees more than perhaps it should."

All right, that was a threat. Throwing caution aside, I set my plate down and stomped up to them.

"Don't listen to him, Signa Blair. Your eye is just fine." I flashed them a reassuring smile, then gave Harking the stiffest, slightest nod. "Dona Harking. Nice party."

"Signa Thorne." Harking's eyes narrowed to gleaming slits. "I must say, I'm surprised to see you."

Oh, I bet you are. "I apologize for skipping the pleasantries, Dona, but I've become aware of an Echo-related security threat that might affect you. Can we talk?"

I was leaning on the fear I'd seen in previous Echoes, and it got exactly the reaction I'd hoped for. Harking's whole face tightened into a blank mask, and he gave a curt nod.

"Of course. Excuse us, Signa Blair."

We stepped aside together, moving to an out-of-the-way nook with walls of rippling cerulean. The filtered light gave his warm brown face an almost purplish cast.

My pulse raced as if I'd been running. I'd give him a chance to come clean first, but if that didn't work, I'd have to push him harder than was probably safe—and I already knew he wanted me dead. I watched him closely for any sign he was about to make a hostile move, so braced to slip into the Veil that the floor felt slightly unreal beneath my boots.

"You have my attention, Signa Thorne," he said, rolling the stem of his wineglass between his fingers. "What is this threat to my safety?"

"I'm going to be blunt, Dona Harking. Someone at this party is involved in Echo business that's getting people killed. You're in mortal danger because of it." I certainly had his undivided attention; his eyes punched holes in me. "Tell me truthfully: Is it you?"

His jaw worked as if he were chewing something. He didn't look nearly surprised enough to be innocent—but then, Harking had never been innocent. I'd phrased my question vaguely on purpose, in case his involvement was more complex than we realized; easier to draw him out if he believed I already knew everything.

"You do love prying into other people's affairs, don't you? A hound with pups should be more—"

"Don't," I snapped. "I'm trying to save your life. You may think you're untouchable, but this isn't a danger that money can protect you from."

"And you may think your guild makes *you* untouchable, but I assure you that is far from the case," Harking retorted. "This had best not be some thin excuse to meddle in my business."

"I never meddle. I'm a Hound. I protect, and I seek, and I find. Right now I'm trying to protect. You knew you were in danger before I told you. Tell me your part in this mess while you still can, before it gets reduced to *victim*."

He eyed me warily. I could almost see him trying to work out how much I knew. I kept my face stony, meeting his gaze.

At last, he sighed. "Fine. Yes, I have reason to believe that I might be the target of an attack by Echoes, or by people armed with Echo relics. No, I've done nothing to deserve it. In fact, I rather suspect it's all a misunderstanding. Does that answer your question?"

"Not really. Is there anything else you'd like to tell me?" I didn't give him time to utter the negative reply I could see forming on his lips. "Because I'm pretty sure the reason we're all in danger from Echo attacks tonight is that someone made a bad mistake and is in over his head. And the only way we're all getting out of this, you included, is if that someone admits it."

"Signa Thorne," Harking said slowly, "you sound almost as if you're trying to pressure me to confess to something."

"Maybe I am."

Harking let out a cultured little laugh, as if I'd made a mildly inappropriate joke but he was being a good sport about it. "Ah, Acantis! The parties are always exciting. Do you know the nature of this *mistake* you speak of? Its full details and implications?"

Time to turn the screws a little. "Worried that you're in more danger than you realized? Or that you've been found out?"

"I *never* worry about being found out. That's a crass and commonplace concern." He slid a hand into his tailcoat pocket, fingering something there, and my whole body thrummed with a readiness to dodge. "I am far more concerned that some churl who fancies themselves my enemy might take dramatic steps to try to remove me. So—you don't know why these Echoes were summoned here to attack me?"

I'd hoped that he'd confess out of fear and we could move on to the uninviting, but he seemed far more interested in fishing for information about how much I knew. If covering up his misdeeds was still his first priority, that meant it was time to play my least favorite party game: trying to goad him into attempting to murder me. Unless he had some way of dealing with my blink step, I was pretty confident I could subdue him, and then if he was so concerned about getting caught at his crimes, it should be simple to blackmail him into complying.

"I have a fair idea of why," I said. "I'd prefer not to make it public.

What I need, Dona Harking, is your cooperation in getting rid of this Echo."

"In that, we are very much on the same side, so you can stop glaring at me." With exaggerated slowness, holding up a hand as if to caution me from any murderous reflex, he drew out a small, gleaming object from his pocket. "Here. For you, in the spirit of cooperation."

It was a round brass disc—like a coin, but not League Cities money. It could be a charm, or maybe some carnival token or ancient foreign currency from the ruined Sigil Empire. The side that winked up at me from his palm bore a symmetrical geometric pattern, a bit like a mathematician's idea of a flower.

Harking watched me as he proffered it with an intensity that suggested he expected the sight of it to cause me to burst into flame.

"What's that?" I asked dubiously.

He regarded me a long, long moment before answering. "My personal token. If you show it to any of my people, they'll offer you their assistance."

Sure it was. If Harking ever made a personal token, it'd be solid gold, bear his family crest, and be the most ostentatious item conceivable. But I played along.

"Why are you giving this to me now? The threat I'm investigating is here at the party, which doesn't seem to exactly be crawling with your people."

"To show my goodwill. You seem to mistrust me, Hound. But if there's a threat, I want you on my side." He pressed the coin into my palm. "Take it."

"I don't accept bribes, Dona Harking."

"It's not a bribe." His lip curled. "What kind of pathetic bribe would a single dull old coin be? If I bribe you, Signa Thorne, you'll know it."

The thing certainly looked like it came from an Echo, but I couldn't be sure whether it had changed along with his clothes to match the local aesthetic, or if it was some Echo relic and had always looked like that. He'd touched it with his own bare skin, so hopefully it was at least safe to handle.

I was about to slip it in my pocket to have Blair look at later when Pearson's voice suddenly came back to me, clear as day: *You know, the Echo relic smuggler. Turned up dead with some highly dangerous cursed coins stolen from him, and the Fisher Queen was furious.*

A spark lit in my brain, kindling one realization after another like a fire spreading from tree to tree. It wasn't becoming a casualty of the year-naming rite that Harking feared. He was expecting an attack not just by Echoes, but by people armed with Echo relics. He'd called his problem *Echo-adjacent.* And he hadn't threatened Blair until they mentioned the Fisher Queen. It was *her* vengeance he was afraid of— her and her network of Echo allies and loyal fishers.

I looked up from the coin in my hand to meet Harking's gaze, putting on a bright, curious smile.

"Where did you get this exactly, Dona Harking?"

His face went neutral and controlled, still as an untroubled pond. "You recognize it, then."

Ah. This would be the moment where he tried to kill me.

I shifted my weight toward my toes, ready to blink step; his hand crept toward his dagger.

The silk hanging covering the doorway flung open with a sudden flourish. In came Dona Marjorie, Carter, and a couple of armed staff in her wake.

"*There* you are, Signa Kembral! I had a security question for— Oh my!" She seemed to sense the tension sizzling between me and Harking; she stopped in midstride, her fan snapping out and lifting at once to cover her mouth.

Harking's gaze lit with panic for an instant, then went cunning. Before I could say anything, he drew himself up, radiating authority.

"Marjorie, thank the Moon, you've come just in time. Guards, seize this woman for attempted murder."

I gaped at him. "What?!"

"You heard me." His face settled into familiar lines of triumph. "By my authority as a City Elder, I place you under arrest."

AVOID CONFLICT WITH THE AUTHORITIES

I had to check myself from reaching for my sword. "With all due respect, Dona Harking, what manner of bullshit is this?"

Dona Marjorie's fan whirred wildly. "Oh my! Oh dear! Are you certain, Ryvard?"

"Quite certain." Harking put on a convincing air of gravity, only the slightest hint of vindictive satisfaction leaking through in his voice. "She's got a death magic Echo relic on her. Look, it's right there in her hand."

"I have a death magic Echo relic because *you* just gave it to me!" I burst out, frustrated. We didn't have time for this.

"Oh, how dreadful!" Marjorie's lashes fluttered almost as fast as her fan. "Signa Thorne, is it true? Can you show it to me?"

Her eyes were wide and gentle, with no sign of the hard edge I knew full well they could display. She was putting on an act, playing along with Harking; I just didn't know why, or for whom.

Reluctantly, I opened my fist, showing her the token on my palm. She gazed at it, her fan rising to cover half her face until she barely peeked over it.

"Oh dear," she murmured breathily. "Oh my Moon and stars! This *is* terrible."

"I don't know what you think you're up to," I told Harking, too furious for caution, "but this isn't going to work. I know where you got this token. I know who you—"

Harking recoiled suddenly, as if I'd attacked him. "Help! Guards! Seize her!"

Carter hesitated, glancing to Dona Marjorie for confirmation. The other guards were newer and didn't know me as well; they leaped into action with the swiftness of instinct and training, responding to an Elder's command.

There was an instant where I could have blink stepped, could have blocked or dodged their reaching hands—could have made it a fight that I'd have won easily enough. But every Hound knew not to start fights with people's house guards, or the Watch, or anyone like that. The guild had our backs, and if we got arrested in the line of duty, we'd be free soon enough—so long as we hadn't actually done anything overtly illegal or caused anyone irreparable damage.

So I let them grab my arms and twist them behind my back. I noticed that they made it look much worse than it really was; I'd never been so politely manhandled in my life, and I was certain they knew as well as I did that I could break free in half a heartbeat even without resorting to a blink step.

There was also the small detail of the potted plant by the entrance that hadn't been there before, shimmering ever so faintly around the edges with illusion. And when it came down to it, well, I trusted Marjorie.

Her guards looked to her for further instructions, seeming uncertain.

"Oh my! Signa Thorne, you wouldn't *dream* of resisting, would you?" She waved a hand at me in an airy fashion. "This is all so distressing!"

"We have an emergency to deal with," I reminded the whole room, frustration building. "We don't have time for your little power games, Harking."

"This is no game, Signa Thorne."

The chill in his tone put a cold certainty in my belly that he had no intention of giving my guild the chance to come demand my release and set things right.

Marjorie laid a hand on Harking's arm. "Come along with us," she urged. "I've never had to hold a criminal in my house before, but I have an idea for a place where we could do it, if you think it might suffice."

I knew for a fact that Dona Marjorie had held a criminal in her house before, from the time I'd helped stop an assassination attempt on her son. *Well now.*

"Fine," I grumbled, playing along and pinning my hopes on Marjorie. "This is a flagrantly false accusation, and you'll be hearing from my guild, Dona Harking."

His lip curled. "The guilds are not the power in Acantis, Signa Thorne."

They were a significant force in all the League Cities, and not one the council messed with. His august Hillside lineage stretching back to the founding of Acantis wouldn't save him from guild reprisals. This was an act of desperation, a move to cover his own guilty ass because Marjorie had walked in before he could kill me for the crime of recognizing that coin.

My nerves hummed as the guards marched me along through the silk-swathed corridors of the mansion, Harking striding at the fore next to Dona Marjorie. No room in this place could hold me; Marjorie certainly knew that, and Harking might, too, depending on how well he understood the full capabilities of a blink step. He must at least know that I'd demand to talk to my guild, and that once I did, he couldn't keep this quiet. But he looked so sure of himself.

He had a plan, and it didn't involve me living out the hour, let alone the night.

This ploy of his was eating time we didn't have, but there wasn't much I could do about it. I could blink step away, but then what? We couldn't get Rai's invitation revoked if I was leading Harking and Dona Marjorie's guards on a chase around the mansion. I'd have to try to get this over with as quickly as possible—and hope that Harking, who was clearly improvising, would make mistakes.

Dona Marjorie and her guards took me down to her wine cellar.

The walls here remained old stone, the air cool and musty. Thin silk panels hung over arched doorways, fluttering in the draft like ghosts. Marjorie had procured a lantern; its flickering light cast eerie shadows through the dim space.

Harking glanced around in distaste. "Is it far? I do need to get back to the party."

"Oh, of course. I do too—it's my party, after all. We're there already." Dona Marjorie gestured with a flourish of her fan at a heavy door, and one of her guards stepped forward to open it upon a dark, damp storage room.

I went loose and ready. If Harking was going to try something, it would be now. I could almost see it: a scuffle as they pushed me in, a faked attack, his entirely excusable defense of his person from my murderous intent. So sad that I didn't survive.

I could feel his eyes on me, sense the sudden tension in the lines of his body. His hand rested on the knife at his hip.

"What do you think, Dona Harking? Will this do?" Marjorie's voice was light and breathy.

"It will serve." Harking slid closer to me.

"Oh, good! I'm so glad you approve!" She fluttered her eyelashes at him. "Guards, lock him in there."

"I— Wait, what?" Harking froze in shock as Marjorie's guards unceremoniously seized his arms. "Marjorie, what in the Void is this nonsense?"

Everything soft and vague and sweet fell away from Dona Marjorie, as suddenly as if she'd thrown off a cloak. She snapped her fan shut, back straight as an iron rod, staring at him with icy disdain.

"I'm arresting you for attempted murder, Ryvard. You went too far. It's over."

The guards started wrestling Harking into the cell. I managed to keep a grin off my face with a titanic effort. It was *hard*, but damn it, I couldn't do something so unprofessional as gloat in front of Marjorie.

"You can't do this!" Harking struggled to hold on to his dignity, lifting his chin and glaring at her with piercing dark eyes. "Would you truly take a lowly Hound's word over mine?"

"I don't need to, Ryvard."

Harking's gaze turned to me, full of contempt and fury. "You can't prove anything, you wretched dog, and I'm a City Elder. You don't have the authority to—"

Marjorie stepped closer to him, a grim smile changing the landscape of her face. "Oh, Ryvard. She *can* prove it. You see, I know exactly where you got those coins. I know who you had killed to steal them."

He stared at her, shock dousing his face, and suddenly stopped struggling.

"You," he whispered, as Dona Marjorie's guards hauled him into the cell. There was fear in his face now, stark and primal.

"You were told those coins weren't for sale, Ryvard." Marjorie's voice had gone cold as the stone around us. "You knew the fisher was disposing of them because they were too dangerous. But you couldn't bring yourself to let them slip through your fingers, could you? And now you pay the price."

"No," Harking gasped, hoarse and raw. "No, wait, I didn't... You can't..."

"You did. And I can." There was no mercy in Dona Marjorie's tone. "I'm afraid you're about to learn what happens when you cross the Fisher Queen."

I stared at Marjorie in shock.

The vengeance Harking had been running from had found him at last. He'd walked right into her house.

Dona Marjorie gave him an exaggerated coquettish wave as her guards threw him into the cell and slammed the door. The sound reverberated through the cellar with the grand finality of a tomb door closing.

She turned to me then, all smiles. It occurred to me that now I knew her secret, and I was in her cellar surrounded by her people, none of whom looked surprised by this turn of events at all. Carter's mustache didn't so much as twitch. They were all her fishers, every one of them.

I'd better hope she liked me as much as I thought she did.

"Well! Stars, this has been an exciting night!" Her eyes twinkled.

I swallowed. "You have no idea."

"Now, I know I can trust your discretion, Signa Kembral."

"Naturally, Dona Marjorie."

"That's what I love about you, dear." She patted my cheek. "You're a professional."

She turned to one of her guards, then, looking them up and down. "And you, too, Signa Nonesuch, I hope? I do a great deal of business with the Cats, as you well know."

I had to pick up my jaw off the floor as one of the guards shimmered all over, her servant's uniform transforming to a silvery gown, her blond braid and pale skin darkening. None of the other guards looked surprised, which made me feel like a bit of a fool.

"Of course." Rika gave Dona Marjorie a sly wink. "We keep our clients' secrets, Your Majesty."

Marjorie laughed fondly at that, returning the wink with a blown kiss.

"Dona Harking might not be so discreet," I pointed out, somewhat reluctantly. The last thing I wanted was for her to decide she needed to murder him in front of me—I'd have to report that.

"Oh, he'll keep his mouth shut. He's got bigger secrets than *this* in the Fisher Queen's ledgers. Even now he's thinking of all the ways I could destroy him, if I chose." She fanned herself as if she could waft her usual breathlessly sweet persona back into place. "So many people underestimate you if you're kind. They don't understand that kindness is a sign of strength. Stars, if I were weak like him, I suppose I couldn't afford to be so nice!"

"Anyone who underestimates you is a fool."

"Oh, don't say that! I work so hard to make sure they do." Marjorie beamed. "Now, why don't you give me that nasty coin? I'll see that it's safely disposed of."

I hesitated. "Will you be cursed if you touch it?"

"Aren't you sweet! No, don't worry, you have to hold on to it for at least a few days before it can hurt you. Otherwise Ryvard certainly wouldn't have been handling it. But if you kept it for a week, well—one morning you just wouldn't wake up."

Her words went through me like lightning. *Exactly like the Redgrave witnesses who died.* And the smuggler had been murdered about ten months ago, around the same time I'd been investigating the Redgrave scandal. This was it—the connection Harking hadn't wanted me to make.

I could trace the coins; they were the link I'd been looking for, the connection I'd been on the verge of making. This must be why he'd tried to kill me. I finally had the proof I needed to bring the bastard down.

And it had absolutely nothing to do with Rai's invitation.

I handed the coin to Marjorie in a daze. She patted it safely away in a hidden pocket in her voluminous skirts, then clapped her hands.

"Now, we'd best get back to the party! A good host shouldn't leave her guests for too long."

Rika fell in by my side as we made our way back through the cellars.

"That was beautiful," she murmured. "I hope this is the reality that sticks. If we could ring in the New Year with Harking locked up and facing criminal charges, it would be amazing."

"I wouldn't mind that," I agreed. With the evidence I had on him now and Marjorie on my side, I even had a hope of landing him in prison despite all his wealth and power.

Our hands brushed together, and Rika's little finger hooked through mine, neat as picking a pocket.

It was a small thing, a gesture that seemed casual, almost accidental, but it asked a question. One I wasn't remotely prepared to answer.

Surely Rika must understand that I wasn't in any position for romance right now. Even setting aside the matter of saving the world, I had a baby at home. As soon as tonight was over, I'd be back to spending every moment of every day struggling to take care of her (and somehow also myself). I'd be a messy, grouchy, sleepless wreck unfit for human company.

I didn't untangle my finger from hers. Maybe that was an answer, or maybe I was just not quite ready to point out to her that she was making a serious mistake.

Rika swept her free hand expansively. "Harking in prison, the world saved, me not on probation, and you..." She gave me a piercing glance. "What *do* you want from the New Year?"

She really was set on making me think about difficult things, wasn't she?

"That's the question, isn't it? Everyone keeps either assuming I'm going back to work, or assuming I'm staying home with the baby. It's nice of you to actually ask."

Earlier tonight, I might have shied away from thinking about it. But now...I could apparently still do the job. And despite all the horrible things that had happened, I was reveling in the sheer dizzying freedom of not having a baby constantly attached to me. Sure, I *also* wanted nothing more in the world right now than to be curled up with Emmi in my arms, warm and sweet and safe (and nursing, for love of the Void—my milk ducts were so full they felt like steel cables). But being out on my own, doing Hound things, was sweeping thick cobwebs out of my brain I hadn't known were there.

"I want to go back. I think I *need* to go back. But there are only so many hours in the day, and only so much energy in my soul. I'm worried that if I try to be a Hound *and* a mother, I'll be half-assing both of them."

Rika gave me a strange look, like she was suppressing a laugh—or something more bittersweet than a laugh, perhaps.

"Leave it to you to take a question about your dreams for the New Year and make it all about work."

"I want to see a lot more of my friends, too." Greatly daring, I added, "Like you."

"Well." She gave me an amused glance. "I suppose that's progress. I'll take it. But, Kembral—you're incapable of half-assing anything. I wouldn't worry about being a bad mother or a bad Hound. I'd be much more worried about you not sleeping, running yourself into the ground, and winding up in the guild infirmary."

"That's also a possible outcome," I admitted.

"*Or,*" she suggested, "you could let your friends help you. Or let your guild help you. Or *hire* someone, for Void's sake. You're a senior Hound—they've got to pay you decently."

"I…They do, but…" I instinctively resisted the idea, but I couldn't articulate why.

Well…if I were entirely honest with myself, yes I could. It was because I didn't want to admit that I couldn't do it all by myself. Because I hated feeling small and inadequate and helpless. Because I didn't want to face that I'd actually needed Beryl.

Bah. I could get better help than Beryl recruiting random urchins off the street.

"All right," I conceded. "You have a point."

Rika's finger was still hooked through mine. She hadn't said anything about it. Maybe I shouldn't say anything, either, and pretend I hadn't noticed. I could have this small, nice thing for myself, in this moment.

We climbed the stairs up out of the cellars; warm, shifting light filtered from above to touch Rika's face. The moment we stepped back into that ballroom, we'd have to scramble to make up the time we'd lost; since Harking's secret hadn't been that he'd invited Rai after all, we'd have to talk to Vandelle next, and if it wasn't her, I didn't know what we'd do. I didn't want to return to the aboveground world of desperation and death, of Empyrean power struggles and the great turning wheels of fate. I wished I could slow down these last few seconds, where I didn't have to think about anything weightier than the feel of Rika's finger linked with mine.

But it couldn't last. In only a few heartbeats, we stepped back through a curtain of fluttering silk into the ballroom.

It was on fire.

Hungry orange flames licked up the delicate silk panels in wicked shifting patterns. Thick clouds of black smoke hid the ceiling, plunging the room into night. The scattered remnants of celebration littered the floor: torn swaths of silk, shattered glass, trampled food, broken and overturned furniture.

Among the wreckage sprawled about a dozen bodies, bloody and still. Everyone else cowered in the one corner of the room that wasn't ablaze, huddled together for comfort. Most were on their knees; others lay protected in the arms of their friends, clearly injured. Jaycel was among the latter, Blair fussing over a dark stain on her side. The Clockmaker crouched behind her clock, hands over her mouth, unnoticed by anyone but me.

Alone in the center of the room, fire reflected in her eyes, stood Tarchasia Vandelle.

BE READY TO IMPROVISE

Marjorie," Vandelle rasped, her voice dragged out from some sharp and ragged place. "It's not what you think."

Marjorie's fan snapped closed like an axe falling. When she spoke, her voice was soft.

"Tarchasia. Oh, Tarchasia. What have you done?"

My hand slid from Rika's. I let my fingers curl into place around the grip of my sword, but I didn't draw yet. This was a moment too dangerous and delicate to cut with bared steel.

"I..." Vandelle sank clawed fingers deep into the grey shock of her hair. "This isn't how it was supposed to happen. This was never what I wanted."

"No," said a deep, familiar voice from the shadows at the back of the room. "But it's a price you were willing to pay."

Rai coalesced from the darkness like a bad dream, trailing smoke and shreds of night sky.

Shit. We were in the cellars too long, and Rai had made his move. Harking's scheming would cost us everything.

Vandelle turned to the Empyrean, her face twisting as if in pain. "You promised me a better Acantis."

Rai advanced on her. "And you shall have it."

She gestured furiously at the flames, the choking smoke that stung my eyes and left them streaming. "This isn't better!"

"You are the conqueror, Tarchasia Vandelle. When the year has turned, in the light of the Snow Moon when all is fresh and new, you can take this city in your hand and shape it as you always wanted." Rai reached out to touch her cheek. "Acantis belongs to you. It is my gift."

He was gazing at Vandelle with something like adoration. As if she were something beautiful, something necessary—his salvation.

His anchor.

Rika and I exchanged an anguished glance. I could tell she'd come to the same realization I had: *ambition*. Rai's equilibrium thread. At first I'd thought of people like Harking, power hungry and selfish, but an idealist like Vandelle wanted so much more than Harking ever could. Because she wanted it not for herself, but for the whole city.

"Tarchasia," Marjorie began gravely, "Acantis *is* its people. You know that better than anyone."

"Of course I do!" Vandelle's hands curled into fists. "Do you think I'd do this for anything less?"

Rai held out his hand to her. "You are a waning Silk Moon. You understand the necessity to unravel the old before you can weave anew. Come. You're in far too deep to stop now. Let's finish this."

Vandelle squeezed her eyes shut; tears leaked from the corners. "Do what you must. But don't kill anyone you don't need to."

"As you will it." Rai turned toward us, and the dry hot wind from the flames seemed to suddenly go fever-cold. "Now. Tell me where you've hidden them—the other Silk Moons."

My pulse quickened. Marjorie must have gotten them to the safe room before Rai arrived. If we could stall him until midnight somehow, we had a chance.

Rai didn't look like he intended to allow himself to be stalled. He drew his great black sword in a long, liquid motion and began pacing toward us. The twisting orange light of the fire gilded his pale, intent face.

I stepped in front of the others. It was the last place I wanted to be, but everyone else seemed frozen with dread—except Rika, who had vanished. I uttered a silent prayer to the Moon that she had a better plan than I did.

I kept my sword in its sheath for now. I had to get him talking.

"Maybe Dona Vandelle is the only Silk Moon here," I suggested, taking a wild stab at the one thing he seemed to care about. "What will you do then?"

"I don't waste time contemplating theoretical questions." Silver eyes fixed on me. "I see that someone has lifted my curse. I hope the price you paid was worth it."

A wide circle of flames sprang up suddenly around me. I recoiled from the heat, cursing. Somewhere beyond the whoosh and snap of them, past the blinding angry light, Rika called my name.

Rai stepped through the wall of fire, its orange fingers caressing him harmlessly before sliding off. His sword tip rose swift and terrible as lightning to hover an inch from my heart. I barely managed to keep myself from stepping backward into the flames.

"Tell me where they are," he said softly.

My fingers flexed on my sword hilt. The flames baked the sweat dry off my skin before it could even form; my throat stung from the smoke. He could kill me in an eyeblink. I met his mirror gaze, hoping he couldn't tell how vigorously my heart thundered with his blade so close to piercing it.

"There's one right behind you," I said. "You've killed her before. What's stopping you now?"

"Before, she was a possibility. Now, she is a promise." Triumph shone from his face like moonlight, the weariness I'd seen before burning away. "I came here to name the year, hoping it would be for her. For one who wants so much, and who has pursued it so relentlessly. She has heard the call and risen to it at last. She's mine now, and has become the one mortal here I will not sacrifice."

"If you push her too far, you'll lose her anyway." I pitched my voice hoping Vandelle would hear me. "Dona Vandelle is a good person. She wouldn't condone a slaughter like this. She'll reject your bargain."

"You think so?" Amusement twisted his mouth. "How little you know her."

He cocked his head as if listening. The crackle and mutter of the flames encircling us made it hard to hear what was going on beyond them, but there was Marjorie's soft, stern voice, and Vandelle's raised defensively. I made out a brief fragment:

"They attacked us, Marjorie! I had no choice!"

"There is always a choice, Tarchasia."

Bitter disappointment struggled with disbelief in the back of my throat. Damn, I really liked Vandelle. How could it have come to this?

"Now." Rai's sword point pricked my sternum. "Tell me where they are, Kembral Thorne. My patience is far from infinite."

"Signa Kembral?" Marjorie called, concern in her voice. "Are you all right in there?"

"I'm fine," I snapped.

I wasn't. I was out of topics and out of time, and I'd only bought a few minutes. We were nowhere near midnight. Rika or Marjorie or just about anyone would be better at this, curse it. I was bad at drawing things out; I always wanted to get straight to the point. And now I was about to die for it.

"Remember," Vandelle barked, "no unnecessary killing!"

"Everything I do is necessary." Rai's gaze never left mine. "Last chance."

I had no clever answer. I eased my mind toward the delicate equilibrium that would let me slip into the Veil, hoping to dodge back through the flames.

"So be it," Rai said. "I'm disappointed. You could have been useful, dog."

BOOOOOOONNNNGGG.

The peal of the clock crashed through us all, shaking the world down to its bones. For one flicker of an instant, I wondered if he'd somehow already killed me.

BOOOOOONNNNG.

The black sword tip wavered, retreating from my chest. Rai's mirror eyes went wide.

"*What?!*" he breathed.

I was just as stupefied. We stared at each other, rendered equals for one brief moment by complete and utter shock.

BOOOOOOONNNNG. The tolling of the clock set reality to wavering. Rai whirled, his starry cloak flaring, and the circle of flames dropped to a mere smoldering ring.

Beyond it, Vandelle slumped, eyes dull, blood staining her mouth. Rika half caught her in one arm, lowering her gently toward the floor.

In her other hand she held a long dagger, shining darkly with Vandelle's blood.

DESPAIR IS THE ENEMY

I was standing in water.

The skirt of my peacock-tail coat dragged in it; a sluggish current lapped at my knees. It was strangely warm, a contrast to the cold damp air in the dark, echoing space that was slowly coming into focus around me. And there was a smell—a terrible, coppery, familiar smell.

It wasn't water. I was standing in blood. An endless lake of it, stretching out between bulky stone columns beneath an ominously low vaulted ceiling. I could have reached up and touched the rough, damp stone.

Of *course* it was blood. It only seemed appropriate, after everything that had just happened.

Rika's face in that last moment stayed seared into my mind. Grim, a little sad, but without regret. And Vandelle's—first with flames reflected in her eyes, then still and empty with death. *Void's teeth, Vandelle.* What had happened since I'd last talked to her, to make her choose something like *that*? She hadn't seemed desperate enough, despairing enough, to stand above a floor strewn with corpses and tell an Empyrean to *do what you must.*

Maybe I didn't understand people as well as I thought I did. Maybe

I was wrong about everyone I'd ever known, and I was the one deluded fool who valued human life.

A wave of trembling took me. I groped instinctively for some wry thought to make everything seem less awful, some morbid joke I could mutter to the dank gruesome emptiness around me to keep it at a safe distance, but I had nothing. Everything had gone so horribly, utterly wrong, and we'd lost again, and now we were nine Echoes down, and I was utterly exhausted and running out of hope.

I looked around, nerves on edge, half expecting to see some scene of carnage already. But there was nothing—just the red lake reaching in all directions. Dull lights flickered on the thick square support pillars, open flames ruddy in the shadows. An odd glow shone from beyond the most distant columns, its source invisible. The vaulted space stretched on seemingly forever, but the massive weight of stone hanging so low overhead made it feel claustrophobic.

There was no sign of Rika, or anyone else nearby. Some distance away, little clumps of partygoers stood in tight backlit clusters, holding glasses of what I dearly hoped was wine. Their laughter echoed strangely over the lake, ricocheting in hollow emptiness beneath the vaulted ceiling. Gowns and coattails trailed in the blood, leaving a wake when people moved.

In the center of everything stood the clock, unchanged, blood lapping at its sides.

I muttered a curse and started wading toward one of the distant clusters of people. They didn't seem to get closer as quickly as they should. It was *work* walking through this stuff; it dragged sullenly at my legs, and the smell was getting to me. I considered taking a standing rest, but no—I didn't dare lose any time.

"Kembral!"

It was Rika's voice, chasing its own echoes across the lake.

My heart jumped. I turned without hesitation, like a compass needle jerking instinctively northward. It didn't matter how I felt about what she'd done; I needed to find her, felt unsafe and alone without her in this accursed place. The pale silvery glimmer of her dress in the darkness between distant columns drew me as sure as a moth to the flame.

Her face emerged from the shadows, edged by flickering torch-light, drawn and worried.

"*There* you are. Thank the Moon."

"Rika." Her name came out jagged edged. All I could think of was the blood-slicked knife in her hand.

She glanced away. "Don't look at me like that. She won't stay dead, and he was about to kill you. It was all I could think to do."

"I wish the one thing you could think of wasn't murder."

"I couldn't just stand there and let him kill you," she said fiercely. "It did the job. No one got permanently hurt. We stopped him."

"You made a blood seal."

"No, I..." Her eyes went wide. "Shit. Did I?"

"The clock rang. It only does that when someone successfully carves a blood seal into that Echo. It doesn't matter whether you meant to or not. You made the seal, Rika."

She bit her lip. "But... can someone who's not a player *do* that?"

I stared at her, the implications settling in like spilled wine into a white tablecloth. "No."

"It doesn't make any *sense*! How am I a player?" She frowned. "For that matter, how are *you* a player?"

It was a damned good question. And it was easier to think about than the other questions sitting heavy in the hollows of my mind, like how I felt about a murder that wasn't a murder and whether I was grateful or upset or a potent mix of both. I nudged my brain into the safe, familiar, logical track of unraveling the mystery.

"According to the Clockmaker, players have to make a blood sacrifice in each Echo to stay in the game." I closed my eyes, trying to remember exactly what she'd said. "It doesn't have to be a death. Those beetles were barely nibbling people to make their sacrifice. And—oh."

"What?"

I opened my eyes and held up my finger. My *cut* finger, with the sparkling little bits of magic clock keeping it from closing up. I'd been leaving a very small, very slow blood trail through every single Echo behind me.

"She never said it couldn't be your own blood," I said.

"That explains you, but what about me? I didn't cut myself until the second Echo."

"But you killed that assassin in Prime, right as you arrived. That counted. And you might not remember, but in the first Echo, you cut yourself somehow—something Cail handed you."

"Fantastic." Rika raked a frustrated hand through her hair. "I don't want this. No, no, I quit."

She reached into what looked like a mere fold in her gown and pulled out a little bit of cloth, the kind you might wipe the lenses of spectacles with—or that you might use to wipe away any smudges left by your touch, if you were a Cat. With brutal efficiency, she wrapped it around an apparently unblemished fingertip, tying it in place with a bit of string from the same hidden pocket. The makeshift bandage looked ludicrous until it shimmered with illusion and vanished.

"Got any more of that?" I asked.

"No," she said sharply. "You should stay in the game. Just in case we need a player for something."

"How come *you* get to be the one to quit?"

"Because I'll kill someone if I need to, and I don't want to make a blood seal again."

"Not killing someone is also an option, you know," I pointed out, with a bit more feeling than I maybe meant to.

I'd had to confront the possibility of needing to kill one person to protect another plenty of times in my career; I'd always wondered if I could do it. In the heat of the fight, yes, probably. The cold calculation Rika had made in killing Vandelle felt different, though, and it fit uneasily in the space I'd shaped for her in my heart.

Rika didn't look away this time; her grey gaze bored into mine. "No. Not if the alternative is watching you die. I will *never* let that happen."

"Vandelle wasn't—"

"What would you do if someone tried to hurt Emmi?"

"I'd rip them apart with my bare hands," I said, without hesitation.

Rika made a gracious *you see* gesture, her wrist fluid, one brow raised.

"That's different."

"Is it?"

I opened my mouth to protest that of course it was—Emmi was my daughter, who I loved past reason, past the bounds of morality, and I'd burn the city down to keep her safe. And then the intensity in Rika's eyes got through to me, and I snapped my mouth shut.

Surely she didn't mean...?

She did.

The thought that I might be *that* motivating to Rika was a little alarming. The inexplicable flush of warmth, like she'd wrapped me in a cozy blanket, was even more so.

My face heated. "All right. Fine."

Rika blinked, taken aback by my sudden agreement. "I...Yes. Glad you see it my way."

I cleared my throat, failing to dislodge the feelings stuck there. I was *not* remotely prepared to deal with all this right now. "So. Right. Have you seen Dona Vandelle?"

She gave me a sidelong look, but accepted the change of subject. "You think it's worth talking to her? After *that*?"

"I don't know. I don't understand how she got there. She didn't seem...well, I'm maybe too optimistic about people." I sighed. "You realize she's his anchor, right?"

Rika's lips pressed together, and she nodded.

"What do you think that means?" I asked, lost. "Is it part of the game? Do *all* the Empyreans have anchors here?"

"I don't see how they could. I rather doubt Dona Swift gave them control over her guest list." Rika tipped her head. "You noticed how Rai's focus shifted rather creepily to Vandelle last Echo, yes? He still wanted to make his blood seal, but suddenly it was all about *her* in a way that it definitely wasn't before."

"Something changed, yeah. He said that she's *his* now."

"She must have agreed to be his anchor while we were dealing with Harking—either explicitly or by accepting some bargain to conquer Acantis. I think it changed everything for him. I don't think it's directly part of the game; I think his priorities have shifted. When

Empyreans get focused on an anchor, they . . ." She shivered. "It can get very intense."

"But we still need her to uninvite him. It's our only option. Look at this place—I don't think it even *has* Dona Marjorie's safe room."

Rika gave me a long dubious look, then sighed. "All right. I want to get this over with and get out of this horrible Echo. Let's go find her and try."

We sloshed through the dim echoing vaults, from one ruddy torch to the next. I sure as stars wouldn't want to try to sneak up on someone in this mess. Rika shuddered, holding her gown up as best she could.

"I guess we know what Moon *this* is," she said.

"Yeah, I—" I broke off as a sudden irrational panic seized me. *My boots.*

With a great flailing and splashing, I pulled one leg up out of the blood in a panic. I stood on one foot, holding my own calf as if it were a wounded animal. The leather beneath my hands was inexplicably dry. Relief washed through me. My Damn Good Boots were okay. I knew it was a ridiculous thing to be worried about, all things considered, but it was one small thing that the night hadn't yet ruined.

I would have felt even more foolish if Rika weren't holding up the edges of her smoke-and-silver gown with a similar sigh of relief.

"Thank the Moon it doesn't stick," she said. "It's still disgusting, though."

"At least it's not raining on us." I reluctantly put my foot back down; the blood swirled sluggishly around my leg.

"Don't give the Echo ideas."

We trudged on. All I could feel was a dull, horrified resignation. This was a far more fitting setting for tonight's squalor than any of the more sparkling and beautiful Echoes, I supposed. Maybe as you got deep enough, they stopped lying and showed you the truth of things.

Oof, I might need someone to talk to after this was over. I imagined trying to explain it to my sister—her eyebrows climbing ever higher, asking me what in the Void I saw in this job and why under the Moon I wasn't staying home with Emmi like a sensible person.

This was why I needed someone in my life who *wasn't* sensible. I caught myself before I could glance at Rika.

"This is horrible," she muttered. "This whole night has been so awful. I wish I could forget it all, like everyone else."

"I don't," I said, without hesitation.

Rika waved me off wearily. "I know, I know, you're glad you're aware of what's going on so you can protect everyone. I mean, I am too, in a less annoying Hound sort of way, but—"

"That's not what I meant." My neck was heating up, but I pushed ahead. "If I forgot everything, I wouldn't remember all the parts with you."

The rhythmic splash of Rika's footsteps paused, a brief hitch like a skipped heartbeat.

"Not all those parts were great," she said cautiously.

"Oh, sure. But if I didn't remember, we'd be back to fighting. Or whatever we were doing." I shrugged self-consciously. "This is probably the worst night of my life. The only gleam of light has been what's happened with us. But I'd rather live with all the bad memories forever than lose what we gained tonight."

Well, now I'd made everything awkward. My whole face was on fire, and I stared down into the murky roiling blood at my feet.

Rika touched my shoulder, feather-light, and I looked back up. Her grey eyes crinkled at the corners.

"You're a strange creature, Kembral Thorne. Your priorities are pretty messed up. But I'm glad we're all right again, too."

All right again didn't begin to sum up what had changed between us, but I couldn't find words to describe it, either. We'd had some *experiences* together, and if someone had crafted the vocabulary for what that did to our relationship, I'd never learned it.

I was spared having to think of how to respond by spotting Vandelle at last. She leaned against one of the rough stone pillars in a jacket of crimson velvet, staring into her wine cup and frowning. The sight of her sent a jolt through my stomach; I remembered her standing amid the ruin of her own making, with fire reflected in her eyes.

When she saw us approaching, she grinned a disturbingly normal grin and raised her glass.

"Signa Thorne. Signa Nonesuch." She lifted the glass to her lips as if she were about to drink, then wrinkled her nose and stared into the cup again. "This doesn't seem quite up to Marjorie's usual standards." Rika gave a somewhat nervous little laugh. "I think it's off. I wouldn't drink it."

I wasn't sure how to deal with the friendly expression on Vandelle's face, or her usual relaxed slouch, or the guileless way she looked at us as if she hadn't just unleashed destruction on everyone here. Being Vandelle, she always looked a *little* like she might be plotting the overthrow of the Acantis government—but not with anything more violent than stinging rhetoric, organized workers, and maybe the rare well-deserved face punch.

I could jump into demanding she uninvite Rai. But we were nine Echoes down; I had no margin of error. If I pushed her too hard and we lost this chance, it would be disastrous.

"How are you?" I asked tentatively, for lack of a better opening gambit.

Rika gave me a disbelieving look.

Vandelle sighed, swirling her glass as if still deciding whether to drink it. I glimpsed enough to be pretty sure it was more blood in there.

"Honestly? I'm angry and I'm tired."

She looked it. Her grey hair seemed even more scruffy than usual, and lines of tension fanned beside her eyes. I wondered if some deep part of her remembered everything that had happened, even if her body and mind didn't—if all the horrors happening again and again to the party guests left marks on their souls, or if they remained clean of it as new-fallen snow.

"Angry about what?" I prodded.

She shrugged, a restless motion. "That warehouse collapse the other day. Something Harking just said to me. This whole rotten city."

"You love this city."

"I love the good parts of it. I love what it could be." She shook her head. "I used to think I could change it within the system, you know. Get elected to the council, make some good speeches, pass some laws. Now... We're a democracy, damn it, but old money rules Acantis sure as if it were the Cathardian monarchy. If there's a good way out, I don't see it. I'm starting to think we've got to throw it all away and start over."

Rika and I exchanged meaningful glances.

"You can't just throw out a system of government," Rika pointed out reasonably. "That's a coup, or a revolution; it requires violence. The council may be half corrupt, but it could be worse—you and Marjorie are on it, after all—and if you tear it down by force, people are going to die."

Vandelle gave us a long, weary look, but I got the feeling she wasn't seeing us. "*Or people are going to die,*" she whispered. "Stars. I can't tell you the number of times I told them that."

"Dona Vandelle?" I asked uncertainly.

"You've got to pass this housing-reform law, or there'll be more building collapses, and people are going to die. You've got to pass this working-conditions law, or the miners will keep getting lung rot, and people are going to die. And do you know what happened?"

I did. Unfortunately. "They didn't pass them."

"And people died. And Harking and his ilk don't care, because they're *poor Dockside scum.*" Vandelle's lips twisted bitterly. "If risking harm to a handful of the city's elite will save the lives of hundreds— no, *thousands*—in Dockside, I'd be no better than a traitor to the people I represent if I didn't take that chance."

"Harking's going to prison," I said desperately. "I've finally got the evidence to do it."

Vandelle laughed, but there was no mirth in it. "It doesn't matter. Fuck, it doesn't matter. He'll buy his way out in ten minutes. No one is ever going to hold his lot accountable. No, there's only one way out."

She tossed her empty wineglass over her shoulder. It vanished into the blood without a splash, as if something hungry had swallowed it.

"It's time to burn it all down."

Before I could reply, a cold breeze set the lake around us to rippling. Lights glimmered in the shadows behind Vandelle—a scattering of stars.

They shone from a swath of greater darkness that unfolded in sudden and terrible grandeur, blotting out the flickering torchlight. At its center, twin silver gleams pierced the vaulted gloom.

"You're ready, then?" Rai asked, stepping forth into the light, his cloak spread around him in wings of celestial glory. His mirror eyes fixed on Vandelle with something like pride; an odd, hungry smile touched his lips.

Vandelle faced him resolutely. "Yes. I'm ready at last."

OWN YOUR MISTAKES

Wait!" I reached for Vandelle in desperation. "Don't listen to him! He's going to—"

"*You* two stay away from her."

Rai's gaze flashed with blinding silver light. An invisible force hit my chest as if a giant had punched me; I went flying backward, the breath whooshing out of my lungs, and splashed down into the blood. It entered my mouth, salty and nauseating; I struggled to rise, straining after breath, blood sloshing thickly around me. By the splashing at my side, Rika was in similar straits.

With a great and terrible grinding of rock, the subterranean space around us began to change.

The low ceiling heaved upward over Vandelle, rising into a vaulted dome. The ground beneath her rose, lifting her up above the red lake; startlement flickered across her face, but she caught her balance and rode it grimly, looming over the rest of us. From all directions, exclamations sounded; some of the distant figures drew closer, coming to see what was going on.

No, I thought at them, *run away*. But my lungs hadn't succeeded at sucking in air yet, and I had no breath to speak with.

"Behold!" Rai called, and his voice was a thunderclap. "The old year is dying! Now is the Sickle Moon, the time of reaping. The time when long-laid plans come at last to fruition, and the old must die so the new can be born."

An audience was gathering, fear in their faces. Vandelle stood above them, arms crossed, glowering down at the elite of the city with indomitable resolve. She had made her bargain, and she was claiming her due.

Rai swept an arm up toward her. His face lit up with an ecstatic, devouring joy.

"Attend now the reaper!"

Vandelle stepped into the moment he'd prepared for her like she'd been born to it. She flung her arms wide, embracing the sudden wind that blew back her tailcoat and reddened her cheeks.

"This city has been sick for a long time." Her voice rang out with all the confident charisma of a Butterfly performing at the Grand Theater. "Sick and suffering with corruption and rot that feeds upon its own people. But I'm here to cure it. To *save* it. To let it become what it always was meant to be."

I'd managed to drag in a few ragged breaths, getting my lungs working again. I started to shout Vandelle's name, but Rika's hand clamped over my mouth.

"He'll kill you if you interrupt her," she hissed. "She's gone, Kembral. It's too late. She's *his*."

"I refuse to accept that," I growled against her hand, which eased when she saw I wasn't about to yell. "We can still convince her to turn on him."

"Even if we did, he's already inside the ward! It's too late!"

"For this Echo," I agreed grimly. "But we can save the next one."

Vandelle had raised her arms as if she could call down the lightning. "It's time to cut out the rot. It's time to burn the old, corrupt system away and replace it with something fresh and new!" Her voice rose to a roar. "And it begins here, tonight!"

Rai smiled like a proud father. A faint silvery nimbus shone around him, as if her moment of glory kindled the light of the stars within him.

"Good," he murmured, his voice carrying across the lake of blood, settling it to shivering little ripples. "Very good. And now, my chosen, let us begin by destroying your enemies."

Oh, *that* didn't sound good. I turned to Rika.

"We've got to stop her. Come on."

I started toward Vandelle, but the blood had grown thick as molasses, its surface seething as if in a furious rain. It was hard to push through. Rika made a noise of frustration and followed close behind me.

A great rushing echoed between the broad pillars, and a wave surged from behind the crowd of onlookers, eliciting cries of alarm as it tugged at their garments and rocked some of them off their feet. It dumped a single figure in an elegant burgundy tailcoat on his knees at the base of Vandelle's platform, his hair bedraggled, his breath heaving with shock.

Harking. Before he could rise, dripping ropes of blood whipped out of the surging lake around him, wrapping his neck and arms, pulling dangerously tight. He made a choking sound that approximated Vandelle's name before they cut his air off.

"Decree his fate," Rai urged Vandelle. "Now is your moment; he is helpless before you. Crush him beneath your boot and climb to your rightful place over his corpse. Remake your city upon the worthless bones of those who stand in your way."

"Dona Vandelle!" I called desperately. "He's using you! He's going to unleash death and slaughter on Acantis in your name! He's here on your invitation—you've got to revoke it!"

Vandelle froze. Her eyes gleamed with a feverish spark in the torchlight.

Out of nowhere, Rika tackled me. We splashed down into the lake of blood, rolling through waves that slapped at us angrily. I barely had time to be shocked before a great chunk of stone crashed down from the ceiling, right where I'd been standing. A red wave drenched us, knocking us back again just as we were struggling to rise.

"I told you I wouldn't let you die," Rika gasped.

Vandelle stared down at Harking, a struggle on her face. He drew in ragged, tortured breaths that barely scraped past his constricted throat, struggling against the red cords that held him, staring at her in a mute and furious plea.

"This...isn't right." She dragged the reluctant words out over gravel.

Rai laid an arm across her shoulders; the look on his face was almost tender. His wings folded the starry sky around them both.

"All is well, my chosen. In blood and death, at the turning of the year, you will rise. And the whole world shall behold the splendor of your glory."

The bonds of blood holding Harking twisted in a sudden, violent jerk. The snap of his neck breaking echoed from the damp stone pillars.

Shit. My breath hissed between my teeth. The crowd drew back with gasps and cries, gowns and coats trailing wetly. Harking's body collapsed into the blood; it swallowed him without a ripple.

Vandelle whirled on Rai. "*No.* I never wanted this."

"Oh, but you did." Rai chuckled, the sound old and full of dark wisdom. "I know you, my anchor. You *wanted* this. You *craved* this. To tear down your enemies and watch them perish. To burn all their works, and to build your own on the ashes. You called to me, and I came. I am here for *you.*"

"There's a difference," she said through her teeth, "between fantasizing about something and actually desiring it with your rational and conscious mind."

You tell him. I surged to my feet, red sloughing off me in stainless rivulets.

Rai lifted a silver brow. "Will you surrender this city to your enemies, then? Without my help, you cannot triumph. Will you truly *let them win?*"

Vandelle stiffened. "No! Of course not! I won't let them have this city."

"Then do not flinch from destroying them."

"Don't listen to him!" Rika called as the two of us splashed closer. "There's *always* another way."

Vandelle's fists clenched at her sides. "But I've tried for so long. *So long.* Nothing makes a difference."

"You don't need him." All my fury at Rai exploded out of me through my voice. "Come on, Vandelle! You're a *Dockside* brat! You don't know how to give up—and you *never* need help from the powerful to get things done!"

Vandelle straightened, and a light came into her eyes. "Of course," she murmured. "Of *course.* That's always been the way."

All of a sudden, she whirled on Rai. "I don't want your help. I don't *need* your help. I'll find another way to win. And if I don't..." She drew in a breath. "So be it. I'd rather lose as a free and honest woman than win as the tool of an Empyrean."

The smile on Rai's face faded. Something almost like grief flickered in his eyes, a deep and bitter disappointment.

"Then you are no use to me," he said softly.

His ragged wings of starry night snapped wide.

A great and terrible groaning of rock began all around us, punctuated by sharp retorts. Cracks ran through the low stone ceiling, one after another, snaking fast as lightning. I grabbed Rika's hand and ran for the dome that arched up over Vandelle, where the cracks hadn't yet reached.

Vandelle stood her ground. She glared at Rai, anger blazing in her face. "Laughing As He Rises, I revoke my invitation. There is no covenant between us. You are hereby uninvited; I sever our agreement, and I cast you off. Three times I declare it."

Her voice echoed through the vaulted cellar, stirring little skittering ripples in the bloody lake. I tensed; everything went quiet and still.

No wave of magic pushed Rai out. No tolling bell sounded from the great clock. He was already inside the ward. Vandelle's repudiation had changed everything and nothing.

The cracks spread through the ceiling, an awful rumbling growing louder. One massive chunk of rock crashed down, then another, sending waves careening in all directions. People ran and screamed, but there was nowhere to go except the dubious stability of the dome, where an angry Empyrean awaited.

A slab of stone as big as my torso plummeted toward the great clock. I glimpsed a flash of pale hair and a smudged smock beneath it, and I sucked in a horrified breath.

The Clockmaker flung her arms around the clock as if to protect it, and a faint shimmer of amber light surrounded her, like a thin golden soap bubble. The rock bounced harmlessly off, landing ten feet away with a tremendous splash.

Was this the protection I'd accidentally given her? *Holy shit.*

Rai ignored the deadly rain of masonry. He radiated fury, his attention fixed entirely on Vandelle.

"I overestimated you, Tarchasia Vandelle, if you cast aside your chance at greatness for the sake of something so petty as a conscience."

Vandelle visibly steeled herself against taking a step back. She looked at him and saw death in his face, and she didn't cringe away. "There's nothing petty about wanting the hands that hold this city to be clean of blood."

"You came to me burning with a hungry light I marveled to see." Rai spoke softly, but the air shivered with his anger. "You *shone* with the consuming worthiness of your ambition. And so I exalted you with my favor. But now you suddenly have no *stomach* for the revolution you craved with all your soul."

Vandelle stared at him, pale and set, her hands curled into fists. "Signa Thorne is right," she said. "I'm a Dockside brat. You can keep your greatness; I don't want it. I just want a better city, and you're making it amply clear that yet again, I can't trust anyone to give it to me. I'm going to have to take it myself."

Rai's voice rose, trembling with some strange Empyrean emotion. "You disappoint me. You *disgust* me. You are a false fire, an empty promise, a snuffed-out candle with no future but blowing dust."

He stepped close to Vandelle. I drew my sword, ready to intervene, Rika a step behind me as we reached the base of the platform; Vandelle saw and gave her head a sharp shake, stopping us.

"I will give you one last chance." Rai reached out with great tenderness, his hand trembling, and touched Vandelle's cheek. "Tell me you're ready, Tarchasia Vandelle. Tell me the time has come to burn this city down so that you may rise like a phoenix from its ashes. Tell me to make your wish come true."

Dust rained down from the cracking ceiling. An entire section collapsed with terrible thunder, crashing down on a huddle of frightened youths in feather-trimmed scarlet tailcoats. My stomach wrenched with horror—there was no way they'd survived. The waves from the impact shoved against us, rocking me onto my toes.

All sound went suddenly distant: the boom and rush of blood against stone muffled, the screams of the wounded and the terrified gone far away. A great listening silence enfolded Vandelle, hanging on her answer. Rika's fingers dug painfully into my bicep.

"Get ready to tackle her if she gives in," she whispered, her breath barely stirring the air by my ear.

"She won't."

Vandelle looked at Rai with something that was very nearly pity.

"Tell me," he whispered.

Her voice firm and immutable as the bedrock of Prime, she answered, "No."

Rai's face twisted bitterly. His hand moved so quickly I saw only a clawing blur, with no time to react. There was an awful tearing crunch, and blood sprayed from Vandelle's neck onto his face.

"No!" I cried, lunging forward. But it was too late.

Vandelle crumpled and slid from the platform, the lake claiming her body with a murky splash.

"I'll still win," Rai said through his teeth, sheathing his sword in a fury. He turned his back on Vandelle's body as it sank slowly into the blood. "I *always* win."

Rika stepped forward, fury in her gaze. "Why did you do that? If Vandelle was your anchor, you don't have a cause anymore! Do you even have a reason to name the year at all?"

He whirled on her. Some molten substance ran down his cheeks, spilling from his eyes in sluggish beads like quicksilver. The rage on his face transcended anything human.

"I can *never* accept defeat," he snarled at her. "Do you understand me, foolish infant? I do not cede this game. I have other paths to victory, and other anchors; I can name this year for them. I can survive. But I must always, always, always..."

He trailed off. Some shudder of immortal exhaustion shook him, older than time itself.

"There will *always* be more rounds," he said softly, and without any particular relish. "There will always be more games, more contests, more wars. And I will triumph in each and every one of them, and cast you all down to perish at my feet."

He sounded as hollow as if he were speaking his own doom.

More stone tumbled down around us, the impacts shaking the ground and riling the lake to chaos. The clock began its deep awful toll, and the world fell into pieces once more.

The last thing I saw in that Echo was the bleak desperation in his ancient, mirror-bright eyes.

DON'T GET COMPLACENT

The new reality assaulted my senses before my feet even seemed to touch down on the ballroom floor.

Everything exploded with bright colors, from shimmering draperies shrouding the walls to vibrant displays of eye-catching fashion; the windows had turned to stained glass, including a great round one in the ceiling, casting shards of color across the dancers. Curtains of light moved and shifted through the room like an aurora: shivering bands of emerald and turquoise, violet and vermilion. As they swept across the ballroom, they changed the color of everything left in their wake. Dresses flipped from purple to gold, wine from red to lightning blue, the mosaics in the floor swapping palettes from cool to warm.

After the oppressive dim tomb of the lake of blood, it felt like an attack. Adrenaline still flooded my nerves, screaming at me to stab something; my nose kept telling me I still smelled blood. All the living, laughing, dancing people around me seemed just as *wrong* as the bodies I'd seen sink into the murk.

Rika stood beside me, breathing hard as if she'd been running.

"Is it done?" she whispered. "Dona Vandelle revoked his invitation. Are we safe?"

"We're ten Echoes down. We're not safe." I struggled to sort out the vibrant sensory mess around me. If things were this chaotic inside the Clockmaker's protections, I could only imagine that stepping outdoors would be downright lethal. "We can't assume the Empyreans won't find some other way in."

Rika let out a strained laugh. "No, no. You were supposed to say yes, we did it, we're safe. We can relax now."

I snorted. "I'm not about to tempt fate like that. Rai made his sacrifice and his blood seal last Echo, pulling the ceiling down on all those people, so he's still a player for now. Arhsta...we haven't seen any sign of her for a while. Do you think she's out?"

Rika grimaced. "No. Not having heard anything is a bad sign. It only means we don't know what she's doing."

"Speaking of which." I hesitated; this felt a little weird to bring up, but it was too important to let go. "That tip you got. The one that I'd be here, and in danger. Was it anonymous? Or possibly in some form that could be forged, like writing?"

"How did you—" She wiped the surprise off her face, going carefully neutral. "I can't answer that."

"Harking got a tip I'd be here, too. Presumably why he knew to send a hired killer after me—thanks for taking care of that, by the way. *And* the Clockmaker knew I'd be here and in danger. But I didn't even know I was coming here myself until two days ago, and I didn't tell anyone but Marjorie and my sister. So who was spreading it around?"

"Arhsta." Rika hissed the name between her teeth. "Why would she do that? Getting her pieces in place, I suppose. What does it mean?"

"I'm not sure yet. We should—"

I broke off as a sheet of snaking blue light wove across us, hazing my vision. For a brief moment, laughter or weeping sounded in my ears, and an itching like the feet of a thousand ants crawled across my skin.

Then the wave of color was gone. It left the floor beneath our feet a glassy deep cobalt blue and turned a nearby tablecloth to an ultramarine so intense it hurt my eyeballs, but Rika and I remained unchanged. Good thing, because I really liked this coat the way it was.

Rika shivered, edging closer to me. "Lovely. I always used to wonder what it'd be like to stand in a rainbow, but I didn't think it'd involve sizzling noises and feeling generally damp."

"Huh, I got something different. Clearly a Rainbow Moon, anyway."

She looked cold. I hesitated, then half lifted one arm, like a bird stretching its wing.

Rika tucked herself in against my side like she'd always belonged there. Every muscle in my body went stiff, and hers did, too; we were like two sticks bundled together.

"You should get a nice jacket," I murmured. "You're so cold."

Rika laughed ruefully. "It wouldn't work with the split sleeves, and I love this dress."

It hit me all at once that she'd killed a man for me in that dress.

She'd come here to protect me. She'd been protecting me all night, and before that, and I'd never known. *Damn.* I was so used to being the one doing the protecting, whether it was a client or Emmi or Acantis itself. Having someone else protect me—and to do it so competently I didn't even notice half the time—was kind of amazing.

Rika was warming and softening against my side, like butter out of the icebox. I wished we could stay here, just like this, looking out at the shimmering rainbow light show and the swirling clothes of the dancers. But I wasn't fool enough to believe that Rai would let us win so easily.

I cleared my throat. "We should talk to Dona Marjorie. Warn her about the threat again, and have her people make sure the wards are all still in place. And I want to check up on Pearson."

Rika shook her head. "That was close. I thought you might be in danger of relaxing for a second there."

"I'll relax when we're home safe."

"Will you? Somehow, I doubt it." She raised an eyebrow. "When this is over, I'm going to force you to sit in Hillcrest Park with me watching the sun go down over the bay and sipping wine just to see if sitting still that long actually makes you explode."

"Can't." I sighed. "Baby."

"Tea, then. I'll hold the baby for you. I like babies."

I stared at her as if she were a stranger. "You do? Bit hard to take with you when you're climbing up walls and swindling unwary Elders out of their secrets."

"There's a lot you don't know about me. Maybe you should find out." The teasing smile didn't quite leave her eyes, but it softened into something more serious.

"Rika…" I didn't want to say this, but I had to. "You know I'm a wreck now, right? Every single moment of my day, I'm taking care of Emmi. My house is a *sty* and unfit for company—but if I leave it, the baby has to come with me. Not to mention I can barely find time to bathe, so I'm not in any state to leave the house half the time in the first place. After everything I give to Emmi, I don't know how I'll have enough left over to not let everyone who's counting on me down. I can't—"

"Shh. You think that matters? I'm a mess, too, Kembral. We can be messes together. And I'm going to make you learn how to accept help if I have to break into your house and give it to you while you're sleeping."

It took me a long, long moment to blink my eyes clear. I swallowed a few times into the bargain, just to be safe.

"All right," I said at last. "Tea."

"It'll be lovely. You'll see." A satisfied smile curled her lips.

To compensate for such utter recklessness, I let her go, tugging my collar straight. "Come on. Relaxing later is all very well, but we can't afford it quite yet. You know as well as I do that the job isn't over until it's over."

She sighed, brushing slim fingers through the dark fall of her hair. "I suppose I do."

—m—

Pearson's color looked a little better, back to a healthy warm brown, his lips no longer alarmingly bluish. Someone had changed the bandages on his head, and his chest rose and fell peacefully. It was weird seeing him sleep. Pearson was always full of quick, darting motion, rarely quiet, never still.

"You look like you're going to live," I murmured to him. "Good. It wouldn't be the same if I had to report to somebody else who was more respectful of my time off."

I felt a bit bad about that (not that he could hear me), so I patted his shoulder.

"You'll be happy to know I decided I'm coming back to work once my leave is over." I sighed. "I wasn't sure, I'll be honest. A baby is a lot, Pearson—you have no idea how much. And I don't want to leave her."

It was easier to say this stuff to Pearson when he was unconscious. Like practice. I drew myself up sternly. "And how I work is going to have to change. Fewer jobs, reasonable hours, none of the really risky stuff, you understand? Except Echo retrieval missions to find lost kids. I'll still take those. Should feel downright easy after tonight." My voice softened on me, despite all my good intentions. "It's going to be a work in progress. You'll have to bear with me. But I don't want to stop being a Hound. I *like* this ridiculous job. So I'll be back on duty before you know it. Stars, I'm even looking forward to it."

One brown eye cracked open, just a thin gleaming slit in Pearson's face.

"Gonna hold you to that, Kem," he croaked.

"Pearson! I swear you'd come back from the dead to make me work." I shook my head, but I couldn't keep from smiling. "Listen, when I say 'before you know it,' I mean maybe in a few months, all right?"

"Right." The shadow of a smile visited his lips. "Three months. Putting it on my calendar."

"That's not a hard number! Oh, I should knock you right out again." I grinned. "Good to see you back, but stay down and keep resting. This isn't over yet. You're safer in bed."

He nodded, his eyes drifting shut. "I'll wait right here. You save the..."

Asleep again. For his own sake, I hoped we were back in Prime when he woke up.

A strange surge of optimism unfolded in me, delicate as the first damp leaves of spring. Pearson was going to be all right, Rai's invitation had been revoked, Rika and I maybe had something like a date planned in the near future, and I was still a Hound. We just had to survive two more Echoes, and everything could go back to normal. Well, some new post-baby normal that I'd have to make up as I went along, anyway.

Humming to myself, I went to find Rika.

"I talked to Dona Swift," Rika reported. "All the wards seem to be in place. The safe room may not exist in this Echo, but a very confused Carter is looking for it. She's going to do a party game to identify the Rainbow Moons either way, just in case. How's Pearson?"

"Awake, briefly. I think he's going to be fine."

A sheet of rosy light swept over us; this one made my scalp tingle and smelled strongly of cinnamon. Beryl's voice whispered in my ear for one brief instant—*Hey, sharpstuff, I got you something*—and then faded as the scarlet wave passed. The clothes of the partygoers around us went vivid pink in its wake.

Rika shuddered. "Ugh, I hate those things. Glad Signa Pearson looks like he'll pull through."

"Seems like we've got all our defenses in place. I'm worried about what Rai said about having other paths to victory, but if that was just bluster, we might be— What's wrong?"

Rika had gone completely still, staring past me, her pupils wide and drowning.

"She's back."

I followed her gaze and froze. We stood near an open archway to a side room that shimmered with coruscating rainbow hues. On the far side of it, a set of tall stained glass doors led out to the garden, which appeared to have mostly dissolved into a jumble of vivid colors, twined and clumped to create the vague texture of landscape. It didn't look like a place where a human could live for long. Someone had left the doors open, which seemed like a very bad idea, though none of the rainbows were leaking into the house . . . yet.

Standing in those doors, just on the far side of the threshold, was Adelyn Cail.

She seemed undisturbed by the chaos of colors around her. Her clawed fingers lifted an intensely violet drink to her lips; she sipped it and watched us with patient, inhuman eyes.

She shouldn't be here. Those shadows had destroyed her. It should have taken her at least a day or two to come back, regathering her form from the stuff of Echoes. But she looked completely fine, as if nothing had ever so much as inconvenienced her. An uneasy shiver crawled across my skin.

I tore my eyes away from Cail, dragging them back to Rika. "You don't have to talk to her. You can just ignore her."

She let out a strained laugh. "No, I can't."

"Fine, but still—"

"No, it's all right. She can't get in. We'd better see what she wants."

She sounded about as happy as if she were going to get teeth pulled, but she started through the archway and across the side room toward the garden doors. I fell in beside her like a bodyguard. Rika moved with her usual liquid grace, but I could feel the humming tension beneath. I didn't doubt she had hidden weapons ready.

I pasted on an unfriendly grin as we got close to Cail's Echo, hoping it would cover my unease. She stood waiting for us in the doorway, the grass beneath her feet a sickly patchwork of blues and oranges that blurred into nonsensically undulating shapes as it got farther from the stability of the house. Normally I'd assume that some time discrepancy between Echoes had allowed her to come back so quickly, but no Echo could pass midnight before Prime did on this night. So either Cail was far more powerful than she'd seemed, or something strange was going on. Neither was likely to be good news for us.

The Echo's eyes fixed on Rika with devouring intensity. "You can put that away, child. I'm not here to hurt you."

"You tried to kill me earlier," Rika accused, but a hand that had been hidden in a fold of her skirts eased reluctantly back into sight.

"Did I?" Cail's slit-pupiled eyes gave a slow, languorous blink. "Are you so certain you know your lady's intent?"

"She's not my lady." Rika nearly spat the words.

"How ungrateful. She has done so very much for you, child. Despite your cruelty, she sends her greetings." Cail inclined her head courteously.

Rika closed her eyes as if the words hurt her. She mouthed something that looked like *Fuck her*, but no words came out.

And there was that surge of violent protectiveness, right on cue. Being a mom did strange things to my emotions, but in this case I embraced it. I stepped forward, deploying my prized skill of looming over someone despite being shorter than them.

"Do you have anything more useful to say than that? Because if you're bothering Rika, I see no reason not to shut this door in your face and leave you to the Deep Echoes."

Cail laughed. It was a terrible music, bright on the surface but with awful dark depths, like a cold winter river. There was a deep, resonant power in it I hadn't glimpsed in her before. It was all I could do not to take a step back.

"Rika," she said at last, "control your dog before I do it for you."

I started to move, but Rika's fingers clamped cold and panicked on my arm. She'd gone still, eyes widening in the stark mortal fear of an animal looking into the face of the predator that will kill it.

"Kembral," she whispered hoarsely, "that's not Cail."

"I know that."

"She's not Cail's Echo, either." Rika took a step back, dragging me with her. "We've got to go."

"You'll stay where you are and listen—both of you."

Cail smiled just as a wave of opalescent purple washed over us, filling my ears with the ringing of sweet tiny bells and my body with the awful plunging sensation of having stepped off a cliff. Her smile spread until it shimmered all over her, or perhaps the veil of color did, or simply the sudden force of her presence. And she *changed*.

She stood impossibly tall and slender, her sweeping fall of hair glimmering like starlight—eyes bright as the Moon, skin dark as the Void, beautiful as the oblivion of death and powerful as the light of creation. I recognized her at once: the Empyrean whose reflected image had spoken to Rika in the mists.

Stars Tangled in Her Web had appeared in person at last.

KEEP THEM TALKING

Rika shrank into herself like a lost, frightened child.

I could see the past as clearly as if I'd been there. She'd slipped through the Veil when I wasn't there to protect her, the Echoes drawing her in at last. And this monster had been there, waiting to catch her, to toy with the terrified prey that had fallen into her web.

I was suddenly angrier than it was safe to be at an Empyrean.

"What do you want?" I demanded.

"I've come to claim what is mine." Her shining eyes stayed fixed on Rika.

"Absolutely not." I stepped forward to grab the stained glass doors.

Or I tried to. My feet wouldn't move. With a plunging sense of horror, I looked down.

Black lines like the shadow of a web spread from the hem of the Empyrean's gown, across the threshold and along the shimmering rainbow floor. They stretched under our feet, rooting us to the ground as if our boots had fused there. More black lines crept up over Rika's ankles, crawling higher, wrapping around her legs.

"No," she whispered, panic stretching her eyes. "No no no, please, no..."

"You've taught me to be thorough in binding you, my slippery one," Arhsta crooned. "I'll weave my webs into every vein in your body, all through your blood, along every nerve. I'll wrap your heart in a cocoon so thick you'll barely feel it beating. You are mine, and this time, the throne I have made for you is one all will tremble to see."

"Leave her alone," I growled, too aware that my threat was empty. There was no one else in this side room; a curtain of shimmering deep green had sealed it off, whether by the Empyrean's Echo-warping efforts or through sheer bad luck. There was no help coming. I itched to draw my sword, but I knew too well it would do me no good. She might be unable to enter the building, but we were entirely at her nonexistent mercy.

Arhsta's glowing eyes turned to me. Her gaze enfolded me like a gloved hand, squeezing too tightly around my heart.

"You have been very helpful, Kembral Thorne. One tug on your strand gained me the unwitting assistance of the Clockmaker. Another let me draw Rika into my web. It would be a shame to destroy a tool that may yet have further use. So rein in your impertinence, mortal."

Pain lanced up into my ankles from the webs around them. I couldn't hide my reaction.

Rika grabbed my arm, her fingers digging into my bicep with the strength of panic. "Kembral!"

I caught her glance, sweat beading on my skin, and tried to give her a warning look. *Don't show her you care.* If I knew one thing about Echoes, it was that you could never let them see what you truly valued. It was blood in the water to them.

Rika faced Arhsta, rallying enough to slip on a cracked mask over the terror I could still see in every line of her body. If I understood what those invisible weblike scars meant about her childhood encounter with the Empyrean, it must have taken phenomenal courage and a will of pure steel. But when she spoke, her voice barely trembled.

"There's no need for that. Tell me what you want. I'm listening."

"I want so much for you, child." Arhsta drifted closer, with agonizing slowness, her star-scattered gown making a noise like a winter breeze through bare branches as it slid across the rainbow grass. "I want all the worlds to tremble in the subtle grip of your power. But for now, what I require is simpler: I want you to name the year."

Her voice was musical, mesmerizing. She stood right at the threshold. An icy breeze flowed over me, scented faintly with ozone. I shuddered beneath its touch.

"But I can't name the year for you," Rika objected. "Cail was your player."

"She was never my player." Arhsta's eyes fixed on Rika, pools of radiance without iris or pupil. "It was always you."

My heartbeat quickened, thudding painfully against my breastbone. Rika made a smothered sound.

I had to redirect Arhsta's attention. Empyreans only cared about their equilibrium—hers seemed to center around her labyrinthine plans. Maybe, just maybe, she wouldn't be able to resist explaining them.

"How is that possible?" I asked desperately.

"I see *exactly* what you're doing, mortal. But very well." The Empyrean's sigh gusted through us, shivering a ribbon of brilliant amber from the air and sending it undulating off through the room. "Unlike my peers, I had the foresight to watch the site of the convergence in advance, learning the pieces available to me in this game. When I discovered that this mortal you care for would be present, Rika, it was a simple matter to alert her enemy so that she would be in danger, then inform you of that fact to draw you here."

There it was: the burning shame of being used, a mere convenience to trap someone I cared about. I kept my mouth shut on the curses I wanted to spit at her. Whatever it took to keep her talking and postpone the part where she filled Rika with spiderwebs and took her away.

"I'd long ago recruited an Echo of your colleague to my service, so I sent her to shepherd you." Arhsta's glowing gaze all but devoured Rika, who stood rigid in its light. "It was her task to make sure you performed a blood sacrifice in every Echo, and to sabotage the other players as she could to increase your chances."

"I don't understand why you had Cail tell me what she did." Rika's voice trembled, so slightly I wouldn't have noticed if I weren't listening for any sign she needed me to intervene. "Why you made me think I was...that my guild..."

She couldn't finish. Thinking she was on probation had left marks. I had to stop myself from reaching out a comforting hand; she was struggling enough to hide her vulnerable spots without me pointing them out.

"So that you would cooperate, child. You have shown me that you lack obedience." Arhsta's silvery voice sharpened to a dagger point. "It's unfortunate that you chose not to deploy the net I gave you. It would have bound everyone linked to the clock to you, so that any blood they shed would be in your name. Now your power over the crux year will not be as great as it could have been, and I mourn that loss. But if you perform the last seal in the final Echo with your own hand, and name the year with your own lips, the crux year will be yours. You will be the spider at the center of my web, the empress in your castle, the nexus of all my plans."

I could see it too clearly: those shadowy webs stretching across the entire world, weaving into everyone's blood, wrapping their minds and hearts and souls, binding them to whatever terrible purpose suited this shining creature's whims. And Rika at the center of it all, bound to a throne with a million tiny strands of web running through her, screaming.

By the terrified look on her face, Rika could imagine it, too.

"Now." The Empyrean's hair fanned out around her like wings, lifted by a shimmering eddy of pale apricot that engulfed us in the scent of burning pine. "The time has come. Offer me your fealty. Acknowledge you are mine, bind yourself to me willingly—and name the year."

A brief tremble washed over Rika. Then she went still, forcing herself back under control. The hollow mask of confidence she lifted to Arhsta broke my heart.

"First, I need to understand something about the blood seal. Everyone who died in the previous Echoes has come back to life." Her tone was detached and curious—fishing for information, or stalling to buy me time to think of something. "Does that still count? Does it take true and final death to bind the year?"

"Perceptive," the Empyrean noted, and a faint flush mounted Rika's cheeks, as if despite everything she couldn't help feeling a traitorous thrill of pride. "The Clockmaker's clever working has placed an Echo shield around the mortals here. Those humans *did* die, but it was displaced; all harm done to them sloughs away when they pass between Echoes, skimmed off by the Veil. But a death revoked is still a death, and suffices to carve the blood seal into the year." Arhsta's glowing gaze narrowed. "Do not expect this trick to work for the final seal, however—that will be a true death. Then the game is over, the year turned, the rite complete. Some things cannot be undone."

So this was the last Echo where we could make mistakes. Whatever happened in the final Echo was permanent. Not that it seemed likely to matter, since by the waning patience in her ethereal voice, I expected Arhsta was about to do some fairly permanent things to us right now.

"Enough." She reached out a commanding hand toward Rika, her fingertips stopping just short of the invisible plane of the doorway. "Swear to me, child. To bind the year in blood and death in the final Echo, and to name it with my voice, as my anointed agent."

Her voice had gone hard and cold. She was done with our delays; this was all the grace we were going to get.

Rika took a deep breath, then closed her eyes and let it out again. The black webs snaked higher around her, creeping past her waist; Arhsta stared at her with a gaze intent as that of the Moon itself, lambent and unblinking.

Rika shuddered and opened her eyes. "No."

I expected Arhsta's wrath to fall on her like a hurricane. I was poised on the cusp of the Veil, ready to blink step, sure it wouldn't do me any good.

Instead, the Empyrean's perfect lips curled in a slow smile.

"It pleases me that your will is strong, little one. But remember, you are mine. You do not get to make a choice."

Rika let out a sudden gasp of pain. My heart plunged.

Black webs swarmed over her gown, her arms, her face. She swayed on her feet, eyes glazed with horror.

"*Rika!*" I reached for her, grabbing her arm in some desperate hope that I could pull the webs off her; my palm burned and stung where I touched them, but they had no more substance than a shadow.

"You will always be mine," Arhsta said caressingly. "You can never, ever escape."

Rika clawed at the webs, desperate, her breath quick and panicky. But the gaze she turned on Arhsta radiated so much fury it almost seemed to glow.

"No!" The word tore out of her in a scream, raw with rage as much as fear. "I am *not* yours, and I say *no!*"

The hair-thin webs covering her stilled, their threads glittering, lying sharp and ready against her skin. Arhsta regarded her as if she'd turned into something entirely unexpected, a new and unheralded creature who must be analyzed to be understood.

"I see," she said softly. "There is a better way to persuade you."

And she turned her searing white gaze to me.

The pressure of her attention was like the bright cold light of the full Moon in winter, stark and inescapable. It made me immediately tiny, insignificant, a mere speck floating in the great river of time. A terrible certainty stole my breath away: She was going to pick me apart to hurt Rika, slowly and surely and as painfully as only a divine child of the cruel Void could manage.

"Don't." There was true panic in Rika's voice now, shaky and uncontrolled, all her furious will broken at once. "Don't you dare, don't—"

The webs binding me to the floor twisted up my calves, tracing lightning-hot paths of pain. Screaming filled my ears; I didn't know if it was Rika's or mine.

With the same unthinking instinct that would pull my hand out of a fire, I slipped out of time.

Golden silence enfolded me. Arhsta blazed in the thick honey of the Veil, bright as a sun, but I didn't waste an instant looking at her. I had no doubt she could be active and present here just like Rai, and I didn't dare draw her attention with anything so foolish as an attack or even a glance.

I slid free of the ghostly images of her webs, meaningless as any other binding when form itself was a figment of the imagination. One quick stride and I popped back into a bright and colorful world where Rika's voice cried my name in pure, ragged anguish.

I grabbed the edges of the stained glass doors and swung them closed—one, two—in the Empyrean's face.

The thing about Echoes is that symbolism matters. Even an Empyrean needs an invitation. An open door is an open path for magic; to shut it is to seal it. Never mind if it's made of fragile glass, if there are cracks around it that shadows could slide under, if it should be the easiest thing in the world to push open again. An open door is a door. A closed door is a wall.

The instant those doors came together and the gap between them into the mad colors of the garden vanished, the shadowy webs along the floor and all over Rika disappeared. Just as surely and swiftly as if they were true shadows and someone had shone a light on them, they were gone.

I stood panting, my palms pressed against the cool stained glass. I had a wavering and discolored view of the garden through the doors—the jumbles of form and hue that approximated bushes, the drooping rainbow tangle that had replaced the weeping tree, the distant shimmering barrier of the wall.

There was no sign of Arhsta. She was gone, as if she'd never been there at all.

"*Kembral!* Are you all right? Are you—"

"I'm fine."

"She's gone. She's gone. Holy Void, she's gone."

Rika staggered back from the door, breathing hard, brushing her arms frantically as if webs still clung to them.

I didn't stop to think. I went to her, grabbing her shoulder. "Are *you* all right? Did she . . . That stuff she said about blood and nerves . . ."

Rika dragged in a ragged breath. "She didn't get the chance this time. I'm all right."

This time. Shit. She'd been a *child.*

"Fuck her," I said with feeling. "So you're not hurt? You're—"

She slammed into me with bruising force, and for one winded and confused instant I thought it was an attack; she'd been playing some long game, and I was dead. Every muscle in my body tensed, unsure how to respond.

But no. Those crushing bands around my ribs were her arms, holding me in wild desperation. That was her face in my shoulder, pressed there as if she could block out the world and all its cruelty. That was her body slim and warm against mine, a piece of elusive shadow made physically manifest at last.

Slowly, with a sort of stunned gentleness, I started to fold my arms around her. But she whirled away from me before their circle could close, ruthlessly scrubbing tears from her face.

"Thanks," she said, her voice tightly controlled. "Looks like you saved me again."

"It's only fair." I kept my tone as light as I could, trying to ignore the lingering warmth the brief press of her body had left on mine. "You saved me in the fog, and a couple other times before that. Got to even the score or you'll get too far ahead."

She let out a brittle laugh. "I think we're past that point. *Stars.* I hate her so much, Kembral."

"Well, you're safe from her for now," I said gruffly. "She can't get in, and she can't win this game because you're not going to help her. Hopefully once she doesn't need someone on the inside here anymore, she'll forget about you again."

"Hopefully," Rika agreed, but I could tell she didn't believe that any more than I did.

"Come on." I held my hand out to her, looking for any way to distract her from the pain still shadowing her eyes. "The year hasn't turned yet, and the party is still going. The Empyreans are locked out. If nothing is on fire, maybe we can have a dance."

I'd meant it as a joke—well, mostly—but Rika's mouth curved

in a secret little smile. She reached out and put her narrow, nimble fingers in mine.

"Why, Kembral, how gallant! I'd like that very much."

Our hands remained joined as we walked toward the shimmering curtain of emerald light that still blocked the archway. My pulse pounded thick in my veins, and my face warmed. I was really going to dance with Rika Nonesuch, despite all the horrors that had occurred tonight. As if I could still have a romantic future, even as a mother. As if the wounds we'd given each other were healed—the rift between us not vanished, but mended with golden thread.

I squeezed Rika's hand. The shifting green wall of light floated loose and dissipated just as we stepped through the door.

What we saw stopped me like a pike thrust to the chest.

I was not going to get to dance with Rika tonight.

First came the assault of color on my senses: a wide swath of red carved through everything, the transformed ballroom tracing an obliging path of vivid, eye-hurting scarlet in a sweeping arc from the ballroom doors to its center. Still, bloody lumps of human wreckage scattered in that wake—dozens of them, in puddles of skirts or the graceful splay of tailcoats. Hands still, fingers curled, eyes empty.

There were scattered survivors: knots of people pressed against the walls in terror, staying as far away from that path of slaughter as they could. The Butterfly with the eye makeup stood in front of his friend, a table knife in his trembling hand, ready to fight; the remnant of Dona Marjorie's guards formed a tight knot in a nearby corner, most of them wounded, holding her bloodstained body slumped in their arms. Carter lay dead at her feet; Vandelle sprawled not far away, cut nearly in half with vindictive force.

At the center of the room stood Rai, resplendent, an ecstatic light shining in those mirror eyes. Blood slicked his terrible black sword as he withdrew it from the chest of a staggered, crumpling Jaycel Morningray.

KNOW WHEN YOU'VE LOST

I froze, shock stealing the air from my lungs. Rika went equally still at my side.

Jaycel heaved a bloody breath, fury in her dark eyes, her sword sliding from slack fingers to clatter on the floor.

"This wasn't what I intended," Rai murmured to her, almost regretfully.

Jaycel clamped her arm tight over the terrible wound that gaped between her ribs and fell to her knees.

"If I'd known... you were such a churl..." A wet gasp swallowed the rest of her retort as her lungs filled with blood.

Blair, who had been standing some distance behind her, made a noise like an animal in pain. They lunged forward to fling themselves down and wrap their arms around their sister, heedless of any danger.

"No," Jaycel gasped. "Blair, stay back!"

"Ah," Rai sighed in something like bliss. "A Rainbow Moon at last."

He raised his bloodstained sword over Blair's bowed and vulnerable neck.

Absolutely fucking not.

I dropped Rika's hand and flung myself out of time, heedless with rage. The golden honey of the Veil enfolded me; I plunged through it, drawing my sword and dagger as I ran.

There was no time to spare a glance for Jaycel's agonized face, or the shattering of innocence into grief in Blair's sapphire eyes; I had to move quickly, before Rai could react. I ignored the part of my brain that screamed that I couldn't fight an Empyrean, focusing only on angle and target and the delicate mental balance that kept me suspended in this liminal non-space between one world and the next.

A glimmer of life and motion came into Rai's mirror eyes, focusing on me through the Veil—and then I was back in reality, sound roaring in my ears, as I shoved his blade aside with a furious *clang* and crashed into him, knocking him away from Blair.

I couldn't hurt him, but he still had a physical body, and I could *move* him.

He staggered back a step and brought his great black sword into a guard position, the full piercing force of his attention shifting to me. I kept my sword tip pointed at his eyes in a firm, high line. My heart pounded wildly, but my blade didn't waver.

His mouth twisted into a displeased frown. "Your interference is becoming tiresome."

I didn't say anything. Jaycel was the one who always had a return quip ready. Her tortured breathing scraped at my senses; I forced myself to stay focused on my enemy, not to look behind me at my dying friend.

"Who was it who broke my curse?" Rai demanded. "Are you making yourself such a thorn in my side because you've allied with my opponent?"

"I serve no Empyrean."

His smile gleamed like a drawn blade. "Then no one will protect you from me."

"That's fine. I'm not here to be protected."

Rai looked ready to talk, some question or grand speech poised on his lips. If I could see any advantage to buying time, I'd let him—but it was a moment of distraction, and I seized it.

Well aware that this was not my best idea ever, I charged him.

His reflexes were good—he barely lost an instant to surprise. His blade was much longer than mine, and he took a cut at me as I tried to close.

I slipped out of reality in midstride, plunging into the frozen amber of the Veil, passing through his sword like a shadow.

He flickered into motion, becoming real in this unreal space, sharp teeth bared in a grin that said I'd made a fool's mistake to face him here again.

But I was already inside his guard.

He might be an all-powerful celestial being, but his hands were full of a massive sword and I was in his face with a shorter blade and a dagger, and he'd made himself real here—here, where *nothing* was real, where there were no Echoes to shape to his divine will, where even the light of the Moon and the dark of the Void couldn't reach.

Where maybe, just maybe, there was a chance he might be vulnerable. He'd probably never had the opportunity to find out. But right now, we were going to do some *science*.

I caught his pivoting sword hilt with my dagger to keep it safely out of line and rammed my sword between his ribs.

Impact jarred up my arm, impossible in this space where nothing had substance, including myself. Dazzling light blasted from the wound in his side, as if he were full of stars, which for all I knew he was. His goat-pupiled eyes widened in shock.

I released my tenuous hold on the Veil immediately, snapping back into time and space, and hurled myself away from him. My heart beat a wild, terrified dance in my chest for what I'd done.

Rai's starry cloak flared like wings from his shoulders in a sudden burst of panicked darkness. He reeled back, hand clamping to a wound that wasn't there in this world (damn it), face startled blank and wild with what might have been his first experience with pain.

A surge of vicious triumph fired my blood. *Take that, asshole.*

I took up a defensive stance, breathing hard, and stared him down as if I actually could meaningfully threaten him. My borrowed sword with its flame-swept hilt was light and lively in my hand, quick as thought; my arm felt precise and fast and *ready*.

I met his stare without flinching. I could hurt him, and that changed everything.

Rai's gaze narrowed. His fingers flexed on his side, becoming claws for a moment. Then he brushed the unmarred gleaming black metal of his breastplate, flicking the pain away.

"Very well," he said softly, and that quiet tone turned my bones to ice water. "Very well, Kembral Thorne. I accept you as an adversary."

Oh, that didn't sound good. I was going to regret this so much. But a fierce energy surged through me, and it didn't know defeat. I doubled down.

"Now you know you're not invulnerable. And I'm not going to let you hurt Blair."

His silver eyes glittered. His cloak floated back into place, a tattered shred of night sky streaming cape-like from his shoulders. Calm and control settled over him once more.

"Are you so sure about that?"

Something about his tone made me hesitate. It didn't sound like standard taunting or boasting—more like he genuinely wanted to know.

Rai flung an arm wide, taking in the whole room. The bodies strewn everywhere. Rika standing at Marjorie's side, head bowed, shaking her head. Jaycel dying in Blair's arms, her breath a ragged, bloody mess.

"If you stop me from killing them, you win. Congratulations!" Rai's voice rang out with the painful clarity of a great bell. "The seal fails. The year turns. The game is done. I am defeated; you are triumphant. And all these people die a true and final death."

He was right. If I stopped him here, *this* was the reality that would stick. So many people dead. Marjorie. Jaycel. Blair making heartbroken whimpers like a hurt dog.

Rai definitively beaten, the year unnamed, the world saved from the machinations of the Empyreans.

Pain lanced through my heart as if he'd run me through. I couldn't make this choice. I couldn't weigh my friends' lives—and dozens of innocent bystanders, too—against the looming doom of unknown cosmic catastrophe. This was an absolutely bullshit choice, and I didn't want any part of it. But now he'd given it to me, and there was no evading it.

"Let him," came a soft voice behind me.

It was all I could do not to whirl around, but I wasn't going to give Rai that opening.

"Signa Blair, respectfully, this isn't the moment for dramatic gestures."

"It's not drama. At least, I don't think it is." Their voice drifted closer, calm now. "I don't know what's going on, but I can see the Echo overlay. It's blurry, like someone erased it and wrote over it."

"Blair," Jaycel began, her voice weak and strained, but she broke off in a wet cough.

"I died here before, didn't I?" Blair's hand touched my shoulder so lightly, like the wing of a butterfly, and they were standing at my side. "I'd rather die again and get better than watch Jaycel die and have it be real."

My sword tip trembled. Ten Echoes down, and only one left. If I let him kill Blair here, I was gambling on being able to save the day somehow in the last Echo. I'd be standing aside and letting him murder an innocent, and I could well be casting the entire world to its doom.

But if I protected Blair, all these deaths would be irrevocably on my hands. Marjorie, Jaycel, Vandelle, Carter, all these others—it would be my choice that sealed their fates. They wouldn't get another chance.

I wanted to catch Rika's gaze, to plead silently for help. But I didn't dare look away from Rai. And she couldn't help me in this anyway. Passing off the choice to someone else would be a choice all on its own.

"Well?" Rai asked, his tone curious.

I hesitated. Damn me to the Void, I hesitated. My sword tip sagged, falling out of line in defeat.

Rai took the moment with inhuman speed, closing so fast he might as well have blink stepped himself, his sword coming down on Blair like the fall of night.

I could have saved them. I could have slipped into the Veil and parried with the knee-jerk instinct Almarah had trained into me for moments like this, so I wouldn't have to think. So I could move faster than Echoes, faster than lightning, faster than time itself.

But surrounded by death, Jaycel's blood-choked breath in my ears, I hesitated for the tiniest fraction of a second. And that was a decision. It was enough. It was a fucking *surrender*, and I hated myself for it.

Blair's blood spattered the side of my face. Jaycel's scream ripped the air, wild with grief and rage, too powerful for her ravaged lungs to contain.

The clock began to toll.

I stared at Blair's blood-soaked body, crumpled at my feet, and a thick wild bubble of grief and shame rose up in my chest, threatening to break loose in a tremendous howl.

Rika's voice cut through my horrified daze, piercing me from across the ballroom.

"Kembral, *look out!*"

I started to turn. Something hit my back, and pain ripped along my side. I staggered, a coppery taste in my mouth, and stared in absolute shock at the hate-filled, bloodstained face of Jaycel Morningray.

"You *let them die!* You *monster*, you let Blair die!"

She was on her knees, her chest heaving sickeningly with each breath, a bloody dagger in her hand.

That was *my* blood. She'd have stabbed me right in the kidney if Rika hadn't warned me. I touched my side with a shaking hand and found it warm and wet.

The clock kept tolling. Rai was laughing; Rika was running toward me, swearing. All I could see was Jaycel's face, twisted with rage and grief; nothing else mattered.

"I didn't—I'm sorry, I—"

"You can die, too, you traitor!" Her eyes were glassy with death. "I *hate* you. Just . . . die . . ."

The clock's terrible bell rang one final time, and I couldn't tell whether I was falling because reality had shattered beneath me, or because I'd just been stabbed, or because I was such a Moon-cursed wretched excuse for a human being that the ground was swallowing me up.

IF YOU'RE HURT, LIE LOW

Kembral, are you all right? Did she get you?" Rika's fingers clamped around my arms like cold iron bands.

I didn't give a fuck if she'd gotten me. All I could do was kneel on the floor in a daze, marveling at what a wretched thing I'd just done. Or allowed to happen, which was damn near the same thing.

"You're covered in blood." Rika's voice had gone flat, almost distant. "Is that yours? *Kembral.* Answer me, or I'm going to slap you."

Her lips were pressed tight together with worry. For a moment, her eyes were dark, some other color that resolved swiftly into their usual clear grey. She searched my face, then drew back her arm, shoulder muscles bunching.

"I'm fine," I said quickly, raising a hand. "Grated off my rib. I just...I'm fine." Except for the sick knot of guilt and grief in my chest. *Blair,* of all people.

"I can't believe that bitch stabbed you," Rika growled, reaching for the buttons on my coat.

I pushed her hand away and tried to surge to my feet, but tumbled back awkwardly onto my ass instead. Wet warmth was seeping all across my side. It was hard to care.

"She had every right to stab me," I said numbly.

"Don't be a diva. This isn't the Grand Theater. Now let me see that before you bleed to death and score points for some Empyrean in this awful game."

Her nimble fingers were undoing my buttons, which was more than a little embarrassing. Everyone had to be staring—but no. We were down behind a buffet table, in a sliver of space between the gauzy white tablecloth and a curving pale wall. A towering display of something like fluffy meringue further blocked off the rest of the room.

I twisted away from her anyway, hissing in pain. "I'll take it off myself, all right? Damn it, I *love* this coat, and now it's ruined."

But my own fingers were clumsy and trembling. Rika laid her hands over mine to still them, met my eyes for a wordless moment, and then patiently took back over like I was a fussy child.

It was kind of nice. *Fuck.*

"Thanks, by the way," I muttered. "For warning me."

"You should have blink stepped," Rika said. "What's the point of being one of half a dozen people in the world who can blink step if you stand there like a dazed chipmunk and let people stab you?"

"I wasn't expecting it, all right? It's been a long day."

Rika helped me struggle out of the coat; I swore a lot as blood-soaked fabric came away from my skin. The shirt under it was torn, too, but that I could just peel up. I looked away from the long, messy gash beneath. It really was bleeding quite a bit.

Rika sucked in a breath through her teeth. "Doesn't that hurt?"

She laid cool fingers on my skin next to the cut. I flinched away.

"Yes, of course it hurts! It hurts like fuck. But it's shallow, and I'm fine." I started to get up, but Rika's steely light touch on my shoulder held me down.

"Once we stop the bleeding, *then* you're fine." She grabbed a bunched-up corner of tablecloth and pressed it against my side. I hissed.

"Sorry," she murmured. "Hold still."

I did, jaw set, not looking at her or at the cut. "I should have stopped him. We're on the last Echo, Rika, and he must have some other invitation. The world is going to drown in catastrophe because I sat back and let an Empyrean kill an innocent."

"No, it's not," Rika said, doing something that sent another flare of pain through my side. "You're going to stop him."

I let out a bitter laugh. "Me?"

"Well, I'm going to help." She reached up onto the table for something, and a nasty suspicion hit me.

"Wait, Rika, tell me that's not—*auuuuughhh!*"

It was wine. It was fucking wine, and I swore like an angry teenager as she cleaned the wound. A couple of middle-aged bankers peered behind the table, got one look at us, and quickly scurried off.

"Shh," Rika hushed me. "My goodness, your kid is going to have quite the vocabulary."

She dabbed at my side with the tablecloth some more and made a distressed noise in the back of her throat. I looked. There was an upsetting amount of bright red staining the white cloth.

"I'd better get some real bandages," Rika said, her voice husky.

I swallowed. "Yeah, probably."

"You wait right here, Kembral. Don't get up, don't move around, don't go *anywhere*," she said fiercely, jabbing an accusing finger at me. "This will only take a minute. If you *dare* move, I'll gut you myself."

I pulled my shirt back down and pressed my arm against my side, trying to stop the bleeding. I knew it looked worse than it was— blood was always so alarmingly *red* that it seemed like there was three times as much—but still, it didn't feel great. Part of me didn't want Rika to leave; I had to swallow down a protest as she hurried off, split sleeves fluttering behind her like trailing wings of smoke.

With her gone, it would be all too easy to sink back into a morass of awful feelings about Blair. I didn't know how I was going to face them again, or Jaycel for that matter. But I couldn't think about that now—we were on the last Echo. I had to figure out who else had invited Rai and get them to revoke his invitation; there was no time for me to sit around on the floor moping and bleeding.

Footsteps approached my hidden corner. Not the deadly inexorable pace of Rai's boots, thank the Moon, but a softer, more casual sound. *Don't look back here,* I thought at them silently. I didn't want to explain what the Void was going on.

The Moon wasn't smiling on me tonight. The figure that rounded the end of the table was none other than Ryvard Harking.

His tailcoat had gone white and grey to match this Echo, with a stormy silver waistcoat and a diamond pin at his cravat. I might despise the man, but I had to admit his outfit was fantastic. It made me all too aware that I was sitting on the floor with my coat off and a great gash in my shirt, covered with blood.

He stared down at me with curiosity that turned rapidly to surprise, then cooled to something hard and pleased and secret.

"This is awkward," I said wearily, getting my legs under me to rise.

"Oh, I think it's perfect, actually." He smiled, with real warmth.

He didn't make a move. If he had, I would have slipped into the Veil to dodge, because I was ready for this—was watching for the sudden motion, the flicker in the eyes, the shifting stance. He was good, and he didn't do any of that. Just brushed an ornate cuff link at his wrist.

A bright green light stabbed from the diamond in it, straight through my brain, and turned all my thoughts to water.

I tumbled to the floor like he'd shot me with a crossbow.

TAKE THE INITIATIVE

There was a time, when I was maybe about thirteen years old, when I was kidnapped.

I'd been training with Almarah for seven or eight years, and I couldn't really blink step yet. I'd only just barely learned to get to the Veil at all, and if I tried to move while I was there, I'd immediately fall over and bounce right out into Prime again. About the only useful thing I could do was lean against a wall and topple through it.

I thought that was pretty pathetic, but as it turned out, some people considered falling through walls a skill worth any cost to obtain.

It was a Hound who originally figured out how to blink step, and since then the Hounds had controlled the knowledge. There were only a couple of people in the world who could teach it, and very few students made it more than a year or two through the training. I wasn't officially a Hound yet—Almarah had told me I'd learned enough that if I wanted to stay on as her student I'd have to join, but I hadn't taken the oath or gotten my guild tattoo.

So some racketeer found out about me, a defenseless kid without a guild tattoo who could walk through walls—or fall through them, anyway—and nabbed me on my way to Almarah's place one day.

But it's very hard to hold captive someone who can blink step, even if they're just a kid and really bad at it. To stop me from flopping my way to freedom, he drugged me until my head was reeling and there was absolutely no way I could attain the delicate mental balance needed to reach the Veil.

Almarah found the racketeer before he could sell me to some high bidder in another city, and let's just say he learned a valuable lesson in why you do not fuck with the Hounds in general, and with Almarah in particular. But the point is, the racketeer did his research, and he knew how to stop someone from blink stepping.

Harking had also done his research. One flash from that diamond and my brain was soup.

I couldn't move, couldn't make sense of what I was seeing or hearing, could barely form an intention. Thwarted adrenaline coursed through my system. I struggled to get up, to run or fight, anything that might keep him from killing me; I might have managed to twitch a little.

Something nudged my wounded side sharply—the hard toe of Harking's boot. The resulting flare of pain across my ribs shocked enough sense back into me to at least understand what was happening, but I couldn't do more than curl slightly around the kick, brain seething with profanities.

"Here you are, alone and injured, like a gift from the Void. This is so easy I'm almost worried it's a trap." A scrape of metal as he drew a knife. "The Sickle Moon is the time for reaping, I suppose. Let's make that wound of yours a bit deeper, shall we? No one needs to know but you and me."

Through the blurred narrow slit between my eyelids, I saw him bend over me. I strove to roll out of the way, but whatever part of my brain handled the business of connecting to my body was still scrambled. I was utterly helpless.

Damn it, I couldn't die like this. But my body wouldn't even respond enough to tense against the cold steel angling smooth and lethal for my side.

The table that shielded us from view went crashing over in an explosion of meringue and bloodstained tablecloth, flung by an enthusiastic arm.

The Last Hour Between Worlds   333

"Villain!" cried Jaycel Morningray, in a voice like a crack of thunder.

She stood there in bold dramatic form, her sword gleaming at her side, her flowing white shirt pristine and unbloodied. The dagger that had stabbed me was sheathed once more at her hip. The sight of her sent a lance through my heart.

For a moment my muddled thoughts were sure she meant me, for sacrificing Blair. But it was Harking her gaze fixed on in righteous fury, her sword pointing a shining accusation. My eyes finally focused properly, first on her, then the rest of the room—she'd exposed us to full view, and the crowd was already pressing back, forming a curious circle as if this were one of Jaycel's paid show duels, excited whispering spreading like wildfire.

Harking dropped the knife with a soft curse and rose, brushing imaginary dust off his immaculate jacket as he stepped away from me.

"Morningray," Harking greeted her, his gaze half-lidded, tone relaxed as if they were having a casual conversation. "What a droll way to greet me."

"If you like how I said hello, wait until you see how I say goodbye." Jaycel swished her sword in a savage flourish. "You attacked my friend. Draw and fight me, or be named a coward before the whole city."

It was classic Jaycel. She would fight the Void itself for a friend; she certainly wouldn't balk at publicly dueling a City Elder. After what had happened in the last Echo, it was enough to twist my heart in two.

My senses were steadying, my thoughts starting to fall into place again; I struggled to sit up, to make sure she wouldn't have to face Harking alone.

"Shh. Lie still." A sudden swirl of mist resolved into Rika, kneeling by my side, a roll of bandages in her hand. "Let her distract him. We have to get that bleeding stopped."

I still couldn't talk, so I couldn't tell Rika that actually, I was pretty sure this wasn't a distraction, and Jaycel had every intention of stabbing Harking in front of everyone. Rika started bandaging up my wound, her gentle hands summoning angry fire from my skin with every touch. I flinched and managed a very slurred curse.

"Draw what?" Harking spread his hands, making a great show of examining himself for any weapons. "You have me mistaken for some cheap entertainer who makes public scenes for spare coin, I think. Should I have someone fetch you a hat to pass around?"

"This is no show, and I'm not playing." Jaycel strode closer, lifting her sword to rest its tip on his collarbone. Harking didn't flinch. "Get a sword and defend yourself, or I'll skewer you where you stand."

"I will not," Harking declared scornfully. "I regret dallying with you in bed, and I certainly won't do it in the dueling circle."

Gasps rose up from the crowd. Not putting on a show, my ass.

"You just hate giving a woman satisfaction, do you?" Jaycel retorted, and the crowd went wild.

Dona Marjorie fluttered to the fore, fan going furiously. "Oh my Moon and stars! Violence, right in the middle of my party! This won't do!" She turned to Harking. "Ryvard, do I understand correctly that you've declined this challenge?"

Harking sneered. "Of course. I have no obligation to waste my time dueling some Southside circus act."

"Nor do I want to tarnish my blade with your Hillside venom," Jaycel retorted. "But *I'm* not a coward, so I don't shy from what honor demands."

"Morningray, my dear, *please,*" Dona Marjorie cajoled her.

Jaycel sheathed her sword with a disgusted flourish. Marjorie beamed at her as if she were terribly proud.

"Now, Ryvard." She turned to Harking, the same sweet smile on her face. "Since you've declined the duel, I have to put you under arrest."

Oh, hello. I wrangled myself up onto an elbow as Rika tied off my bandages and smoothed down the bloody remains of my shirt.

"What?" Harking drew himself up in outrage. "I'm a City Elder, Marjorie!"

"Yes, dear, and you *did* just attempt a little bit of murder." She said it almost sympathetically, as if she were informing him he'd committed an obscure faux pas against the Cathardian ambassador. "Signa Nonesuch, is Signa Thorne all right?"

Everyone turned to look. My face burned as I shrugged my coat back on, smothering a hiss of pain at the motion.

"Fine, Dona Swift, no thanks to *him*." Rika gestured to Harking's knife still lying on the floor, its elegant ivory hilt a conspicuous match to the empty sheath on Harking's hip. Playing up the scene like she was Jaycel's trained sidekick.

"Oh, good!" Marjorie waved her fan at Harking as if he were a fly who'd gotten into her ballroom. "Guards, please do make Dona Harking comfortable in a secure place."

I hoped the world wasn't going to end tonight, because I wanted to savor the look on Harking's face as Carter and the rest led him off to the cellars forever.

The crowd broke up into excited milling chaos, the murmur of gossip rising like applause. People were already surging toward us, eager for all the scandalous details.

I finally had enough control of my body to stumble to my feet. A rush of dizziness hit me, and pain seared my side at the motion; I couldn't suppress a grunt.

"Come on," Rika murmured, slipping her arm through mine. "Let's shake them off."

Dona Marjorie's house had turned into a single round tower of grey-veined marble, stairs spiraling up along its inner walls to high balconies that circled the airy room, one after another, until the ceiling was lost in the puffy white underside of a cloud. Windows ringed the tower, every one of them showing nothing but dense fog. Eleven Echoes down, I'd bet cold money that fog was lethal to humans.

"Up to the balconies," I suggested. "People hate climbing stairs."

I wasn't too fond of them myself when I was wounded and shaking off the effects of an Echo relic, but I got a little steadier with every step. The cut in my side wasn't great, and it hurt a distracting amount, but it didn't seem to be hampering my movement at least.

This had been one absolutely rotten rat carcass of a day, and Harking's arrest was like a precious gem lying in the muck of it. But it didn't help us avert the disaster that was looming closer every moment.

"That took up too much time," I muttered as we reached the blessed quiet of the first balcony. There was no one up here; we had it to ourselves.

"Yes, it did." Rika's voice was subdued. Her fingertips trailed down my sleeve as she released my arm, lingering near the gash in my coat. "We're eleven Echoes down, Kembral. *Eleven.* This is our last chance to get this right, and now you're hurt on top of everything."

I blinked her into shape as if I'd only now finished settling into this Echo. Her smoke-and-silver gown was getting tattered around the edges; she looked like a wraith, her grey eyes haunted and urgent. Everything in the moment seemed crystal clear: the little baby hairs plastered to her temples with old sweat, the teasing honey-and-clove scent of her perfume, the soft quickness of her breath.

"It's all right," I said instinctively, even though it clearly wasn't. "We can do this."

"Can we?" Rika let out a harsh little laugh. "You're just saying that. What possible reason could you have to believe it?"

I put my hand over hers where it clenched my arm. "Because look how much trouble we've caused for each other all these years. Now that we're working *together*, there should be nothing we can't do."

"Well, if you put it that way." She took a long, shuddery breath, and her shoulders relaxed a little—not into rest, but into readiness. She met my gaze, resolve hardening her clear grey eyes. "We've probably got less than an hour left. What now?"

"We don't have time to be subtle. I was thinking we could make an announcement—"

I broke off. Footsteps sounded on the marble steps, climbing up from below with slow deliberation. It sounded like multiple people, too labored and shuffling to be Rai, but my whole body tensed anyway, ready for danger.

Blair appeared first, looking a bit winded, their visible eye wide with alarm. My gut twisted, but I shoved the memory of their bloody, lifeless body from my mind. They were fine now, and that was what mattered. And after them came—

"Pearson! Shouldn't you be in bed?"

He was leaning heavily on the railing, his face a little grey beneath the bandages on his head. But he flashed me a quick smile.

"Felt a bit better, so I came to see what I missed. Turns out I missed a lot. We've got a problem, Kem."

Rika leaned heavily back against the wall. "We have an unreasonable number of problems."

"Well, maybe this one isn't such a bad one!" Blair smiled a sweet, room-brightening smile. "I think it probably isn't good, though. Look up."

We all looked up. The room stretched above us, one balcony stacked above the next until everything vanished in a cloud ceiling some five balconies above.

"Yes, clouds," Rika said. "Very nice. How are they a problem?"

"Oh, the clouds aren't the problem. Well, sort of." Blair pushed their bangs away from their brilliant shining Echo eye and gazed upward, then let out a disturbingly low and impressed whistle and added, "All right, maybe they are."

"Blair," I reminded them. "To the point, please."

"They're getting lower," Blair said simply.

Shit. They were. I couldn't remember exactly how many balconies I'd been able to see when we arrived in this Echo, but it had been more than this, and the disc of fluffy cloud had definitely seemed smaller and farther away.

Rika shot me an alarmed look. "What happens if the clouds reach us?"

Blair tilted their head thoughtfully. "Well, so far as I can tell, when the walls and balconies and windows and things go into the clouds, they cease to exist. So probably we would, too."

Everyone exchanged some very uncomfortable glances.

"Let's not do that," Rika suggested, with false brightness. "I like existing."

I didn't want to think about Blair's little observation. I'd never heard of anyone returning from eleven Echoes down. My Raven friends had never heard of anyone going to the Deepest Echo and surviving, not in the oldest accounts in their library. So far as I understood, it was so close to the Void, so chaotic, that it was utterly inhospitable to humans, and anyone foolish enough to try to explore there would presumably die within minutes.

It had to be the clock keeping us safe. A weird sense of pride for the Clockmaker surged through me. Sure, she wasn't Emmi, but she was an Echo of my daughter, and she was *amazing.*

"Okay," I said, "That's pretty bad, but first things first. We've got to—"

Someone was on the stairs *again,* this time bounding up with a distressing amount of energy. I knew that jaunty stride.

Jaycel Morningray burst onto the balcony, her eyes at once fixing intently on me. A pang of guilt twisted my heart. All I could remember was her dying face screwed up in rage, blood on her lips, crying out *I hate you.*

"Kembral darling!" She took a few quick strides to my side, looking me up and down. "Are you all right? I saw you positively drenched in blood!"

I forced my mind to unclench around what had happened in the last Echo. Jaycel was all warmth and concern; she clearly didn't remember. And making hard decisions was part of the job, something Hounds had to do. I could absorb and process everything later; right now, she was my friend, and she deserved my smile rather than whatever strange expression was trying to stiffen up my face.

"Just a scratch," I assured her.

"Who did this to you? Was it Harking, or did he find you that way? Tell me, and I swear I'll run them through."

"Will you, now," Rika said icily.

"I can't go into it right now." And nor was I going to later, so I'd better hope she forgot about it. "We've got an emergency, Jaycel. We need to figure out who..."

I trailed off, staring into Jaycel's keen brown eyes, realization not so much dawning on me as knocking me down like a runaway cart.

Jaycel's playful tone when she'd first faced off with Rai: *You have a lot to account for, darling.* The regret in Rai's voice when he'd told her

This wasn't what I intended after stabbing her. Her unfinished response: *If I'd known you were such a churl . . .*

And way back in Prime, a thousand years ago, Jaycel's mischievous grin as she said *If you think* he's *a bad idea, wait until you see my date for tonight!*

"Jaycel Morningray," I said slowly, "did you invite an Echo here tonight as your mystery date?"

She blinked. "How under the Moon did you know? It was supposed to be a big surprise! Not that he's showed up, the cad. I suppose they like to be fashionably late."

Rika and I exchanged stunned looks. I shook my head in wonder.

"I didn't see *this* coming," Rika murmured.

"I should have." I turned to Jaycel. "I'm sorry, but you're going to have to dump him."

"What? Darling, you haven't even *met* him!"

"I'll give you the quick explanation, because we don't have much time." I kept an eye on the graceful, rounded marble arch framing the double doors that presumably led outside. It was early yet for Rai to appear, but I didn't trust time in the Echoes. "I'm sure he was genuinely attracted by your indisputable charms, but he's also got his own agenda. Any minute now he's going to arrive and start murdering people, and if he kills someone from the wrong Moon . . ." I trailed off as the truth hit me.

"Kem," Pearson said nervously. "That's not a good place to stop."

"Cloud Moon." I swallowed. "It's got to be a Cloud Moon this time. Jaycel, do you know of any Cloud Moons here besides me and Rika?"

Jaycel thought about it a moment, then shook her head. "No, but believe it or not, I don't actually know *everybody*."

Blair leaned over the railing, far enough that Jaycel grabbed the back of their shirt with the ease of long practice.

"Hey! HEY! Excuse me, but is anyone here a Cloud Moon?"

The murmur of the crowd fell silent for a moment. A few scattered replies called back—*No* and *Not me* and *Flower Moon here!*—and then the sound of conversation flowed back in to the empty space it had left.

"Nope!" Blair reported cheerfully. "Just you two."

I stared at Rika. "Then he'll be coming after us."

She let out a hopeless sort of laugh. "How does it keep getting worse? It was already impressively bad! But it keeps getting worse."

"No, this is good." I rested a hand on the comforting pommel of my sword, trying to convince the sick feeling in the pit of my stomach that my words were true. "If he's coming after us, we don't have to worry about him finishing the blood seal before we can react."

"If this is your definition of good, Kembral, your standards have dropped to unacceptable levels."

Blair's head snapped suddenly up, Echo eye all but glowing. "Oh! Here he comes."

On the far side of the room, the doors slammed open, as if a powerful gust of wind blew them. Thick clouds filled the archway but didn't spill inside.

From that blank white wall strode Rai, sleek black armor gleaming, mirror eyes blazing. Wisps of fog clung trailing behind him like a mantle of power, an exhalation of the flaring starry darkness of his cloak. He moved with the lethal, arrogant purpose of a being who knew that only one easy death separated him from absolute victory.

His gaze snapped at once up to the balcony, fixing on me and Rika. My own death waited dark and final in those Void-black rectangular pupils.

"Too late," I breathed. "He's here."

Party guests streamed away from Rai in a panic, pushing against the walls, clearing a space. He stood in the middle of the room, gazing up at us with hungry anticipation, and slowly drew his great black sword.

Jaycel let out a tragic sigh. "I mean, look at him! Can you blame me?"

"Jaycel," I urged her, "you have to uninvite him. If you do that, and we can get him outside the building, he won't be able to come back in. Otherwise he's going to kill us, and unleash far worse on Acantis. And he's an *Empyrean*, so we won't be able to stop him."

One wonderful thing about Jaycel was that if her friends were in, she was in, no questions asked. And if she was in, she was *all* in.

"All right," she said. "But you owe me a drink for this, Kembral darling." She straightened and stepped forward with her best dramatic swagger.

Rai's gaze caught on her and narrowed. "Stand aside," he called. "This doesn't concern you."

"Darling, I'm so sorry to tell you this, but it does." Jaycel braced herself on the balcony railing in an artful lean, raising her voice to project with all the precise clarity of a celebrated show duelist. "I can think of nothing more gauche than to show up to a date with the intent to ignore your partner and murder her friends. It's *embarrassing*, darling, and I'm downright offended. Our date is hereby off—you are no longer my *'and guest'* for this occasion. Consider yourself uninvited!"

A cold wind swept through the room on the heel of her words, swirling around Rai, rustling in the dried bundle of herbs and bones still hanging on the open door. I tensed. Had it worked? Did he have yet another invitation to fall back on?

A look of genuine regret softened Rai's gaze, a strange visitor among the hard lines of his face.

"How unfortunate. Were this any other night, I'd be here solely for your company, Jaycel Morningray. Alas, I lack your mortal freedom to choose my priorities, and victory in this contest must take precedence." Everything about him sharpened—his voice, his gaze, even his shadow. "And I'm afraid you're too late. I'm already past your little ward; I need no invitation."

Well, shit. I'd suspected as much, but the confirmation still sent a chill of dread down my spine.

"What a brazen churl," Jaycel muttered, with a note in her voice that sounded disturbingly like admiration. "Overstaying his welcome. Absolutely no shame."

"We've got to get him out." Rika gave me a glance wide with alarm. "Before he kills you."

"Right." I was more worried about him killing Rika, but I wasn't going to start an argument about that.

Pearson's gaze darted around the room below, white-rimmed. "I don't think Dona Swift's guards will have any luck evicting him."

A calm came over me. All I had to do was get him out the door. Sure, he was an Empyrean with terrifying power who could snuff me out like a candle, while I was a mortal with a couple of sharp pieces of metal and one neat trick. I didn't stand much of a chance. But here, at last, I knew what I had to do—and I was exactly the right person to do it.

I might be a nursing mom in over my head, but I was still me: Kembral Thorne, senior Hound, master of the blink step, and pretty good with a blade even on an off day, if I did say so myself. And if there was one thing I knew about myself, it was this: I always brought the dog back, even when anyone else would have given up.

I drew my sword. It felt good in my hand, ready as a living thing.

"Leave it to me."

Rai's starry wings unfolded, the ragged tips of his cloak spreading to gently test the air, his mirror eyes locking on me. At last, after a long night of dancing around each other, he was coming to kill me.

His knees flexed, and he launched upward toward me, disdaining the stairs.

Fine. I didn't need stairs, either. I stepped back and drew in a breath.

Before I could think better of it, I vaulted over the railing to drop down on him from above.

DON'T PICK A FIGHT YOU CAN'T WIN

Pain ripped across my side as my wound reopened, with a duller echo across my abdomen as I wrenched muscles not wholly recovered from the dramatic disarrangement of pregnancy. I barely noticed it. The clear, sharp focus of the fight was on me. Irrelevant information like pain got ruthlessly jettisoned to the back of my mind along with other useless thoughts, such as *Oh shit, why did I just jump off a twenty-foot-high balcony?*

Air rushed past my face and swept back my hair. Rai flew up at me, black sword lifting to skewer me as I plummeted down at him.

Perfect.

I flickered out of reality, sliding into the golden frozen instant, where concepts like *falling* had no meaning. Rai hung in the air, cloak-wings stilled midbeat. I threw myself at him, mind humming with electric readiness.

The light of awareness came into those eyes, his face quickening with the illusion of time, his sword tip starting to move.

Now. Before he could bring that great dark blade into line to stop me, I slashed down into his wing.

My mere idea of a sword met *something*, some divine essence of him, more real here than I was. The shock of meeting substance in a place without form or matter jarred through me, and dazzling white light erupted from the gash in the Void-black shadows of his cloak. A soundless shriek made the Veil itself tremble.

I didn't stick around for him to retaliate. I ducked back into reality maybe six feet off the ground—close enough to land with the soft flexibility Almarah had taught me, rolling to be safe, sword held carefully out to the side.

Rai reeled out of the air, staggering backward on his landing, clutching his shoulder. His great starry wings beat once for balance; then he was stable on his feet, and they slumped back into a cloak again with a broken haste that suggested lingering pain.

I rose to my feet, wincing at the wetness spreading on my side. He stared at me with a strange expression—it wasn't quite fear, and it wasn't quite anger. It was colder than that, more assessing, more implacable.

"Enough," he said, his voice soft as falling rain. And he raised his hand.

A curling rope of fog wound in through the door several paces behind him, questing toward me like a snake. Something about the mere sight of that wisp of mist sent a primal chill through me. I knew, *knew* somehow, that its touch would mean annihilation.

I couldn't fight that. I knew my limitations. But just maybe, I also knew his.

"Laughing As He Rises!" I barked. "Are you really going to kill me with Echo tricks? After I've challenged you with a sword?"

"The idea of fair play is a mortal concept in which I have no investment."

The tendril of fog lifted over his shoulder almost affectionately, reaching in my direction. It was all I could do to force myself to hold my ground.

I gave him my nastiest smile. "So you're acknowledging that you can't beat me without magic."

The wisp of fog froze. Rai went utterly still.

"I understand," I said, with taunting condescension, my heart beating wild in my chest at the risk I was taking. "You know you can't win with a sword, so you're conceding and resorting to other methods. You're not even going to try to fight me."

All right, *now* he was mad. His eyes glowed with molten fury. He seemed to grow; his black armor sprouted spikes like gleaming thorns, and his horns curled to sharper points. The air around him shimmered as if with scorching heat.

He knew exactly what I was doing, and he couldn't do a damned thing about it. His nature—his equilibrium thread, Laemura had called it—demanded that he pursue victory, crushing his opponents. I'd challenged him in a way he couldn't walk away from without losing who he was.

And now he sure did look like he was going to murder me for it.

"Very well." He flicked a finger, and the fog slithered back through the door, obediently banished. It left a gouge in the threshold as if a hot knife had carved out a scoop of the marble, easy as butter. "You'll have your fight, dog."

Thank the Moon. I tried not to let my relief show.

Rai grasped the hilt of his massive sword in both hands, sliding one foot back and angling his hips, flowing into a distressingly competent-looking guard. "But you should know that I've wielded a sword for as long as there have *been* swords."

"I'm sure you have." I drew my dagger in my off hand and dropped into a low stance myself, ready to lunge. "But I'll bet you've never fought anyone else who can blink step."

And I launched myself at him, like an arrow from the bow.

He was ready for me to blink, so I didn't. Almarah had trained me to save it, always save it as long as I could. If you exhausted yourself early when you had other options, you could wind up unable to pull it off when all other recourse was gone.

He had so much reach on me—ridiculous, decadent amounts of reach, between that enormous black sword and his greater height—and he knew how to use it. As I came rushing in low and fast, he took a leisurely step back, then another, flicking lightning-fast cuts at my hands, my face, my shoulder. I barely parried most of them, taking a light kiss of a cut along my cheekbone and a slightly deeper one on the outside of my arm.

He didn't let me close, maintaining his distance with those liquid backward paces and the indisputable argument of his steel. He kept me right in the worst possible place to be: the small and terrible zone where I was within his reach and he was outside mine, so he could strike at me at will but no amount of skill or effort would let me hit him. It was an absolutely disastrous opening for a swordfight; the advantage was entirely his, and it was all I could do not to get cut to ribbons.

But I didn't care about hitting him. I cared about moving him toward that door. And the distance between him and the exit was vanishing with every taunting backward step he took.

He started to circle, sliding to the side, and I couldn't allow that. Time to change tactics.

This time, when I lunged at him and he flicked one of his rapid warning cuts at me, I skipped into the Veil just long enough to close and sidestep—only the briefest flash of gold across my vision, an instant of sullen silence and then the pop of sound and air against my ears. A small movement, but it put him back in line between me and the door again—and let me inside his guard.

He pivoted to match my new angle, bringing his sword in tight with admirable speed and nearly smashing my temple with a sweep of the pommel. It clipped me; I staggered back a step, pain flashing through my head, the impact disorienting.

My own departing sword swipe passed harmlessly through his side as if he were made of mist.

Shit. That had lost me ground. My temple throbbed, and my cuts stung—but it had almost been much worse.

He watched me almost pityingly as I caught my balance outside his range, lifting my sword up into a high guard pointed at his eyes, trying to keep him at bay long enough to pull myself together. My breath came hard, and my limbs felt heavy already. It didn't help that I'd come into this already wounded.

"You can't win," Rai said, with the exasperated patience of

someone explaining something to a stubborn child. "I am a creature of divine blood and starlight. Your mortal steel can't touch me."

He wasn't wrong. But if he hadn't figured out why that didn't matter, I wasn't going to tell him.

"I don't expect you to understand this," I said, "but not everything is about winning."

"Nonsense," he scoffed.

"Kembral darling!" Jaycel called, from somewhere behind me. "Do you want to share the fun, or should the rest of us stay out of it?"

"If anyone intervenes," Rai said sharply, "this match is over, and I finish my business with expediency rather than finesse."

"Please don't do anything that will make him kill me," I urged Jaycel fervently.

"If you're sure, darling! Good luck!"

I'd caught my breath, and I was at a good angle to Rai again, with the door behind him. Break time was over. I needed to finish this, before he finished me.

Rai didn't wait for me to charge him again. I just had time to register the warning flicker in his eyes before he came at me with a brutal overhand slash that nearly bisected me from shoulder to hip.

I barely jumped back in time. The tip of his sword ripped down the front of my poor mangled coat, and a few buttons skittered loose across the marble floor.

A ragged gasp rose up around us. I registered distantly that everyone was watching, rapt and silent as a tournament audience in the final round, then dismissed that information as irrelevant. The pain from my cuts, the watching eyes, the lowering clouds above, the sawing of my own breath—none of it mattered. I had no time for anything but staying alive.

Rai followed up his first attack with more, brutally fast and hard. He was deadly serious about killing me now. The wind of his sword cut by my face, forcing my parries to get quicker and quicker, the shocks reverberating in my wrist. I had to take a step back, then another. *Shit.* I couldn't afford to lose ground like this.

I dug in, both blades working furiously to keep his at bay. I tried flicking a cut at his eyes to get him to back up, but he didn't so much as blink. This was no good—I'd picked up too many injuries, and my stamina was near its limits. He was going to finish me in a few more moves, and he knew it. A slow smile curved his lips.

And there it was. On the brink of victory, his intensity eased. He didn't quite get sloppy, but he gave me the fraction of an instant I needed to shift the tide and attack.

Time to climb up in his face like a rabid weasel.

I hurled myself at him, forcing his black blade up and aside with my dagger and lunging at his chest. Almarah would have been proud; I was fast, I was precise, it was perfect. The point of my sword took him straight through the heart.

I might as well have stabbed the wind. There was barely any resistance; my blade ran in almost to the hilt. I'd thrown so much force behind the thrust that I crashed into his armored chest, which was as solid for me as it had been airy for my blade. At least *that* knocked him back a little.

Without warning a spiked bracer slammed into my shoulder blades, knocking the wind out of me.

He crushed me against his chest, my sword still caught in him, clasping me close. A fierce grin lit his face as the cold edge of his blade came for the back of my neck.

Fuck. I jerked sideways and up out of reality just in time, into the liquid amber of the Veil, throwing myself through an insubstantial arm and a great black sword that had been *far* too close to ending my life. Panicky energy jolted through me, the last dregs in the bottom of my barrel.

A glimmer of motion flickered along the edge of Rai's blade, but I was ready for that. The instant light came into his eyes and his presence here was real, I rammed my dagger into his stomach.

He jolted with the impact, a ripple like a cry of pain shaking the Veil—but he'd expected it this time, too. His hand shot out and grabbed my sword wrist.

You can hurt me in this place, his voice hissed in my mind, *but you can't kill me. While killing* you *is as simple as holding you here.*

He wasn't wrong. Panic leaped in my insubstantial throat.

Starlight poured from the wound in his stomach, coursing over my hand and scalding it. Already a terrible pressure was building in me, a desperate drowning need to duck back out of the Veil and into reality. It came faster this time, my limits strained from pushing myself too far all night. It wouldn't take long for me to die here, in this time-forsaken place, from a cruel asphyxiation of the soul.

I wrenched against his grip, struggling to break free. He released his sword, leaving it hanging in midair, and seized my dagger arm, too.

Almarah had taught me how to fight in the Veil, in preparation for the unlikely event that I ever squared off against someone else who could blink step. *You and your opponent both move in a constructed space your brains made up so you can fool yourselves into believing you understand what's happening*, she'd told me. *But you're outside reality; none of it is truly real. You're as strong and fast as you believe yourself, deep down, to be.*

Rai thought pretty damned highly of himself. He was strong as a mountain; I couldn't break his grip.

I twisted my knife in his gut, desperate to make him let go, but his hands only tightened as his silent hiss of pain shivered through me. My nonexistent lungs ached to scream, my imagined veins ready to burst from the pressure of maintaining the idea of myself in this unreal place.

Kill me here, I tried to tell him, *and my death is wasted. If it's not the eleventh Echo, it doesn't count for the blood seal.*

He snarled, silver eyes mad with unaccustomed pain. *Then I'll bring you to the brink of annihilation here and finish you back in reality, cur.*

Black spots pulsed in my vision, as if holes were opening in the Veil into the Void itself. I didn't want to die here. I *couldn't* die here. Any longer in this place and my essence would spiral away into those expanding dark gaps, unmade utterly.

In desperation, I slammed my head forward, headbutting him right in the face.

It startled Rai just enough. His hold loosened, and I dropped out of the Veil, sound and color and light crashing into my senses.

The marble floor hit me hard as a falling building. I lay there gasping, pain stabbing viciously through my skull. My sword clanged down beside me.

I didn't understand at first that I'd collapsed. My whole body shuddered uncontrollably; my hands were twitching. It was all I could do to cling to some tattered shred of consciousness. Getting up to fight was out of the question.

"It's done," Rai said, his voice ragged at the edges. "I'll grant you this, mortal—you fought well. But it's over."

I forced my eyes into focus. He was standing over me, black blade in his hands once more. Unwounded and whole. He straightened, shaking off even the echoes of pain; his voice smoothed out, all traces of suffering vanishing from his sleek, composed presence. Damn it, I'd worked so *hard* to hurt him, almost killed myself to do it, and it hadn't even stuck.

He was going to kill me. Run me through with that murderous sword of his and pin me to the Echo and the year beyond it, using my life as nothing more than a sort of cosmic adhesive.

No. Fuck him. I was more than that.

"It's not over," I rasped. I hauled myself onto an elbow, and then my hands, and then my knees. It was unexpectedly hard. I couldn't stop shaking.

"Don't be a fool, little dog." He gazed at me with pity sliding inexorably into contempt. "You've lost. Make this easier on yourself and accept a clean death."

The door was right behind him. If he were just a couple of paces farther back, I could push him through it. But I doubted I could even stand.

He raised his sword. I reached for mine, fingers trembling, knowing I'd be too late.

The black blade came down.

SOMETIMES, YOU HAVE TO MAKE SACRIFICES

A flutter of white sleeves blocked my view of the sword rushing down to kill me, and the sweet chime of steel on steel rang through the ballroom.

Jaycel Morningray stood between us, close enough to Rai to kiss, her blade angled to catch his.

"If it's over and you've won, that means it's my turn, darling."

Rai grinned as if nothing could delight him more than her sudden appearance between him and his prey. "This wasn't the kind of dance I wanted with you."

"I'm afraid tonight's a wash, but I might be free next Thursday."

She lifted her other hand to the flat of her sword and shoved his blade away two-handed, then swept into a dramatic guard position, sword pointed at him, off hand curling gracefully up behind her head.

The whole maneuver forced him to take a couple of steps backward. *Yes.* Either she was brilliant, or her unerring sense of drama had saved the day. Knowing Jaycel, probably both. I braced myself to lurch to my feet; we had a chance.

"*Now,*" Dona Marjorie barked from behind me.

Jaycel ducked nimbly aside. Marjorie stood proud and indomitable in the middle of her transformed ballroom, resplendent in acres of puffy white tulle, fan in hand—the same fan, I realized with a start, its metallic filigree unchanged through every Echo from the way it had looked in Prime.

It was an Echo relic.

She snapped it open at Rai in a swift sideways cut, as if it were a weapon. A burst of air scythed over my head, ruffling my hair.

It hit Rai square in the chest with the force of a cannonball, staggering him. The cloud-filled door was right at his back.

This was my chance. I surged to my feet and hurled myself at him.

Or I tried, and sprawled flat instead. Something had a grip on my legs, locking them in place with a weight like stone. Shit, not just *like* stone—he'd shaped the marble floor over my legs, trapping me.

"I admire your spirit," he hissed, mirror eyes narrowing. He didn't sound like he meant it at all. "But your struggles are pointless. I am the blood of the Moon, fount of all creation; Echoes are like clay in my hands."

"And I," came a ringing, terrible voice, "am the blood that is starlight."

Rai's head jerked up in shock.

"You may not harm this one, Laughing As He Rises. She is mine."

I knew that voice. I couldn't help it; I glanced over my shoulder, stunned.

It was her, invitation or no invitation. Stars Tangled in Her Web, radiant as the Moon, terrible as the Void—long hair trailing moonbeams, gown shimmering with stardust. Oh, this wasn't any better. We were absolutely screwed.

Wait. *Rika, you brilliant scoundrel.* This was an illusion.

Rai recoiled a step, staring in shock. "*You!* How are you— I thought—"

I didn't let him finish. Bracing against the stab of pain through my head, I slipped once more into the Veil.

You can walk on a broken foot. Don't let anyone tell you that you can't; I know from experience that it's possible. It's just a terrible idea, and it hurts like the Moon's own wounds. But you can make yourself do it, in a crappy limping kind of way, swearing the whole time and regretting your choices.

Blink stepping when I'd just overextended my time in the Veil nearly to the point of unmaking was like that, only worse. Blinding agony shot through my head, through my whole body, through my *soul*, and it was all I could do not to bounce right back out into reality. But I held desperately to that fragile state of between-ness, just long enough to stumble forward a few steps, clumsy as if I were still a half-trained teenager. Rai was so busy staring in horror at Rika's illusion that he didn't notice and shift into the Veil after me; I was too insignificant in the face of a challenge by one of his own kind.

I popped back into reality right in his face, hooked his heel with my foot, and shoved him as hard as I could in the chest.

He toppled back through the door, eyes widening with sudden comprehension. But it was too late; the clouds swallowed him whole.

I had no chance for relief. Tendrils of fog reached for me at once, promising utter oblivion. I was too exhausted to get out of the way quickly enough; they were going to get me, pulling me into undoing after him.

Jaycel grabbed my shirt and yanked me backward. The double doors slammed shut on the misty void beyond with a reverberating crash, Pearson pushing one and Blair the other.

"Good riddance." Pearson panted with exertion, his eyes a little glassy. "Nice job, Kem."

"Thanks, everybody," I slurred, my words running together like water. "G'job."

My knees folded under me. The universe had slid a paring knife into my brain and was coring it like an apple. It would be so easy to flee into the grey borderlands between unconsciousness and sleep.

Something soft and warm and clove-scented draped over my shoulders—Rika's arm, trailing a fluttering silvery sleeve.

"You're a mess, Kembral," she murmured. "Are you going to pass out on me?"

"Trying not to." I pressed the heels of my hands into my temples and squeezed. "Did it stick? Is he locked out?"

"So far. The doors just rattled, but the ward is holding."

Thank the Moon. I trembled all over in some combination of relief and shock. We'd done it. Somehow, despite the impossibility of it, we'd bested an Empyrean. The nightmare was over, the world safe. I could go home and sleep for... well, for about two hours, until Emmi needed to nurse again.

"And no one is hurt?" I pressed, still scarcely able to believe it. "Everyone's all right?"

"Everyone but you."

There was a certain strain in Rika's voice. I looked at her past the sourceless glare of my headache—really *looked* at her—and whatever that expression was on her face, it wasn't good.

"What's wrong?" I demanded. "Blood on the Moon, I just want to be done. What is it this time?"

Rika didn't say anything. But she raised her eyes, her chin tilting slightly upward.

The clouds. The swirling, ominous ceiling had descended farther while I fought Rai; now only three balconies remained.

This close, it was all too clear that the stone walls didn't disappear into the clouds, exactly. As the underside of the foggy barrier eddied and shifted, sometimes it lifted just enough to reveal uneven edges of stone—some rough and broken as if the top of the wall had crumbled away, others smooth and slick as if it had been scooped out.

The clouds were devouring the walls as they descended, annihilating them as thoroughly and instantly as that tendril of fog had carved a gash in the floor by the ballroom doors.

"That doesn't look good," I said uneasily.

Marjorie and Jaycel and Pearson and the rest clustered around me; beyond them, the other party guests were hesitantly drawing near. Everyone looked up at the ceiling in fear and vague confusion; they still didn't know we were in an Echo, so they weren't sure what was going on, but by the strain in their faces they had an inkling it was bad.

Another heavy impact hit the door, and it quaked on its hinges. Everyone flinched. *That* they understood all too well. For now, at least, the invitation ward seemed to be keeping him out.

"What does this mean?" Rika asked, a pleading note creeping into her voice. "We defeated Rai, didn't we? He didn't kill either of us. There's no blood seal in this Echo; no one can name the year. Shouldn't we go back to Prime now?"

I shook my head. I had no answers. The others exchanged worried glances; they understood even less than we did. All they knew was that an Empyrean had attacked the party and that something was decidedly wrong.

"That's not how it works," said a small voice.

The Clockmaker stood nearby, big brown eyes nervous, one hand twisting her apron and the other clutching a pair of pliers. I rose and moved toward her, that same foolish protective urge surging through me.

"How *does* it work?" I asked, keeping my voice gentle. I swept a warning glare around at everyone else, trying to say *scare her and I'll break your arms.*

"The game isn't over yet. The year hasn't turned; someone could still name it. The clock needs the power from either a blood seal or the year-turning itself to take you back to Prime, and it's still two hours until midnight. You can't go home." She gave the pliers a helpless, halfhearted wave. "I did everything I could. I'm sorry. It wasn't enough."

"You don't have to be sorry," I said immediately. "You've done great."

Blair drifted closer; the Clockmaker's worried expression softened to a smile. They blinked at her pliers in amazement.

"It's a wonderful clock," they said. "I've been looking at it between all the fuss. You're very good."

"Thank you." She glowed under the praise, but then her face fell. "It's shielding this place against the outside for now, but it's just not powerful enough. The shield keeps shrinking. It's not going to last much longer."

My chest squeezed. "What does that mean for us?"

The Clockmaker's chin tightened. She looked as if she might cry.

"You can tell me," I said encouragingly, even as my stomach sank.

"The clouds will eat away your ward first, and he'll get in." Her voice started small, and got even smaller. "But even if you somehow kept him out, it wouldn't matter. The safe place will keep shrinking and shrinking. There'll be nothing left by midnight."

I struggled to keep the horror from my face. After everything we'd done—after facing Empyreans and Echoes and murder over and over, all night long—we were going to have to watch death creep closer and closer until the clouds pressed down on us and unmade us. It seemed impossibly cruel.

"I'm sorry," the Clockmaker whispered miserably.

Blair nodded, thoughtful and solemn. "That's what I thought. Oh well. I suppose we're all going to die."

"No. Fuck that. We can't die. I won't allow it." My voice had sharpened too much; I smoothed it out, trying to wrestle helpless panic into calm assurance, for everyone else's sake if not my own. "There's got to be something we can do. Some way to get back to Prime before then, or to stabilize this place, or—"

"There's one way," the Clockmaker said, her small voice heavy with reluctance.

I knew that I was going to hate the answer, but I had to ask. We were out of good options.

"What is it?"

The Clockmaker closed her eyes briefly, then opened them. They were so much like Emmi's, except wise and wary far beyond her apparent age.

"You could name the year."

"No," I said immediately. And at the same moment, Rika said, "Yes."

I whirled on her, incredulous. "Have you forgotten what we'd need to do to name the year? One of us would have to *die*."

She gestured furiously up at the lowering clouds. "If we don't, we're all going to die anyway!"

A great surge of muddied emotions swamped my chest. Anger at her for even suggesting such a thing. Fury at the Empyreans and the world for doing this to us. And a sick gaping fear, dark as the Void itself that waited below us, just beyond the paper-thin barrier of the Veil.

"Absolutely not," I snapped. "I don't accept that choice. Neither of us has to die. *None* of us are going to die. We'll find a way."

Rika threw up her hands. "There *is* no other way! What are you going to do, go out there and find your way back to Prime through the instant death clouds? The time for finding other ways has run out, Kembral!"

Jaycel frowned, staring at each of us in turn. "What are you *talking* about? Nothing you're saying makes any sense! You're worse than Blair all of a sudden."

Everyone was staring at us. Not only my friends, but the people I didn't know well, like Vandelle and Carter, and the people I didn't know at all, like the two Butterflies and the physicker. They were scared—I could see it in their eyes—but there was trust there as well. We'd just kicked out an Empyrean, and they were clearly confident that whatever was happening now, we'd find a way to save them.

Rika gave them all a brilliant smile. "We might have a plan, but Kembral and I need to discuss it for a moment. Excuse us."

"We don't need to *discuss* this." I crossed my arms. "There's nothing to discuss. I'm not going to—"

"In private," Rika said firmly. She grabbed my hand and towed me toward the stairs with the implacable determination of a parent removing a misbehaving child from a candy shop.

I stumbled, and suddenly she had to catch my arm, cursing. It was too much—the blood I'd lost, the stabbing awful headache, the shuddery exhausted weakness of a body I'd pushed too far before I even walked into this accursed party. And now the welling up in my chest of some hopeless, angry, miserable feeling—the knowledge that we were in a bad, bad corner, and it didn't look like I'd be able to get everyone out of it alive.

Not Rika. Damn it, not Rika, after all we'd been through tonight.

"Come on," Rika whispered. "Everyone's watching, and you're their best hope. Up those stairs, and then you can fall down all you want once we're out of sight."

"Fine," I grated through my teeth. "But your plan had better not be what I think it is."

"We can talk about that once we're out of sight, too."

She had to help me up the stairs. My side had fully reopened, and between that and the cuts Rai had given me, I was leaving a modest blood trail—nothing to panic about, just a few drops per step, but I should probably do something about that once I got through the more pressing crisis. Everything hurt, my legs were useless trembling mush under me, and the clouds loomed ominously low overhead. I could feel everyone's eyes on us.

I would have stayed on those stairs forever if it meant never getting to the top and having to hear Rika's horrible idea. I knew what it was by the way her hand trembled on my arm, the way she wouldn't meet my eyes.

We got to the top and moved away from the railing, out of sight of the subdued gathering below. Murmurs rose up from the crowd—people demanding to know what was going on, Jaycel making some kind of witty quip to dissolve tension. Dona Marjorie's voice bright and airy, assuring everyone it would be fine, she knew and trusted Signa Thorne to handle the situation. That put a lump in my throat.

"All right." Rika squeezed my arm. "You can sit down."

She flopped to the floor in a graceless way that made me realize she was tired, too, and leaned back against the wall. I joined her, wincing at the pain of folding myself. The marble wall was cold at my back, leaching my heat away through my poor slashed-up coat.

It felt almost companionable, like we were collapsing here to complain about how tired and sore we were after a long day. I wished I could fool myself into believing that was all we were here for.

"Kembral," Rika began, in the careful tone of someone determined to be reasonable.

"No."

"You heard what she said. We need to name the year."

"There's *got* to be some way to do this without killing anyone." I dragged the unraveling strands of hair back from my face, coming away with a smear of blood on my palm. "Maybe if we got help from an Empyrean who *doesn't* want to name the year—"

"No Empyrean is going to make a deal to save us without naming the year for them. It's too important, and they all want it too badly, and we have no leverage whatsoever to bargain." She shook her head, not meeting my eyes. "We're out of choices and out of time. You've got to name the year. You're the only one who can. I didn't bleed on the last Echo, so I'm out."

"*Rika.*" Her name twisted out of me like a blade bursting through my chest. "I'd have to kill you. I won't do it. I *can't.*"

She looked up at that, showing me the naked fear she'd been hiding. It was in every line of her face. She was *terrified.* But she reached out one trembling hand and laid her long, cool fingers against my cheek.

"It's okay." Her voice came out husky and cracked. "I think . . . it'll be all right."

"No it won't!" I grabbed her shoulders as if I could squeeze sense into her. "The clock doesn't protect us. You *know* that. If you or I die here, we die for real."

"Listen." She swallowed, her throat jumping. "There are things I still haven't told you."

"Don't give me any of that last words bullshit!" My voice cracked and broke. Not this. I could bear all the rest of it, even Blair, but not this.

"You're right." Her hand left my cheek, mouth twisting. "We don't have time for it, *or* for your moral crisis. Look at the clouds."

I glanced up, despite myself. The ceiling had gotten lower; the clouds rested on the railing of the balcony above us. *That* wasn't good.

Rika grabbed my wrist, turned my palm up, and slapped something cold into it.

The hilt of a sharp, wickedly pointed knife.

I tried to drop it in horror, but she closed my hand around it, firmly, staring into my eyes. "There's no fucking *time*, Kembral." She was shaking all over, the tears spilling out now. "Just do it."

"No. I'm not taking part in your little drama." I was angry now, and it boiled over in words that rushed stumbling from my mouth. "I looked for you for my whole *life*, Rika. I finally found you tonight, and I finally found out I was wrong—you didn't betray me, and you *do* care about me—and now maybe we could be friends, or . . . or something. And we're supposed to have that picnic up in Hillcrest Park." I took a wild, shuddering breath. "I *like* you, is what I'm trying to say." Moon above, I was bad at this.

Rika bit her lip, the tears spilling over. "Kembral . . ."

Now *I* was crying, the salt stinging in the cut on my cheek. It didn't feel like a good, healing release; it only felt terrible.

"I have to go home to my daughter after this, Rika. How in the Void can I raise her and show her how to be a good person if I'm only alive because I killed someone I care about?"

The ballroom doors shuddered in their hinges, and there came the sound of splintering wood. Scattered gasps of fear sounded below in response, and then Marjorie's voice assuring everyone it would be all right.

Rika's mouth quirked ever so slightly. Her lipstick was still perfect, and some small corner of my mind that wasn't completely losing its shit figured it must be an illusion.

"Glad to hear that you care," she said softly. "I like you, too."

Her long black lashes dropped down over those clear grey eyes. She drifted closer to me, her lips parting, and I realized in panic that she was about to kiss me.

Did I want to kiss Rika Nonesuch, here at the end of the worlds?

Yes. In defiance of the death closing in on us and the ruin of the year's ending, yes, I did.

Her lips brushed mine, feather-light. All my focus narrowed to this moment, that exquisitely gentle touch, warm and full of a tenderness I would never in a thousand years have guessed lived within Rika at all. But here it was, unmistakable and heartbreakingly genuine, tasting faintly of salt.

"I'm sorry," she whispered, her breath mingling with mine.

Her grip closed like iron around my hand—the one she'd placed the knife in. And she drove it up in a sharp, sudden movement between her ribs.

NO TIME TO GRIEVE

Rika! No, damn it, *Rika!*"

I dropped the dagger in horror, but it was too late. She pressed both hands over the wound, curling around it in pain, and let out an agonized little cough.

"Sorry," she gasped. "Had to...distract you..."

Something was wrong, something beyond the obvious wrongness of Rika dying by my hand, Rika stabbed through the heart, Rika blue-lipped and shaking and utterly undone. Something that pulled at my Hound training, a piece that didn't fit—but I was shattered into pieces myself, and I couldn't pick any of them up. Only hold her, crying, no longer able to do anything else.

"You little brat. How could you do this to me?" I was as wrecked as she was, holding her too tight, desperately trying to think what kind of first aid I could possibly perform—but that dagger had pierced her heart. I'd felt it. It would take one of the city's most powerful Echo workers to do something about that, and we didn't have one.

"Shh. Don't want anyone to see." Her voice was thick with blood. "Didn't want you to see, either."

She was changing.

The planes of her face sharpened; her hair went from a normal, human brownish shade of black to a deep velvety darkness like the night sky. Her eyes subtly shifted shape, becoming catlike, with large bloodred irises and slitted pupils. Something feather-soft intervened between my supporting hands and the pain-taut muscles of her back, though I didn't see any sign of wings.

"You *are* Echoborn," I breathed. "No, wait, you're...you're an *Echo*."

"No!...No." Her voice weakened, ending in another cough that twisted her face in agony. "My father...was human. Please, don't look at me...I don't want..."

She couldn't finish. She might as well have stabbed me in the heart right back.

I bent over her face—and it was still her face. Still Rika's expression, frustration dimpling her brow even through the throes of death, the same complex shadows in her eyes even though they had become so alien. Her hair still smelled the same—and fuck, *how did I know that?* I wasn't going to examine that, not now.

I placed a kiss on her forehead, right on that angry little crease. Leaving tears on her brow.

"You look fine," I murmured. "You look great. Anyone says otherwise, I'll punch them."

"Name the year," she said hoarsely. "As soon as the clock starts tolling. Name it, or this is all for nothing."

"*Fuck you*, Rika."

"Name it, you little..."

Her eyes turned glassy, and they slid closed. Her body went utterly limp in my arms.

BOOOOOOONNNG.

"No," I whispered, the word cracking in my dry throat. "*No.*"

BOOOOOOONNNG.

The ballroom doors blasted open, wood shards flying everywhere. Fog poured in; everyone ran to the far side of the room below, screaming. It all barely registered. I was staring at Rika, the knell of the clock shuddering through my soul.

BOOOOOOONNNG.

An animal howl tried to rise up in my chest. I cradled Rika's body close, rocking as if I were holding a fussing Emmi, as if somehow I could make this all right. But it was only agony that drove the motion; there was no comfort in it, not for me, not for anyone.

BOOOOONNNG.

Rai sauntered through the ruined door, blade in hand, cloak swirling around him like a great cloud of darkness. His eyes glowed an intense silver, and he looked wilder, crueler, more powerful than ever.

BOOOOONNNG.

He was going to come kill me. To drive that black sword through my heart, the last Cloud Moon alive in this place. I might almost welcome it—except Rika had sacrificed too much, and I was far too stubborn to give up so easily.

BOOOOONNNG.

I had to do this. I couldn't just sit here and let the whole world fall apart. I had to name the year—for Rika. For everyone downstairs who would otherwise die. For Emmi.

My hands tightened on Rika's limp shoulders, her body too light in my lap, too unresponsive. Her head tipped back, that Void-dark hair spilling over me. I needed a name for the year. Something good, that wouldn't wind up screwing the world over. Something safe. And I needed it fast, before Rai got up here and killed me and named it himself.

BOOOONNNNG.

My mind went horribly, terrifyingly blank. I was some random Hound, unqualified to shape the future. I had my hand on the destiny of the world, and the responsibility paralyzed me.

BOOOOONNNNG.

Boots rang on marble, ascending. Rai was coming up the stairs.

I couldn't think of a name for the fucking year. I was going to die, tragic and pointless, because I couldn't think of anything that wasn't a recipe for disaster. Rika had died for this, and I was going to let her down.

BOOOOOONNNNNG.

Rika's hands slipped away from her wound, lifeless.

What poured out of it wasn't blood.

It was light. A glorious white radiance, dripping and running like liquid, white-hot and brilliant.

I froze.

BOOOOONNNG.

A little tendril of warmth unfurled in my chest, weak and fragile and miraculous. That bleeding light caught in my eyes, wormed its way into my heart. Rika's utter stillness in my arms couldn't kill it.

Neither could Rai's shadow falling over me.

"Now," he whispered, "you die at last, Kembral Thorne."

BOOOONNNGG.

No. I wasn't ready to die.

A river of emotion boiled up in me like a great volcanic eruption, fierce and hot, full of rage and grief and love and something else, something wild and inexplicably joyous. The spark lit in me by that liquid spill of light from Rika's heart caught fire and leaped into an unstoppable inferno.

I met Rai's gaze and gave him a big fuck-you smile.

"I name this year the Year of Hope!" I shouted.

His expression twisted at once into too-late desperation, the bitter and frantic disappointment of someone who knows they will never catch the fragile thing they just dropped before it breaks beyond repair. He reached for me—not to lash out in violence, but almost as if he were pleading for help.

BOOOOOONNNNNGG.

The clock struck for the twelfth and final time, and the world shattered all around me. I closed my eyes and let myself shatter with it.

ALL IS NEVER TRULY LOST

Reality shook itself like a wet dog and settled around me. The familiar lines of Dona Marjorie's ballroom came into focus—her *actual* ballroom, with its tall arched windows and tasteful curtains and crystal chandeliers. The comforting solidity of Prime surrounded me, everything stable and ordinary and mundane. I'd landed in the little second-floor balcony where Marjorie sometimes hid musicians, guards, spies, or whatever else suited her current need and fancy behind a decorative screen; I knew it, and others like it, from when I'd helped protect her son.

I didn't give a rotten rat's tail about being back in Prime. I only had eyes for Rika, still and limp in my arms. Light gleamed from the wound in her chest, but it was fading, like the slow dulling of drying blood.

The spark it had ignited in my heart still burned, a thin, desperate flame in my chest.

"Come on," I whispered, as the last echoes of the clock faded. "Come on, wake up, you dramatic little wretch."

A great cheer rose up incongruously from the party below.

Jaycel's voice, blurred at the edges with alcohol, called out, "Happy New Year!"

The sounds of celebration grated on me like sandpaper in an open wound. I couldn't stand it. I wanted to scream down at them to shut up—there was nothing to celebrate, because Rika was dead.

Except that possibility thrummed in the air, an exciting electric tingle I could feel even through exhaustion and grief. Something seemed to slowly stir inside me, raising its exhausted head.

And there was the light.

Echoborn didn't bleed light. Pure Echoes sometimes did, but Rika had said her father was human.

Her lashes fluttered, the smallest bit. Her lips parted. I held her close, not daring to breathe.

Rika Nonesuch opened her eyes.

They faded from bloodred to grey quick as a kid throwing a blanket over contraband when their mom walks into the room. The angles of her face shifted just as swiftly back to more human lines, her hair losing the bottomless depth of the Void and becoming mere black again. She blinked a few times, her gaze fixing at first on my face, then tracking down to the ragged hole in her gown in time to see the last glimmer of light wink out.

"Shit," she muttered. "So much for this dress."

There were so many things I could have said. But I couldn't bear to say anything tender, and I was too shaken for anything witty.

All I managed was a weary "I can't believe you didn't tell me you're a fucking Empyrean."

"I'm not," she protested, sitting up as if she were totally fine, unhurt, hadn't been dead in my arms seconds ago. I could have strangled her if I weren't so desperately, soul-shakingly relieved. "I'm really not."

"But your mother is."

It was the thing I'd realized the moment I saw her bleeding light. Like moonlight or starlight—same as Rai had, in the Veil. *Celestial ichor.* I only felt like a fool for not figuring it out before.

Rika's gaze darted around as if seeking some means of escape, and she licked her lips. "Well..."

"Stars Tangled in Her Web. That's your connection with her—she's your mother."

"Not so loud, you oaf!" Rika made frantic shushing motions. "And she's not my *mother*. Not in any real sense of the word. She abandoned me in Prime right after I was born. I didn't even know until she...until I fell into that Echo and met her." She shuddered, drawing her knees up to her chest.

"You could have *told* me that, so I wouldn't worry!" I threw my hands up. "Damn it, Rika, I thought you were *dead*!"

"I...It was too complicated. We were out of time." She bit her lip. "Besides, I didn't know for sure that it wouldn't stick. I don't think I've ever died before."

"You're the worst. You could have said 'Oh, Kembral, don't worry, I'm born of the divine ichor of the Moon and the Void, no mortal can truly slay me,' or something like that."

"Don't say it like that!" She glared at me. "It's not like that. I'm as human as any Echoborn. Besides, I was...scared."

That softened my anger a little. "Well, anyone would be scared of being stabbed to death."

"Not of that." She flushed crimson. "I was scared of...of you finding out."

I stared at her, astonished. "What? Why?"

"Because I didn't want you to..." She waved her hands helplessly. "Look, no one else knows. I didn't want things to get...weird. Between us."

"Rika," I said, "things have *always* been weird between us."

"Weirder, then. Look, Kembral, I—" She broke off, eyes narrowing. "Are you all right? You've gone really pale."

I almost laughed. *All right?* My head was still splitting open, I was bleeding from multiple wounds, I'd survived an Empyrean's curse *and* being trapped in the Veil twice, and I hadn't had more than three consecutive hours of sleep in two months. Not to mention that I'd just named a fucking crux year, whatever that meant, and anything bad that happened for the next century or so would probably be my fault.

"I'm fine," I said instead. "Just fine."

But maybe Prime wasn't as solid and steady as I'd thought, because it wobbled and lurched to the side, and I felt the sick swooping sensation of a fall. For an instant, I panicked, thinking I was dropping down another Echo and we were starting all over—but no, I was just fainting.

Well, that's all right then.

I blacked out.

—⚏—

I was dimly aware of yelling, and Dona Marjorie's voice exclaiming something suspiciously like *Oh my Moon and stars*, and then being carried. Which was an awkward business and rather embarrassing, but I was too far away to put a stop to it. There was a frantic bustling interlude of my beloved scarlet coat being peeled off and wounds being treated, each poke and prod bringing me a little closer back to myself with stabs of pain.

Finally I returned enough to croak out a plea for water. Someone held a cup to my lips, but they were cursed bad at it, and it all poured down my front.

I spluttered, coming fully awake at last.

I was in a very nice, soft bed in what must be one of Dona Marjorie's guest rooms, lying on top of the covers, which I'd ruined by bleeding all over them. The same poor physicker was washing blood from his hands in a basin set in his lap, muttering something about having no idea what happened to all his medical supplies. Bandages wrapped tight around my ribs, and my arm, and another cut on my thigh I hadn't even noticed. A plaster stuck to my cheek.

Several people crowded into the room, making it feel small: Marjorie and Jaycel and Pearson and Rika, all of them looking worried. Rika was the one who'd just dumped half a cup of water on me as she turned to say something to the physicker, because of course she was.

"Void's teeth, Rika, I wanted water to *drink*, not for a bath!"

She turned to me with impeccable poise. "You could use one of those, too."

The physicker made a tutting noise, but Jaycel drowned him out with a robust laugh, slapping me on the shoulder. I winced.

"I'm so glad you're all right." Marjorie placed a hand delicately over her heart. "I must say, I was worried when you were fighting that Empyrean!"

I blinked. "You remember that?"

"Stars, it would be hard to forget!" She fluttered her fan, which made me a bit more nervous now that I knew it was an Echo relic weapon. But then, she clearly knew how to use it.

"Thank you for loaning me that sword, by the way," I said. "It's really nice."

"Did I loan it to you? Oh, you should keep it then! Why, after that spectacular duel, it was clearly made for you." She beamed at me.

My heart leaped like a kid getting a festival present. "Really? Thanks!"

Rika glanced from me to Marjorie, a little smile lingering on her lips. "If you recall the Empyrean, do you remember everything now, Dona Swift?"

Marjorie's fan paused, and she frowned. "I'm afraid my memories are rather blurry for a few hours before that, up until just before that whole dramatic business with the Empyrean. Signa Pearson tells me we were in an Echo, which seems terribly alarming!"

That was downright funny now that I knew she was the Fisher Queen. I had no doubt she could navigate the shallow Echoes more adeptly than I could. But I wouldn't dream of compromising her cover, so I played along.

"We were. But we're back in Prime now?" I knew the answer—I could feel the difference in the sheer solid *realness* of the bed beneath me, the blessed mundane solidity of the ceiling, the ordinary dull absence of any sort of effervescence in the air. But it still felt so good to see everyone nod, confirming it. "How much time has passed?"

"What you'd think," Dona Marjorie said, with airy unconcern. "It's about half an hour after midnight. Happy New Year, by the way!"

I sure hoped it'd be happy. If it wasn't, that was now probably my fault.

"Happy New Year," I mumbled. At least I'd still make it home in a reasonably timely fashion, without keeping my sister up too late. It was an enormous relief to know Emmi and I were on the same layer of reality again.

The physicker launched into some long description of things I should do for wound care and how I should be certain to get plenty of rest, especially since I was a nursing mother. *Ha.* That showed what he knew about nursing mothers. I mostly ignored him, my gaze wandering to Rika sure as water flowed downhill. She looked back at me, her grey eyes troubled, then seemed to realize she was staring and glanced down at her hands instead.

Soon enough everyone else returned to the party, one by one, with all sorts of congratulations and wishes for a speedy recovery. I asked for Marjorie to stay long enough to explain in private about the token in her pocket, to make sure she'd remember to get rid of it; then even she was gone, and it was just Rika and me.

Rika didn't look up from her hands. Her fingers wrapped around one another in increasingly complex patterns.

"You really didn't figure it out?" she asked abruptly. "Before the end, I mean."

It took me a moment to work through what she meant. "Oh. No. I did start thinking you might be Echoborn, but not until tonight. I didn't even know Empyreans could *have* children."

She shook her head in affectionate disgust. "Come on, Kembral. You've seen my illusions—do you know any Ravens who can do them so quickly, without any gestures or words or relics?"

"No, but I . . . I just thought you were really good."

"As if the Ravens would allow that kind of knowledge outside their guild at all, let alone in the hands of a Cat!"

"Look, I'm a Hound, not an expert on Echo working. What *do* you tell the Ravens?"

"I let them think I'm a regular Echoborn. And for most purposes, I really am." She forced a laugh. "You're the first person to know the truth."

"I won't tell anyone," I assured her. "It's your secret."

"For now. Arhsta—my mother . . ." Her voice dwindled to a whisper. "I don't think she's going to let me go so easily this time."

"I won't ever let her take you again," I promised, reaching for her hand. Rika gave it to me with a swiftness bordering on relief, her slender fingers feeling fragile in the cradle of my rough ones. "I spent all those years learning to blink step so I could rescue you if you fell into an Echo. If that bitch tries anything, she'll find out what I can do."

Rika flashed me a smile that held a faint reflection of the little girl I remembered. "And I'm going to keep watching your back. Harking might be out of the picture, but you're terrible at looking after yourself."

"Right. Harking." I released her hand to haul myself up higher on my pillows, wincing at the sharp twinge from my side. "I can only *hope* he's out of the picture. It's awfully hard to get any kind of consequences to stick to a City Elder, even if they commit crimes in front of a room full of people."

"Oh." Rika hesitated, biting her lip. "That's right. You haven't heard."

"Haven't heard what?" I asked, wary.

"In that last Echo... You remember how the clouds were descending on us from above, annihilating everything?"

"It would be kind of hard to forget."

"Well, apparently they were coming up from below, too. Flooding the cellars and consuming them."

Realization dawned on me. "Harking was locked up down there."

"Yes." Rika met my gaze, her expression perfectly schooled into neutrality. "Yes, he was."

Well. That was equal parts horrifying and...all right, there was some satisfaction in there, too. I wasn't proud of it, but there it was.

"I mean, he did steal children and murder people," I mumbled. "But no one should ever die that way."

Rika's neutrality crumbled. "But if someone *had* to, Harking is the one I'd have picked," she concluded, with a certain vicious relish.

Silence fell between us. A question loomed in it, uncomfortably large and complicated. What we were to each other now, after everything that had happened between us tonight. What that kiss meant—which had been a distraction, just like the café had been a trap, but I knew Rika well enough now to understand that didn't mean it wasn't real.

What did you say to the girl you'd kissed and killed and saved and been saved by, in the first hour of the New Year?

Something stupid, probably, given my record to date.

"We're both going to need new outfits," I muttered awkwardly, confirming it.

She let out a deeply aggrieved sigh, the tension broken. "Don't I know it. I'm devastated." A gleam came into her eye. "Maybe we can shop for them together."

"I've got the baby," I said, out of reflex.

"Bring the baby. We'll get her an outfit, too. It'll be adorable."

I swallowed. "That...sounds wonderful. I can't wait for you to meet her."

We were talking about a future that had both of us in it, and Emmi, too. We'd actually made it back to a Prime where a future like that existed. I had to blink my stinging eyes a few times.

On the topic of the future...it occurred to me that we still had one very dangerous loose end to wrap up.

"Rika," I said quietly. "What are we going to do about Vandelle?"

She shook her head. "Only you, Kembral. Only you could lie there, cut to ribbons after saving the entire damn world, and come up with a way for there still to be more work to be done. Bask in your laurels for a while, will you?"

"I'm hardly cut to ribbons," I objected. "And we can't just let her go off into the night thinking she still has some sort of active deal with Rai to overthrow the government."

"Oh, fine." She rose, weariness putting a hitch or two in her usual economic grace. "Let's go save the city one last time. But *then* we're going home."

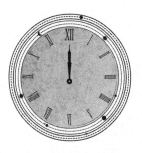

DON'T TAKE THE JOB HOME
WITH YOU

Rika and I found Vandelle alone and despondently slouch-shouldered in a corner, away from the giddy relief and drunken laughter of the rest of the partygoers, one hand stuffed in her tailcoat pocket and the other holding a drink. She was staring into its depths as if desperately seeking wisdom there.

"Excuse me, Dona," I began.

Vandelle jumped as if we'd snuck up on her by surprise, her drink dancing in its glass.

"Oh! Signa Thorne. Signa Nonesuch." She gave me a closer look, and her brows flew up. "Blood on the Moon, Signa Thorne, you're a mess. Should you be up and about?"

"No," Rika said sweetly, at the same time I said, "Yes."

Vandelle grimaced, glancing in her cup again, and then nervously at the ballroom doors. "I'm sorry. That he...That the Empyrean attacked you. I'm glad everything turned out all right."

"It nearly didn't," Rika pointed out, stepping a little closer at an angle that shielded our conversation, making it more private.

"Listen, Dona Vandelle," I said. "I don't know how much you remember, but that wasn't the first time the Empyrean attacked this party tonight."

Vandelle's eyes widened. Her throat moved in a convulsive swallow. "It...wasn't?"

"I'm going to cut through all the dancing around, because I'm tired." I held her gaze unflinchingly. "I know you had a deal with Laughing As He Rises. You don't remember, but you broke with him after realizing what he was, and the violent methods he uses. It was the right call."

I was leaving out so much—Rai slaughtering people in her name, Vandelle giving in and accepting the deal, Rai killing her himself, the fact that he'd been using her as an anchor for his own existence. The real feelings that had flickered across his face when she'd repudiated him. Maybe she had a right to know; maybe it was wrong not to tell her. But she looked like she had plenty to struggle with as it was. I sure as stars did.

Vandelle's face tightened. "Did...Do you know what he promised me?"

"Yes." Rika gave her a cool, assessing look. "And anyone who thinks they can overthrow a government without people getting hurt is a fool, Dona Vandelle. I don't think you're a fool."

Vandelle glanced around, but no one was close enough to eavesdrop. "I don't want to overthrow anything," she hissed. "I just want real reform. And you've got to admit that's never going to happen with the people and the systems we have in place."

"Maybe," I admitted. "But you do this city much more good continuing to try than by bathing it in blood. Besides, with Harking dead—"

Vandelle blinked. "Wait a minute. Harking's dead?"

"Apparently." I rubbed my aching temple. "The point is, you have a chance. You don't need to bring in an Empyrean to help you."

There was that electricity in the air, the charged and giddy feeling that had infused everything since we came back to Prime. Maybe it was just relief that we weren't dead, or maybe something else kept everyone here and partying rather than running home in terror. Just in case all this hadn't been entirely pointless, I dared give voice to it.

"You have hope."

Vandelle's head lifted, a certain gleam coming into her eyes. "Yeah. Maybe I do."

"And," Rika added with a broad smile, "if you ever even *think* about making a deal with an Empyrean again, I will personally make sure you don't live to regret it."

Vandelle blinked at that. A struggle broke out on her face as she tried to decide whether she was offended that Rika had just threatened a City Elder, then seemed to consider the context and accept that she'd deserved it.

"That's fair. But it won't come up." She straightened. "I'm from Dockside, and we don't need help from the powerful to get things done."

"Damn right you don't," I agreed.

—m—

Rika caught my elbow as we walked away from Vandelle, steadying me. "You should probably go home and sleep," she murmured. "Like the physicker told you."

Sleep sounded wonderful. More than that, though, I wanted Emmi. I needed to see her, to hold her warm and small against me, to know she was safe. And to nurse, because holy Moon, so much milk had come in during all this time that my chest felt like it was going to explode.

"Yeah," I agreed, exhausted. "Much as I've enjoyed this party—" I broke off. The Clockmaker was staring urgently at me across the room, hovering near her clock. "Looks like there's someone I need to talk to first."

Rika followed my gaze and sighed. "Fine. Go talk to her, but I'll make your goodbyes for you. I'm not interested in having to carry you home because you stayed too long chatting with friends and keeled over."

I was about to retort, but honestly, staying and chatting with friends now that no one was in danger of imminent death sounded lovely, and I *would* probably find it hard to leave. The party was only now getting into full swing; the musicians had struck up dance music—not

"Under the Flower Moon," thank goodness—and drunken revelers were taking to the floor. Dona Marjorie was loudly declaring to Carter that he should go to the cellars and bring out the good stuff.

I supposed this party would be remembered for a long time, except for the bit where only Rika and I recalled more than a small fraction of it. But I not only needed to get home, at this point I desperately *wanted* to get home.

"Thanks," I said simply.

Rika gave me a long look, and squeezed my arm before letting it go.

The Clockmaker waited for me, practically radiating tension. The sheer worry on her face put a dreadful sinking feeling in my stomach. Surely, *surely* we were done now. The year had turned, the midnight hour had struck, and the game was over.

I tried to keep all of this out of my voice and give her an honest smile. "Hi."

"You did it," she breathed. Her fingers twisted together. "You named the year."

"Apparently. Is that good? Did I mess it up?"

"You did fine." She bit her lip, seeming to think how to put it. "Maybe too fine. You . . . you named a crux year. That marks you."

"Shit." I rubbed my forehead. "This is going to be a long year, isn't it."

"It's a *crux* year," the Clockmaker emphasized. "You *named* it. It's yours. And it'll affect everything, in all the Echoes, until the next crux year comes."

I was no Raven, but I could guess that would make me about as interesting to Echoes and Empyreans and such as the single heir to a massive fortune was to every bachelor in town. Which was absolutely, positively *not* what I needed when I was trying to just live my damn life and raise my kid.

"They're not going to let me forget this, are they."

The Clockmaker shook her head vehemently. "You're bound to the year by your blood. So your mastery of the year is *in* your blood." She stared at me, imploring me to get it. "You know how some Echoes are about that sort of thing."

I felt suddenly unsteady. "Did I just make my blood the most valuable substance in the eleven Echoes?"

She nodded, grimacing.

"Well, shit."

"Most people won't realize. But the Empyreans will know, and word might spread. I'm sorry."

A cold, cold thought bloomed in my mind, spreading veins of frost through my whole body. "This is going to put Emmi in danger."

"It's going to put *you* in danger." The Clockmaker drew in a deep breath, as if steeling herself. "I want to thank you. For keeping me safe. I want to protect you, like you've protected me. So if you let me, I can rework the clock to preserve you."

"What do you mean?"

"It was really hard to make it protect everyone here, and ward the building against the Echoes as well." She waved her hand around the ballroom, excitement sparking in her eyes as she warmed to her topic. "But if I only tie the clock to *one* person, the effect can be much more powerful, and I don't have to bind it to a location. I'm pretty sure I could rework it to give you the same sort of protective Echo shield, no matter where you were. So if you were going to die—if you were going to be seriously hurt, even—it would shed the Echo shell and turn you back to how you were before. Just like it did for everyone tonight, but responding more quickly, and I think I could let you keep your memory." She frowned, her serious little girl brows contracting, and it was a look I knew from my own face. "I hope that made sense."

I went very still. "You're saying you could protect me from— what, accidents, violent death, curses, generalized murder?"

She nodded vigorously. "Yes."

"For how long?"

"For your whole life." The look she gave me was strangely intense, full of silent pleading.

A powerful, eager, almost desperate swell of feeling surged up in me. "Could you—"

"Wait." She raised a hand, stopping me, and her eyes grew

suddenly damp. "I know what you're going to say. I *know*. Because it would protect me, too. You want me to do it for Emmelaine instead."

"*Yes*." I could barely keep myself under control. I wanted to fall to my knees and beg her, hug her, show her how much this meant to me. Nothing in the whole world terrified me more than the idea of something happening to Emmi; the thought was an awful, yawning chasm that could open below me and swallow me whole, into light-less and unfathomable depths. And she might be able to close that horrifying abyss forever. "Can you? Would you?"

Her small hands made fists at her sides. "I used to hope you would ask that. Because it would keep me safe from just about anything. But you're in so much more danger than Emmi is, and you turned out to be so nice. Please, take it for yourself. I don't want you to die."

I laughed. I couldn't help myself, even though the Clockmaker gave me a strange look. "Thank you. I'm sorry, I shouldn't laugh— I'm deeply touched. But it's just..." I wiped my eyes. "There's nothing I want more than for Emmi to be safe. Nothing even comes close. If I can make sure my messing around sticking my fingers into cosmic nonsense with this year-naming business doesn't put her in danger, well, it'd be the greatest gift anyone could ever give me."

The Clockmaker let out a breath that was half defeat, half relief. "You're sure?"

"Yes. Absolutely. I've never been more sure of anything in my life."

She nodded, smiling. "I'll do it, then."

The Clockmaker looked as if maybe she might want a hug, so I kind of twitched my arms in that direction, just in case. And she stepped into them like she'd always belonged there.

"Be careful," she breathed as she hugged me back.

"I will."

"You won't." She stepped back out of the hug, giving me an exas-perated look. "But maybe a bit *more* careful, anyway."

I smiled back at her. "I'll do my best."

—⁓—

Dona Marjorie offered to have her carriage brought around for me, since she didn't want me walking home alone past midnight in my condition. It was a bit embarrassing—I wasn't *that* bad, just really tired and a bit banged up—but it was easier to say thanks than to argue. And honestly, I wasn't completely sure I could make it through the entire half hour walk home without needing to lie down on the cold, damp cobbles and take a nap.

Rika and Jaycel walked me to the doors, and through them out under the night sky. It was strange to breathe in nothing but the crisp air of the first fresh hours of a Snow Moon, the year a blank page ready to be written—though apparently I'd already given it a title. The street looked so *normal*, all fine grand mansions like Marjorie's on carefully sculpted parcels of garden designed to make the grounds look bigger than the dense Tower district allowed, windows lit up blazing gold as people celebrated the New Year within. Lanterns cast bright illumination across Dona Marjorie's circular drive, and the two old trees flanking her door sighed in a dry, leafless breeze beneath the velvety night sky.

Our breath formed little puffs of frost as we did the age-old shuffling dance of people waiting outside in the cold for a carriage. I wrapped my arms around the thin silk of the shirt Marjorie had given me to replace my torn and bloodstained one, mourning the loss of my beautiful scarlet peacock-tail coat.

Rika's arm settled around my shoulders, slow and careful, and her slender side pressed warm against mine.

"You're going to freeze out here," she muttered.

Jaycel shook her head with mock reproof. "That's how it is, darling? Ignoring all my advice? A waxing Cloud Moon and a waning Cloud Moon are oil and water."

"Oh, shut up," I said affably. "You're one to talk about relationship choices."

"One date is *hardly* a relationship. I mean, two if you count when we met, but that was in a pub down by the river, and I thought he was just a regular Echo."

I couldn't wrap my brain around the image of Rai in some seedy pub, so I let that go.

There was a clop of hooves and a rumble of wheels as the coach rolled up the drive from the carriage house. Jaycel clapped my back with ginger care, as if she were worried I would fall apart.

"Well! Happy New Year, Kembral darling! You go get some sleep. I've got a party to get back to."

She sauntered away whistling. As if she hadn't brought down a City Elder and set up a date with an Empyrean tonight—and stabbed me, though of course she didn't remember that. Just another day for Jaycel Morningray.

I let out a long sigh. It rose in the cold air as a little white cloud, swiftly dissipating. "I suppose I should—"

Rika stiffened. "Kembral. *Look.*"

Dread rose in me with the trembling, aching reflex of an overused muscle. I followed her gaze.

Just beyond the warm lanterns of the carriage circle, among the flat black shadows of the trees and bushes, a cluster of shapes waited—ones that didn't match the careful aesthetic composition of the front garden. Three of them, two large and one small, like some bleak parody of a human family.

My heart flipped over. But no—surely my jumpy brain was assigning undue menace to some innocent shrubbery, strung out from a night of violence. It couldn't be *them.*

Twin silver gleams opened in the dark outline of one of the figures. Wind rattled the bare branches of the trees; it carried a horrifyingly familiar voice to my ears.

"You should know by now that I cannot accept a loss, Kembral Thorne."

Well, shit. Rika's fingers laced through mine; I could feel her pulse pounding in them.

"And *you* should know by now, Laughing As He Rises, that there are no true losses," she said. "Only more rounds in the game."

I stared at her in surprise. Rika's voice had gone deep and velvety, infused with a power I could feel resonating in the Veil. The grey of illusion had drained from her eyes; they stared red and baleful into the darkness. But her tone was one I knew well, rich and teasing, crafted to be compelling to a mark. Offering him an easy path to avoid conflict without losing his equilibrium.

The chuckle that emerged from the shadows chilled me to the bone. "Well said, Rika Nonesuch. So be it." The figure swept into a mocking bow, a dusting of tiny lights glimmering around it like the sweep of a cloak. "I look forward to the next round, then, Year-Namer, as this crux year of yours unfolds."

A shimmer of silver caught the light along the edges of the other tall figure, like a fall of shining hair.

"It pleases me that you drop this foolish mask and show your true nature, child," came the vibrant voice of Stars Tangled in Her Web. I could suddenly hear the resemblance to Rika's, and I shuddered.

Rika's eyes went grey again, quick as snuffing a candle. Her fingers twitched in mine, and she took a half step back.

I squeezed her hand, but didn't take my eyes off that willowy patch of darkness. "Mask on or mask off, she's herself," I said, with rock-stubborn surety. "Her *own* self, not yours."

A chiming sweet cascade of a laugh. "That remains to be seen. I'll be watching you this crux year, my precious changeling child."

"Then you can watch me turn my back on you," Rika said, her voice gone hard and cold and brittle.

"You tell her," I whispered.

The third, smallest figure bobbed gently as if on the winter breeze, edges fluttering and streaming into the night.

"No human has ever named the year before." Ylti's young voice brimmed with delight. "You've scattered every Empyrean's plans for the next hundred years. No one knows what will happen! Well done."

"Thanks," I said weakly, because *fuck you* seemed likely to get me in trouble.

Hail the New Year, Year-Namer. A strange tripled voice hissed on the wind itself, a mix of all three of them—and maybe others as well. *Hail the New Year, child of starlight.*

I couldn't suppress a shiver as the wind slid icy fingers through my hair and trailed its touch along the back of my neck.

A cheery whistle sounded incongruously behind us. The elderly coachman approached with a lantern; its swinging circle of light lurched out into the garden, illuminating the dark patch where the three Empyreans waited. My heart spasmed.

A pair of slender trees and a small statue of a faun stood there. Nothing more. The sense of deep, awful portent vanished from the night.

"Ready, Signa?" the driver asked, flashing us a wide smile.

"As I'll ever be," I muttered, and headed for the carriage, a collection of aches and worries.

To my confusion, Rika inexplicably mounted the steps ahead of me and settled into the carriage seat, smoke-and-shadow skirts pooling around her, expression serene. She extended a hand to me.

"Well? Aren't you going home?"

"Right." I hesitated, then let her help me up. Maybe I needed it, and maybe I just wanted to hold her hand—or both, to be honest. "Are you getting a ride home, too, then?"

"No." She patted the bench next to her, moving over to make room for me. "I'm coming with you."

"Sorry, what?"

She lifted an eyebrow. "You're *supposed* to rest. My understanding is that it's hard to do with a small baby around, so I thought I'd help."

I blinked at her. I couldn't find any words. Of all the surprises tonight, this one caught me completely unprepared, and suddenly my throat was thick and my eyes were stinging.

"If that's all right?" Uncertainty entered Rika's voice. "If you don't want—"

"Stars, yes," I said, with a desperate swell of emotion. "Yes, I want help. She's only been sleeping a couple of hours at a time, and I... *Thank you.* But you have to be exhausted, too. Why...?"

"You may remember that you asked me to take care of Emmi if anything happened to you." Rika arranged her ragged skirts on the bench with great dignity.

"I remember that you slapped me."

"Yes. And I said that maybe I'd take care of *you* instead." Her smug little smile softened. "Besides, I want to meet her."

"I..." I swallowed. I was right on the brink of bursting into tears. "I'd like that very much."

Approaching footsteps crunched on the gritty cobbles. Shit, the coachman was going to come around to shut the door, and I was going to be absolutely *bawling*.

"Kem. Hey, Kem."

It was Pearson, alert and downright sprightly despite the bandage still wrapping his head. I tried very hard not to give him a death glare. "Yes?"

"Before you head out, I just wanted to say good job. You know, back there with the Empyrean. All this messy business with the year-turning." He was back to his usual rumpled self—not dressed in rainbows or silks, not glowing and floating, very much normal and unassuming and alive. "Always great to see you in action. One of our best."

"Thanks."

A pause. He flashed me a nervous sort of smile. "So, ah, since you're clearly in fighting shape—I mean, except for all the injuries, of course—when do you think you can come back to work?"

"Pearson," I said, with affection. "Pearson, listen to me carefully. I'm going to tell you something very important."

"Yes?"

"I'm *on leave*."

I shut the door in his face, and the carriage rolled into motion. In our enclosed box of bumpy privacy, I leaned into Rika's arms, letting go of the night's tension at last.

Together, we went home.

The story continues in…

**Book TWO of
the Echo Archives**

Acknowledgments

This book began in 2019, when I sat down in a sudden fever of inspiration and wrote the first ten thousand words and three Echoes in two days.

Before that, this book began in a DM conversation with my agent, Naomi Davis, where I made a joke about how, since I liked party scenes so much, I should write a story that took place entirely at a party that sank through different layers of reality and kept getting weirder and more dangerous, and they told me actually, yes, I should absolutely write that.

This book would never have happened without that conversation—and all their help and enthusiasm in making it a reality.

It would have happened a lot later, if at all, without the patience, support, and love of my husband, Jesse, and my daughters, Maya and Kyra, who cooked meals and took over my chores and wrangled the dog so I could write.

It couldn't have existed in its current form—and would have been a lot worse—without the incredible work of my editor, Nivia Evans, who never lets me get away with less than my best. I'm immensely grateful to my UK editor, Emily Byron, who lent so much insight and enthusiasm to this project. Huge thanks also to Angelica Chong, assistant editor, who did a ton of excellent work on this book at absolutely blistering speed.

I remain in complete awe of the Orbit art department, and especially Lisa Marie Pompilio, whose design witchcraft adorns my cover.

Gazing at its gorgeousness gave me the strength to get through edits! Heartfelt thanks also to my excellent copyeditor, Kelley Frodel, and my wonderful managing editor, Bryn A. McDonald, for polishing this book into its final shape. And my deep gratitude to Ellen Wright in the US and Nazia Khatun in the UK, publicity goddesses, for their tireless work to get this book into the hands of readers. The whole Orbit team is a pleasure and privilege to work with, and I'm honored to have them at my back.

This story has benefitted immensely from the feedback of my loyal beta readers, Deva Fagan and Natsuko Toyofuku—thank you for still being willing to read my cruddy first drafts after all these years! And thanks to my daughter and brainstorming buddy Maya King for being my sounding board, giving me great feedback, and lending her expertise on time loops.

Writing can be lonely, and I could not ask for a more wonderful group of author friends than the Bunker, who've been with me through the highs and lows. And big thanks also to the authors of the Powerhouse for all your friendship and support! This career is so much better with a great heist team / pirate crew / adventuring band at your side, and I'm incredibly lucky to have you all on mine.

And finally, thank *you*, my readers, for letting me tell you this story.

extras

orbit

meet the author

Erin Re Anderson

MELISSA CARUSO was born on the summer solstice and went to school in an old mansion with a secret door but, despite this auspicious beginning, has yet to develop any known superpowers. Melissa has spent her whole life creating imaginary worlds and, in addition to writing, is also an avid LARPer and table-top gamer. She graduated with honors in creative writing from Brown University and has an MFA in fiction from the University of Massachusetts Amherst. Melissa's first novel, *The Tethered Mage*, was shortlisted for a Gemmell Morningstar Award for best fantasy debut.

Find out more about Melissa Caruso and other Orbit authors by registering for the free monthly newsletter at orbitbooks.net.

if you enjoyed
THE LAST HOUR BETWEEN WORLDS

look out for

NOTORIOUS SORCERER
The Burnished City: Book One

by

Davinia Evans

Welcome to Bezim, where sword-slinging bravi race through the night, and where rich and idle alchemists make magic out of mixing and measuring the four planes of reality.

Siyon Velo, Dockside brat turned petty alchemist, scrapes a living hopping between the planes to harvest ingredients for the city's alchemists. But when Siyon accidentally commits an act of impossible magic, he's catapulted into the limelight—which is a bad place to be when the planes start lurching out of alignment, threatening to send the city into the sea.

It will take a miracle to save Bezim. Good thing Siyon has pulled off the impossible before. Now he has to master it.

CHAPTER 1

Siyon couldn't get the damn square to line up, and the hangover definitely wasn't helping.

He squinted at the ash lines on the floor. The tiles tessellated in a not-quite-repeating pattern of swirls and spirals that could probably cause headaches all by itself. It was left over from before this place was taken over as the Little Bracken bravi safe house, when it had been a...temple? Church? Whatever. They called it the Chapel now, so probably one of those. Siyon didn't know much about all that religious stuff. He'd been born and bred here in Bezim, where they preferred the certainty of alchemy instead.

The building was nice; tidy brickwork, tall pitched roof, narrow windows of coloured glass. From the pale hair and impressive beards on the figures, Siyon thought the stories probably drew from the cults and myths of the North, not the remnants of the Lyraec Empire he was more familiar with.

The Chapel was quiet right now, with the morning sun cutting through the dust motes dancing around the lofty beams. The bravi were denizens of the night—the feet that rattled fleet as a passing rain shower over your roof tiles, the midnight laughter that promised mayhem and crossed blades and adventure. Last night they'd been all of that, the stuff of the dreams of children and poets, and now they were sleeping it off. So the tall, vaulted space—which might otherwise be cluttered with the scrape of a sharpening sabre, the clatter and call of training duels, the bicker and bellow of arguments over style—was all at Siyon's disposal.

He still couldn't get his delving portal square.

Siyon's tea had gone cold on a pushed-aside pew. He lifted the tin-banded glass, high and higher, until the light through the stained-glass windows both made him wince and turned the remaining liquid a fiery golden orange. A colour burning with righteousness. An *Empyreal* sort of colour.

Siyon *reached* through that connection and snapped his fingers.

And then nearly dropped the suddenly scalding glass.

Allegedly Kolah Negedi—the long-dead father of alchemical practice—had strong views about casual use of the Art. Something about the essence of another plane not being a dog to fetch your slippers. Poetic, but frankly, the great Kolah Negedi didn't seem all that applicable to the life of Siyon Velo. Let the fancy azatani alchemists, with their mahogany workbenches and expensive bespoke glass beakers, debate his wisdom. All Siyon did was fetch and carry for them. And that's all he'd ever do, unless he could scrape together enough hard cash to pay for lessons. Today's work would barely add to his stash, but one day, maybe…

In the meantime, at least he could have hot tea.

Siyon blew gently across the surface of the liquid, took a careful sip, and sighed as the blissful heat smoothed out the jagged edges of his hangover.

"Sorry," someone said. "I can come back later if you're enjoying your alone time."

Not just any someone; that was the tight, pointed accent that went with leafy avenues and elegant townhouses and lace gloves. That was an azatani voice. Siyon cracked one eye open, and looked sidelong toward the doorway.

The young woman wouldn't have come up to his chin, but

she stood straight and tall, barely a trace of a girl's uncertainty in the way her weight shifted from one foot to the other. She was clad head to toe in bravi leathers—sturdy trousers, tight vest, bracers laced up to her elbows. They creaked with newness, and the sabre at her hip gleamed with oil and polish. The tricorn balanced atop her tied-back ebony curls had an orange cockade pinned on with a Little Bracken badge.

They'd probably run the tiles together, two fish in the great flickering school of the Little Bracken, but Siyon never paid too much attention to the azatani recruits. They joined, they had their youthful adventures, they left to take up their serious adult responsibilities. None of his business.

But here she was, getting in his business. "What are you doing here, za?" he demanded, though he had a bad feeling he knew the answer.

"I was sent by the Diviner Prince to..." Her words petered out, uncertainty conquering the assurance she was born into. "Er. Assist you? Hold something?"

Siyon snorted. "I need an anchor, not a little bird. Go back and tell Daruj—"

"No," she interrupted, her chin coming up in a belligerent jut. "I can do it. I'm bravi. Same as you."

Siyon sauntered out into the aisle, where she could in turn get a good look at him. At the fraying of his shirtsleeves and the scuffs on his boots, at the battered hilt of his own sabre, at the lean length of his limbs and the freckles and even the glint of red in his brown hair that said *foreign blood*. That confirmed he was a mongrel brat.

She could probably trace her family back a few hundred years to the end of the Lyraec Empire. They'd probably helped overthrow the Last Duke and claim the city for *the people*. People like them, anyway. They'd renamed the city *Bezim*—in Old Lyraec, that meant *ours*.

"Yeah," he drawled, stretching the Dockside twang. "We're peas in a fucking pod. How old are you, anyway?"

"How old are you?" she demanded right back. There was a flush of colour in her warm brown cheeks, but she wasn't backing down. Was it even bravery when you hadn't heard the word *no* more than a dozen times in your life?

"Twenty-three," Siyon said. "Or near enough. And I've been on my own since I was fourteen, delving the planes since seventeen. That six years of crossing the divide between this plane and the others tells me I'm not trusting you"—he jabbed a finger at her, in her new leathers with her boots that probably got that shine from the hands of a servant—"to hold the only thing tying me back to the Mundane. No offense, princess."

She hesitated in the doorway, but then her chin came up again. "Fuck you," she stated primly. "I can do it. And I'm all you've got, anyway. Daruj went down to the square; Awl Quarter have called public challenge." There was a twist to her mouth. It stung, to be sent to do this, rather than being included in the party to bare blades against another bravi tribe, even in a small morning skirmish.

Siyon knew what that felt like. He drained his tea and set the glass down on the pew next to him. "You're well out of it. It'll be dead boring. Lots of posturing, barely three blades getting to kiss daylight. No audience in the morning, see? So no pressing need to fight."

She really did look like a doll playing dress-up, but she hadn't fled. And if Daruj was off playing *Diviner Prince* (Siyon never found his friend's bladename less ridiculous, whatever its proud history), then she probably was the best Siyon was likely to get until later this afternoon. Which would be cutting it fine to make his deliveries.

He sighed. "What's your name again?"

She grinned, sudden and bright and blindingly pretty. She was going to carve her way through society when she set aside the blade to take up a ball gown. "Zagiri Savani. And I'm eighteen. If it matters."

Siyon shrugged. "Not to me. Come on."

His ash square still looked a little skewed at one corner, but he wasn't redoing it again. "How much did Daruj tell you about what's involved?"

Zagiri stayed well back from the lines of ash, so at least she was sensible. "You're going to raid one of the other planes. For alchemical ingredients."

Basically right, but she'd need more than basics. "I tear a hole between the planes," Siyon elaborated. "Which is what the square is for. Keeps the breach contained. There's no risk—not to you, not to the city." The inquisitors might feel differently, but they weren't here, and what did they know anyway? "That also cuts me off from the Mundane, so to get back, I need a tether."

She nodded. "Which I hold."

"Which you hold." Siyon watched her for a moment. Clearly a little nervous, but she had a strong grip on herself. That irritating azatani arrogance might be good for something after all.

He unhooked his sabre from his belt and set it down on a pew, picked up a coil of rope instead. It was rough stuff, thick hemp and tarred ends, liberated from docks duty. As mundane—as *Mundane*—as rope could get, heavy with work and sweat and dirty, fishy business. "One end ties around me," Siyon said, looping it around his waist, under his shirt and the weight of his cross-slung satchel. "And you hold the other. You hold it no matter what you see, or what you hear, or how much it jerks around. You hold on to this."

She wrinkled her delicate little nose as she set a hand just above the thick knot tied in the end. She'd probably never put her pampered hands on anything this coarse in her life. "What happens if I don't?" Not a challenge, more curiosity.

Siyon smiled, tight and brittle. "I get stuck in there. Since I'm delving Empyreal today, that means I'm trapped in unforgiving heat with the angels on my back until either I can find a way out or you"—he prodded at her shoulder—"scarper off and find someone to summon me back. I recommend Auntie Geryss, you can find her through the tea shop near the fountain in the fruit market. If, y'know, you fuck up completely."

Zagiri swallowed hard, wrapped the rope around her fist, and braced her heels against the tiled floor. At least she was taking this seriously. "All right."

"Don't worry." Siyon grinned, the thrill of what he was about to do starting to tug at him as surely as a tether. It never got old. "I'll be right here. Well. Right here, and on the other side of reality at the same time."

She didn't look reassured.

Siyon stepped into the ashen square and vanished into heat haze.

Between the planes was the void, and the void was perfect; it flashed by in a fraction of a blink, and Siyon was through.

It was like stepping into an open oven, snatched up in the Empyreal plane's hot, dry fist. Siyon staggered, dizzy and dazzled, as the universe tilted around him. It always took a moment to get his balance, like he'd jumped from a moving cart.

Doing this with a hangover had been an awful idea.

Sand skewed beneath his boots, and whipped up on a keening wind. Or at least, it looked and felt like sand, abrading his skin and gritty between his teeth. Not actually sand, not here. Tiny grains of duty, or conscience, or something equally uncomfortable and insistent. Stung like a bitch, making his eyes water, and Siyon pulled a thin scarf over his face. Easier to see through it than with his eyes scrunched closed against the blast.

Dunes undulated away in all directions, toward shimmering horizons. The not-sand was white—scalding white, pale as purity, clean as righteousness—and the sky was seething fire that sizzled in sheets of orange and yellow and incandescent blue. It was dangerously beautiful; easy to overlook the tiny black specks within the burning gyre.

First rule of delving: The longer you gawk, the less time you have to harvest. Get in, load up, get out.

Siyon lowered his head again, and concentrated on slithering down the side of the dune without falling. This not-sand was so fine, it ran like water. You could drown in it, if you didn't look lively.

In the gully between dunes, there was a little shelter from the sandstorm. Siyon could crouch without fear of being buried, and shovel aside the fine, flyaway grains at the surface. Deeper down, the sand took on a molten glow, clinging to his fingers like an itch. Siyon scooped up a stinging handful, funnelling it hurriedly into a flask. He shook the excess off with a wince and wiped his hand against the rope around his waist; the roughness of the hemp was great for stripping away the last little bits, or maybe it was the sheer Mundanity that did the trick.

He got one more vial of firesand using the other hand, and tucked them both away safely inside his satchel. Trying to get any more would be asking for burns or—worse—recurring attacks of guilt back in the Mundane.

Standing, he laid a hand on the rope around his waist again. The tether leading back to the Mundane wasn't visible, but

extras

Siyon could *feel* it, tugging at him when he moved. The pull wasn't too much right now, so Zagiri didn't seem to be getting impatient. It was always difficult to tell how much time had passed while he was here. Tears were nudging at the corner of his vision, but Siyon could blink them away. The breath still came easily—though harsh and burning—to his lungs, and he wasn't experiencing any strange urges toward crusades, justice, or self-improvement.

Perhaps he could try for a little more.

He shouldn't. Get in, load up, get out, remember? The vials of firesand were what he'd been commissioned to deliver.

So if he could find something extra, it could be bonus cash. If he could find something *good*, he might be able to get his hands on a book—a real one, a proper alchemic tome. One that might *teach* him something. Make him more than just an interplanar errand boy.

Hey, a guy could dream.

Siyon flipped his satchel open again, running a finger blind along the dozens of little loops and pockets sewn into the lining. He needed to move fast; he needed something that might lead him to something powerful and lucrative.

Ah. Perfect.

He pulled out a feather—small, plain, grey, notched at one end. Just a pigeon feather. But like called to like, and in this place there were far more interesting—more powerful—things than pigeons on the wing.

Siyon lifted the feather and let the breeze pluck it out of his grip.

It zipped away, moving fast, and Siyon had to scramble after it. Up the dune and down, crosswise along the next, hauling himself up a rocky outcrop that surely hadn't been here a moment ago. The pigeon feather danced up and over the lip, smudgy

extras

against the fire-bright sky, and Siyon dragged himself after it. The rocks scraped against his ribs like pious privation, but he pushed onward. If he lost the feather, it would all be a waste.

Just over the lip of rock, atop the outcrop, the feather snagged on the sharp black edge of a nest. Siyon could've whooped in victory, if he'd had the breath for it.

The nest wasn't built of sticks, but of slabs and shards of obsidian, razor-keen and gleaming. It wasn't big, barely wider than the length of Siyon's arm, and there were only two eggs within, nestled among smouldering embers. When Siyon peeled back his scarf to peek over the edge of the nest, the heat nearly took his eyebrows off.

He didn't want an egg, though. What the hell would he do with a phoenix chick? (Answer: Set fire to his bunk in the Chapel and be left in the ashes for the inqs to pick up at their leisure.) Instead, Siyon edged carefully around the nest, peering into the nooks and serrated crannies, until he spotted the butter-bright gleam of a trapped feather. Extracting it was like sticking his hand into a shark's mouth, sliding careful fingers between knife-like obsidian and the roaring heat of the nest itself. The feather felt like a wisp of silk between his fingertips, hot as a Flower's underthings and just as full of promise. Siyon teased it out, wrapping it in a length of actual silk before tucking it away in his satchel.

He was so focused on it that he barely heard the whistle from above. Not like a bravi signal, no human sound at all; more like the sigh of air ripped through a grate. The sound of an angel's wings scything through excuses.

But he did hear it, and his body was already moving before his mind caught up, hurling him sideways a moment before the broadsword came slamming down right where he'd been crouching.

402

The force of it buried the edge in the rocks as though they were cheese. Flames licked blue-bright along the length of the blade. Light washed dazzling over Siyon—not from the sword, but the one who wielded it, looming above him resplendent in armour even whiter than the sand. The brutal white of perfect virtue, the unflinching white of implacable justice.

The shattering white of an angel.

Her face was a smudge in the searing light; Siyon just got an impression of a wild halo of fire around diamond eyes and hawk beak.

That beak opened and she *screamed*, like a raptor diving upon its prey.

"Zagiri!" Siyon shouted. "Pull m—"

The angel backhanded him, slamming the words from his mouth and the sense from his head. Air spun wild around him; he bounced against the rocky outcrop once, twice, before plummeting to the sand.

This wasn't his physical body, Siyon reminded himself, trying to drag breath back into his lungs. Not real, not him.

Still hurt like a motherfucker.

Sand sucked at him as Siyon heaved up to hands and knees. His satchel pulled him off balance; at least he still had it. Tears crawled down his cheeks, actually cool against the heat around him.

"Pull me out," he said, but the words were barely a scrape in his throat. No power to them at all.

The world shook as the angel landed in the sand next to Siyon. Her arm wrapped around him, binding as a solemn promise, and she hauled him effortlessly up. His legs dangled, ribs creaking beneath her grip. "*Thief*," she snarled in his ear. It wasn't speaking so much as a stone-chiseled statement of immutable fact. "*You must earn what you would steal.*"

Siyon had no idea what that meant. But her fingers—or talons, by the sharp sting of them—dug into him as she closed her fist around the rope at his waist. It grew warm against his skin, and something shimmered into being in front of him; a twist of connection, spiralling away into the air like a faint and billowing umbilical.

Siyon gaped. He'd never seen his tether in the planes before. It was sort of beautiful.

The angel lifted her sword.

Siyon thrashed against her grip, but she only clutched him tighter, and his ribs cracked and his lungs spasmed and no sound at all came from his throat.

The sword flashed in its descent, bright with blue-hot flames.

Her grip around him tightened, impossibly, and then yanked. No, wait, it was the rope itself, and Siyon popped fish-slippery from the angel's hold, whipping into half a moment of dizzying blackness—

—and then there was stone under his feet, and his knees giving way as he crashed into another body and they both went down.

A whistle in Siyon's ears—no, in reality. "Look out," he gasped, and shoved hard as he rolled in the other direction.

Something slammed down where he had been with a screech of ironwork and a frustrated hiss, and then there was silence.

Siyon sat up too fast, and paused for the whirling sparks to dance away from his vision. Zagiri was backed against the end of the pew, knees drawn up to her chest and eyes wide. Between their bodies, the ash square was nothing but a smear across the floor.

Except the tilework—and the stones beneath—were sliced through in a deep gash the length of Siyon's arm.

Zagiri's dark eyes were wide. "It just—it was—"

"Angelic broadsword," Siyon croaked. His throat still felt scorched. His cheeks were stiff with dried tears. He reached out to the wound in the floor, but stopped short; the heat was still rising from it, with a smell like midday-baked stone paving. "Thanks," he said. "You did well."

She made a noise somewhere between a squeak and a sigh, and lifted her fist. The rope was still wrapped around it, but there was barely an arm's-length left before it ended, abrupt and fire-blackened.

The end was still smouldering.

Siyon scrambled over and pried it carefully from her trembling grip. He held it gently, moved it slowly, to avoid killing the flame or dislodging ash. There could be good use—good *money*—in angel ash. How much more in a still-burning fire?

Never mind the phoenix feather, what could this earn him? More books? Equipment? *Lessons*? Proper ones from a Summer Club alchemist, not just occasional tips from Auntie Geryss.

Zagiri wiped her hands on her trousers. Her fingers were still shaking, but only a little. More backbone to her than many Siyon had seen tangle with the fringes of alchemy. "We're done now, right?" she asked, evenly enough.

"Change of plans," Siyon said, eyes still on the smoking rope. "Delivery time. This is too important to wait."

if you enjoyed
THE LAST HOUR BETWEEN WORLDS

look out for

THE HEXOLOGISTS
A Hexologists Novel

by

Josiah Bancroft

The Hexologists, Isolde and Warren Wilby, are quite accustomed to helping desperate clients with the bugbears of city life. Aided by hexes and a bag of charmed relics, the Wilbies have recovered children abducted by chimney-wraiths, removed infestations of barb-nosed incubi, and ventured into the Gray Plains of the Unmade to soothe a troubled ghost. Well acquainted with the weird, they never shy away from a challenging case.

But when they are approached by the royal secretary and told the king pleads to be baked into a cake—going so far as to wedge himself inside a lit oven—the Wilbies soon find themselves embroiled in a mystery that could very well see the nation turned on its head. Their effort to expose a royal secret buried under forty years of lies brings them nose-to-nose with a violent anti-royalist gang, avaricious ghouls, alchemists who draw their power from a hell-like dimension, and a bookish dragon who only occasionally eats people.

Armed with a love toughened by adversity and a stick of chalk that can conjure light from the darkness, hope from the hopeless, Iz and Warren Wilby are ready for whatever springs from the alleys, graves, and shadows next.

1

THE KING IN THE CAKE

"The king wishes to be cooked alive," the royal secretary said, accepting the proffered saucer and cup and immediately setting both aside. At his back, the freshly stoked fire added a touch of theater to his announcement, though neither seemed to suit what, until recently, had been a pleasant Sunday morning.

"Does he?" Isolde Wilby gazed at the royal secretary with all the warmth of a hypnotist.

"Um, yes. He's quite insistent." The questionable impression of the royal secretary's negligible chin and cumbersome nose was considerably improved by his well-tailored suit, fastidiously combed hair, and blond mustache, waxed into upturned barbs. Those modest whiskers struck Isolde as a dubious effort to impart gravity to a youthful face. Though Mr. Horace Alman seemed a man of perfect manners, he sat with his hat capping his knee. "More precisely, the king wishes to be baked into a cake."

Looming at the tea cart like a bear over a blackberry bush, Mr. Warren Wilby quietly swapped the plate of cakes with a dish of watercress sandwiches. "Care for a nibble, sir?"

"No. No, thank you," Mr. Alman murmured, flummoxed by the offer. The secretary watched as Mr. Wilby positioned a triangle of white bread under his copious mustache, then vanished it like a letter into a mail slot.

The Wilbies' parlor was unabashedly old-fashioned. While their neighbors pursued the bare walls, voluptuous lines, and skeletal furniture that defined contemporary tastes, the Wilbies' townhouse decor fell somewhere between a gallery of oddities and a country bed-and-breakfast. Every rug was ancient, every doily yellow, every table surface adorned by some curio or relic. The picture frames that crowded the walls were full of adventuresome scenes of tall ships, dogsleds, and eroded pyramids. The style of their furniture was as motley as a rummage sale and similarly haggard. But as antiquated as the room's contents were, the environment was remarkably clean. Warren Wilby could abide clutter, but never filth.

Isolde recrossed her legs and bounced the topmost with a metronome's precision. She hadn't had time to comb her hair since rising, or rather, she had had the time but not the will during her morning reading hours, which the king's secretary had so brazenly interrupted, necessitating the swapping of her silk robe for breeches and a blouse. Wearing a belt and shoes seemed an absolute waste of a Sunday morning.

Isolde Wilby was often described as *imposing*, not because

she possessed a looming stature or a ringing voice, but because she had a way of imposing her will upon others. Physically, she was a slight woman in the plateau of her thirties with striking, almost vulpine features. She parted her short hair on the side, though her dark curls resisted any further intervention. Her long-suffering stylist had once described her hair as resembling a porcupine with a perm, a characterization Isolde had not minded in the slightest. She was almost entirely insensible to pleasantries, especially the parentheses of polite conversation, preferring to let the drumroll of her heels convey her hellos and her coattails say her goodbyes.

Her husband, Warren, was a big, squarish man with a tree stump of a neck and a lion's mane of receded tawny hair. He wore unfashionable tweed suits that he hoped had a softening effect on his bearing, but which in fact made him look like a garden wall. Though he was a year younger than Isolde, Warren did not look it, and had been, since adolescence, mistaken for a man laboring toward the promise of retirement. He had a mustache like a boot brush and limpid hazel eyes whose beauty was squandered on a beetled and bushy brow, an obstruction that often rendered his expressions unfathomable, leading some strangers to assume he was gruffer than he was. In fact, Warren was a man of tender conscience and emotional depth, traits that came in handy when Isolde's brusque manner necessitated a measure of diplomacy. He was considerably better groomed that morning only because he had risen early to greet the veg man, who unfailingly delivered the freshest greens and gossip in all of Berbiton at the unholy hour of six.

Seeming to wither in the silence, Mr. Alman repeated, "I said, the king wishes to be baked into a ca—"

"Intriguing," Isolde interrupted in a tone that plainly suggested it was not.

Iz did not particularly care for the nobility. She had accepted Mr. Horace Alman into her home purely because War had insisted one could not refuse a royal visitor, nor indeed, turn off the lights and pretend to be abroad.

While War had made tea, Iz had endured the secretary's boorish attempts at small talk, made worse by an unprompted confession that he was something of a fan, a Hexologist enthusiast. He followed the Wilbies' exploits as frequently documented in the *Berbiton Times*. Mr. Horace Alman was interested to know how she felt about the recent court proceedings. Iz had rejoined she was curious how he felt about his conspicuous case of piles.

The royal secretary had gone on to irk her further by asking whether her name really was "Iz Ann Always Wilby" or if it were some sort of theatrical appellation, a stage name. Iz patiently explained that her father, the famous Professor Silas Wilby, had had many weaknesses—including an insatiable wanderlust and an allergy to obligations—but none worse than his fondness for puns, which she personally reviled as charmless linguistic coincidences that could only be conflated with humor by a gormless twit. Only the sort of vacuous cretin who went around asking people if their names were made-up could possibly enjoy the lumbering comedy that was the godless pun.

Though, in all fairness, she was not the only one to be badgered over her name. Her husband had taken the rather unusual step of adopting her last name upon the occasion of their marriage. He'd changed his name not because he was estranged from his family, but rather because he'd never liked the name Offalman.

Iz had been about to throw the royal secretary out on his inflamed fundament when War had emerged from the kitchen pushing a tea cart loaded with chattering porcelain and Mr.

Horace Alman had announced that King Elbert III harbored aspirations of becoming a gâteau.

His gaunt cheeks blushing with the ever-expanding quiet, Mr. Alman pressed on: "His Majesty has gone so far as to crawl into a lit oven when no one was looking." The secretary paused to make room for their astonishment, giving Warren sufficient time to post another sandwich. "And while he escaped with minor burns, the experience does not appear to have dissuaded him of the ambition. He wants to be roasted on the bone."

"So, it's madness, then." Iz shook her head at War when he inquired whether she would like some of either the lemon sponge or the spice cake, an inquiry that was conducted with a delicate rounding of his plentiful brows.

"I don't believe so." Mr. Alman touched his teacup as if he might raise it, then the fire behind him snapped like a whip, and his fingers bid a fluttering retreat. "He has long moments of lucidity, almost perfect coherence. But he also suffers from fugues of profound confusion. He's been discovered in the middle of the night roaming the royal grounds without any sense of himself or his surroundings. The king's sister, Princess Constance, has had to take the rather extreme precaution of confining him to his suite. And I must say, you both seem to be taking all of this rather in stride! I tell you the king believes he's a waste of cake batter, you stifle a yawn!"

Iz tightened the knot of her crossed arms. "I didn't realize you were looking for a performance. I could have the neighbor's children pop by if you'd like a little more shrieking."

War hurried to intervene: "Mr. Alman, please forgive us. We do not mean to appear apathetic. We are just a bit more accustomed to unusual interviews and extraordinary confessions than most. But, rest assured, we are not indifferent to horror; we are merely better acquainted."

"Indeed," Iz said with a muted smile. "How have the staff taken the king's altered state of mind?"

Appearing somewhat appeased, the secretary twisted and shaped the points of his mustache. "They're discreet, of course, but there are limits. Princess Constance knows it's a secret she cannot keep forever, devoted as she is to her brother."

"Surely, you want physicians, psychologists. We are neither," Iz said.

The secretary absorbed her comments with an expression of pinched indulgence. "We've consulted with the nation's greatest medical minds. They were all stumped, or rather, they were perfectly confident in their varying diagnoses and prescriptions, and none of them were at all capable of producing any results. His condition only worsens."

"Even so, I'm not sure what help we can be." Iz picked at a thread that protruded, wormlike, from the armrest of the sofa.

The secretary turned the brim of his hat upon his knee, ducking her gaze when he said, "There's more, Ms. Wilby. There was a letter."

"A letter?"

"In retrospect, it seems to have touched off His Majesty's malaise." The royal secretary reached into his jacket breast pocket. The stiff envelope trembled when he withdrew it. The broken wax seal was as sanguine as a wound. "It is not signed, but the sender asserts that he is the king's unrecognized son."

Warren moved to stand behind his wife's chair. He clutched the back of it as if it were the rail of a sleigh poised atop a great hill. Iz reached back and, without looking, patted the tops of his knuckles. "I imagine the Crown receives numerous such claims. No doubt there are scores of charlatans who're foolish enough to hazard the gallows for a chance to shake down the king."

"Indeed, but there are two things that distinguish this particular instance of blackmail. First, the seal." Mr. Alman stroked the edge of the wax medallion, indicating each element as he described it: "An *S* emblazoned over a turret; note the five merlons, one for each of Luthland's counties. Beneath the *S*, a banner bearing the name Yeardley. This is the seal of Sebastian, Prince of Yeardley. This is the stamp of the king's adolescent ring."

"He identified it as such?" Iz asked.

"I did, at least initially. Of course, I like to believe I'm familiar with all the royal seals, but I admit I had to check the records on this occasion. Naturally, there is much of his correspondence that His Majesty leaves me to open and deal with, but when something like this comes through, I deliver it to him unbroken."

"The signet was no longer in the king's possession, then?"

"No, the royal record identified the ring as lost about twenty-five years ago, around the conclusion of his military service, I believe."

"That's quite a length of time to sit on such a claim." Iz reached for the letter, but the secretary pulled it back. She looked into his eyes; they glistened with uncertainty as sweat dripped from his nose like rain from a grotesque. "What is the second thing that distinguishes the letter?"

"The king's response to the correspondence was... pronounced. He has thus far refused to discuss his impressions of the contents with myself, his sister, or any of his advisors. He insists that it is a hoax, that we should destroy it, though Princess Constance won't hear of it. She maintains that one doesn't destroy the evidence of extortion: One saves it for the inquiry. But of course, there hasn't been an inquiry. How could there be, given the nature of the claim? To say nothing of the fact that the primary witness to the events in question is currently raving in the royal tower."

"The princess wishes for us to investigate?" she asked. Though Isolde held little affection for the gentry, she liked the princess well enough. Constance had established herself as one of very few public figures who continued to promote the study of hexegy, touting the utility of the practice, even amid the blossoming of scientific discovery and electrical convenience. Still, Isolde's vague respect for the princess was hardly sufficient to make her leap to her brother's aid.

Mr. Alman coughed—a brittle, aborted laugh. "Strictly speaking, Her Royal Highness does not know I am here. I have taken it upon myself to investigate the identity of the bastard, or rather, to engage more capable persons in that pursuit."

"I'm sorry, Mr. Alman, but what I said when we first sat down still holds. I am a private citizen. I serve the public, some of whom come to me with complaints about royal overreach, the criminal exploitations of the nobility, or the courts' bungling of one case or another. I don't work for the police—not anymore. Surely you have enough resources at your disposal to forgo the interference of one unaffiliated investigator."

"I do understand your preference, ma'am." The royal secretary rucked his soft features into an authoritative scowl. "But these are extraordinary circumstances, and not without consequence. The uncertainty of rule only emboldens the antiroyalists, the populists, and our enemies overseas. You must—"

Isolde pounced like a tutor upon a mistake: "I *must* pay my taxes. I *may* help you. Show me the letter."

Mr. Alman tightened like a twisted rag. "I cannot share such sensitive information until you have agreed to assist in the case."

"There is another way to look at this, Iz," Warren said,

returning to the tea cart. He poured water from a sweating pitcher into a juice glass and presented it to the dampened secretary, who readily accepted it. "You wouldn't just be working for the Crown; you would be serving the interests of the private citizen who has come forward with the claim...perhaps a *legitimate* one." The final phrase made Mr. Alman nearly choke upon his thimble swallow of water. "If the writer of this letter shares the king's blood, and we were to prove it, I don't think anyone would accuse you of being too friendly with the royals."

Isolde bobbed her head in consideration, an easy rhythm that quickly broke. "But if I help to prove that he is a prince, I'd just be serving at the pleasure of a different sovereign."

"True." Warren moved to the mantel to stir the coals, not to invigorate them, but to shuffle the loose embers toward the corners of the firebox. "But if you don't intervene, our possible prince will remain a fugitive."

"You think we should take the case?"

"You know how I feel about lords and lawmen. But it seems to me Mr. Alman is right: If there's a vacuum in the palace and a scramble for the throne, there will be strife in the streets. We know who suffers when heaven squabbles—the vulnerable. Someone up on high only has to whisper the word 'unrest' and the prisons fill up, the workhouses shake out, the missions bar their doors, and the orphanages repopulate. And when the dust settles, perhaps there'll be a new face printed on the gallet bill or a fresh set of bullies on the bench, but the only thing of real consequence that will have changed is the number of bones in the potter's field. Revolution may chasten the rich, but uncertainty torments the poor."

Isolde patted the air, signaling her surrender. "All right, War. All right. You've made your point. Mr. Alman, I—"

A heavy, arrhythmic knock brought the couple's heads around. The Wilbies stared at the unremarkable paneled door as if it were aflame.

Alman snuffled a little laugh. "Do knocking guests always cause such astonishment?"

"They do when they come by my cellar," Warren said.

The door shattered, casting splinters and hinge pins into the room, making all its inhabitants cry out in alarm. It seemed a fitting greeting for the seven-foot-tall forest golem who ducked beneath the riven lintel.

Its skin, rough as bark and scabbed with lichen, bunched about fat ankles and feet that were arrayed from toe to heel by a hundred gripping roots. Its swollen arms were heavy enough to bend its broad back and bow its head, ribbed and featureless as a grub. The golem lurched forward, swaying and creaking upon the shore of a gold-and-amethyst rug whose patterns had been worn down by the passage of centuries.

"A mandrake," Iz said, tugging a half stick of chalk from her khaki breeches. "I've never seen one so large. But don't worry. They're quite docile. He probably just got lost during his migration. Let's try to herd him back down."

With hands raised, Warren advanced upon the mandrake, nattering pleasantly as he inched toward the heaving golem that resembled an ambling yam. "There's a sport. Thank you for keeping off my rug. It's an antique, you know. I have to be honest—it's impossible to match and hard to clean. I haven't got one of those newfangled carpet renovators. The salesman, wonderful chap, wanted three hundred and twenty gallets for it. Can you imagine? And those suck-boxes are as big as a bureau. I have no idea where I'd park such a—"

The moment War inched into range, the mandrake swatted him with a slow, unyielding stroke of its limb, catching him on the shoulder and throwing him back across the room and violently through his tea cart. Macarons and petits fours leapt into the air and rained down upon the smashed porcelain that surrounded the splayed host.

The mandrake raised the fingerless knob of one hand, identifying his quarry, then charged at the royal secretary, who sat bleating like a calf.

Follow us:

/orbitbooksUS

X **/orbitbooks**

/orbitbooks

Join our mailing list
to receive alerts on our
latest releases and deals.

orbitbooks.net

Enter our monthly
giveaway for the chance
to win some epic prizes.

orbitloot.com